A New Beginning

The Smoke of One Thousand Lodge Fires

STEVEN G. HIGHTOWER

This book is dedicated to my grandchildren:
Caleb, Kelby, Gracie, Faith, and Noah.
You are my inspiration…

Preface

Given the chance to relive history, what if anything would any of us do differently? That opportunity is afforded to my characters. What will David J. Ross, a modern-day cattle rancher, choose or live out differently than his ancestors chose? How will the legal system behave toward Tabbananica (Voice of the Sun), a Comanche Warrior living in modern times. How might the government of Texas deal with a New Comanche Nation…when given a second chance to do so?

I have heard it said many times, "If I could live my life over, I would change nothing." This mindset guarantees with certainty that we might never learn from our mistakes, and that history will indeed continue to repeat itself.

Acknowledgments

I am forever grateful to Debra L. Butterfield for her editing wonders. Thank you, Debra. Special thanks to Nan Chisholm of Nan Chisholm Fine Art LTD, New York, NY (used by permission). Thank you, Nan!

Special thanks to Ellie…you are the love of my life.

Prologue

October 1844
San Saba River Valley

Topusana (Prairie Flower) lay upon the soft sand of the cavern floor, dreaming fitfully. She could hear the songs of Tosahwi (White Knife) faintly in the distant recesses of her mind. She was clinging desperately to this world. She could still remember.

Thoughts floated through her mind. She had seen the attack on the Home Camp coming. She had witnessed her daughter's cruel violation and brutal murder. She had watched her child's spirit rise from the burning camp. The silhouettes of the bodies of her friends blurred in and out of focus within her mind.

The tears rose again. She cried out, a pitiful whimpering cry like that of a wounded fawn.

How could these men be so ruthless?

The words of the songs Tosahwi sang penetrated deeply within her soul. The Dream Time ultimately overcame her.

Tosahwi, the Shaman, knew in his heart that Topusana needed to let go of this place and time. He rested his hand upon her brow. He could feel her pulse slow within his palm, the warmth of her skin…the surrendering of her spirit. He let the song drift from his soul, quieting now.

Then Topusana slept.

Chapter 1

The Cavern
Present Day

In the darkness of the hidden cavern along the banks of the San Saba River, Topusana awakened.

Her awareness dawned…as the Dream Time came to an end. The pungent charcoal smell from the old cave fires brought forth her memories. The feel of the soft sand and cool stone against her skin awakened her senses. The sound of dripping water echoing softly through the cavern reached her ears and brought further awareness to her mind, bringing her alive. Topusana was alive!

She wondered how long had it been? An hour? A day? A year or longer? Had she been in the Dream Time long enough…long enough to escape the rangers? Would they now finally be safe?

She sat up abruptly. She was alone, suddenly cold. Reaching for the flint and stone stored against the cave wall, she located it easily in the darkness. She struck the stone, the shower of sparks lighting the prepared torch. Topusana watched the upper rooms flicker before her in the glow of the small torch. Shadows danced across the vast open room as the flame wavered in the light airflow that moved throughout the cavern continuously. As her vision adjusted, Topusana peered across the open space of the hidden cavern. There, just a few feet from her, under the warmth of the huge buffalo robe, she could make out the shape of her husband, her beloved Tabbananica (Voice of the Sun). In the dim light, she could detect the movement of her husband's shallow breathing. Tabbananica was still in the Dream Time.

The gentle movement of the air that flowed throughout the cavern brushed across her skin like a soft feather. This whisper touch brought further awareness. That movement of air was the last thing she remembered as she entered the Dream Time.

Her memories again drifted into the forefront of her mind. She thought of only her daughter, Topunicte (Prairie Song), and her heart seemed to skip, a dull ache making its way into her very being. Topusana recalled the gentle spirit of Prairie Song. As her mind awakened, she began to remember all that had taken place. The reasons for the preparation, the planning, the escape…

She thought of Tosahwi. His medicine was indeed powerful! Topusana knew not where he was now. He seemed to be able to travel great distances and to be where he was most needed at the most appropriate time. She needed him now. She would pray to the Great Spirit for Tosahwi to come to her in her little cavern in the Texas Hills.

Tosahwi, the Shaman, seemed to have no years. No one from the Numunuu (Nuh-Muh-Nuh), *The People,* knew his age or even his birthplace. Tosahwi would say he was born of the prairie in the time of Topusana's grandfather Buffalo Hump, the great Comanche Chief. However, her grandfather told her Tosahwi was an old man during his time as Chief and leader of *The People.* Her grandfather taught her about Tosahwi, revealing that he had been given special gifts from the Great Spirit. He taught her that she should always respect and trust Tosahwi. She always did. She trusted him even now.

Topusana thought of her *People*, the once great Numunuu, the Comanche Nation.

The People had offered peace and agreed to peace. Those agreements were violated by the government soldiers and rangers time and time again. *The People* were promised a Homeland, promised ceasefires, and in later days even promised food when they were starving and the buffalo gone.

Those promises were always broken. It seemed the terms from the white leaders were never sincere, as within a few days or hours of any terms, the treaties were violated.

Bands of Comanche were hunted down and wiped out in the same way the whites hunted and slaughtered the once great buffalo herds. It is true the Comanche fought back fiercely as any people would who were fighting for their very existence. It was also a fact that the Comanche Nation was losing this fight.

Topusana knew in her heart they would never survive the struggle. She had seen her family murdered before her own eyes, including the brutal violation of Prairie Song by the white soldiers. She would never understand that level of cruelty. Topusana knew she would forever walk with the wounds and pain of that day.

The Comanche always showed mercy toward the children of war. Why could the white soldiers not do the same for her daughter? The whites called it taking captives. *The People* saw it as a chance for those children to learn the Comanche ways. The white children would have a chance of a new life by integrating into the culture and a chance at true life with *The People*. For centuries this had been their practice, and by far the majority of those adopted never wanted to return to their old life. Most were much happier and content in the simple nurturing life of the Comanche culture and in the acceptance and love of *The People*.

Topusana thought she would never understand the death of Prairie Song. The details of her death she hid away in her heart and mind. She could never share with her husband, Tabbananica, what had happened to Prairie Song. She knew it would mean his death. He would attempt to enact revenge on the entire white nation, but their numbers were too great.

In answer to his question, "Did Prairie Song die well?" She simply answered, "Yes." She knew in her heart they must survive.

She also knew revenge was not a way to live well. To live well, Tosahwi taught her, was to forgive, a thing most Warriors did not understand.

Her husband was a Warrior.

She also knew something must be done to preserve a remnant of their way of life and the culture of *The People*. That would be her focus, a way to live through the horrors of war. In the incredible pain of losing her beautiful daughter, the only choice she had was indeed forgiveness—and survival.

Tabbananica, Topusana, and Shaman Tosahwi were willing to live a new way. They had planned well for their escape. They had escaped not into a place or new land or even into hiding. They had escaped into the Dream Time.

The Dream Time was a place where the enemy could not go, nor did they understand. There, for a time, they would be safe from the bullets, safe from the broken promises, safe from the rangers and the white soldiers. The once great Numunuu were no more. Topusana thought perhaps never again would this great proud Nation of people walk this earth as they had in their time.

Topusana, or Sana as her mother referred to her, was alive in her little cavern near their former Home Camp on the San Saba. She had awakened from the Dream Time. She would now await her husband's awakening. Perhaps they could find a new beginning, and then possibly once again walk and live and love upon this land the Great Spirit had given to them all. Sana thought perhaps they were now safe from their enemy, those who would see the Comanche People, culture, and way of life brought to an end.

She had seen that this pursuer was so hungry for land that nothing seemed sacred to them. No person, no place, no people could stand in the way of what this adversary called progress.

She knew her enemy well, although this foe seemed to appear in many different forms: white soldiers, cavalry, Texas Rangers, politicians, Indian agents, even missionaries. That formidable force she felt deep in her spirit she would somehow now face again—the Government of the United States of America.

Sana rose from the sleeping area and gently swept the soft sand from her skin. She could hear faintly the shallow breathing of Tabbananica, or Tabba as she called him. She moved the few steps across the elevated sandstone room. Kneeling beside her husband, she watched for a moment as he slept. Tabba was her life, her everything. Their love had endured the most tragic events that a family could ever imagine. Sana knew she needed his strength; she needed his protection.

"Oh, my husband, how long will it be before you awaken and join me?" she whispered softly to him. She stared across the empty space of the cavern in the direction of the perilous route toward the cavern entrance. What would await her once outside the cavern in this new world and time in which she had awakened?

Chapter 2

June 24
Present Time

Sana needed to move. She struck a second pre-prepared torch with her flint and stone. She knew from Tosahwi that food and drink were now essential. Sana had no way of knowing how long the Dream Time had lasted. Her body was speaking to her, and she knew in order to recover, hydration and nutrition were needed quickly.

She surveyed the cavern for the supplies she and Tabba had spent months preparing and storing away. There was nothing.

No dried meat in the tightly packed skins. No dried corn nor seeds. There was nothing left of what they had stored for the very purpose of living in the cavern, perhaps for an extended time. The cavern floor was void, nothing but clean sand and stone. Even the fire pit where so many fires had been laid was now just vaguely detectable against the stone wall. The smoke hole that Tabba had so expertly disguised some seventy feet above her head was no longer visible from below. Now there was only a small darkening of the cave wall where so many fires had been kindled. Very little evidence was left of the nights and days spent here preparing with her husband and Tosahwi.

All those nights and days spent in planning, talking of the Dream Time, and preparing for their eventual exit; those plans would now have to change. Now it would be necessary to leave the cavern to survive. She knew from experience hunger could drive a person to make decisions that were not sound. She needed food, but she also knew she would have to be extremely careful of detection. Sana had trained well and knew what must be done. She would need all her skills and intellect to perform everything necessary with excellence.

What had become of the supplies was a mystery. Doubt was creeping in. Was she awake? Was this a dream? What was real? Was she in her little cavern in the Texas hills?

Yes, answered a voice from within, startling her. Did she hear an audible voice? Peering across the room, she heard again the shallow breath of her husband, soundness returning to her. She also heard running water. Sana was suddenly aware of her thirst.

The cave water was cool and clear. She saw her reflection in the pool for the first time in how long?

Sana was still young, still beautiful. With high cheek bones, shining black hair, beautiful dark eyes—her man would say her eyes were like the night moon—a glimmer in them always. Tabba had always said to her that she was a delicate, beautiful creation, just as her name suggested. Sana was slender, but her body strong, muscular even. Her mind was keen and aware.

As the chosen leader of her Tribe, Sana had been trained, conditioned even, in the skills required for a Warrior. She had been educated concerning the history of her *People* and the struggles they had faced, as well as instructed in the art of negotiation and diplomacy. Sana was well versed in the ancient tales of her *People*, their creation. She knew of the love of the Great Spirit.

The leaders of her tribe, including her grandmother Kota (Friend to Everyone), had seen the signs even in Sana's childhood; the special giftings she had received from the Great Spirit were clearly evident. Sana's giftings also included that of visions. Her elders had set her apart at a very early age for her training. Those elders knew and could see Sana's life would have a distinct purpose.

Sana was beginning to understand that purpose. She continually heard the voice of the Great Spirit whispering within her heart. She knew without a doubt the Spirit was directing her steps. She knew the calling and purpose that had been placed on her life at such a young tender age. The purpose was not complex or confusing to her. Now that she had survived the attack on her camp and survived the travel through the Dream Time, she knew her survival was not a coincidence but a destiny.

She wondered how many of the others might also now be awakening.

Sana reached to her side and felt the completely healed wound. She spied her reflection in the pool and saw the distinct scar that would become a lifelong reminder of the day the white soldiers had taken everything from her.

Her clothing was worn and tattered, another mystery, as they were new when she had entered her Dream Time. She would need to make new skins, which would be a risk in itself. She drank deeply again from the pool. The cave water instantly revived her mind and body. It also awakened her soul while bringing the glimmer of the moon back into her beautiful eyes.

The Comanche in her knew water meant life. Life was why she was here, one of the last of her little tribe to survive. Sana needed to be strong. She had been given a gift. The marvelous gift of life, a blessing from the Great Spirit. Resolve was settling in her mind and soul, along with something else too, determination.

At that very moment, Sana made a decision. She would live, not just survive as she had in the days of the past. Topusana would live! She would set in motion this very day the reason for her survival, her living for purpose. This day to live would be to continue who the Numunuu, *The People*, could become. The quest of establishing a new Homeland for her people would begin here and now.

Sana paused for a moment in the silence of the cavern. In her heart, she knew this was a good day.

Little could she know this day was June 24, 2020.

She began to think again of all that had taken place. The struggle to survive, the constant pursuit of *The People* by the white soldiers. Her mind drifted into the scenes and horrors of the past, the reasons for the preparation, the planning, the escape…

Chapter 3

Kansas Territory 1838

The freezing wind cut across the prairie with nothing to slow it for hundreds of miles. Ice crystals formed on the buffalo grass, giving the prairie the appearance of a frozen white ocean, as far as the eye could see.

In this windswept frozen land moved the little band of Comanche. They had covered nearly 500 miles in just over one month, searching for the buffalo. Chief Maguara (Spirit Talker) ordered the movement to begin. He knew they must find another deer today just to keep *The People* alive. Sending out two of his strongest Warriors, Neeko (One Who Finds) and Tabbananica, and having Tosahwi pray over them first, they rode farther north directly into the fierce wind. A fine sleet was beginning to fall as the Warriors disappeared over the low hills. Maguara also prayed for their success. Surely today they would catch up to the buffalo herd.

They had left the San Saba in beautiful autumn weather, hoping to reach the hunting grounds in just a few days.

The prairie had continued to change with the settling of the Texans, who were building cabins even in the Llano now, their presence ousting the buffalo from their wintering grounds. The pursuit of the buffalo, with the entire camp in trail, had proved futile to this point. Tosahwi thought possibly today the Great Spirit would hear their prayers and they would find buffalo. The movement had not been without pain and suffering; they had lost several horses. Starvation was a real threat to animals and *The People* alike. The little band was now only one day, at most, from having no food stores at all.

The older ones and the younger children could not keep up the pace much longer. Tosahwi would lead the way today, praying as they moved ahead.

Prairie Song, the young daughter of Topusana, stumbled as she was packing her things for the day's walk, skinning her knees on the frozen ground. She began to cry, her mother gently helping her rise, encouraging her. Sana gently dabbed the trickle of blood that quickly froze to the exposed skin on both of Prairie Song's knees. Six-year-old Prairie Song was cold, tired, and most of all hungry. She wanted nothing more than to have a day of rest. Even at her young age she understood the necessity of continuing to move with *The People*. *"Can we please just rest today, Mommy?"* she pleaded with her mother through the tears. *"We could stay by the fire, and perhaps we could play a game."*

Her mother simply embraced her daughter while drawing her into the warmth of her skins and bosom, turning to shield her from the harsh bitter north wind and the hunger that gnawed at them both.

Sana thought, how could a mother protect a child from such a thing as hunger? *"Be strong Little One; we will feast tonight,"* Sana gently whispered in her ear. *"I have had a dream. I have seen and understood clearly. We will be upon the buffalo before the sun sets. You will be full, warm, and safe with me tonight."*

Prairie Song lingered in the embrace and love of her mother's arms. The tears were still coming, but in her heart, the comforting words of her mother warmed her from the inside out. The two stood together for a few moments on the frozen prairie, wrapped in one another's arms. Prairie Song's heart was filled with hope from this caring, loving embrace.

From a bluff overlooking the camp of the Comanche, Karl Bodmer opened the spy glass and focused on the scene below. What came into view was obviously a Comanche mother and her daughter in a loving, protecting embrace. He closed the glass and began to sketch immediately the image burned into his mind's eye.

Never had he witnessed such emotion and love in a single moment. In this brutally harsh environment in which he supposed the Comanche's very lives were in the balance, the sight before him was both heart-wrenching…and heartwarming.

Karl and his guide had set out from Fort Leavenworth along the banks of the Missouri river. The two men had traveled for seven days continuously and not seen another living soul or even an animal. The weather displayed a fierce cold, frozen rain and a brutal wind.

Karl thought the conditions nearly unbearable for human survival. It seemed as if all life on the open prairie had simply vanished in the silence of the frozen windswept plain. However, sensing as he recorded in his journal, "How do I explain this inner calling to continue on in these brutal conditions?" Karl and his guide pressed forward upon the freezing winter plain.

On this now the eighth day of the foray, his guide had risen early, and then returned quickly to camp as Karl was preparing a morning fire. Upon hearing the news of a band of Comanche moving just a mile or so away, the two men quickly covered the mile, completely hidden due to the gently rolling terrain. The sight before him in the spyglass was exactly what was missing from his pictorial record of their expedition.

Love, emotion, tenderness appeared before him, none of which the American or European press was presenting in the daily stories of the settling of the American West.

In fact, this scene he had just witnessed was exactly what he had found in his travels, research, and documentation.

Most of Karl Bodmer's encounters with the Native peoples had been quite friendly. The Indians were enthralled with his ability to re-create on paper things from everyday life within just a few moments of introducing himself. The Natives were especially in awe of the sketches he would produce of themselves, and Karl found the laughter and lighthearted sense of humor as the Natives gazed upon a likeness of a family member or friend, simply enchanting.

He really had no intention of trading his sketches, but the Natives simply would not take *"No trade"* for an answer. Karl ended up with more artifacts, valuable tools, and weapons than he could possibly carry with him back to Europe.

On his return to New Orleans and then ultimately to Paris, he felt he would have a lifetime of work ahead of him. The art patrons of Europe were completely overwhelmed with the American West. His gallery would be a busy place for years to come.

He wondered to himself this frozen miserable day, would he be able to re-create this scene once back in Paris? He would need his viewers to feel the cold bite of the wind, sense the compassion, relate to the universal embrace of mother and daughter. This re-creation would be a masterpiece if he were able to do so.

He turned silently to his guide and whispered, "We may return home. I have seen all I need to see."

Paintings of this beautiful land and these beautiful people would soon come forth from his brush, he thought. The story of human compassion and love would also now be a centerpiece of that work.

Karl knew this love, compassion, and tenderness he had witnessed this day was truly a universal gift to all mankind. To put on canvas that emotion, to re-create that universal gift in still life was a skill not taught in art schools but rather a gift, he thought, that came forth from one's soul.

****

The little band of Comanche had been moving about half a day when, on the crest of a slight rise, Tosahwi called for all to stop. They would rest a moment, drink the last of the water, and eat the last few pieces of dried meat. One small piece only per person. Tosahwi thought it seemed the temperature was dropping further with the wind stiffening, freezing the skin of his face while his lungs burned with the cold in every breath.

Gazing into the distance, Tosahwi dismounted his pony and fell to his knees in gratitude as he made out the distinct figures of the returning Warriors. They were dismounted and walking, leading their war ponies; both horses were loaded with buffalo meat.

Chief Maguara led his little band toward the east just a few hundred yards. Following a frozen creek, he spied the cottonwoods along and below a small bluff. Firewood was gathered from the huge cottonwoods. Lodges were set up quickly. The lodge fires lit. Within the hour the lodges began to warm. The aroma of roasting meat wafted along the frozen creek bank and within the teepee lodges.

Prairie Song nestled further down into the huge buffalo robe between her mother and father. The fire crackled as the warmth spread within the protection of the teepee.

Outside, the darkness settled across the frozen prairie. The wind whistled in the treetops; the ice pelted the sides of the lodges. The wolves began their songs.

For the first night in many, Prairie Song, the daughter of Topusana and Tabbananica, was full and warm and safe.

Chapter 4

The Council
San Antonio, Texas
March 1840

Buffalo Hump, grandfather of Topusana, knew in his heart the white leaders could not be trusted. The twelve Chiefs had urged him to join them in the peace negotiations. Perhaps the white soldiers and the leaders of the Republic of Texas would finally agree to establishing boundaries and a sovereign land for the remaining Comanche tribes. Upon the offer he had received from twelve Chiefs to attend a peace conference, Buffalo Hump declined. Speaking as few words as possible, the Comanche way of attempting to make his point, Buffalo Hump said simply, "The white soldiers cannot be trusted."

Chief Maguara drew closer to the night fire to warm himself. He was surrounded by the other Chiefs, the women, children, and a few Warriors. Their delegation numbered sixty members…tomorrow they would enter San Antonio in all their finery. Dress, beads, paint, even hair was to be prepared for a display. The women and children would serve them respectfully. The Warriors would offer a show of protection. This would be a presentation of the proper and excellent Comanche culture to the white leaders. This display would be a sign for all to see they were still a powerful nation of people to be reckoned with and respected for future negotiations.

Tonight, they were camped outside San Antonio. The stars were bright overhead and the air quite cold for March. The wind whispered lightly in the trees above them. Why were the others not listening? Why could they not hear?

Maguara thought there were simply too many words to hear. The Spirit was speaking in the wind. Listening to the talk of the other Chiefs, Maguara was deeply troubled, troubled by the refusal of Buffalo Hump to participate. Troubled by so many words and talk from the other Chiefs. But more than anything, Chief Maguara was troubled by the vision he had seen. Should he speak of it now?

He decided no.

In his vision he had seen a massacre. He knew in his heart the vision had been given him as a warning and as a preparation. He also knew the others would not listen. He could not change the truth revealed in the vision. He had simply seen the future of tomorrow. Chief Maguara knew this would be his last night to walk the earth. He tried to concentrate on the gifts surrounding him: children sleeping, a wife, the whisper of the wind, the pictures the stars painted in the sky. Life was a treasure and a gift. Chief Maguara was grateful.

He knew tomorrow they would all leave the land to walk with the Great Spirit.

The white leaders, indeed, could not be trusted.

****

In a warm office near the Council House in the center of San Antonio, Albert Stanley Johnston, the Texas Secretary of War, consulted with his officers. He had just ordered the entire Comanche Delegation to be taken hostage upon their arrival, without bloodshed if possible. He was determined to have the Texas hostages returned. The Comanche bands were continuing to take captives, many of them young children. Johnston would see to the return of these hostages…no matter the cost.

****

The Comanche procession entered San Antonio, proud and quite elegant. The dress and finery were a brilliant contrast to the drab streets and dull appearance of the south Texas spring that had not yet flowered or budded. The streets were dusty with a windblown sky overhead. The sun shone bright on the delegation, highlighting the colorful, yet fierce appearance of the Comanche as they rode slowly down Market Street.

People had come out in droves to see the real-live savage Comanche Chiefs. Children cowered behind parents while women backed inside the doors of local shops as the procession neared. Fear permeated the crowd, empowering the Chiefs and Warriors who could always sense fear in any enemy.

Chief Maguara led the way, mounted upon his beautiful war pony. The delegation approached the Texas leaders who met them a few blocks from the Council House. Albert Johnston, escorted by fifty or more Texas Militia, greeted the Chiefs with a wave and a gesture to follow him. No words were spoken.

Johnston was fuming, he saw no prisoners with the savages. However, one prisoner was present; he simply did not recognize her in her splendid Comanche attire. Na'Ura (Someone Found) walked proudly beside her new mother Kota.

From Johnston's perspective, this meeting was solely for that purpose, the return of prisoners. He decided to lead them to the Council House, which adjoined the jail. The Texas Militia now surrounded the entire group as they proceeded in parade-like fashion along the streets of San Antonio.

Chief Maguara could sense the tension with the other Chiefs and the Warriors. None of this was a surprise to him. He had seen it all in his vision, a sense of calm enveloped him as he rode his fine stolen mount for the last time. His eyes bored through any who dared even make eye contact with him. He possessed a defiant look, a challenge to these innumerable whites who had invaded the land of his people. He would die a good death this day!

Entering the Council House, the Comanches, in their tradition, seated themselves on the floor. The Texans sat in chairs on the wooden platform above them, and within a few minutes, the Texas Militia lined the room along each wall. There were no pleasantries exchanged.

Speaking through an interpreter, the Texans demanded to know the location of the hostages. Chief Maguara responded, "*The hostages are being held by other bands with whom we have no control. I have spoken with the Chiefs of these bands. It is a possibility they can be negotiated for in exchange for a great deal of ammunition and blankets.*"

On hearing this, the Texas officials, while speaking through the interpreter, said to communicate to the Chiefs that their entire band would be taken hostage and placed in jail until all captives were returned.

When hearing the reply from the Texans, the interpreter became alarmed. However, speaking not to the Chiefs what had just been spoken, the interpreter informed the Texans, "If I communicate that to the Comanche, they will surely fight their way out of the building!" The Council officials instructed him to inform the Comanches anyway.

On hearing they were now to be imprisoned, the brave little group of Comanche Chiefs and handful of Warriors, a few women, and children attempted to respond with force.

Time slowed for Chief Maguara as he saw the bullet enter his chest as if watching a dream. Maguara saw his body fall as his Spirit floated upward, no longer indwelling his body. He watched the entire battle from the top of the room, although it was more a massacre than a battle…just as in the vision. He saw the Texans begin to fire on the others from the Peace Delegation.

Very few arrows or knives found their mark. In a few moments, the Chiefs were all dead. Now they each joined Maguara's slow-motion vision, watching the massacre beside him. Even the women and children began to fall. Na'Ura, his new daughter, fell face down on the platform, the blood pooling around her slight, lifeless body. In a hail of bullets, one Warrior after another joined them, as did most of the women and young children. His children.

A few of the women and children escaped into the street. Somehow, all the dead now joined them outside the building, still viewing the slow-motion scene from above. Several were shot in the street. Even some Texans along the street were killed by the bullets of the Texas Militia. The few remaining Comanches attempted to flee. None of the survivors would escape.

Fifty-two members of the delegation of sixty Comanches were slaughtered in and around the Council House. All fought bravely, but they were badly outnumbered and out gunned.

Theirs was a good death this day.

The eight survivors were taken captive and placed in the jail. A few hours later the Texans decided to move them to an undisclosed location, to avoid talk of immediate hanging. The crowd demanded revenge for the bystanders who had been killed in the streets; although the bystanders had, in fact, all been killed by the bullets of the Texas Militia and not by the Comanche women and children who had escaped the slaughter in the Council House.

Chief Maguara and the others rising higher above the scene, floated away from the massacre, into the presence of the Great Spirit.

****

In the vastness of the Llano Estacado, Buffalo Hump paused and listened quietly to the voices in the wind. The voices were crying out…singing their death song.

Tomorrow he would begin to gather his forces.

Chapter 5

March 1840
The Following Day

Kota (Friend to Everyone), wife of Maguara, walked along at the rear of the procession of captives.

Each of the captives was bound with rope, hands tied behind each captive's back. As the eldest, she would now be the leader and looked upon for a plan. How to escape? she thought. She closely observed the men overseeing their movement.

It became very apparent lesser men had been assigned the task to move a few old women and children. Kota noticed the shared bottle being passed between the men. She also noticed the eyes of the leader continually upon her. It was quite plain what the man was considering. She felt for the knife she had easily concealed beneath her skins. Patience was a thing Kota knew well. She would wait, for now.

Late into the morning, the Texas sun began to bare down on the Comanche captives and the soldiers alike. The lead soldier halted the march within a mesquite thicket adjacent to a small spring. A light wind stirred; little puffs of dust rose from the trail. On Kota's signal, the plan was clearly communicated to all using sign language.

The captives were allowed to sit on a slight embankment, rest a moment, and drink from the spring. Kota communicated a need for privacy and knew the soldier would follow. What made these Texans think Comanches could not remove and cut flimsy ropes? The soldier had drunk much whiskey during the move. The white soldiers smelled of whiskey and human filth. Kota could smell the man's stench as he approached her from behind. She was alert and ready. The wind seemed to settle; the birds quieted. A stillness fell about the scene.

The "Big Fool" attempted to grope her, grabbing her hair from behind… and did not expect a fight from an old woman. The man surely looked surprised as the dagger sank deep into his chest, the blood from his black heart pouring forth, covering Kota's hands. Kota whispered the name of her husband in the white man's ear as he fell.

"Maguara, Maguara, Maguara!"

He collapsed to the ground…dead at her feet. Kota signaled the others with the faint call of the night bird.

The women and children sprang into action. The two soldiers were drinking from the spring; Kota had timed the move perfectly. Both soldiers were dispatched easily in their drunkenness—by old women—drowned while face down in the pool. The women approached Kota; without words she handed over her knife. The women went to work leaving evidence intended to frighten any pursuers. The bodies would be found with no manhood. For the first time in her life, Kota, in a deep and personal seething anger, took three scalps.

This was the first time in her seventy-five years she had felt such satisfaction. She now knew what all Warriors must have known, to kill an enemy, to exact your power over evil, was an emotion she had never felt, but now understood.

****

Kota walked through the night. She was not in a hurry, as she knew no one followed. The survivors had agreed to each travel in different directions. They knew this would confuse any pursuers and leave less sign to follow. The younger ones would survive just fine; they had been taught well in the Comanche way of movement.

Her heart was breaking for her husband and the others. What kind of people would welcome a Peace Delegation and then slaughter them? Kota prayed as she walked, trying to erase the scene from her mind, yet going over it again and again. There was comfort in knowing the dead would now walk with the Great Spirit. But she would miss the closeness, companionship, comfort, and love of her husband for the rest of her days on this earth. It was a comfort to her also, to know in her heart, that her remaining days on Earth would be very few.

She would walk back to the Camp on the San Saba. It would be a long and dangerous journey. She estimated ten days, fifteen miles per day. If she just kept moving, it would not be a difficult thing to do. She had survived much longer journeys. As a young child, a young mother, and now as an old grandmother, walking, moving with the land, was a way of life for the Comanche.

Movement of *The People*, whether for buffalo hunts or simply moving to warmer grounds for winter, walking along the ancient trails was how the Numunu traveled. Kota knew how to move steadily without detection. She knew where the water was, the water that flowed along every trail in Texas.

Water, and knowing where it was found, was of the utmost importance. Traveling out onto the Llano, or west toward the Pecos, or even to the east and south toward the Great Water, Kota possessed this wisdom and the ability it brought for survival.

Tonight, as she walked along the trail by moonlight, she softly sang. The sky above her was clear, and a light wind whispered in the trees, accompanying her songs.

She paused and listened. The air was again quite cold for March although Kota hardly seemed to feel its effects. She began again to quietly sing the song of mourning for her husband. She also sang the song normally reserved for Warriors, the song of victory over one's enemy.

Though Kota considered killing those three soldiers and her escape a small victory, it was enough to drive her on. She must reach the San Saba and her people. She needed to tell the story. She would have no problems recounting the events that played over in her mind. The story of the massacre would be told along the rivers and trails of the Comanche Homeland. As she walked along under the starlight, she sang the songs her ancestors had sung for hundreds of years.

Kota was not alone. The stars, the wind, the trees, even the river she followed, sang along with her.

Chapter 6

San Saba River Valley
October 8, 1844
Four years Later

The trees along the river glowed a golden hue in the late afternoon sun. The camp of the little band of Comanches was still and quiet. The gurgling of the river could be heard throughout the camp; the light wind rustled the fall leaves. Several leaves drifted like feathers in the sky, landing here and there on the surface of the water, gently floating downstream in the mild current.

Sana had exited the hidden cavern located just up the small canyon north of the Home Camp. She knew instantly something was wrong. No birds were singing, the atmosphere was quiet, too quiet.

She saw the first of the troops approaching from the other side of the river, moving in columns toward the camp.

What to do…Tabba was at the rear of the cavern. It would take her fifteen minutes or more to travel to him in the cavern, another fifteen minutes to return to where she now stood. Deciding not to return to the interior of the cavern, she did the only thing she could. There was not enough time.

From the top of her lungs she yelled a *War Cry*, warning the others of the impending attack. Teepee flaps began to open as friends and family scattered into the trees and underbrush.

Sana raced toward the camp, screaming her *War Cry*. The few Warriors remaining in the camp charged toward the enemy on the other side of the river. Their numbers would not be enough. The group was made up mostly of young boys and a few old grandfathers. The Warriors of the tribe had not yet returned from their hunting. They had been gone now only two days, traveling toward the south and west, toward the bend in the great river the Mexicans called Rio Grande.

The white soldiers began to fire on any and all targets. The small band of Comanche remaining dispatched a few with their first few shots. Sana's heart sank as she saw the flanking movement from the east.

Dozens of soldiers poured forth from the brush, firing directly into teepees and lodges.

Where was Prairie Song? Topusana began to call her name. Running directly toward her lodge, she was rapidly closing the distance between herself and the camp. Suddenly something struck her in the side; she stumbled, not understanding. Feeling no pain, she attempted to press on toward the camp. Struggling to regain her footing, her legs not working correctly, she stumbled again. There, exiting the lodge, was Prairie Song.

Sana called out to her. "*Little One...run!*"

From nowhere, the butt of a rifle struck Sana on the back of the head. The world began to turn around, the earth tilted sideways, the ground racing upwards toward her vision.

Then there was only blackness and pain.

The terrible dream came to her. The soldiers were hurting Prairie Song. Sana tried to call out. Each time she attempted to scream no sound would come forth. She begged for them to take her instead. She pleaded with the white soldiers, each effort to scream, or yell, or speak produced no sound. Sana became aware. What she was seeing...was not a dream.

Prairie Song, from beneath a white soldier, looked across the camp directly into the eyes of her mother. She made the sign of love.

Prairie Song then attacked the soldier, biting his face and removing a large chunk of flesh from the man's cheek. Blood poured out of the man's face. The white soldier rolled over, screaming in pain. Prairie Song reached for her clothing, attempting to cover herself while crawling away from the man. Her innocence and modesty even in the midst of violation cost her a few precious seconds. She stood to run, coming face to face with the bloodied man. The white soldier had located his revolver near his clothing. He took aim and fired one shot into the forehead of Prairie Song. She fell dead at the man's feet.

Topusana could hear the laughter of his companions.

She somehow became aware of the unseen Spirit World and saw the beautiful spirit of her only daughter, Prairie Song, rise from the burning camp.

Light enveloped her. She was singing softly, her hands lifted upwards as if being greeted by a friend. Overwhelming peace and comfort reflected and shown forth on the face of Prairie Song…and then she was gone.

Then the darkness overcame Topusana again.

****

The heavens gave forth no light. The sky was completely blackened by the high overcast. No stars shown through the veil, even the half-moon gave no light. Sana had finally awakened; she was tied and bound, hand and foot.

As the soldiers strode about the camp, Sana heard laughter encircling some of the campfires. Teepees and lodges smoldered in the darkness. She could see bodies strewn about the camp. She lay there motionless, crying silently. Her family, her friends, were all gone now.

Prairie Song also was gone, departed forever from this cruel world.

Topusana wanted to die right here and now. How could this happen? One more day and the remaining tribal members were going to enter the caverns for the Dream Time. One more day, she drifted away into the pain and darkness.

When she awakened again the fires had died down; the white soldiers were silent. All were sleeping in their drunkenness.

For the second time this day Sana sensed it was too quiet. She heard the faint call of the night bird.

Tabba was calling to her! She lay there in silence, listening.

Sana, knowing the signal, chanced a faint reply. At the count of twenty-five came the confirmation in a return call.

Tabba was coming for her! She lay there in the darkness awaiting.

It took less than three minutes for her to sense his presence. Hearing the slight scuffle just a few feet from her, Sana caught the scent of the fresh blood spilling to the ground from the group of white soldiers nearest her.

For Tabba, it was an easy thing in the darkness to lock onto the enemy's throat. Then with his strong forearms, the sharp knife slicing deeply, hold the man in the death lock a few seconds. Unconsciousness coming quickly as the blood drained from the man's open throat.

Tabba thought the death much too easy for the evil these men had done this day. The faint shuffle again as one by one Tabba opened the throats of the group of soldiers nearest Sana.

The last man Tabba killed had received a wound to his face. The stench of the man was overpowering. The fear in his eyes as he died was somehow deeply satisfying to Tabbananica, the Warrior.

Then he was beside her, cutting loose the bonds that held her prisoner. Rising from the ground with Sana in his arms, he silently moved away from the camp. Only after a safe distance he lowered her to the ground.

"*Prairie Song*?" he spoke her name to Sana as a question.

She lowered her head, tears flowing freely.

Fierce anger arose from the depths of Tabbananica.

Taking Sana again in his arms, Tabba silently worked his way up the little canyon across from their former Home Camp and entered the cavern.

With a burning in his heart, Tabba wanted to return and kill the rest of them one by one. After lighting the torch, he could see Sana was injured; she had lost much blood. Gently, he moved her through the difficult descent in the front of the cavern. Reaching the area of the lowered ceiling, Tabba laid her gently onto the travois he had fashioned for the purpose of moving supplies into the rear of the cavern. He carefully pulled Sana along behind him and toward the large room. Tabba knew he could not return to the camp. Sana needed him.

He had supplies, food, water, and Tosahwi had his medicine.

Exiting the area of the low ceiling while praying his way along, Tabba now lifted Sana and carried her to the upper sandstone rooms, gently laying her on the prepared sleeping area.

Upon seeing Sana, Tosahwi began his prayers for her also, preparing the medicine she desperately needed.

He had never sent a person into the Dream Time that was injured. It would be necessary to do so this time. Tosahwi began his songs.

Chapter 7

October 9, 1844
The Following Day

In the large cavern one mile north of the cavern where Sana and Tabba now slept, Tosahwi began the sacred ceremony by lighting the cave fires surrounding his family.

His surviving family included his wife, and his two sons and their wives. The other survivors of the small band were four young girls found along the riverbank after the attack. Two old grandmothers, along with his own five grandchildren, had also survived. Seventeen people plus Tabbananica and Topusana would survive the attack on the San Saba band of Comanches. Little could he know they would be the last survivors in Texas of the once great Comanche Nation.

Tosahwi knew he had made all the necessary preparations. The dried food was stored in place. The water flowing freely through the cavern would supply their needs. Clothing, firewood, even some craft and bead work was set aside. There would be work for the days ahead while the few survivors awaited one another to awake.

He paused a moment, emotion overcoming his soul as he looked upon his little family. When would they exit the Dream Time? What would await them in the new time where they would awaken? He had no way of knowing. Tosahwi was certain of one fact. None of them would ever survive the invasion of their present Homeland by the whites.

The enemy was ruthless, unbending, unwavering in their pursuit of the land and the destruction of any peoples in their path.

The Dream Time, he knew, was their only hope of escape.

Tosahwi knew his instructions to the survivors would be followed explicitly. They would wait for each other. No one would exit the cavern until all had awakened. Tosahwi had chosen the larger cavern located nearly a mile farther to the north from where Tabba and Sana now slept. The access was much easier, as a person could simply walk through this entrance and stay upright while traveling its length. In this cavern, however, the sheer size and the complexity of the maze of dead ends, switch backs, and deep-water pools made entry, or more importantly, exit from the cavern very difficult. Tosahwi knew they would be safe here in the Dream Time.

The pungent smell of the incense as it burned brought a level of comfort to him. The fragrance reminded him and the others entering the Dream Time of the many sacred ceremonies they had participated in as a people. The cave fires smoked and crackled, reflecting dancing light on the walls of the cavern. The elder grandmothers began the songs. Each one of Tosahwi's remaining family and tribe drank the medicine from the sacred bowl. Joining in the songs and prayers, *The People* moved one by one into each sleeping site. The Dream Time came quickly for them.

Their faith was strong.

Lastly, Tosahwi lay upon the sand-covered floor of his sleeping chamber. His prayers were fervent, his medicine exact and powerful. He was grateful for the gifts he had been given from the Great Spirit.

Perhaps these few survivors were enough to continue. They could possibly continue the life, the love, the reverence of their special way of life.

The Numunuu may possibly survive, despite the plans of the white man.

The tunnel seemed to spin rapidly as it encircled him. He felt light, as if floating through some space or time. He felt a distinct peace indwell him.

Then Tosahwi slept.

****

Later the same day, Kota, wife of Maguara, observed the Home Camp from the ridgeline above and to the south. Concealed in the brush, she could make out the figure of Captain Ross. Though she could not clearly hear or understand the man's words, Kota understood he was angry. The body language and instructions were clear. Bodies were being buried in a large hole. Several Texas militia soldiers were in handcuffs. Ropes were strung high in the trees.

None of what the white soldiers were doing at this moment concerned her. Her heart was simply empty. Even her mind was somehow now numb. She wanted to feel, to feel something, revenge, sadness, any emotion. Kota could somehow no longer feel anything.

She had ventured far up the river the previous day. Late in the evening she could smell the fires from miles away. She knew in her soul many had died in the previous night's attack by the rangers and Texas Militia.

Kota turned and walked away from her destroyed Home Camp alone. She began her journey. Walking this time toward the south and west. Toward the Big Bend. She knew the men were not more than a day or two away. It would be best to intercept them and lead them away from the massacre. They would join Buffalo Hump in the Llano Estacado stronghold.

Chapter 8

Present Day

The cavern lightened as Sana quietly moved toward the entrance. She extinguished her torch as she worked her way closer to the small opening. The temperature rose rapidly now as the smell of the Texas summer made its way into the front of the cavern. Here the cave began to shrink in size; no longer were there huge rooms like those that opened up farther back in the cavern. The expansive area was where they had slept in the elevated chambers formed in the sandstone. In this area toward the front of the cavern where she was now, the distance from floor to ceiling lowered to less than four feet.

Sana began to crawl. She moved silently as Tabba had taught her, feeling her way, more than seeing. "Quieter than the deer, quieter still than the fox," Tabba's voice echoed in her mind. Silently, skillfully, she moved as her muscles awakened. Bone, muscle, tendon, all working in harmony and grace. She paused briefly to gain her breath, her arms relaxed. She moved another three hundred yards, which revealed more light and slightly more warmth. It had been harvest when the three had last entered the cavern, but the temperature now was the first indication of time passing. Some months had obviously gone by, at least in the world outside the cavern. Sana sensed something was off, something was not right.

She paused and listened as the sounds from outside echoed into the cavern. Strange sounds she had never heard. Slowly she feathered another one hundred yards, moving silently. The ceiling here lowered further, less than three feet separating the ceiling from the sandstone floor, with a severely sloping upward grade. Climbing now more than crawling in the confined space, Sana inched her way upward. Foothold, handhold, pressing her back and shoulder against the upper rock, bracing her knees and toes against the lower floor then pressing forward. Foot hold, hand hold, she pressed forward. The climb was not difficult for Topusana…the sounds were.

She paused again to listen as the sound became distinctly louder now. What could this be? It did not sound like any animal she had ever encountered. Roaring and rumbling, but not like thunder, the sound then faded away and ceased. The sound began again, softly at first, then grew louder, a little louder still, then at its peak, the sound changed pitch.

Like the sound of the eagle as he passed overhead, the sound grew louder as he approached, then as he soared away on the wing his sound slowly receded into nothing.

Fear crept into her mind again. What would she find of her Home Camp on the San Saba? Would the rangers still be there? Were *The People* really all dead, killed by the rangers?

She had seen with her own eyes and knew the answer…Yes, they had, in fact, all passed on, to walk now with the Great Spirit in the Great Land.

She was climbing the last few yards of the cavern as here the slope was long and steep. This drop from the entrance was the reason Tabba had chosen this particular cavern from the beginning. He knew it was unlikely anyone would venture inside given the difficulty of the entrance. Sana paused on the small step-like shelf at the narrow opening.

The debris, small stones and gravel in the entrance, was piled inward until there was only a small opening. It was as if someone had intentionally attempted to close off the entrance. Who would have done this? Had someone attempted to hide their resting place?

Sana had many questions. Perhaps the answers lie in the world outside, just within her reach.

The ingress itself was now so small that even with her slight stature Sana could not negotiate the opening. She thought it best to remove as little of the debris as possible so as not to give away any evidence that someone had entered or exited the cavern. Digging and scraping aside rocks and dirt, she managed to enlarge the opening of the entrance an additional six inches on the bottom and opening the entrance another six inches along one side. The opening now left just enough room for her to maneuver upward and through. Very slowly she inched her way forward on her belly while fighting against the loose debris.

She eased only her head out of the narrow opening. Sana peered across the open valley ahead of her. She saw her former home on the San Saba for the first time…in apparently a very long time.

The copse of brush that hid the entrance from the outside to anyone passing by had grown into a thicket of huge oak trees. The sound came to her faint at first, then she realized as the sound grew, whatever it was, was becoming louder and drawing closer. She immediately shrank back into the cavern as the sound continued to grow, then diminish and finally fade away. Peering out again while scanning the river below, she took in the scene with disbelief. She froze for a few moments as her mind attempted to understand.

Sana again quickly receded farther from the entrance, sliding down the slope and back into the cave. She could not believe or even comprehend what her eyes had just seen.

She paused at the base of the slope, resolve settling her emotions. She knew she must be brave. Taking the metate in her hands, Sana worked her way back up the slope and out of the opening.

The tribe had worked for months developing the elaborate system of signs to communicate to one another who had awakened. The first sign for Sana would be the placing of the metate. She concealed the sign in an outcropping of rocks just above the entrance to the cavern. Now if any of the others ventured near the entrance, they would see the metate and know she had awakened.

The sound began again, faint at first. As the sound grew, Sana once again quickly entered the cavern, descending into the darkness.

Chapter 9

The Ross Ranch, Grove County, Texas
The Following Day

Although only mid-morning, June in Texas was sweltering. Abigail Ross felt the perspiration across her back trickle along her torso like a feather and come to rest on her hips. Her garden was bursting forth with summer squash, okra, cucumbers, tomatoes, even the cantaloupe and watermelons were swelling daily in the hot Texas sun.

Abigail was content. She felt really at peace at this time of her life. Tending the garden was not work, but more like therapy. These days in the autumn of her life were filled with goodness and grace for all those whose lives she touched. She now spent most of her time giving her time away. It felt good to do so.

Giving offered her peace.

Besides tending to her garden and household chores, which she loved, she maintained an immaculate and stunningly beautiful home, which gave her a personal pleasure. She also volunteered a couple of days a week at the local library and even put in one or two shifts per week at the local coffee shop owned by a lifelong girlfriend.

Abby had spent the last thirty years of her life as an elementary school teacher. Those years had included the busy hectic life of raising her own children. She knew it was now time to spend the rest of her years serving, serving others, serving the community. It was her way of saying, "Thank You." Thank you even to God for a life well lived. Abby knew that was where her peace and contentment came from, a loving, grace-giving God.

The Ross home was spectacularly beautiful, as was Abby herself. After the two children she bore—a son, Jonathan, and a daughter, Grace—Abby had never showed the physical wear that most women did post pregnancy. Her body almost instantly returned to her normal weight of 120 pounds. Her face was still lovely, though slightly showing the effects of the Texas sun. Her beauty was apparent with soft kind sky blue eyes, gentle graceful features, her hair a soft golden blond. Her figure now, even in her sixties, still resembled that of her college years at the University of Texas. In fact, she could still fit into her college cheerleader uniforms, which she had done on several occasions or at special events or parties through the years. However, she had learned from the experience. This had evoked jealous comments from old classmates and even lifelong girlfriends.

Not to mention the reaction from her husband, David, who somehow thought since she was in her cheer outfit, they should relive some of their college escapades…in the backseat of his double cab ranch pickup. She had quite enjoyed the experience herself but had decided it best to put the cheer uniforms away for good.

Abby was the quintessential Texas ranch woman. Evoking a sense of pride and accomplishment in all she did, no matter how big or small the task. Abby Ross had only one way to do whatever was put before her, and that was to do it with excellence. Whether teaching a six-year-old immigrant to read or managing a multi-million-dollar building project for the University of Texas Alumni Association, Abby performed all with excellence, beauty, and grace. Although, Abby considered the teaching so much more important than the alumni work. Her politics could never quite line up on either side of the isle. She was quite conservative on many issues, but when it came to caring for those families who were in her country illegally, Abby was a champion defender of those children.

She was not just a teacher but gifted to teach. Her parents never understood why she chose such a lowly profession. They simply did not understand Abby's compassion and true gifting.

She never saw the poor families pouring across the southern border as criminals, but rather individuals in need, in a foreign land, desperate for help. She often provided help, both monetarily and physically, by providing basic needs to them. However, more than in any other way, Abby, by educating the children of the workers, gave those children hope. She offered hope that they might have a chance, an opportunity at a better life, even the kind of life she and David now led. After all, wasn't that what was written in the Good Book? Loving her neighbor was something Abby would always attempt to do… politics be damned.

Abigail Ross, former first grade teacher, daughter of former Texas Governor Clive Sutton, wife to David Ross (a direct descendant of the famous Texas Ranger Sullivan Ross), one of the most respected and admired cattle ranchers in Grove County or all of Texas for that matter, was at peace, content and happy.

Life had not been without trials and heartache. She suffered through the loss of their only son to a war in Iraq, which she as a woman did not understand, the "War on Terror" as it was called.

Jonathan's death was more than Abby thought she and David could ever bear. With that tragic event, Abby and David now wore a symbolic badge of triumph and honor. The pain was always there, just under the surface, but life and time had dulled it to the point of overcoming the loss. She chose to recall the love, chose forgiveness, and finally, chose to accept, move forward, and live.

Moving on was what Jonathan would have wanted. It was what they were doing, living contentedly in spite of such great loss.

Abby loaded her garden basket with choice produce and headed for the coolness of the covered porch that ran on three sides the entire length of the ranch house. Here the gentle breeze instantly cooled her skin, sending goose bumps along her graceful neck and arms. It was at least twenty degrees cooler here in the shade of the porch.

David was making himself busy with the repair of the screen door. She had been after him for days to do that chore.

"Hot enough for you?" The touch of his hand against her cheek still made her flush.

"Iced tea?" he asked.

"Yes, thank you, David." The tea was dripping condensation from the glass overflowing with ice, sun brewed tea, a slice of lemon, a sprig of mint from the garden. The cold tea washed over her as she drank, the hint of mint and lemon on her tongue. Abby wondered if it was her contentment that allowed her to notice such small details these days. In the former busyness of her life, she had not noticed such details. But now, even the quick look of desire from David she instantly noticed. The goose bumps returned.

After forty years of marriage, David could still cause her heart to skip with that slight glance she knew so well.

"Forget it, Mr. Ross, I'm a busy woman today." He gazed at her beauty, the look was back, and she knew his thoughts. "Maybe if you play your cards right."

"Playing the cards right for me means never bluffing," he said.

"Indeed, Mr. Ross." She smiled, replying. He kissed her gently on the cheek. She smelled the faint scent of her favorite aftershave, felt the touch of his warm face against her cheek, the touch of his body against her. Then Abby Ross, daughter of a Texas Governor, queen of her empire, went weak in the knees.

Perhaps it was the time they had spent apart, both physically and emotionally, after Jonathan's death. Maybe they were still healing in many ways. Is that what brought this new awareness of touch, sound, sensations? Abby loved that she was now so in tune with life, and my what a life, swooning over her handsome husband after forty years of marriage.

"I think that you think you're still twenty," she said.

"Come let me show you my latest find," he said, smiling.

Chapter 10

Present Day

David took Abby by the hand and leaving the porch, led her through the Great Room toward his study.

Abby paused a moment as the two entered the room. "Let's just look again this morning."

David knew the little game they played very well. Abby loved to simply stop and soak in the beauty, the fullness, the life, that surrounded them. For Abby it was always a moment to count her blessings, become aware, and express her gratefulness.

For David the little game was troubling. His mind always seemed to drift to his son Jonathan. He would play along and not share with her where his heart and mind truly went...to that place of deep brokenness and heartache.

Abby stood at the entrance to the beautiful room and thought only of her husband this morning. David J. Ross was a unique man. His great-great-grandfather, Sullivan Ross, was a former Confederate General and Texas Ranger. David favored him in more ways than one. Mr. Ross was his name to all who knew him. Whether by a ranch hand or United States senator, all addressed him as Mr. Ross.

David Ross cut a tall figure, both in stature and in life. Although six feet tall, he seemed taller. His body remained lean and muscled, even in his sixties, from the hard work of life on a Texas cattle ranch.

Abby knew David never demanded respect or admiration. It was simply bestowed upon him. He was a natural born leader of men. With that came the respect of most, the envy of some. Abby thought what might best describe her husband and partner was trust. David Ross was a man you could trust.

David released her hand and moved toward the huge fireplace in the center of the room as Abby observed.

He was a handsome man with graying hair, dark blue eyes, a strong jaw, and strong features. He often carried a look of seriousness that covered over the soft, kind heart hidden beneath that Abby knew all too well. Sometimes she would say, "You can fool most of the people with that *look,* David, but I know your heart is smiling on the inside." David had learned to use this particular *look* when he tired of a conversation or had decided whoever might be speaking was simply "a fool with a limited vocabulary."

Abby admired David's brilliant intellect more than anything. To her, intelligence was stimulating, both mentally and physically. Although, he never attended college, a fact at which her parents were appalled. David was self-educated in every sense of the term, a student of history, science, geography, and archaeology. He was an expert at cattle growing, breeding, and animal genetics. He was an excellent horseman and possessed an aptitude for range management that he put into practice on his land even before it was taught in the agricultural colleges. David's hard work and intelligence had, in fact, earned them all of these blessings that surrounded their life.

Abby moved toward her husband. He opened his arms and embraced her.

"What do you see today, love?" he asked.

"More than I could ever ask or imagine," Abby said.

David led her through the Great Room to his private study.

Abby could not walk through the room without admiring the beauty that surrounded them. The finest Western art adorned the walls of their home. Works by Remington, Terpning, and Russell enveloped them. Depictions of Native American life and early culture, including pictures of cattle drives on the Great Plains surrounded them.

But Abby's favorite from an unknown artist depicted a beautiful young Comanche mother and daughter. The faces were not clear in the painting, the emotion was. The two were simply clinging to one another in a loving, protecting embrace. It was as if the mother was trying to shield the child from something, the young girl lost in the embrace of her mother.

As a mother, Abby knew that embrace. She was always drawn to the sadness in the painting, never quite understanding the reason for her attraction and the emotion it produced in her.

The bronze cowboy scenes and sculptures were spectacularly captured by known and unknown artists alike. The home was, for all practicality, a living museum. The texture, the color, and life of Texas ranching surrounded them both as they walked through the room.

The two entered David's study. From his desk he took in his hands an ancient stone bowl.

"I found this, this morning, must have passed it a thousand times. I was on my way to the north pasture near one of the caverns. There it was lying in plain sight. What do you think?" he asked, smiling at the object.

"David, it's magnificent!" Abby said, taking the bowl from his hands, feeling the smooth texture, the coolness of the rock. "Do you know what it is?"

"According to my research today..." David referred to a book from his extensive collection on Native American history and artifacts that sat open on his desk. "It's a grinding bowl. The proper name is *metate*."

"Magnificent!" Abby stated again, now feeling the surface, instantly imagining who might have used this piece. She wondered who might have prepared meals for their family, working tireless hours in preparation for winter. How many centuries had it been used and passed down? What could have become of its last owner? "How old is it, David?"

"It's hard to say. Sometimes these were passed from band to band or traded after they had been used for hundreds of years; it is probably very old." David often reminded Abby that Texas history, in terms of the planet or European history, was still quite young. In fact, just over 100 years ago this very ranch was part of the vast Homeland of the Numunuu, the Comanche people. They had actually occupied a camp not far from their present-day home, along the banks of the San Saba river.

David gently placed the bowl on the mantle of the fireplace that warmed his study during the cold Texas winters. He set the bowl alongside other ancient treasures he had found over the years: a Comanche bow, several intact arrows, a Comanche medicine bag, and an assorted collection of arrowheads, two old silver coins, and a few musket balls.

He moved behind his desk, his eyes on the open research book. He sat in his huge overstuffed leather chair, perusing a few pages of the book.

Abby seated herself across from him, lost in her own thoughts. She reflected that they had come so far.

David Ross owned one of the largest ranches in Texas. Abby knew David did not consider the land his. She knew Mr. Ross considered himself a steward, simply a man who had been entrusted with this land for a time. He was a man who would do his very best with that to which he had been granted. He had seen neighbors and friends alike lose what had been entrusted to them, whether to the banks, the government, thieves, or just poor financial decisions. Abby knew David Ross would see to it, through prudent and wise management, that losing this beloved land would never occur. In fact, ever the shrewd manager, David had taken the opportunities presented with the foreclosures of neighboring ranches. He had purchased those adjoining properties for pennies on the dollar. Wisely investing in cattle and land, adding to the already extensive ranch holdings. David had more than tripled the size of the ranch over the last forty years.

More importantly, he had made certain all land holdings included 100 percent of any and all mineral rights.

Abby knew David had been approached by the big oil companies concerning exploration on his land. After sorting through several proposals and meeting face to face with the executives of the huge companies, he said no to all of them.

Abby remembered well the meeting years ago in this very room. David had wondered aloud why anyone would allow an oil company to keep 88 percent of the production, leaving the owner of the oil a paltry 12 percent of the income, in perpetuity. That was the standard agreement offered to all landowners in Texas. Times were changing, he had shared with her. He explained the standard deal offered since the 1940s and 1950s didn't seem appropriate any longer. It was the 2000s, oil markets and supply were unstable and subject to the Saudi's whims. West Texas Crude was reliable and the standard for quality. Quietly, David had hired his own geologist, researched neighboring production, hired an independent drilling company, and began his own exploration.

That was nearly twenty years ago with the first fifteen wells in and producing. The price was high. Pipelines were still being built and plans for additional drilling were in place. Abby knew the net income from the production was now approaching $3.2 million dollars…per month.

Before they married, David Ross inherited his father's ranch in 1971. Cattle prices were at rock bottom. The ranch itself was in disrepair with broken and downed fence lines, and many of the water sources were inoperable. The income from the cattle could not support the loans his father had taken out on the property. Upon his father's death, foreclosure was in process. Through sheer knowledge, determination, and hard work, David Ross had become successful.

He had not simply inherited a wealthy ranch from his father, quite the opposite. David had built an empire out of a failing poor West Texas ranch.

For Abby, her husband was trusting, kindhearted, yet fierce when necessary, intelligent, and quite handsome.

Abby Ross was forever…deeply in love with him.

David Ross closed the research book and noticed Abby watching him. He was in awe this fine morning of all that surrounded him. The ranch, the history books, and especially his beautiful wife, Abby, who noticed the look in his eyes again. Gently she took his hand and led him up the stairs.

Chapter 11

Afterward in the glow of fulfillment and intimacy, David said, "I need to call Grace."

"What are you thinking?" Abby said.

"Well, I've been watching the weather. Looks like a few days of clear sailing."

Abby knew David was suggesting a sailing trip to California.

Another of the unique characteristics of David Ross, a true Renaissance Man, that Abby so admired about him was his love and knowledge of the oceans.

David's interest in the ocean had begun early in his life when he spent a couple of years on the Texas coast. While other classmates went from high school to college, David was drawn to the Texas coast. He worked as a mate on offshore fishing charters and as a deck hand on charter sailing vessels out of South Padre Island.

South Padre was where they had met when Abby was on a sorority weekend getaway. She was instantly in love with the tanned handsome young man and blushed at his advances. Who knew she would say yes to that first date on the bow of his employer's sailboat?

The sorority girls giggled and teased one another and whispered behind Abby's back. But she knew any girlfriend would be thrilled to have the attention David was directing toward Abby and Abby alone.

Those who didn't know him well would not be able to put together David's love of ranching and his fascination with the earth's oceans. To a narrow mind, a Texas rancher might seem out of place as captain of his own ocean-going sailboat. This was not the case with those who knew him well. He seemed to Abby to be more at home on the ocean sometimes than on the ranch he had built.

David dialed the number on his phone. Steve, his pilot, answered, listened a few moments, and said, "See you at noon." Turning to Abby, David asked, "Can you be ready in an hour?"

Spontaneity…she loved it!

The jet climbed rapidly across the west Texas sky reaching flight level 440, (forty-four thousand feet above sea level) in just twenty-one minutes. There were some storms across southern Arizona. However, according to Steve, the tops were around thirty-nine thousand feet. The CJ3 business jet would cruise in smooth air nearly a mile above those storms. Traveling at an astounding 530 miles per hour, flight time would be only two hours and six minutes. Grace would be overjoyed to see them.

Grace was their daughter who now lived in California. She was a free spirit as a child, and now the same as a woman. She had acquired the best features of both her parents and was simply "super model beautiful," as her father would say. Indeed, her talents, striking looks, and graceful figure, along with her father's work ethic, had insured her access and success in the world of fashion and modeling. Although with her success in those desirable worlds, Grace was left somewhat empty, even bored with the lifestyle, and what she called "eccentrics" who permeated the fashion industry. Grace was now an art student quickly becoming a talented sculptor in her own right. She was a woman whom the ranch back at home in Texas could never hold. Her parents both knew that and celebrated that fact with her, although Abby did so more than David. David and Abby encouraged her in her interests, even though they knew she was gone to California in her mind before she ever left high school.

They would touchdown in Santa Monica, California, in time for an intimate dinner in Malibu with Grace.

Chapter 12

Later that Day
6:00 P.M.

Sana stood motionless outside the cavern entrance. She had been studying the black ribbon for the entire afternoon. She had never imagined something like this could exist.

She had heard stories of the stagecoaches crossing the great Llano Estacado in a day, drawn by four or even six horses. But these stagecoaches had no horses, no reins, while the sounds they made were an affront to the ears. This was the sound she had heard from inside the cavern. Some stagecoaches were much louder than others, some huge, with great tall boxes that followed. Some were much smaller and quieter. She could see the Texans inside the stagecoaches. The speed at which they traveled was unbelievable to her, much faster than the swiftest horse. Evidently the Texans in the stagecoaches could not see her or did not attempt to. They seemed quite busy steering the great stagecoaches as you would steer a horse. The Texans paid no attention to what was happening outside the black ribbon on which they traveled.

The black ribbon crossed near the center of her old camp on the San Saba, following the river as far as she could see out toward the west. The last time she had gazed on her home it was burning. Sana recalled it was harvest season, the trees along the river displayed a golden hue. Bodies were strewn about the camp, the bodies of her family, her daughter, Prairie Song, and those of her friends.

What had taken place here in her Home Camp since that day? This great long ribbon, the strange stagecoaches with Texans in them, there were so many changes. Was this some kind of new weapon? She could not begin to understand, but Topusana would watch and listen and learn.

There in the meadow just below her, between her and the black ribbon, was an enormous log shelter. The shelter was larger and taller than any shelter she could have ever imagined. She had heard the talk of the whites building enormous shelters in San Antonio, or what Tabba had called "barns," for horses and cattle, but she never imagined anything of this size could be built. It seemed as if there were no people, either Texans or rangers, about the large shelter. It appeared, for the moment, to be abandoned.

Along the rear, toward the west was another large shelter with openings on both ends. Perhaps this was what Tabba had meant when describing to her barns the Texans had been building along the ancient trails. From her vantage point above and behind the barn, she could detect, when the wind was right, the scent of animals.

What interested her most was the garden. It was ripe with vegetables and melons, even squash and corn. Sana thought she would like to walk right up to the fencing, crawl over and gorge herself on the food just waiting there. She needed to be patient for now as she knew she must wait for the cover of nightfall to do so.

Hunger and curiosity had driven her back out of the cavern. Her mind curious as to the sounds that were emanating from outside the cavern. Sana was discovering more about this new time to which she had awakened.

Her intention was to set snare traps around the large oak trees near the cavern entrance in hopes of a chance of a meal by morning.

Using the sinew from her supplies, Sana shaped and fashioned the green branches expertly. Within a few moments, she had the snares expertly laid and concealed. Patience here was her priority and what was required. Sana knew hunger. She could last a few more days, if needed.

As she studied her former Homeland before her, she noticed the deer herd approaching the black ribbon. They had crossed the ribbon earlier, moving toward the river, just as they had in her former days at the camp. Sana had been waiting for them to return from watering, her bow at the ready. Perhaps…

The sound came to her ears, distant and soft at first, from a large stagecoach. It was approaching from the east, steering into the evening sun.

Sana had counted how long it was from the first faint detectable sound, until the stagecoach became visible, and then the count until it passed. The count of thirty-eight was the time that elapsed between the first faint sound and the change in pitch when the stagecoach was passing in front of her. Then another count of twenty until the sound disappeared to the west.

Sana began to count. The deer herd could also hear and were aware of the stagecoaches and their coming and going. She watched, as did the deer herd, their nervous tails twitching, noses in the air. At the count of twenty, several of the deer bounded rapidly across the black ribbon. At the count of twenty-seven the sound from the stagecoach was much louder now, five more deer ran full speed directly across the black ribbon. Several of the deer clumsily stumbled, hooves sliding on the smooth ribbon surface. At the count of thirty-six, one last deer, a fat doe, started across the black ribbon, much too late, as Sana counted, thirty-seven, thirty-eight.

The horseless stagecoach with a tall box collided with the deer, sending it sprawling. The stagecoach didn't even seem to slow its progress as the deer went under its noise-generating belly. The stagecoach continued down the black ribbon as if nothing had happened.

The deer was obviously severely injured. It struggled to escape the black ribbon. Sana thought surely the stagecoach would slow and retrieve its harvest; it did not. By the count of twenty it was out of sight, the sound of its great belly receding into the evening dusk.

Sana carefully watched the animal crawl through the underbrush and up the hill to within fifty yards of where she was standing. After ten minutes had passed with no further movement from the deer, Sana silently stalked through the underbrush, locating the now lifeless body of the animal. She whispered a prayer of thanks to the Great Spirit.

Within two hours, venison was roasting on the fire pit in the rear of the cavern. The smoke hole she had reopened above her gently pulled the smoke upward and out, invisible in the growing darkness of the Texas sky.

Sana had staked out the deer hide in a hidden opening outside and above her cavern. The hide would suit perfectly for new skins. For the first time in many days Sana would once again be fed by the bounty of the earth. She thought to herself, what a strange way to harvest an animal. She would be weary of the black ribbon and the horseless stagecoaches. She also had discovered a food source that would possibly prevent her detection in the future.

Sana was learning of this unusual new world to which she had awakened. She would sleep well tonight, full, beside her husband. She would dream of this strange new world, and the possibilities now before her. She drifted into a deep sound sleep.

12:30 A.M.

Sana awoke suddenly, the dampness of the cavern enveloping her. It was always cool in the larger rooms, a relief in these summer months. She had willed herself to awaken around midnight. She wanted to explore further the area around her cavern, the log shelter, and especially the garden, while under the protective cover of darkness.

Moving close to her husband again, she observed Tabba for a few moments. What could be happening? Why had he not awakened? She recalled that Tosahwi had instructed them both this was a possibility, awakening at separate times. But how long could this go on? Would his body be able to recover?

Her heart felt heavy within her chest as she arose from his side. She prepared for the nighttime ascent out of the cavern.

Even though she knew most of the land by heart, it was so different now with the addition of the black ribbon, the log shelter, and barn. She took from her small collection of beads a delicate necklace and a pair of bracelets woven by her daughter. She placed them in her day pack, which she hoped to load with fresh vegetables.

The climb out of the cavern had become easier. Sana could feel the strength she had gained from the meat of the deer. Extinguishing and leaving her torch one hundred yards from the exit and covering the last part of the climb, she spied the nearly full moon shining through the small entrance. Once outside, her night vision came to her quickly. She could see clearly the outline of the log shelter and nearby barn. There was no sound from the black ribbon.

Cautiously, Sana worked her way down the slope to the rear of the garden. From her vantage point here, she could see into the rear of the log shelter through one of the openings. The interior of the shelter was completely dark, no firelight, no sound from within.

Observing the huge structure, she noticed a covered area that surrounded the shelter. Under that cover were sitting chairs with colorful decorations on them and flowers in pots of all sizes and shapes, aligning the covered area.

Taking in the scene, Sana decided this was the work of a woman. Clearly to her, a feminine hand had designed the outdoor areas surrounding the shelter. Was this the camp of a Texas woman?

Working her way closer, she circled around the large fence that enclosed the garden. Sana had seen fencing before. A story was told of some foolish Texans that had attempted to fence some open prairie to the north out on the Llano; the buffalo had made quick work of the fence and the Texans that attempted to save it.

Days of storytelling and laughter seemed so far away now. The Comanche thought it an impossible thing to fence in a prairie. Sana had seen the fencing aligning the black ribbon; now she was not so certain. However, here the fence served its obvious purpose, enclosing the plantings safely from the deer herds. Silently, she worked her way through the opening and farther into the garden. Sana could smell the delicious scents of ripe fruit and vegetables all around her. She began to feel her way in and out of rows, filling her pack with corn, melons, squash, a few carrots, some onions, and beans. She did not want to take so much as to be noticed; however, she did not know how many opportunities she would have to enter this garden with evidently no people inhabiting the shelter.

Satisfied she had enough for several days, Sana paused before exiting. Here in the moonlight, she knelt against a post and reached into her day pack, then gently hung one of the bracelets made by Prairie Song. She left it dangling from a notch in the wood, the bracelet glistening as it hung there in the moonlight.

She did not fully understand why she left the gift. She knew she needed to avoid detection. There was something about the garden that was also like the sitting chairs and flowers surrounding the log shelter. It felt so feminine, the layout, the borders of flowers, the neatly spaced rows, the watering cans placed near the entrance. Topusana was not a thief; perhaps an offering, perhaps a thankful gesture was in order to the feminine hand that had planted, cared for, and unknowingly shared her bounty.

It meant life to Topusana. A thank you may have been foolish, but she knew in her heart what she had been taught by Tosahwi. Kindness was never a wasted gift. Kindness, once planted, like the garden surrounding her, always produced a return.

She wanted to have a closer look at the shelter Tabba had called *barn*. Carefully silhouetting herself against a backdrop of scrub oak, she silently made her way toward the animal shelter. She froze against the edge of the shelter, waiting, she had heard movement from within. Standing perfectly silent, she could smell the familiar scents of horses and grass feed. A gentle breeze stirred against her cheek and hair. The moon shone brightly down around the structure, glimmering in her eyes again. Peering around the structure, she could now see a dim light coming from the barn. Then the scraping sound of footsteps on a wooden floor. She clearly heard the voice of a man speaking quietly!

Sana's heart began to race. Her body froze in the moonlight. Should she run? Again, she heard the man's voice speaking gently, along with the sound of brush strokes. Thinking through the sounds, the man was speaking to his horse. Gently he called it by name. Sana heard again, "Easy, Brother, easy now," as the brush strokes continued. The language she did not understand, the tone, and meaning was obvious.

The Comanche always had known the way of the horse. While frozen in the moonlight, Sana at first was more concerned about the horse sensing her presence than the man. Now she knew the horse would not give her away; the animal would be distracted by the man's gentle voice. She slowly backed away from the barn. Reaching the edge of the scrub oak, she silently entered the cover. She was now concealed in the brush. Sana knew she was beyond detection. Slowly making her way up the hill toward the entrance to the cavern, she finally began to breath normally.

A large rabbit was struggling in one of the snares. She quickly dispatched the animal as she had been taught, with a quick twist of the neck. Sana whispered a prayer of thanks for the animal's life. Another meal and the perfect size for a new medicine bag.

Taking the rabbit, her pack filled with vegetables, and retrieving the deer hide, she paused a moment, standing in the moonlight, observing the scene outside her little cavern.

It was a frightening night for Sana, yet she felt exhilarated from her late-night exploration. She had learned a great deal. The barn was occupied; the shelter was not, for now. She now had food for several days. As she stood observing the moonlit Homeland before her, clouds began to block out the light of the moon. The sound of distant thunder reached her ears. She could feel the change of the wind; the moisture of the air and cool wind against her skin sent a chill across her body.

The coming storms, from the south and east, could mean days of rain.

Sana entered the cavern, pushing out some of the rocks and dirt, covering any sign of her exit and entrance. It might be several days before she exited again. She was not afraid. She had provisions, work to do, a safe dry home for now. Tonight perhaps, in the exchange while not just taking, but also giving, there were new possibilities in this world to which she had awakened.

Was there now a possibility of friendship?

Chapter 13

Los Angeles, California

On the same early morning Sana had completed her exploration of the Ross home, garden, and barn, David and Abby prepared the sailboat for their early morning departure. There was no marine layer for the first morning in over a week. A brisk north wind drove the sailboat an astonishing fourteen knots, while sailing on a full broad reach.

David was filled with awe and wonder again. The smell and taste of the ocean air filled his lungs. Under the surface of the water, the huge rudder separated the turbulent flow of the ocean. Each slight swell attempted to upset the vessel, creating a need for constant vigilance on David's part. From beneath, in the dark cold waters of the Pacific, David could feel the slight rumble. He could sense the separation as tons of water flowed under the boat and around the rudder as he lightly gripped the helm. Here, under the surface of the water, the large rudder at this speed became sensitive to the slightest change in wind or swell. David stood behind the wheel, detecting each subtle movement, correcting constantly as the unseen forces affected heading, speed, sail trim. Sailing, as David knew, required constant awareness and skill, combined with experience and knowledge…and David Ross was in love with it.

He could see and hear the splashing of the dolphins as they led the way along both outer hulls of the forty-four-foot Hammerhead Trimaran. The Pacific Ocean lay ahead, the land astern already receding from site. He thought it a perfect day for sailing; how could a man be any further blessed!

Abby bounded the ladder from the galley with a piping hot mug of his

47

favorite coffee blend, a quick answer to the question he had just posed to himself. David thought this must be a little piece of heaven on Earth.

They had motored out of Marina Del Ray as the dawn was breaking behind them. A few stars were still visible on the western horizon. The rhythmic swell of the Pacific was lulling them, not into sleep, but somehow into a peaceful comfort in the midst of full awareness. David reached to cut the engine.

There was always much to do in the first few minutes of a sail. Preparing and attending the boat, navigating just offshore, hoisting sails, securing gear, and then with the sails filling and the boat picking up speed, it was time.

David turned the switch and cut the engine. It was always his favorite moment on a sail. The sound of the eighty-horsepower turbo diesel faded into silence. The prop folded away beneath the hull. The quiet of sailing, the sounds of the sea, enveloped them.

A light breeze flowed across the bow while the gentle lapping of the ocean along the sides of the boat could be heard. The seabirds calling to one another and an occasional splash of a dolphin, even the spouting followed by the intake breath of whales as they took in massive volumes of air could be heard. This was what called to David Ross, again and again.

The Sea.

He set the auto helm on a course for the Channel Islands National Monument. The anchorage on the southern shores should be perfect, he thought. Perfect for an afternoon of watching the sea life, reading, possibly a hike onto the island, if the swell permitted a landing in the dingy.

One of the things David enjoyed most about sailing, and often proclaimed, was, "A man simply could not be in a hurry on a sailboat."

"About four hours at our current speed," he announced.

Abby smiled approvingly. It warmed her heart to see David so excited, so childlike about his adventure. She knew the ocean, and the time he spent upon it, was healing his heart. She would not mention Jonathan unless he did. Then she would mostly listen.

David clearly was finally becoming whole again. At one time, Abby had thought their marriage would not survive the loss of their son, Jonathan. David had spent the entire first year or more sullen, withdrawn, even becoming bitter and angry. The months turned into years of heartache. Abby, for a season, thought she was possibly losing both her son and her husband. Gradually, he had begun to open up. The grief therapist had contributed immensely. The journaling David had agreed to brought forth the stark facts of his fatherhood in black and white. Abby recalled the day David had eventually realized, like many fathers, he had missed much in the raising of his children. It was the first giant stride in David coming to grips with the loss of Jonathan. That realization became a place from which he could move forward…dealing with his own guilt. But it seemed the time upon the sea was his greatest helper. She thanked God for the few days away.

The satellite phone rang loudly over the speaker system from below deck. Abby went below and answered. "I can see you in the telescope, Mom. Just wanted to give you a wave from Malibu," Grace said.

"Good morning, sweetheart, and thank you for the dinner. It was perfect," Abby said. The two women chatted a moment; Abby ended the call, promising to check in later in the evening.

Climbing the ladder to the deck and helm above, she paused to watch her husband. His body was slightly tense. She noticed David feeling the wind on his skin and face, making minor adjustments to the sails and heading, based on that feel. The man was indeed in tune with his boat and at home on the ocean.

"Let's explore a little more of Santa Rosa Island this afternoon," David said from above.

"Sounds perfect. You think we can get a shot of one of them?"

"It's possible. I was reading the Park Service has released another two breeding pairs onto the island," answered David.

This was the only place on Earth the animal existed. The species was only found in the Channel Islands. David was speaking of the island fox, a beautiful animal that had fought back from near extinction in the 1980s. There were only fifteen of these animals left on San Miguel Island, and only fourteen left on the island of Santa Rosa. Those few animals were the only ones of their kind on the planet.

It was a success story in wildlife intervention and management, a subject dear to David's heart. He had contributed a great deal to the research and breeding program. To see one of the animals in the wild would be a dream come true. To be a part of saving an animal from extinction was priceless to David Ross.

The sea life in the Channel Islands was simply unbelievable. Since its designation as national park in 1980, several species near extinction had returned to healthy populations, including a huge population of northern elephant seals living and breeding in a rookery on San Miguel Island. These creatures had been hunted to near extinction just one hundred years ago.

Now with the protection and the island's designation as a national park, the population of elephant seals numbered in the thousands. To see the successes of species' recovery in this lonely wind-swept place, where just an hour away were the freeways of southern California and fifteen million people, was, to David, simply a miracle.

The bald eagle had completely disappeared from the Islands in the early 1900s. Now a healthy population was on the rebound. It was quite common to see them fishing in the waters surrounding several of the islands.

David could have used his donations in the recovery of the island fox as a means to be escorted by park rangers out into the middle of their habitat. He was not that kind of a man. David Ross believed his acts of charity should be kept secret. No one knew where the donations for the program had originated, except Abby. If he was to ever see an island fox living in the wild, it would be as anonymously as possible. His heart jumped at the thought that he could possibly see one in his lifetime.

He changed course to pass to the south and west of Anacapa Island. Its beautiful lighthouse gleamed in the distance. He found himself dreaming, dreaming of his few years on the Texas coast.

The sea and land along the Gulf of Mexico, off Texas and Louisiana, was quite the opposite of what was found in the deep waters here off southern California. The Texas coast was, in many places, *dead*, void of its once teaming wildlife.

In his days on the Texas coast, they would often fish for hours, or even days, without catching anything. The oil industry had polluted the waters to such a point that in many places it was no longer safe to swim. The contrast was absurdly disturbing. David Ross's ability to support from oil revenues on his ranch the research and breeding programs around and under the waters of these islands was quite an irony. However absurd or ironic, he would continue to do so.

It caused him to pause. How could he use his own ranch in recovery of native species to the Texas Plains? This seemed a question he had pondered many times over. Buffalo he had considered, could be the answer. The research from the handful of ranches raising and managing buffalo herds was amazing. Native plants and grasses had rebounded rapidly. David had recently read of a study that showed favorable results in grass growth. The simple difference in the hoof shape of the buffalo as compared to cattle was the primary factor in the results of the study. The buffalo hooves tilled the soil and seed within that soil to a greater depth. That depth just happened to be, according to the research, the perfect depth for springtime germination of those native grasses. In the same study, cattle actually reduced germination of native grasses by as much as 50 percent less than the buffalo pastures in the study. Within just a few short years after removing cattle and establishing the buffalo on those ranches, many ranchers documented the earth beginning to balance and correct.

The success here on these remote islands and the recovery of several near extinct populations was inspiring a new dream in David's heart and mind.

Abby, not wanting to interrupt his thoughts, sat quietly lost in her own world of thought. These were some of the best days of her life with David. She could feel the movement of the ocean beneath her. She could taste the salt air while surrounded by the sound of the sea birds: the brown pelican, the cormorants, the western gulls. David had taught her the names and how to identify each. She listened to the splashing of the dolphins as they played in the wake of the sailboat's amas. Her vision was full of the engrossing seascape before her. She sat here by her husband, in silent gratefulness, comforted by the sea.

David had shared with her a famous quote by the researcher Jacques Yves Cousteau that suddenly came to mind. "The Sea, once it casts its spell on you, holds one in its net of wonder forever." Amen, she prayed silently, amen.

Chapter 14

10:30 A.M.
Channel Islands National Park

Riding the surf across the swell at an angle, David expertly landed the dingy ashore on Santa Rosa Island. The wide beach before them was filled with seabirds of all types. California seals and a few sea lions also dotted the beach. These islands were inhabited by more than two thousand different species of birds, animals, and plant life. One hundred-fifty or more of these species were not found in any other place on the planet but only here on these five small islands.

David dragged the dingy up the beach to a point above the water line. "That should do." Hoisting the day pack onto his shoulders, he and Abby strode away from the beach into the beautiful pristine wilderness of Santa Rosa Island.

They spent the afternoon atop an inland ridge where they could see a great deal of a wide valley spreading before them. Abby had packed a delicious lunch that she spread on a blanket. The picnic included hard salami slices, Italian ham, an assortment of cheese, a fresh baked loaf of rye with butter, and lemon squares that she and Grace had baked together the previous evening. A perfect bottle of Pinot Grigio capped off the delightful assortment of flavors and textures. The delicious meal was followed by a dreamy afternoon of reading and napping on the blanket.

Here, just below the ridge line overlooking a little valley on the Island of Santa Rosa, in the bright southern California sun, they dined and napped, and watched the sun work its way across the great Pacific Ocean sky.

Feeling the warmth of the beautiful day, David removed his shirt. "Just need to soak up some of this sun. Doesn't it feel wonderful?"

Abby watching her handsome husband lay back onto the blanket and said, "Perfect idea," as she also removed her soft flannel shirt. Then Abby staring into the longing eyes of her husband, slowly, seductively, removed her top.

David reached for her, her body warm and soft against his skin. Their lips met. The kiss was intimate, deep, and filled with passion Abby had not sensed in many years. David wanted her completely. Not just as a woman, not just for sex…she could feel and sense his longing to be a part of her, for who she was as a woman. As his woman. Abigail Ross gave herself unreservedly to her man.

Later as the sun slowly lowered in the western sky, David asked, "How are you feeling about Jonathan these days, Abby?"

Not sure how to reply, Abby answered as honestly as she could. "Terrible, some days, other days, I'm okay. How about you, David?" Abby waited for his response, then listened quietly, sensing he just needed to talk some more.

"He was doing exactly what he wanted to do, wasn't he?"

"Yes, he was," she said to the question he had asked her a thousand times.

****

Jonathan Ross was sixteen years old in 2001 when the Towers fell. He and his friends had just arrived at school when the word came over the loudspeaker system for all students to report to their homeroom classes. Arriving there, his history teacher, Mr. Clark, who was a former Marine and veteran of the Gulf War, sat glued to the television news station. The students also gathered around, watching in horror and fascination, as the story began to unfold before them.

Jonathan admired Mr. Clark immensely. To Jonathan, Mr. Clark was that one teacher every parent and every student hoped to be lucky enough to encounter. That encounter with a man of integrity made high school forever worthwhile for Jonathan.

Mr. Clark actually cared. He cared enough to invest time and energy into each and every student. He often made home visits or called students if they were falling behind. He would schedule whenever and wherever a student would agree to meet with him.

Mr. Clark gave freely of his time, assisting in many students "Getting their act together, before real life starts," as he would say.

His moral character was something Jonathan admired and wanted to emulate. Mr. Clark also taught wood shop. Jonathan would never forget the first day of that freshman class while Mr. Clark was going over all the rules and regulations for using the power equipment. One of the many regulations he set forth was to never wear watches or rings while operating the equipment. He presented a few grizzly stories of irresponsible students being maimed for life, hands or ears being sucked into the blades of gruesome flesh-eating machines. The injured students each had foolishly not removed said items.

Mr. Clark stated there would be one exception to that jewelry rule, and it applied to Mr. Clark only. He, and he alone, could operate the machinery with his wedding band in place.

The class waited in silence for an explanation, or someone to ask why. Mr. Clark obviously baiting them, waited.

Jonathan spoke up. "Ok, I'll ask, why is that, sir?"

"A great question young man and posed properly," Mr. Clark said. "Because this ring never comes off. I put it on the day I was married. I wore it through two tours of duty. I clung to it many nights, longing to be home. This ring never comes off! You young men take note, marriage is for life! Any further questions?"

That example put forth that day was worth a thousand sermons or lectures. A man honoring his wife, his vows, and his faith were priceless examples to Jonathan, examples to each and every student that would attend Mr. Clark's class throughout the years of his career.

Major Lynnwood Clark was, in action and deed, a man of honor.

That day, as the students watched the Towers fall, as they listened to their president make a speech, as word of the innocent dying, as the death toll began rising…Mr. Clark said nothing.

The students in his class searched for answers. Upon reaching the end of the class that memorable day, Mr. Clark simply posed one question.

"What are you young men and women going to do about this?"

Jonathan did not answer that day, but something was burning within, a fire had been kindled.

He knew in his heart he would do something about "this."

He began to make plans to study more; he would never make less than an A again. He began to improve his athletic training, specifically in the pool. To this day, Jonathan still held several state records in aquatics.

Jonathan Ross would graduate valedictorian of his class. His application and appointment to the Naval Academy, with the assistance of his grandfather, a former Texas governor, would follow, as would his application to the SEAL teams be accepted four years later, after the successful completion of BUD/S training (Basic Underwater Demolition/Seal).

The Navy strategically placed commissioned officers in the elite teams. Jonathan Ross would prove to possess the skill, physical ability, and intelligence to be one of the "chosen few," a Navy SEAL.

Perhaps it was the blood of patriots that ran deep in his veins or the lineage of military men and warriors in his family history. Jonathan Ross would live a life that mattered. A life of sacrifice. He would, in fact, make the ultimate sacrifice for his country and his family.

Jonathan Ross would have sacrificed his life willingly many times over if that had been possible.

David Ross was extremely proud of his only son, Jonathan. His son was a hero. The Navy had awarded him the Navy Cross, posthumously. David could not fully understand the pain of losing his son. He felt sometimes he had simply made friends with the pain and loss.

****

David and Abby sat in silence for a few moments. David peered through the powerful binoculars across the little valley. He caught a flash of movement on the adjacent hill. Tapping Abby on the shoulder and pointing, she, too, raised her binoculars just in time.

There across the valley, sitting on its haunches, the little fox sat perfectly still. For five full minutes the island fox sat before them, seeming to relax in the sun, warming himself. His eyes nearly closed, dozing, even yawning a few times.

The minutes passed. Opening his eyes, seeming to peer directly toward them, he sniffed the air. Then the little fox casually turned and wandered over the ridge and out of sight.

Chapter 15

The Ross Ranch
Three Days Later

Sana exited the cavern before the sun had risen. Three days had past since her last exploration. The rains had finally ended. She was anxious to learn more of her surroundings. In the darkness, she worked her way across the ridge to the west. Then moving away from the log shelter, out of sight of anyone within, she crossed the black ribbon. Sana's Home Camp was just down the river from where she now stood. The moon, resting on the western horizon, gave an eerie light to the scene. Silently, she moved along the riverbank toward the camp. A cool wind followed her, giving her presence away to any game. She was not concerned with that now. Foremost in her mind was what had become of her Home Camp?

Finding the approximate center of her old camp, even the exact place where Prairie Song had died, there was nothing. No signs that her people ever existed or lived upon this sacred beautiful land. Her heart grew heavy within her chest. How could it all vanish? What had the white man accomplished? What had become of her people? For now, Sana had no answers.

Her tears sprung forth as she thought of the many nights, days, seasons, even lifetimes that had been lived out right here along this sacred quiet river.

A resolve settled within her spirit again. This was her people's Homeland. Who claimed it now? The Texans living here? Texas? The white leaders?

She determined in her heart again this day...to have this Homeland returned to *The People*.

Lifting her gaze toward the eastern sky, Sana, just as she had on many other dawning mornings in this exact place, began to pray. She slowly lifted her hands, the songs coming forth from her soul. Songs of mourning, songs of lament. Songs of remembrance. The voices of her people accompanied her. Their voices sang in the light wind as it rustled through the trees. The voices harmonized within the gurgle of the river. The voices of her people cried out softly from the fading starlight.

It was mid-morning when she became fully aware. She was lying in the buffalo grass. The sun shone brightly down on the former camp. The birds sang in the trees. Sana arose from her spirit worship and carefully made her way back across the black ribbon, up the west ridge, to the entrance to the cavern.

The grinding bowl was missing! She had placed it exactly as Tabba had instructed, upside down in an outcropping of rocks that were similar in size and color. This was to be the first of several possible signs they had agreed to leave one another in the event they were separated from one another by awakening at different times, a thing Tosahwi said could possibly occur.

Tabba had awakened! It must be; it was the only explanation. However, something about the scene on the ground caused her to pause. Examining the area around the cave entrance, disturbing signs were present. Horse prints, a place where the animal had been tied, boot prints in the soil. The signs were obvious. Texans had been here. Had Tabba really awakened only to be encountered by the Texans? The only way to know was below her feet, in the darkness of the cave.

She quickly entered the cavern, nearly closing over the entrance again. Moving as quickly as possible, working her way through the maze of the tight closed cavern she wondered, would he in fact no longer be in the Dream Time? Her heart raced as she hurried through the cave, lighting the torch and calling out softly, "Tabba." There was no response. Sana made her way into the larger part of the cavern and up the steps to the sleeping rooms.

Tabba was still there. His breathing seemed steady and quiet. Tabba had not yet awakened from the Dream Time.

What had happened? She silently considered the facts. Someone had discovered the sign she had left. That someone was on horseback. They had collected the metate. Would this give her away? Who was this someone? Should she investigate further? She would return to survey the site more completely, perhaps a better clue had been left. Or even perhaps someone had simply stumbled upon the metate, this too was a possibility.

It had been three days since the night of her garden exploration. The rains had indeed come from the south and east. Steady soaking rains during which she had spent the days cooking, preparing new skins, and praying. How long could a person sleep? She had watched Tabba closely; there were no signs of awareness whatsoever. She had even felt for his heartbeat. It was very slow when she compared it to her own.

Topusana would continue to hunt, explore, and perhaps study from much closer, the log shelter and the barn. She needed sleep now. Her sleep patterns were changing. She would sleep into the night and awaken sometime after midnight. The dark nights were now coming with only a sliver of moon. In the darkness she could explore more freely. Sana would cover herself with the darkness. Then she could indeed move very close or perhaps even enter the log shelter or the barn.

It was also time to check the other cavern. Sana had not been able to find any of the agreed upon signs from the others. She continued to check each time she exited the cavern. Could she have missed the signs? Or might those signs also have been found by the Texans? Might the others still all be in the Dream Time? The route would be difficult to travel in the darkness. To travel the full mile to the north in daylight might possibly expose her to discovery by the Texans.

So many decisions. One thing was certain, each decision was critical for her survival and the survival of the others. Strategy and information were decisive and what her husband, Tabba, the Warrior, would advise. Knowing as much as possible about her surroundings, who her enemies were, what they were planning, and even what they were capable of, was of the utmost importance.

Thinking of the past, her history, thinking of Prairie Song, Sana knew what the Texans were capable of. She needed to discover all she could about the Texans living on her former Home Camp, just above the river called San Saba.

Chapter 16

Present Day
11:30 P.M.

Darkness draped the little valley as Sana exited the cavern near midnight. The sliver of moon had already set, a light wind coming from the west. Only the dim starlight guided her as she worked her way down the slope toward the garden.

All seemed quiet in and around the log shelter. The barn she had encircled twice seemed unoccupied, with the exception of two beautiful mares kept in pens. They had nickered to her but were easily calmed by her quite voice and experienced way with horses. Her confident manner settled them as they became familiar with her touch and voice, something she would use to her advantage in the days ahead.

Silently moving toward the log shelter, she climbed the steps to the side covered area. She could smell the potted flowers as she gazed through the clear solid openings around the shelter. She had never thought of such a thing, a solid cool surface, yet completely transparent. Peering through one of the openings into the large room before her, there were little glowing lights all through the shelter, lighting the interior. The room before her had a large tabletop with a chair next to it. Many beautiful carvings had been placed around the room. She recognized buffalo and cattle, and even carvings of Texans on horseback. She could see a large fire pit and the wall above it covered with many river stones.

Above the fire pit was a flat area, evidently carved from a great tree. There were several objects placed upon the huge flat piece of wood over the fire pit.

As she gazed at what was resting above the fire pit, her heart leapt inside her chest. There, above the fire pit, was her grinding bowl!

Sana's first thought was to enter the shelter and retrieve the metate. A calmer voice of reason said simply wait. How had the Texas woman found it? Possibly it had been dislodged by the rain, or an animal had unknowingly disturbed its resting place. Sana decided to leave the item in its new home. Perhaps later, it too could be useful to her. She silently left the covered area and headed for the garden in the cover of darkness.

Once inside the gate, she paused. The bracelet she had left here on the wooden notch was gone. Observing the scene, listening intently, Sana decided to continue into the garden. She began silently working her way through the plantings. She loaded her small pack with a variety of vegetables, selecting ripened fruit from different areas so as to be as unnoticeable as possible. Satisfied she had enough for a few days, she made her way back toward the opening.

Reaching the gate, suddenly a bright light blinded her. She heard the voice of a woman calling, "Who's there?" Sana did not understand the words, the light shown all around her. She ran.

The voice following behind her called out, "Hey, who's there? Stop!"

Entering the brush, Sana dove to the ground, quickly changing course, the light now shining where she had dropped.

The Comanche knew how to evade any tracker or follower. Within a few moments, she was across the side hill, moving away from the cavern, back toward the black ribbon.

The bright light was moving all around, but still shining mostly where she had entered the brush. Now she was moving south toward the black ribbon, and nearly behind her pursuer.

The woman moved the light in the direction of the barn, calling out in what Sana recognized as Spanish *"Quien está ahí?"*

Sana rose from her crawling position. She was up and moving swiftly now, around the little valley, and climbing up the adjacent canyon. Within ten minutes she was atop the adjacent ridge watching the shelter from above.

Standing there in the darkness, Sana could see the bright lights had been extinguished. Several rooms of the log structure glowed with light from within.

Sana had been discovered.

The Texas woman had to have seen her clearly in the bright light. Would they call the rangers and hunt her down tomorrow? Would the white soldiers now return? She had the presence of mind to not drop the vegetables.

The soldiers could hunt her for days. Topusana would not be found. Entering the cavern, she gently covered over the entrance, leaving it as nearly undetectable as she could in the way she had first seen it.

Descending the steep entry, she wondered aloud, "How did the Texas woman know I was there?"

Chapter 17

Abby sat at the kitchen table, too excited to return to bed. The motion alarm had awakened her when the motion detector in the barn had been activated. How long had she taken to finally awaken, find a flashlight, get some slippers? She was particularly groggy this night after the flight home, the unpacking and settling in from the California trip. She thought she was quite exhausted from her and David's latest adventure. This interruption in the middle of the night was adding to her level of fatigue.

Checking the barn from the darkness of the house, she could see nothing. Switching on the barn lights from the remote switch brought no movement or activity. Glancing toward the garden, with the powerful flashlight, she was surprised to see the Mexican woman exiting the gate.

Abby had seen "illegals" many times on the ranch before, but never in or around the house. She was sure the poor woman was simply hungry. If they would only ask, I would help, she thought. But this was a first. She decided not to call David, who was away for one night in Austin; it would only worry him.

She heated a cup of milk and drank slowly, enjoying the smoothness. The milk warmed her, working instantly to relax her as it had since she was a young girl. She made her way to the bedroom. Snuggling under the covers, she whispered a prayer for the poor young woman.

She wondered, as she lay in the comfort of her warm bed, what the woman's life might be like. Was she so hungry she risked sneaking into a garden in the middle of the night just for a poor meal of vegetables? How long had she traveled to get here? Where would she sleep this dark night?

Replaying the event in her mind, Abby knew something was off. She thought of how to describe the event to David. He would want to know how many people. What time? Was anything missing? What did she look like? Abby thought, what did...she look like?

Abby dozed off, the milk doing its job. Her sleep was restful; she felt no threat at all from the encounter.

Awaking at 6:30, going through her morning routine, she thought again of last night's events. Preparing to call David, she went over in her mind the description he would want to hear in detail.

Then it came to her suddenly. The thing that had bothered her, what it was that was "off" about the late-night encounter.

The young woman was not a Mexican National, as she had so naturally assumed, having seen so many over the years. The woman she would describe to David was an American Indian!

She was dressed in buckskins and moccasins! With a bow strung over her shoulder!

Abby picked up the bracelet she had found on the post of the garden. She ran the bracelet through her fingers, feeling its polished texture, admiring the striking colors, and the incredible detail of the beadwork.

She knew it was Native American bead work from David's reference books.

What in the world was going on out in her little garden? She started to pick up the phone yet hesitated. This story she would need to tell David face to face.

Chapter 18

The Following Morning

So, you're telling me, that a we have a Comanche woman in full native dress, raiding our garden in the middle of the night?" The question was not really being posed as a question, but a dismissive statement from David to Abby.

"I know it seems farfetched to believe me, David, but I'm telling you exactly what I saw. I didn't say she was Comanche."

The silence between them an awkward moment. "Well, as you know, I would have to see that with my own eyes to believe it."

"I'm sure that's true, David, but it doesn't make what I saw with my own eyes untrue."

David had arrived from Austin, after a meeting with his longtime friend, confidant, and attorney William Travis. He had time for a quick lunch with Abby, then had planned on heading out to the north pasture to check on the cattle. But this story of a nighttime intruder, alarms going off, missing vegetables, and of all things, the bracelet before him on his desk. David rubbed his forehead in thought, digesting the story. The bracelet was authentic; he knew that instantly. "And this was just hanging on the gate post?"

"Yes," Abby answered.

"Alright then, let's go out for a little explore. If what you say actually happened, there may be some other evidence of the activity."

"Let's do!" Abby had not thought to look around the barn and hillside behind the house, the direction in which the woman had disappeared.

Loading a camera, water, and two trail cams in his day pack, David changed his plans for the day. Abby, in excitement of another adventure with David, donned her hiking boots and packed a light snack in her day pack.

The two explored the area around the barn first. David looked for signs on the ground. He could find nothing. He thought if the intruder was, in fact, Mexican, there would have been more than one woman. These families usually traveled in fairly large groups, leaving a trail of tracks and even litter as they traveled. This made tracking them fairly easy.

David, on several occasions, found the need to track the large groups of illegals making their way north across his ranch. Border Patrol agents, who continuously patrolled both his ranch and many of the surrounding properties, did the same daily.

They decided to move farther up the low valley that slowly ascended behind the ranch toward some of the caverns. Moving through the low brush, Abby directed David to the exact spot she had last sighted the woman as she was diving into the cover of the undergrowth. "So, this is where you last saw her?" David asked.

"Yes," Abby replied. "It must be pretty close anyway." Abby sighted the line between their location and the side porch of the home where she had stood with her flashlight last night. David began to make a slow circle, trying to not disturb the ground around him. Once around and seeing nothing unusual, this time he widened the circle. Continuing the search, he circled the area again and suddenly froze.

"Don't move, Abby," David ordered.

There, under his boot, several things were out of place. Footprints, light indentations, were pressed into the damp soil between a few scrub oak.

He motioned Abby toward him, having her circle around on the side of the site.

"What is it, David?"

"Definitely footprints," he answered, "but not like any I have ever seen before."

There below them and all around the damp area, small footprints could be seen. They had not made a distinct imprint like most of the Mexicans left behind. Those groups with their athletic shoes, with no thought at all of being tracked, left an easy to follow trail. These fresh imprints were clear, small, smooth, made by someone with a shoe without a sole pattern.

Abby was first to speak. "Is it a human track, David?"

"Yes, it is, but how unusual, a soft sole shoe?" he said.

"Moccasins?" Abby replied.

"It couldn't be," David stated in wonder.

"Yes, it could be, it's what I saw her wearing, David., Abby said firmly.

David did not reply. Taking a few steps farther uphill, he could find no other trace. "How could she just vanish?"

Abby watched as David started the circle pattern search again. "And she disappeared heading up the canyon?" David asked.

"Yes, I think so," Abby said.

David began to think like someone trying to escape. "You know, from what I know in all the historical research of Comanche evasion tactics, she would never have simply run in a straight line up the valley."

"So it's a she, and you think that she is a Comanche?"

"I did not say that," David said, rather sternly Abby thought.

"But you're thinking like she would think, aren't you?" Abby asked.

"Yes, I am."

Just about to complete his latest circle, David moved in the opposite direction they had been traveling, back downhill toward the barn. Abby followed closely behind.

Abby saw it first. They had only moved a few feet back toward the barn. There at their feet lay a medium sized squash.

"I'll be damned," David whispered to himself.

The squash was surrounded by indentations in the damp ground where someone had fallen or dove into the ground. A clear trail of scuffling tracks led back toward the barn and across the hillside. It appeared as if someone had not walked here but crawled through the underbrush. Whoever had left the sign had moved in the opposite direction of where any pursuer would expect. It was a precise move, a Comanche move, David thought.

"Have we found some evidence of my story, David?" Abby asked.

David stood in thought, wondering who might have left this light delicate trail clearly before them.

"I suppose we have," David said. "So, if you were trying to escape detection, or pursuit, from right here, where would you go?" David asked.

Abby, looking around, pointed up the hill to the ridge just west of the house and barn.

"That's where I would head also," David said.

Moving toward the ridge, they lost the trail within a few yards.

"She is up and walking now," David said.

"How do you know?" Abby said.

"No more tracks." Indeed, there was no sign on the ground in any direction. "But let's follow your thought. If you climbed up over the ridge, you would be completely out of site, correct?"

"Yes. There are no tracks now because of moccasins?" Abby asked.

"Maybe. And then once over the ridge, you could resume your escape on the route intended," David said, speaking out loud as he thought through what he was visualizing. "You would be out of site of the house and barn," he said. The two paused.

"But you would not travel toward the highway, right?" Abby asked.

"No, probably not," David said. "So where would you go now?"

"Away from the woman with the flashlight," Abby answered.

David smiled inwardly at the quick logic of his wife.

They made their way up the ridge, cresting the top in half a mile. Atop the ridge they paused again, observing their world below.

Before them, their beautiful home shone in the afternoon sun. They observed the grounds, the garden, the barn, and across the highway, the San Saba River could be seen slowly winding its way below them.

"How about we call on another picnic?" Abby said as she began to unload her pack. David poured them coffee from a thermos.

"Penny for your thoughts," she said.

"I'm stumped." The little trip of discovery had posed more questions in David's mind than answers. "This is quite unusual. She's heading north, Abby. What's north of here?"

"Nothing for miles," she said.

"Exactly," David said. "Just cattle and grass. The next town is more than fifty miles away."

"What is there in between here and there?" Abby asked.

David thought through the terrain, the water sources in his mind's eye.

"Just the caverns," he said softly to himself.

Chapter 19

David set two trail cameras to activate on motion and record for up to one minute. One camera he set near the entrance to the first of several caverns that dotted the hillside above the house and barns. The other he attached to a tree above and adjacent to the garden. Carefully, he pointed it toward the house and garden. These were sure to record any activity night or day as they were both equipped with low light sensors and motion activation functions. He then paired the cameras to his and Abby's cell phones. Now, either camera would immediately send notification to them, if they began to record anytime twenty-four hours per day.

The technology was amazing to David and Abby both. They were adapting to and living in the modern technology that permeated their world. They both knew this new era of technology was a huge benefit to society. They made every effort to educate themselves so they would function in this brave new world of technology. The information they were looking for could now be gathered in real-time. The plan for investigating exactly what was going on in their own backyard was in place.

Now they would simply wait.

Topusana watched the two Texans from the ridge to the east of the log shelter. The hillside opposite where she had escaped the night before provided a hidden vantage. It was clear they were tracking her. She became very alarmed as the Texans worked their way toward the cavern entrance. As they surveyed the area around the entrance, the Texans made no move to enter. She was grateful they did not attempt to do so.

Perhaps they knew the difficulty of the descent?

"Isn't this the area where you found the metate?" Abby asked.

"Yes, just a few feet up the hill from the entrance here."

"When was the last time you entered the cavern, David?"

"Years ago. Actually I think I was still in my teens. Several of us from school had planned to spend the weekend exploring the caves. We didn't quite make it the full weekend."

"I remember you telling me the story of your friend Will flipping out and just wanting to get out," Abby said. She was speaking of David's longtime friend and attorney William Travis.

David, lost in the memory, began to retell the story. "Yes, it was quite an adventure. We carted Coleman lanterns, food, ropes, sleeping bags, flashlights, and most important, we trailed a full mile of kite string behind us so as to find our way out. That was quite an exploration party, literally. My dad told me stories of finding Indian artifacts at the entrance to the caverns in his days, but he would never venture farther in than a few feet.

"When you're seventeen and fearless and with buddies, you can do things you might not otherwise consider," David said, chuckling to himself. "I remember the entrance here in the first cavern drops pretty steeply, and the distance from floor to ceiling is only two or three feet for several hundred yards."

"Icky," Abby said, making a squeamish face. "I would never make it past just that part. That gives me the creepy crawlies!"

"We were young and in very good shape, I suppose. As you know, I never ventured in again, although it was a fascinating place." David paused, recalling more. "I remember how huge the rooms were toward the back of this cavern. Seems like we thought the ceiling to be higher than fifty feet with stalactites hanging above. The most interesting feature to me was the live water that runs through the cavern system. That, and the constant airflow. If you stood motionless just about anywhere, you could feel the air moving softly against your skin."

"What does the airflow mean?" Abby asked.

"It means there must be other openings throughout the cave system. We found several over the years above ground while tending the cattle. The water pools were amazing to me also. The water looked to be about six inches deep. It is quite a trick the cave can play on your vision. Reflecting the top of the cavern into the pool when bright light is shined on the water. I actually stepped into one of the very shallow pools to walk across it and sank deep over my head… never touching the bottom."

"Oh my, how deep do you think it was?"

"I can't really say, but none of us tried to walk across even the smallest puddle after that.

"We made a camp in these upper rooms that were formed along the sides of the large room. It was so otherworldly. We were all so tired out and thought we would just get a little sleep and then head out first thing the next morning.

"None of us slept a wink. As a matter of fact, after a couple of hours of lights out, we lit our lanterns and spent the rest of the night telling horror stories. We told tales of trapped miners, ghosts, and all kinds of teenage boy talk, none of it fit to repeat."

"So how did the trip end?" Abby asked.

"Well, to be honest, I think we set a record pace getting out the next morning. I know Will did. It was hard just to keep up with him. We pulled the string back out behind us so as not to disturb. I don't know what…" David said deep in thought, remembering the distinct feeling he had experienced that day. He felt very much like they were disturbing something or someone in their exploration of the cavern. He had often regretted the group had not been able to explore the huge cavern rooms more thoroughly.

"On the way out, we did see etchings on the wall about a half mile in. I remember thinking these must be very old, but none of us wanted to pause long enough to even take an instant Polaroid photograph. The little camera we carried all the way in and out, we never used," David said.

"It seems so exciting that this world is literally right under our feet on the ranch," Abby said. "Why did you never return?"

"I'm not sure, but as I grew older, I thought about how dangerous that trip actually was. Rescue would be practically impossible due to the size of the ceiling in the front of the cavern. The world on the top side seemed interesting enough to me. That world underneath, while fascinating, just seemed plain dangerous."

"I'm glad Jonathan never ventured in there," Abby stated. David did not comment. He just stood there looking sheepish.

"What, David! You never told me!"

David quickly changed the subject. "You remember the study Dad allowed to take place before I inherited the ranch?"

"I remember you talking about that vaguely, tell me more," Abby said, looking quite annoyed at David.

"Texas A&M sent a team in to map and explore, with my father's approval. I still have some of the drawings the team made. They were even able to transport some dive equipment all the way down there. The team spent three days in the first cavern and never found an ending to the system. They explored one of the largest pools and found it to be forty feet deep, with water flowing from the bottom of that pool from a great spring. They were also able to swim under a cliff wall and into another huge room adjacent to the large room we spent the night in."

"That is amazing, David! "Abby stated in wonderment.

"That dive into the adjacent room is where the researchers found the silver coins."

"The two that you keep on your mantel?"

"Yes, that was quite a mysterious find also. The researchers had no idea how one hundred-fifty-year-old silver coins could have made their way into the bottom of a pool in that cavern. It's a mystery still.

"The team also dye-tested the water flowing through the cavern system. The dye surfaced in the San Saba some twelve miles downstream from here," David said.

"So, what were their conclusions?" Abby asked.

"Several observations were noted in their logs. For one, the wall drawings are authentic Comanche pictographs."

"That's amazing."

"Another conclusion, or recommendation from the research team…never enter the caves alone; they are filled with dead ends and circular switchbacks. I often think of what might have happened if part of our kite string was cut and floated away on that light breeze. One of my own conclusions was, if a person wanted to hide from anyone, or anything…the caverns would be a great place to do so."

"Why is that?" Abby asked.

"Because they contain several elements for human survival just naturally built in."

"How so?" Abby asked.

"Lots of fresh water for one, and an excellent, permanent shelter here for another. The researchers believe the temperature inside the caverns is constant year-round, around fifty-eight degrees. So, let me ask you, Abby, what else would a person need to survive in the cavern for an extended period of time?"

Abby thought for a moment and answered, "Just a few vegetables now and then from my garden."

David stood in silence for a moment, taking in her logic. "That would just about do it," he said quietly again, deep in thought.

"And the researchers never returned?" she asked.

"They have asked repeatedly over the years. I've denied access. These caves are ancient and undoubtedly have somehow been occupied in the past. For now, I am preserving them my own way, by keeping them closed."

As the two concluded their talk on the little hillside above the ranch, David checked the operation of the cameras one last time.

Sana watched as the Texans worked with the box attached to the tree outside her cavern. What could this possibly be? She could tell it had a kind of dark eye in its center. Was this some new Texas medicine?

As she watched the two Texans work their way down the canyon toward the log shelter, Sana began to devise her strategy. How was she to deal with this box, with the eye?

She would go on the offense. If she were to be captured or taken by these Texans, it would be her choice of when and where. It would not be because of some medicine eye…watching her.

Chapter 20

Later that Same Afternoon

Sana circled the back of the canyon well above the cavern. Here, just below the ridge, she was out of sight from the log shelter and out of sight of the medicine box the Texans had attached to the tree adjacent to her cavern. Silently moving above and behind the medicine box, she approached it from behind the tree to which it was attached. What to do with it was the question? She was afraid to touch it, but she also did not want the thing to see her through its dark eye.

She had waited the entire afternoon atop the canyon, observing the log shelter. The Texans had eventually departed in their own horseless stagecoach and had not returned. She knew they were no longer in the area. The stagecoach had traveled toward the east, riding away in a cloud of dust and smoke trailing from the stagecoach's belly fire. The stagecoach then had disappeared to the east, traveling along the black ribbon.

Sana needed to enter her cavern and rest, but there was something about the medicine box, a presence even, she thought.

It seemed her awareness of being watched was not her imagination. She possessed a sense, as did many Comanche, that brought this awareness. Anytime someone was watching Sana, she was aware of it.

This was a form of self-defense, a learned skill that was taught even. This sense or skill helped on many occasions to ensure survival for the Comanche.

Sana knew the medicine box had the ability to see her.

As she thought of the activities of the last few days and her detection by the Texas woman, perhaps there were other medicine boxes in or around the log shelter that she had not sensed or detected? It could possibly explain how the Texas women had known she was in the garden and barn the previous night.

She stood silently wondering about this strange medicine.

Sana moved farther uphill from the medicine box then toward the side, then downhill until perpendicular, at a hidden angle to the tree. There were no eyes on the sides of the medicine box. Evidently it could only see forward with it's one eye. She decided to take action. Moving away at a ninety-degree angle to the box, she knelt and chose two smooth shaped medium sized stones from the ground the perfect size and shape.

Sana had learned at an early age to use stones as a hunting weapon. She had used just such stones on many occasions to take quail, squirrels, even rabbits and other small game.

Taking careful aim, she loosed the first stone with expert precision. The stone struck the medicine box dead center. The damage after the second stone struck the box appeared to be complete. The medicine box shattered, its side breaking open, several thin colorful strings now hanging forth loosely from its insides. Most importantly, the eye was now protruding outward and pointing straight down toward the ground.

No longer was it peering toward the entrance to her cavern.

Sana moved quickly, entering the cavern, taking care to gently cover any tracks while smoothing over the ground surrounding the entrance. Again, she carefully covered any evidence of her entrance. She descended to a point only about twenty yards inside the cavern. Here she could listen and hear any outside activity, yet escape quickly farther into the cavern in the event anyone approached the entrance.

She waited and prayed in the silence of the cavern. Perhaps now she would determine the truth about this strange Texas medicine eye.

****

Abby and David were just finishing a delightful late lunch at the Downtown Coffee Shop, as it was referred to by locals. Set on the courthouse square in downtown Little Grove, Texas, the charm and quaintness of the setting was serene. Beautiful one-hundred-year-old pecan tress surrounded the old stately courthouse with its spires and gold leaf dome gleaming in the warm Texas afternoon. A perfectly manicured lawn and beds of roses in full bloom lined the walkways. Abby could smell the fragrant rose beds while walking the square or even driving past with windows of her car open. The crisp sweet fragrance permeated the beautiful scene.

The park benches were occupied by retirees and a few tourists enjoying the perfect late afternoon weather in the shade of the pecans. The square itself was surrounded on four sides by walkways, old fashion streetlamps, and flower baskets that hung from the lamp poles. Running around the square on all four sides was a single lane road paved with red brick. Artisan shops, bookstores, antique dealers, and even a sports bar, lined the square's sidewalks.

"I wonder how long it might take for the trail cameras to record something?" Abby said.

"The nice thing about the technology is the cameras will tell us within a few seconds of any activity," David said. The two sat in wonder for a silent moment.

"So, your trip and meeting were a success? Abby asked.

"Yes, Will had all the contracts prepared and signed. The buffalo should begin arriving next month. The crews will have to work overtime to get the special fencing in place before they arrive."

Abby could see again the excitement in David's expression as he told of the plan to introduce the buffalo onto the ranch. Catching the sparkle in his eyes, Abby listened intently. David was so animated when he pursued his dreams… she knew him so well. His passion always brought forth her attraction to who David was as a man. She noticed *the look*…his response to her interest and attentiveness.

David had set aside 100 sections of land—sixty-four-thousand acres—specifically for this purpose. As David continued, Abby gazed out the window of the café momentarily. She was just thinking how much she enjoyed the flavor of her hometown when her and David's cell phones vibrated simultaneously. They paused and, looking into one another's eyes, glanced at the message flashing on the cell phones.

The *camera disabled* message was flashing on the trail cam icon. Quickly studying and opening the app, it was apparent to both what the message meant.

The trail cam nearest the cavern entrance had been disabled!

David, motioning toward the waitress and reaching for his wallet, rose from the table as Abby gathered her keys and purse. While David paid the check, Abby exited the coffee shop, started the truck, and was waiting alongside the curb. David jumped in the passenger seat, and they made a hasty departure to the questioning looks of the people relaxing in the shade of the courtyard park.

Sana estimated it had taken less than an hour since she had destroyed the medicine eye for the Texans to arrive in their horseless stagecoach. Then another few minutes or so for them to work their way up the little canyon toward the cavern entrance. She could hear their voices from inside the cavern. She had no way of understanding their language, but clearly, their voices expressed surprise and wonderment at what had happened to the medicine eye.

She now knew the medicine box could somehow talk to the Texans.

Topusana began to move back into the cavern. She was certain the Texans would attempt to repair the box, or even replace it with another. She decided to stay hidden for a few days. She would pray for wisdom.

How could she avoid detection now with the presence of this strange, powerful medicine? She knew the next time she exited the cavern the medicine box, with its leering eye, would know. Then the Texans would know soon after.

David and Abby slowly made their way up the little canyon behind the house. The sun was just resting on the horizon to the west. Daylight slowly fading, the first cool drafts of a mild breeze descended the canyon, cooling them from the summer heat.

Winded from their second hike of the day, the two paused to catch their breath by the tree where the camera had been mounted. Examining the scene, the camera lens hung by a wire, pointing toward the ground. The inner working of the trail cam hung out of its side, the plastic housing shattered into pieces and scattered along the ground below the large oak tree David had attached it to.

"What do you think, David?" Abby asked.

"I don't know what to think. It obviously was intentionally destroyed."

"Why didn't we get any shots before it's destruction? Wouldn't it have recorded video or still shots if someone approached it?" Abby asked.

Thinking through those questions, David arrived at the only logical conclusion.

"The camera can only see forward and out on about a forty-five-degree angle to the left and right. It cannot see behind it and up the hill. It must have been approached from behind."

"Exactly!" Abby stated.

"So, she knew it was here?" David said.

"She?" Abby said.

"OK, I'm with you, Abby. She, your garden visitor, she knew it was here. The question is how did she know?" David said.

Abby thought for a moment. "The only way she could know it was here was if she had been watching us when we put it up."

"You are correct, Abby. She must have been watching us."

The two paused in silence, gazing around in all directions. David spoke the thought first. "Do you suppose she is watching us now?"

Abby began to analyze every stump, tree, and large boulder on the small hills surrounding them. A few moments passed in silence as the two searched in vain in the fading light, scanning the terrain around them.

"Well, if she is, we would never know it or see her," Abby said. "What should we do with the camera?" Abby asked.

"Let's just remove it."

"Will you replace it with another?" Abby asked.

"I don't think so; it would only be destroyed again."

"You really are all in on my story now, aren't you, David?"

"Yes, I am, Abby. I believe your story now…every word of it."

The two stood there in wonderment above the ranch house. David turned, beginning the walk down the little canyon above the river San Saba. Abby followed, both lost in thought, the feeling of being watched as they descended was palpable.

Chapter 21

Three Days Later

Topusana knew the time was now. She was aware of Tosahwi's foreknowledge of her gifting of visions. Tosahwi had understood clearly the gifting and attempted to explain the importance of such to her. Yet, she doubted. Her first *seeing* had been a dream about the frozen winter hunt. She had dreamed of finding the buffalo. She had seen the event in her mind's eye, or heart. Sana knew the Warriors would find the buffalo that frozen day on the prairie.

Today was the day she would meet the Texas woman. Sana had seen it clearly. That was all she knew from the vision.

She had remained out of sight for three days. While venturing this morning near the cavern entrance again, she had listened quietly until she had heard that sound of the Texan's stagecoach leaving, again riding away toward the west. Knowing that the pattern she had observed the last three mornings would repeat itself, it did so, as she had expected.

She waited a full hour. She had dressed completely, cleaning her clothing, brushing out her hair, even washing in the pool, and cleaning her teeth with the cedar trimmings, which left her teeth shining and her breath fresh.

Sana had no idea how this day would end. There was a possibility she would be taken captive this morning. She was prepared for the possibility; she had thought through every scenario. The most positive outcome would be establishing a friendship with the Texas woman. The worst scenario caused her to think…of Prairie Song.

Sana exited the cavern and was quite surprised; she did not see the expected medicine box. She quickly worked her way down the slope, nearing the garden. She did, however, become aware of another medicine box there in the tree above her route as she approached the garden.

She ignored it's leering eye, knowing full well it was watching her. She moved quickly onto the covered area of the log shelter and knocked on the huge front opening.

It took only a few seconds for the entry to open. There before her, just as she had seen, stood the beautiful Texas woman. She was alone, smiling a warm welcoming smile.

Abby's phone began to vibrate at the same time the knock on the door occurred. Silencing her phone, she gently opened the front door and gazed into the eyes of the strikingly beautiful Indian woman. Abby sensed the kind yet cautious look in the visitor's eyes.

Motioning her to enter, Abby led Sana toward the kitchen, gesturing for her to sit. Sana followed her lead and sat in a fine-looking chair, the first she had ever sat upon.

Abby sat opposite Sana, and thinking introductions were in order, she simply said, "Welcome." Abby smiled at the young, beautiful, Native American woman sitting at her kitchen table.

Sana, sensing the welcoming gesture and smile, spoke in her native tongue. "*Nu nahnia tsa Topusana.*" Gesturing at her chest, again repeating, "*To...pu... sa...na.*"

Abby understood the gesture and motioned toward her own chest. "Abby."

Topusana repeated the name awkwardly, "*Ah...Bee,*" while smiling as Abby nodded in approval.

Abby quickly did the same. "To poo sa na."

Sana responded as Abby had, with an approving smile.

Oh my, this will be difficult. No English, obviously, Abby thought. She stood, motioning toward her mouth then patting her stomach. "Food?"

Sana, in the universal nodding of her head, agreed. Abby understood.

Topusana smiled as Abby began to prepare a quick breakfast.

What to prepare? She wondered. Meat? Yes, perhaps that would be best, and a cup of tea seemed in order. Abby began to prepare the tea while taking some roast and a few potatoes, and yes, some carrots, she thought, from the previous evening's meal. She began to warm them on the stove top in a small iron skillet.

Topusana sat in silence and disbelief as Abby prepared the tea. The water came forth on command from a small opening above a shallow basin. Fire started from a large black box at the touch of the Texas woman's hand.

Topusana was stunned. What kind of power did this woman possess?

Making her best effort to remain calm, Topusana surveyed the room. It was quite lovely, adorned with the feminine touch she had seen on the covered area and garden.

Shiny metal pots decorated this area clearly meant for cooking and the preparation of meals. Beautiful paintings covered the walls. Not unlike the cave art many Comanche would create, but with much more detail and color. Flowers and beautiful decorations of all shapes and sizes surrounded them. Somehow, shining light made its way throughout the entire room from small openings in the roof.

Topusana wondered how this woman had even captured light.

A large shiny box stood against one wall, covered in more art. Topusana studied the art on the shiny box. It was much smaller, depicting people in all kinds of dress, and different scenes. Several of the small paintings contained the likeness of the Texas woman, *Ah Bee*, herself.

Abby, noticing Topusana staring at the photographs on the refrigerator, removed one of her favorites, a picture of her and both Jonathan and Grace. The photo had been taken seven years ago at Christmas. Where had the time gone?

She handed the photograph to Topusana, smiling. Topusana took the photograph from Abby's hand. Holding it up toward Abby's face. She instantly recognized the likeness in the painting, the detail was so perfect, the likeness was an exact image of Abby. Sana could see the other people in the painting. They were obviously the Texas woman's son and daughter.

Topusana spoke "*Onaa*," pointing to Jonathan, "*Kahni*," pointing at Grace.

Abby smiled again, understanding, nodding in agreement. "Yes, *Onaa* and *Kahni*, my son and daughter," Abby said. Although how to explain, she thought.

While pointing at Jonathan, Abby made the sign of the cross over her heart, while moving her head left and right, she then placed her hand over her heart. Then bowing her head, the real tears from the storehouse of her heart came forth. Rising again from the place of brokenness, those innumerable tears held just below the surface, the tears stored away in that secret place within a mother's heart.

Topusana understood. The *Onaa*, her son, was no more.

Topusana, pointing at her own heart then toward Grace, made the same sign over her heart. Then rested her hand on her breast and bowed her head, just as Abby had.

Abby instantly understood. Her daughter was gone also.

A flood of memories began to overcome Topusana; she, too, knew the loss, the brokenness only a mother could feel, as tears came forth from her heart.

The two women sat together in silence, unable to communicate verbally the heartache so palpable between them, the atmosphere of the respective loss permeating the room. Even without words, the meaning, the understanding clear.

They had both lost children.

Little could they know the similarities of the death of those children. Both losing their lives…to war.

However, a lifelong knitting of two hearts and two souls was taking place in the frozen surreal moment here in Abby's kitchen. Here on Topusana's Home Camp, along the San Saba River, lifelong friends were made.

When the tea pot whistled, Topusana was so startled she leaped from her chair, backing away from the table. Abby instantly reassured her as she removed the kettle from the stove top. Pouring the teacups full, she served Topusana the hot tea. Topusana again seated herself, sipping the tea as Abby did. The taste was distinct on her tongue, a hint of mint, the tea warming Topusana. Nodding her head again in confirmation. "*Haa*," Topusana said.

"*Good*," Abby said.

"*Good,*" Topusana repeated.

Abby's cell phone lying on the kitchen table vibrated again. She answered quickly. "Yes, she's here, David. …No, you don't need to come home. I'll call you later." She silenced the cell phone and placed it on the table.

Topusana stared at the little glowing box in wonderment. *Ah…bee* had just somehow spoken to someone.

The trusting smile was back on Abby's face, but what had just happened? Was it a signal of some kind? Topusana decided to speak the few words of English she knew.

Pointing at the phone, Topusana questioned, "White soldiers? Rangers?"

Abby was shocked at the question, but more concerned with how to alleviate the obvious fear growing on Topusana's face.

"No white soldiers. No rangers." Abby quickly moved back to the refrigerator, finding a picture of David and her together. She pointed to David, then placed the photo over her heart. Taking the picture Topusana held, Abby pointed again at Grace, then Jonathan, then herself, then David, then David again, then the phone. Abby could see the understanding on Topusana's face.

Topusana understood what Abby was saying to her.

This was *Ah Bee's* husband and family.

Somehow through the little light box, Abby had spoken to her husband! In awe of the medicine the Texan's possessed, Topusana was certain now the soldiers would not be coming. Abby seemed very unconcerned. Topusana was in awe of the medicine with which this woman was gifted. Perhaps, given the time, Topusana would learn of these gifts and how to use them herself.

Sensing that a time for giving of her gift was now appropriate, Topusana opened her medicine bag and removed the pestle that was the match to the grinding bowl. She knew the bowl was located here in the log shelter. Through a silent gesture she offered the gift to Abby.

Chapter 22

Later that Evening

David stood in his study in disbelief, holding the pestle that fit perfectly into the grinding bowl. Over and over again he had run the video clip of the Native American woman approaching the house, walking up the steps, then disappearing from the view of the camera.

Abby sat in the comfortable chair opposite David, answering his questions as best she could.

"So, you spent the entire morning and afternoon with her?"

"Yes, David. It was, for lack of a better term, wonderful."

"And she speaks no English at all?" David asked again.

"Evidently she only knew three words of English, *white soldiers* and *rangers*." Abby again repeated the story of the phone vibrating and the short conversation she had had with him. "David, she became very afraid; it must have been a brave thing for her to do, to walk right up and knock on our door."

"OK, just stay with me a moment. Let's review what we know. A Comanche woman lives in one of the caverns up the canyon. She dresses in traditional animal skins, she speaks no English, but evidently does speak the Comanche dialect. You know her name, Topusana. I found the translation for that name, by the way, Prairie Flower."

"Beautiful, isn't it," Abby said, interrupting David.

"Yes, it is." David continued. "She has lost a daughter, evidently to the white soldiers or the Texas Rangers, and you are teaching her English, starting tomorrow."

"Well, we started today but do plan to continue tomorrow," Abby said, completing David's observational report, smiling broadly to him. "Oh, and evidently she is still living in the stone age," Abby added. "Can you think of a better way to learn to communicate with her? Teaching English, was, in fact, what I specialized in for thirty years."

Thinking through the confusing set of events, David had no answer. "And she returned to the cavern?" he asked.

"Yes, she did."

"Abby, I hate to ask this, but is there any chance this is some kind of hoax? Could this really be?"

"I don't think it's a hoax, David. Our tears were real, our communication as mothers, my intuition as a woman. No imposter could ever behave, speak, and be in such wonder as Topusana was in my presence today."

"Again…I believe you Abby. I can't help but be in wonder myself at this. I know you understand it's my nature to be suspect." David paused a moment in thought.

"I can help." He gazed at his research library. "I'll put together a list of basic Comanche words and a chart of some of their sign language that I've found in my reference books. It should help you some. And you think it's a good idea if I'm not around during the lessons?"

"Yes, I do think that's a good idea," Abby answered. "I think she has an amazing intellect. We were able to communicate quite well, considering. That was mostly due to her, not me. I think if we spend the time together, she will be able to fill in the blanks of her story in a very short amount of time."

"How long do you think it will take?" David asked.

"Probably just a few months."

"Months?" David asked.

"Well, how long did it take you to speak and understand English?"

David did not reply. He sat in the chair behind his desk, working the grinding bowl and pestle with his hands, deep in thought.

"I suppose we should keep a lid on all of this for now?" he mumbled to himself.

"Whatever you think is best, David." Abby turned and exited David's study. Making her way through the great room, she paused a moment before the huge rock fireplace.

She gazed at her favorite painting that hung above the mantle. The frozen prairie, the embrace of a mother's love, the blurred faces. Her heart was moved again at the raw emotion the painting contained. How strange ,she thought, this young Comanche mother embracing her daughter in this very old painting reminded her somehow…of Topusana.

Chapter 23

San Antonio, Texas
1901

Jean Leon Dubois had arrived in the city of San Antonio, Texas, just three days ago. This was now his third social event in as many days. The affluent seemed to be flocking to the fastest growing city in Texas. Indeed, the population had soared to over fifty-thousand and was growing daily as entrepreneurs, cattlemen, sheep growers, an assortment of mill owners, and businessmen from all walks of life scrambled to earn a piece of the ever-growing Texas markets. Texas was indeed providing a mecca for those seeking fame and fortune.

Since the destruction of Galveston in the great storm just over a year ago, many of the wealthiest Texas families had relocated their businesses to the more central secure location San Antonio offered. With the completion and joining of five major railroads, all linking San Antonio to the entire United States markets, the building of mansions and factories was in full swing. The money to be made in this bustling, thriving city for someone like Jean Leon Dubois seemed limitless.

Jean Leon was born in Paris, into the poverty of the Parisian slums. He literally fought his way through the streets of Paris. He struggled to remove himself from the hovel of his birthplace by simply becoming a trader of goods.

He left school at the age of eleven and lived in the streets, surviving off rubbish thrown into the alleyways and trash piles of the slums. Whether looking for food, or something with which Jean Leon could barter, he learned how to survive.

Jean Leon also began to learn his craft and trade. He quickly realized truth from the old adage, "One man's trash was indeed another man's treasure." That treasure for Jean Leon was beginning to multiply.

Jean Leon Dubois was a complicated man. He loved his poor mother dearly. His father was a brute of a man, given to bouts of rage and violence, most often directed toward Jean Leon or his mother. Many days and nights he wandered the streets considering how he could escape the nightmare of life within his own home, if a person could call such a hovel a home. He decided at an early age he would escape. Knowing in his heart and mind, his mother would be safer if he simply left, creating one less mouth to feed. Perhaps his father would not be so filled with anger.

He struggled and fought and saved every penny he could possibly earn. He would rise above his past, and eventually grow his business into one of France's largest exporters of European furnishings and fine art.

Once he escaped, Jean Leon would never again return to the slums of Paris. He did, in fact, send an allowance regularly to his poor mother. At his first opportunity, he purchased a small apartment for her. He had learned through his contacts that his father had died in a drunken brawl over another man's wife. He felt no emotion upon learning of this news, just emptiness, or possibly even relief. Jean Leon kept forever a distance between himself and his mother, fearing her rejection if she should discover his chosen lifestyle.

Having become a voracious reader and self-educated businessman, he studied in the newspapers of the development and wealth being created in America. Jean Leon recognized the opportunity and began his plan to export rare European furnishings to the wealthiest of families who were building and spending fortunes on their homes and estates.

New Orleans seemed a logical place to land. The city, with its French influence and raucous culture, was a perfect match for the ambitious young businessman. Jean Leon quickly worked his way into the pomp and upper class of New Orleans society.

He spent twenty years in the city, eventually working with some of the most influential and wealthiest families of New Orleans. He grew his fortune beyond his wildest dreams. This hard-earned success allowed Jean Leon to travel the world.

Investing wisely, he had built and completed his factory on the outskirts of Paris. He was now prepared for a new adventure. Jean Leon, having spent the last twenty years earning consignments for furnishing the grandest mansions in New Orleans, would repeat that success in the city of San Antonio, Texas.

Gathered around him this evening were all the prominent women of San Antonio society. These very women would, in later years, form what would be known of as the Junior League of San Antonio.

With great pride, Jean Leon read the recommendation letter of the Dautrive family of New Orleans. With this letter, he had immediately secured a contract to furnish and decorate one of the largest mansions yet to be completed in San Antonio, the Hatton Estate.

The Hatton family was ripe for his sales pitch. The matriarch, Mrs. Clarice Hatton, took the bait "hook, line, and sinker," an American expression he had grown to know and love.

While speaking to the lady's group in broken English, although he understood and could read and write English in perfect fashion, Jean Leon addressed the group gathered around him with his strongest French accent. He told enticing stories of grand mansions he had personally furnished and decorated. He would forever paint his stories with colorful, vivid rants in the French language. Those tales told to his Texas audience were, in reality, veiled insults to his listeners. They never knew.

Dubois was certain to impress such a dull mind as Mrs. Hatton. In his past, Jean Leon had worked for many such pompous fools. As the agreement was completed and the terms of commission, travel expense, and bonuses were discussed, Mrs. Hatton agreed to all in writing, with a twenty-thousand-dollar upfront fee.

He would provide the Hatton family with many treasures from Europe to adorn the mansion throughout. Some would be authentic, if he could locate them. Other pieces would be produced in his factory on the outskirts of Paris and made to look authentic and quite old.

The key to the artwork and furnishings was always provenance. Each piece would have a story, some bit of royal history, some items from a duke's castle, or a legend that followed a piece of art hundreds of years old. The details would be easily created, and Jean Leon would relish in creating the fiction behind each piece. It was, he thought, his most creative work to conjure the stories and history. Those stories added exorbitant value to something that had very little value, until it came to life and blossomed within his creative mind.

"The greater the provenance, the greater the profit," was another of his favorite expressions. *"Plus la provenance esta grand, plus le profit est grand."*

With each shipment, Jean Leon would personally accompany the goods on their voyage across the Atlantic and overland by rail from Houston. This opportunity would be his greatest financial gain thus far. With the help of Mrs. Clarice Hatton, the word was already spreading down the hallways, around the tables, and into the ears of the important women of San Antonio society. Mrs. Hatton knew this group of social women would guarantee Jean Leon's work for years to come.

He would depart immediately for France to begin his quest for the drooling Mrs. Hatton. However, a few days delay in New Orleans would certainly be a welcome respite. An intimate evening or two with Stephan would be a delight. Yes, he decided, a respite from these boring Texas women who were fawning over him.

They were like stray dogs that wandered the streets of the slums of Paris he had escaped, he thought. Then he spoke those thoughts in rapid fire French to the smiles and cooing of the small gathering that had surrounded him.

A few more unintelligible insults spoken in French about their hair, dress, and breath, and Jean Leon Dubois exited the room. With a gracious bow and the blowing of a kiss directed toward Mrs. Clarice Hatton, Jean Leon departed in dramatic fashion.

Turning and feeling the check in his pocket while thinking of the many more to come, he walked directly to his hotel and upgraded his room to the penthouse.

Chapter 24

Paris, France, 1901
One month later

Jean Leon Dubois arrived home to Paris with a huge list of inventories needed for the furnishing of the Hatton Estate. He had spent several days in Texas with the atrocious Mrs. Hatton. Going over each room individually, he received explicit instructions from Mrs. Hatton as to even the dimensions of possible artwork to adorn specific rooms throughout the mansion. Jean Leon took tedious notes as the two had walked the construction site in San Antonio each day.

He never felt quite so constrained as to his creative abilities as he did now. He had reviewed his drawings and notes daily on his return crossing. His conclusion…he needed the work but was no longer very excited about the project.

Mrs. Clarice Hatton, Jean Leon had decided, was a frigid, controlling shrew.

He initially thought it odd that he never met Mr. Hatton during his research for the project, nor for that matter, their only daughter. After a few days with the demonstrative Mrs. Hatton, he knew why.

If he were Mr. Hatton, he would be conveniently busy most days and evenings also.

Reviewing his notes and conversations with Mrs. Hatton he recalled that when asked about the child's room and furnishings for such, it seemed the room would need very little. However, the expense afforded to Mrs. Hatton and her separate bedroom, which Jean Leon also thought odd, funds would be unlimited.

90

The *dernière paille*, or last straw, for Jean Leon was the sketching of herself presented to him. He was instructed to have the rough sketch reproduced, by someone famous, of course.

"Possibly Monet?" Mrs. Hatton wasn't asking but instructing. Jean Leon did his best to not roll his eyes in front of the woman.

He recalled his biggest disappointment came on the last afternoon he had spent with Mrs. Hatton when he posed the question to her concerning the purchase and display of Native American art subjects.

Some of the finest galleries in France were featuring the incredible works being created in that genre. He had in mind a painting he had been trying to acquire for several years. The magnificent piece by Karl Bodmer entitled "Mother and Daughter."

Many of the mansions he had formerly consigned contained broad collections of the Native American genre. Jean Leon thought it a wonderful opportunity to preserve some of the history of the Native American culture that was so quickly disappearing from Texas.

Mrs. Hatton would have none of it. Victorian, Victorian, Victorian.

"What a bore!" he said aloud closing his notebook.

After the explicate instruction, he made a decision. He would still attempt to acquire the masterpiece from Bodmer. Jean Leon did, after all, have plenty of the shrew's money...

****

The gallery was one of his favorites in Paris. He thought the setting along the Rue des Martyrs intoxicating with its colorful storefronts, coffee and pastry shops, the smell of flowers blooming in the manicured flower boxes along the store fronts.

Lingering over his late breakfast and a second cup of the delicious coffee was, for Jean Leon, a warm welcome home to the niceties and civilization of Paris. He was early for his meeting with the gallery owner. He had known Bridgette for many years, and they trusted one another explicitly.

He didn't want to seem too anxious, but the painting was still there. It was displayed prominently in the front window of the gallery. Simply magnificent, he thought to himself, caught again in the warmth of the embrace between mother and daughter that Bodmer had captured so exquisitely.

Strolling the nearby store fronts, he lingered a few moments in front of the gallery while observing the painting from several different angles.

He knew in his heart he must have the painting.

Entering the store front, Jeon Leon greeted Bridgette with a light kiss on each cheek. The two were truly glad to see one another. Exchanging pleasantries, Jean Leon quickly got down to business.

"You know I simply must have it," he said.

"But of course, my friend, it is but a question of price. You know that many of Karl's works are being reproduced by other fine artists?" Bridgette asked.

Surprised at this new fact, he asked, "What is this, you are adding to our negotiations, simply due to students' interest?" He spoke while smiling.

"Not merely students, my friend," Bridgette replied. "Yes, Jean, it is true. Come and see." Taking his hand in excitement, she led him toward the rear of the shop.

The painting entitled *The Bodmer Oak* was spectacular in every aspect. It was evident to Jean Leon who the artist was.

The painting had been created from an earlier Karl Bodmer piece, *La Forêt en Hiver* (The Forest in Winter). The painting before him was a stunningly beautiful scene.

Jean Leon glanced at the artist's signature and confirmed his initial thought. It was in fact a Monet.

"So, the new price for 'Mother and Daughter'?" he asked.

"Ten thousand American dollars," Bridgette replied quickly.

Jean Leon thought for a moment. "*Vendu*," he said. Sold.

He would deal with the presumptuous Mrs. Hatton at a later date.

The painting was shipped to Jean Leon's factory. He searched the city in vain for the perfect frame for the masterpiece. He finally designed a frame with his own craftsman and had it custom carved to the exact dimensions. The painting looked absolutely superb in the elegantly carved frame.

Three months later it would be carefully packed, along with many other rare and quite expensive pieces of European art and furnishings, several with splendidly created provenance.

The painting would arrive in San Antonio Texas, along with Jean Leon in the fall of 1901.

****

Mrs. Clarice Hatton, upon viewing the painting, hated the piece, if one could "hate" a piece of art! She simply could not see the emotion.

Jean Leon attempted to explain to her the emotion and brilliance of the piece.

The underlying truth was Mrs. Hatton quite disliked her own mother. None of what Jean Leon explained, masterpiece or not, made sense to her.

She could tell Jean Leon loved the piece himself. Mrs. Hatton made sure that even though she disliked the painting, Jean Leon would never own it. It had been purchased for her, with her money.

She would remain the boss and would prove so to Jean Leon. The painting was never installed in its beautiful frame. Mrs. Hatton made certain it was hidden away quite intentionally in the basement of the Hatton Estate.

A cheap canvas tarp covered several of the most valuable pieces chosen by Jean Leon. Those few artworks that in the end were rejected for use by Mrs. Hatton, were stored away.

Hidden away under the tarp in the basement of the estate, "Mother and Daughter" would remain untouched for eighty-five years.

Chapter 25

85 Years Later
San Antonio, Texas, 1986

A bby was extremely excited! She had seen the estate sale ad in the San Antonio paper and had planned the overnight getaway with David for months.

The new ranch house was complete, and now Abby was taking her time with furnishings and artwork. Being as frugal as possible, frequenting weekend garage sales and perusing consignment and antique shops became her knew hobby. The sale at the old Hatton Estate would be great fun, she thought. Even if she bought nothing, which happened more often than not, the weekend with David would be a welcome getaway from the two little ones at home.

The Hatton Estate had been abandoned in the 1960s. Like many other fine homes from the turn of the century, it simply was too expensive to maintain. Outdated and no longer meeting city code, a renovation would have cost the surviving family hundreds of thousands of dollars.

The simplest solution for some owners was to lock and board up the old estates. Many of the mansions of San Antonio's bygone era sat unoccupied. The once lavishly manicured structures deteriorated slowly as the decades rolled by.

The stately old mansions were a living testament to the once thriving city where fortunes had been made and lost. Those estates now awaited a possible investor who might be interested or could see the potential in the restoration of the properties.

The Hatton Estate was, however, just one of the many once magnificent properties lining the half empty streets of the historic districts of San Antonio.

History was proving, in the Hatton case, to not be worth much on the open market.

Upon the death of the only daughter of the once prominent Hattons, and the last to actually live in the home, the estate quickly fell into disrepair, losing even further value.

There was one surviving granddaughter living in the suburbs of Dallas who had no relationship with her elderly mother. Once she inherited the old estate, the property contents were quickly consigned to an auction house from Houston. The company was given full authority, in any fashion they chose, to simply liquidate. Any and all furnishings, artwork, or other assets found in or within the grounds of the estate were to be sold.

The one surviving family member never made the trip to San Antonio, as requested by the auction house. The family member chose not to interfere in any fashion. The request made of the auction house was contractual, in the event there may have been some item that contained sentimental value, a family heirloom, or some keepsake. The woman adamantly declined. She had terrible memories of her childhood spent in the home. She had no intention of keeping anything.

The company did as instructed and sold everything at auction. A few pieces were sold at close to market value; however, most were sold at give-away prices based on the actual market for authentic European imported furniture and art. The problem was no one attending the sale, even some so-called experts, could differentiate the reproductions from the authentic pieces.

As the employees went about the task of sorting through the huge estate and the innumerable pieces, many of the workers helped themselves to some of those pieces that appeared authentic. A few items were found in the basement of the estate under a dusty old tarp. The event manager, upon inspection of those items, thought the "Indian painting," might bring a good price if framed for the auction. She directed her staff to use whatever could be found on site for the framing. Following orders, the workers did locate a frame about three inches too narrow on each side. The frame was much too small for the painting. Using ingenuity and not wanting to waste too much time with the piece, it was simply folded over on all four sides, about two to three inches, and then tacked into place in the frame, covering over the signature of Karl Bodmer.

Abby Ross spotted the painting right away and fell in love with it. Even though the piece was unsigned and the artist unknown.

Never had she been so drawn to a piece of artwork. The emotion that sprang forth from the scene was breathtaking. As a mother, Abby knew that protective embrace, as all mothers must.

She thought the depiction of the cold prairie, the frozen sea of buffalo grass, the muted colors of the dress and bead work of "Mother and Daughter," as the painting was entitled on the back on small strip of paper, was breathtaking.

Abby splurged. She told herself she would not be drawn into a bidding war, but she knew in her heart this was a special piece. So much so, she thought it could become a center piece for her new home on the San Saba. Hoping she wasn't in too much trouble with David, she was, in the end, the successful bidder. Abby purchased the painting at the auction price of eight hundred-fifty dollars.

She hoped the future value of the painting might possibly increase beyond her investment.

"Mother and Daughter" would be hung in the great room of the Ross home. Abby quite liked the frame and decided to hang the piece as she had purchased it. The artist's signature would remain concealed. The painting had been in place exactly as purchased for over thirty years now.

Chapter 26

Present Day
2:30 A.M.

Abby was awakened by the dream...again.

The meeting with Topusana must be the reason, she thought. The revelation that they had both lost children to war. Her own tears, the photographs of Jonathan, even the pain in Topusana's eyes as Abby revealed that her son was gone. The understanding within both hearts of that pain and loss.

She hadn't revisited Jonathan's death in more than a year. The fresh reminders must have been what brought the dream back. David and Abby had pieced together the story of Jonathan's death with the assistance of William Travis, David's long-time friend and attorney. It had taken the entire year following Jonathan's death to do so. The events that led to the death of her son, Jonathan, Abby knew in complete detail.

August 4, 2012
Location: Classified
Somewhere in Afghanistan

The SEAL team worked its way across the ridge in the darkness. Lieutenant Jonathan D. Ross was always surprised at how cold it could become after the sun set in these remote mountains. The stars were bright overhead, but the last quarter moon produced little natural light, requiring night vision goggles to be in place on the entire team. They had the location, a small hut, within sight one quarter of a mile below them. The camp was silent for now. The target was high value, in fact on the Top 10 list. There were two sentries posted; both appeared to be soundly sleeping. As the team leader, Jonathan knew the intel was good. This should be a routine "Grab and Go" mission. Except he knew that nothing in this remote, godless place was ever routine. So, the possibility of "Kill and Go" was always in play.

They had rappelled from the CH-47 Chinook just twenty-four hours ago. The difficult terrain would not permit a landing of the huge helicopter. The team had rappelled out and remained within one half click of the landing zone, LZ Alpha. The team was patrolling their surroundings, getting a feel for the terrain. "Nothing substitutes for actually being on the ground and discovering what you have gotten your ass into," the words of wisdom from his Tactics instructor ever-present in Jonathan's mind.

He was glad to be here. The work the teams were doing was impacting the enemy. Osama Bin Laden had been captured and killed just over a year ago by some of Jonathan's own friends and colleagues.

The missions of the teams were evolving; they were becoming specialists in deep reconnaissance and counter insurgency. Jonathan often said jokingly, "Deep reconnaissance, here we come, that's what the brochure says men."

In reality, this activity and evolution put the Special Forces teams in the most dangerous places and exposed them to the highest risk of any other units in the entire War on Terror.

Their results were, however, very effective.

His own team had captured or killed more than a dozen Taliban leaders in the previous year. Jonathan was aware these were the evil cowardly souls that had attacked his country. He would not trade his abilities and line of work for anything on the planet. He loved his men; the bravery of their daily lives was beyond compare. Jonathan thought the work of eliminating evil was, for lack of a better term, "Bad ass!"

All elements were in place. The green light had been given; however, Jonathan hesitated. The sense that something was wrong in the scene below would not leave him. It was now his call. He had felt this awareness before on other missions, always dismissing it to nerves and pre-battle jitters. Tonight, this was different; he could sense the sleeping of the sentries was feigned.

"Campbell," he whispered in his earpiece. "How close are you to Sleepy and Dopey?" referring to the two guards.

"Within thirty yards, sir," came the faint reply.

"Give them a little pebble wake-up," Jonathan ordered.

"Roger that," replied Campbell.

Tossing a small pebble and landing it about ten feet away from the two, it should have never awakened either. However, both instantly jumped to their feet, raising their weapons, scanning the surrounding terrain.

Campbell reported back quickly. "They know we're here, sir."

As the team leader, the decision was completely Jonathan's...go or no go. What was happening here? How could the enemy know they were here? Had someone seen the Chinook? No matter what had taken place, the team's biggest advantage, the element of surprise, was now gone. Jonathan analyzed the possible scenarios. Just two days ago intel had reported less than twenty Taliban on location. In terms of intel, two days was ancient history. However, twenty Taliban fighters were no match for his sixteen-man team. That intel could be incorrect, but he doubted it. Even if the enemy knew they had landed twenty-four hours ago, it was not enough time for the Taliban to send word and move other fighters to this location. Jonathan hated that surprise was no longer on their side. Considering all factors, he decided to proceed with the mission.

"Campbell, give Sleepy and Dopey a permanent reason to nap."

"Roger that, sir."

The silenced rounds entered the heads of the two sentries, both slumping to the ground, dead before reaching it.

Then all hell broke loose. The slight muzzle flash gave away Campbell's position and was met with a volley of automatic weapons fire from three different directions. The firing was directed toward Campbell's location in the sparse brush.

Jonathan immediately called for a withdrawal to LZ Alpha. He spoke into the headset distinctly and clearly. "Fall back now! Meeks, get the chopper inbound now!"

Several of the SEALs returned fire on the flashes that had fired at Campbell, giving their positions away also. The action provoked another massive round of automatic weapons fire on their positions. Jonathan raced down the slope, quickly covering most of the distance to Campbell, calling to him on the headset. There was no reply.

Jonathan radioed to Commander Hadley circling high overhead in the AC-130 gunship.

"Uncle Z, what's going on, are you painting the enemy shooters?" Jonathan asked.

The officer in the command center several hundred miles away began to see, at the exact same time, what the gunship was seeing. Dozens of enemy fighters, appearing from what seemed like nowhere, coming from down the hill behind the small hut where the target was located.

"Control, Uncle Z, permission to fire on the hostiles, sir," asked Commander Hadley. The AC-130 crew could clearly paint the enemy troops and distinguish them from the SEALs due to the technology implanted in their equipment and in their bodies.

The naval commander in charge in the operations center had already made the call to his superiors, requesting permission to fire.

Meanwhile, Jonathan called the gunship crew again.

"What's happening, Uncle Z? We're taking heavy fire!"

"Must be a cave, sir," came the reply. "They are still coming out, painting one hundred fifty enemy targets now."

Jonathan's heart sank at the number. They were now out manned ten to one.

Jonathan called again for pull back and rendezvous at LZ Bravo immediately, thinking LZ Alpha could be compromised.

"Meeks, you got that?"

"Yes, sir. Jumper One is up, he can hear you now, sir."

Meeks was referring to the chopper pilot who was now within range of all communications.

"I copy," replied Jumper One. "Nine minutes from LZ Bravo."

"Listen up," ordered Jonathan. "Everyone check in now."

One by one the team checked in over the comms. The AC-130 crew and the command center were both recording the valuable data.

"Who we missing?" Jonathan asked.

"Just Campbell and Jones," came the reply from the AC-130. "We're painting both of their positions…There's no movement, sir."

Again, Commander Hadley in the AC-130 asked the command center for permission to fire.

"We are losing the window to make this neat and tidy, sir," transmitted Commander Hadley from the AC-130. Speaking to his superior in the command center hundreds of miles away he relayed, "They're spreading all over hell and back!"

The most foolish political questions in the history of warfare came back over the comms. Everyone, from the SEALs, to the gunship crew, Intel,

Operations, maybe even the bad guys thought Jonathan, all heard the questions transmitted from the command center.

"Can you verify the enemy is armed? And are there any non-combatants in the field of fire?"

Jonathan, and everyone else in the op…knew they were screwed.

The higher-ups and appointees, and the Commander in Chief for that matter, in Jonathan's mind were gutless chicken shits. They had no will to win this war, and now once again they were leaving the best, brightest, and bravest men on the planet exposed to a potential massacre. The military had the technology in the AC-130 gunship to wipe out all one hundred fifty of the enemy within one minute. The commanders in the field for the last three years had been practically hamstrung with new rules of engagement coming forth from Washington. It was to the point that sometimes Jonathan thought he nearly had to ask permission from the enemy to shoot at them.

Jonathan answered the question from his commander in a tone that could have repercussions, but at the moment, he really did not care.

"Damn it, we're under heavy fire! It's the middle of the night, on the side of a mountain, in the middle of flipping nowhere. We have two men down. You want me to go out there and ask for some stinking ID…sir? Because I'll damn sure do that, if that's what you need," he added.

The commander at the control center reluctantly gave the order from his superiors.

"Uncle Z, stand down for now…awaiting authorization to fire."

"Jumper One, zero six minutes from LZ Bravo," the helicopter piloted reported. "How we doing, men? Anyone close yet?"

The commander in the AC-130 could see most of the SEALs were still ten minutes or more from arriving at LZ Bravo.

"Jumper, Uncle Z, you need to stand off ten, they are still moving toward you."

"Roger that," the chopper pilot replied. He began flying away from LZ Bravo in an effort to confuse the enemy further of his intended landing site. The chopper hovered, backing away. His position in the darkness remained well below the ridgeline ahead and the brave men making their way toward LZ Bravo.

Jonathan checked his GPS display, the data clearly showing the position of Campbell. Locating him visually through his night vision, Jonathan spotted Campbell one hundred fifty yards below his location. He began to belly-crawl through the sparse cover.

"Ross, you need to get out now. Hostiles in all quadrants, sir!" The transmission coming from Uncle Z high overhead.

"Got a little problem with that for now," came the reply over the comms from Jonathan.

Jonathan was closing the distance and could see Campbell again through his night vision, now fifty yards ahead. Reaching Campbell without detection, Jonathan was surprised to find a pulse and hear the light wheezing. Knowing this meant a lung wound, he knew time was of the essence.

"Uncle Z, get a medical chopper up now. He's still pumping!"

"Roger that," came the reply from Commander Hadley in the AC-130.

Jonathan began to drag Campbell through the underbrush toward the LZ. At least it was downhill, Jonathan thought, as he struggled with the weight of his fallen friend.

"I've got six hostiles at your twelve o'clock and one hundred yards, Ross, hold your position," radioed Commander Hadley from the gunship.

"Shit," Jonathan swore under his breath.

Then Commander Hadley disobeyed an order for the first time in his twenty-eight-year career. The gunship descended and targeted the hostiles with deadly precision.

Commander Hadley gave the order, and all six hostiles were obliterated within ten seconds. Jonathan heard the impacts of the rounds and knew instantly what had happened.

The commander in the control center, observing, remained silent.

"Thank you, Uncle Z," Jonathan whispered into his mic.

"Clear to LZ Bravo now, Ross, one click to go." Commander Hadley could see and feel and imagine the struggle as Lieutenant Jonathan Ross dragged his fallen brother one kilometer through the difficult terrain.

Eighteen minutes later Jonathan arrived at LZ Bravo. Within a few moments the smaller, more agile Huey medical chopper, was touching down. There in the darkness on the hillside, the medics began taking over the rescue of Petty Officer Campbell. Jonathan continued toward his men who were now gathering strategically, taking up positions in and around LZ Bravo.

Commander Hadley, in the AC-130, ordered the Chinook to land, as the Huey medical chopper lifted off from LZ Bravo. He knew the terrain surrounding LZ Bravo would allow a landing and evacuation of the team. He could see the hostiles slowly making their way toward the LZ.

"OK, men, let's clear out!" Jonathan ordered.

After making sure all were aboard, Jonathan pressed his comm button. "Get me another medical chopper, sir, and a position on Jones."

There was no reply for a moment as Commander Hadley considered the request.

"Son, there's no movement from Jones. He's over two clicks away. Time to count our losses. We can send in a team under daylight tomorrow for a possible recovery."

Just then a volley of small arms fire could be heard through the comms. Several rounds began striking the sides of the huge Chinook. Jonathan gave the thumbs up to the pilot, who instantly lifted off, however, not before two other SEALs exited the helicopter. The eyes of Petty Officer David Toons and Master Chief Petty Officer Mikey Sanders locked on Jonathan's, their communication clear.

"We're with you, sir."

Other SEALs attempted to jump from the chopper, but Jonathan waved them off. "Sorry, men, just need two. Write if you get work."

As the helicopter accelerated ahead and began a descent below the ridgeline and out of sight, the three men disappeared into the brush. They slowly worked their way toward Jones's location. Commander Hadley, high above in the gunship, swore under his breath, as he tracked the three brave young men crawling across the mountainside below.

He swore again as he saw the number of hostiles. However, he, of all men understood perfectly. He would never have left a man behind either. He silently applauded the bravery of Lieutenant Ross.

Jonathan's team decided to give as wide a birth from the Taliban fighters as possible. Circling well over two clicks to the north and west, they moved away from the enemy and away from Jones. How to get to him was the problem.

Taking directions from Uncle Z on combatant positions, Jonathan gave the order to fan out, a move that would offer some protection from discovery as well as better fire cover.

Now the element of surprise was back on the side of the SEALs. Commander Hadley reported the enemy, from their actions and movement, were all returning to the initial target or disappearing back into the cave.

"I'm sure they think we all evacuated, Lieutenant Ross," came the transmission from Uncle Z.

So far none of the Taliban fighters had discovered Petty Officer Jones.

"Men, you still have a dozen or so hostiles slowly scouring the mountainside."

"Roger that," Jonathan said, and they began to move toward the position relayed to them from above.

Spotting an enemy target at his twelve o'clock, Jonathan raised his weapon and fired the silenced round. The man dropped instantly; no return fire came.

"One down," he whispered into his mic.

Another distinct *pfft* sound from his left, and Toons reported, "Make that two dead bastards."

Miraculously the small team made it to Jones's position within another forty-five minutes without further contact with the enemy. Unfortunately, Petty Officer Jacob Jones had taken a shot under his right arm, the bullet completely missing any Kevlar and penetrating his heart. The soldier had died instantly.

After a moment of silence and a report to Commander Hadley, the men began the dangerous descent. Jonathan strategically decided not to use LZ Bravo again. Instead, the three men took turns carrying the body of their fallen friend to LZ Alpha.

There the medical helicopter would evacuate them to safety. To conserve fuel, the chopper crew landed fifteen kilometers out. The crew sat in the darkness awaiting orders, a short seven minute flight from their position to LZ Alpha.

Under direction from Commander Hadley, the medical chopper crew would launch in time to rendezvous with the SEALs at LZ Alpha.

It took over two hours for the exhausted men to reach the landing site. Upon arrival, they took a defensive position to await the chopper.

As it approached, the chopper began to take on small arms fire. Instantly, a transmission from Uncle Z was received.

"Enemy targets now closing on your three o'clock, three hundred yards."

The SEALs returned fire in the direction of the enemy shooters.

"Mikey, get Jones in the chopper, now!" Jonathan ordered.

Mikey hoisted the body of Jones into the open door of the Huey. Chief Petty Officer Toons, along with Lieutenant Ross, began to lay down fire cover toward the approaching Taliban fighters. The men backed toward the helicopter, the years of training making the movement and actions of the team completely rote. For the moment, the return fire stopped. Toons and Ross turned and ran for the chopper. Petty Officer Mikey Sanders seeing the movement now began laying out cover fire from the chopper over their heads. Sanders continued firing into the trees where the enemy was fast approaching. The two jumped for the safety of the chopper floor as it was lifting off. The pilot quickly flying away and descending down the mountainous terrain and of out of sight.

All three men made it inside the chopper, along with the body of Jones, as the last few bullets pelted the sides of the aircraft.

Lieutenant Jonathan Ross slowly leaned over the body of his fallen friend. His fellow SEALs thinking perhaps he was just saying some final words, turned their eyes away.

A few moments later in a medical helicopter flying across a mountainside somewhere in Afghanistan, Lieutenant Jonathan Ross closed his eyes, lost consciousness, and died.

After a few awkward minutes, Mikey saw the blood pooling under Jonathan. Reaching for Jonathan and rolling him over, he screamed for the medic. It appeared a stray bullet had struck Jonathan in the upper thigh.

It would later be determined a bullet had severed Jonathan's femoral artery, rendering him unconscious within one minute. By the time the medic discovered the wound, and began treatment, the blood loss was so great, despite his best effort, there was nothing that could be done to save Lieutenant Jonathan D. Ross.

****

Abby Ross had just finished her day with the new first grade teacher. This would be a first in many years of her not returning to her classroom for the beginning of the new school year. She had looked forward to her retirement and was excited to have the time to spend with David. She was also looking forward to the travel and the freedom of her new uncluttered schedule.

On the drive home, she suddenly could only think of Jonathan, a terrible feeling of foreboding overcame her. She began to pray as she did every day for her son. Having no idea where he was or what his duties were, she knew he was constantly in harm's way.

Her prayers seemed empty and futile. As only a mother can somehow know or perceive, Abby knew something had happened to Jonathan. The terrible thought would not leave her. She knew deep down in her soul…Jonathan was gone.

August 7, 2012
Three Days Later

For the last three days, Abby and David had attempted to contact Jonathan. The complex system of secure cell networks, phone messaging, even texting the names and numbers Jonathan had supplied to her and David, proved frustrating and unsuccessful.

Abby decided to run to town and take care of a few errands. She had been so preoccupied with worry, she felt like she just needed to get away from the house for a few minutes.

On her return to the ranch, she noticed the black Suburban parked at the entrance to the ranch driveway, just off the highway. She thought it strange that two men were seated in the vehicle. Pulling up the drive, Abby saw the four other black Suburbans lining the drive.

Stopping her car in the middle of the drive, the tears came forth.

The vehicles were all the confirmation she needed.

David came to her, assisting her from the car. No words were spoken; he simply embraced her. Abby had never seen the hard, pain filled, tortuous look she now saw on the face of her husband.

"This is an unofficial visit, I've been told," David whispered, as they walked together up the few steps onto the porch. The Secret Service detail opened the door for them.

Former President of the United States George W. Bush and his wife Laura greeted Abby in her living room. Abby attempted to compose herself.

President Bush moved toward Abby, put his arm around her shoulder, and simply began to pray.

She could never remember the exact words he prayed, but the kind, comforting heart of President Bush was revealed in the prayer. It was, for Abby, one of the most emotionally comforting moments in her life. His compassion and gratefulness for Jonathan's service and sacrifice was truly heartfelt and genuine. It was a day she would come to lean on for comfort for many years to come.

It was also a day she would forever hate.

Abby thought no mother should ever have to endure the pain and heartache of losing a child to war. But that day Abby joined the ranks of many mothers and fathers, wives, brothers, sisters, friends, and families who would share, and forever have in common, this kind of loss. She would never wish membership in this fraternity, this fellowship of the broken hearted, on any person. Especially a mother.

She began to ask the universal question. The question to which there is no answer in the physical world we inhabit.

Why?

Why my son?

Chapter 27

Present Day

Abby sat at the table with Sana going over the sight words contained in her first-grade curriculum. Abby was astounded at how quickly Sana was learning.

In just three days, she had learned the entire alphabet. Sana would quickly repeat the sounds of vowels long and short and all the consonants. The fun rhythmic learning songs seemed to be Sana's favorite.

The sincere innocent spirit that was coming easily now was an amazing and wonderful sight for Abby to behold. The two worked together diligently. Abby's decision to include how to write the letters at the same time Sana was learning them was proving invaluable. The precision with which Sana began to print astonished Abby.

Today basic sight words were being learned in rapid succession: *and... the...it...I*. Sana already putting together the sounds of the letters, forming them into words.

Eager to understand more about the log shelter and the things located within, Sana rose, touching the *table* as Abby instructed. "Table, plate, fork, cup, fire." Sana remembered each just a few moments later when quizzed by Abby.

Perhaps six months was an overestimate, thought Abby.

The following day, Abby decided to move the learning session to the great room where there would be even more common items to identify, name, and write.

The two enjoyed a light breakfast of muffins and tea. Sana had never enjoyed food quite so much, the warm muffins with fresh butter melting in her mouth.

The sweetness of the baked muffins with honey was distinctive. How could food be such a pleasure, Sana thought. She had always considered food simply a necessity, but now she was learning a brand-new thing. Pleasure in eating. What a wonderful thing, to not rush, but to savor the delicious taste of food.

Abby prepared another cinnamon-apple muffin for Sana, who eagerly accepted, and the two of them lingered over another cup of hot tea.

Entering the great room, Abby and Sana sat next to one another on the *sofa*, with Abby patting the cushions beside her. Sana repeating the word *sofa*, smiling.

Sana surveyed the beautiful surroundings. The paintings and sculptures were magnificent. Suddenly rising and moving toward the large painting over the grand fireplace, Topusana cried out, tears flowing instantly down her cheeks. Reaching to the painting, touching the smooth oil, recognizing the image of herself and Prairie Song. How could this possibly be?

The buffalo hunt…the frozen prairie…her daughter, her only child.

The memories washed over her in a flood of emotion.

The pang of hunger, the bitter cold, the biting wind, frozen blood on skinned knees. The memories brought to her mind even the smell of Prairie Song's hair. This flood bursting forth, the memories awakened the feelings, emotions, and fear, and even the comfort of that day.

Motherhood, the warmth of embrace, the sweetness of Prairie Song's beautiful spirit. Memories…

Topusana could not stop the tears, emotion overcoming her entire being. Both hands now caressing the painting, she sobbed uncontrollably. How could this possibly be?

Abby moved beside Sana, embracing and attempting to comfort her. Abby, while not understanding, could clearly see and feel the heartache the painting evoked. She wondered what was it this painting contained? Listening to the sobbing cries from Sana and the distinct words being formed and coming out of her soul…

"Prairie Song. Prairie Song."

"Your daughter?" Abby said in shock and disbelief.

Nodding, Topusana slowly knelt to the floor, the tears ebbing now, the loss of her child in perfect focus.

She sat on the floor at the foot of the great fire pit in this beautiful home gazing into the kind eyes of her only friend. In the quite stillness of the moment, Sana knelt upon the hearth, wondering if she could breathe in her next breath.

"How…can…this…be?" she asked Abby in broken English.

Chapter 28

July 5

Sana had returned to the cavern later that morning. Abby had unsuccessfully pleaded with her to stay, having done all she could to console Sana. The lesson for the day ending abruptly, tearfully.

Abby was perplexed and at a total loss to explain how Topusana and her daughter Prairie Song could possibly be the subjects in a painting that had hung in her home for over thirty years. David had returned home at Abby's request. They now sat together on the sofa in the great room with Abby going over the details of the morning with David.

"There is not a doubt in my mind that Sana knows this is her in the painting," Abby said.

"So, where did you purchase the painting again?" David asked.

"Remember the trip to San Antonio, just as we were completing the house? It had to be 1986 or so, I would guess, the year we finished the ranch house. We went to that estate sale. Remember the huge Victorian home?"

"Yes, I do remember that." Studying the painting, he saw new details coming to him from the canvas. "The setting is bitter, isn't it?"

"Yes, it's what I loved so much about the painting to begin with. The contrast of the actual physical setting, evidently a frozen plain, with the warmth and love of the embrace between the two."

Abby now was studying the image and noticing the possible resemblance of Sana to the woman in the painting.

"We need to find out more about the painting, if possible," David said.

"How do we do that?" Abby asked.

David rose from the sofa. "I have a few ideas, but we can start with this."

David gently lifted the painting from its anchor and removed it from the rock wall.

Together they proceeded to his study. Clearing his huge desk and placing the painting on its back, they began to examine every inch of the piece. David located a large magnifying glass and began to examine the surface of the painting.

"There simply is no signature at all. I was thinking maybe it had faded or was blurred, but there is nothing here," David said.

Abby had an idea. "Let's look at the back." Turning the painting on its front, the two began to examine the frame and mounting. "That's strange, isn't it?" Abby asked.

"Yes, I see what you're asking," David replied. "It looks as if it's been folded in several places."

"That's not a normal way to frame a painting, is it?"

"No, it's not." David answered.

Opening a lower drawer in the desk, David located a small set of pliers and a screwdriver and began to gently remove an inner trim piece that had been tacked around the entire area of the frame.

"Careful, David. Oh my!" Abby exclaimed as David removed the trim piece from one side.

There beneath the trim was easily another two inches of painting that had been folded inward and hidden in the frame.

"Quite a careless way to frame a painting," David mumbled to himself.

"Does that go all the way around?" Abby saw the answer to her question as soon as she asked it.

David was already working the next frame piece loose from its tacks. In a few moments they had removed all four trim pieces from the rear of the frame. Working together they carefully unfolded the newly exposed painted canvas surface, attempting to smooth the surface as they gently worked the piece out of the frame and face down on the desk.

David removed the frame and set it aside. Working together, they turned the painting onto its back. Now clearly the artist's signature could be seen on the lower right of the magnificent painting.

"It says Karl Bodmer, 'Mother and Daughter,'" Abby stated. "What do we do now?"

David was already looking up the artist's biography on his computer.

It quickly became apparent to David that this was, if it proved to be authentic, quite an important piece of art.

"I think we better call Nan right away." He was speaking of Nan Chisholm, a family friend and art consultant with offices in New York. She had helped them in the past with acquisitions and appraisals of their art collection.

"Nan is an expert in that time period and can fill in the blanks for us, I'm certain," David said.

Abby had already dialed her number and was waiting on hold.

Nan was always glad to hear from Abby, and the two spent a few moments in casual conversation, catching up. Pleasantries aside, Abby relayed some of the basics of the painting to Nan.

"Very intriguing, Abby," Nan said.

"The artist?" Nan queried.

"Karl Bodmer," Abby answered.

"Oh, my goodness, is there a way you can snap a photo and send to me while we are talking?" Nan asked.

"Yes, of course." Abby motioned to David, who quickly snapped photos on his cell phone. Finding her contact information, David forwarded the best of the few shots he had taken to Nan.

"David just sent you a quick cell pic of it. It's not going to be the best light, but it will clearly show the signature," Abby said.

"OK, great. Let me do some research and call you back in a few minutes. Tell me again where the painting was purchased." Abby went over the story with Nan and remembered the name of the estate.

"Yes, the Hatton Estate in San Antonio. Yes, that was it, I'm certain." Abby ended the call.

"Well, Mrs. Ross, I'm not sure what in the world we have gotten ourselves into, but my research is revealing this artist actually was on an expedition to the Great Plains in the 1830s. He sketched a recorded history of the Native American Plains Indian Tribes, and, in fact, painted many famous scenes of that time."

"You learned that already while I was on the phone?" asked Abby.

David studied his computer screen. "It says here he was actually a contemporary of one Claude Monet. They evidently were friends and studied together."

Abby's cell phone began to ring as she stood digesting the information

111

David continued relaying to her. Looking at the phone, she saw Nan Chisholm's contact info on the screen and answered quickly, listening and nodding in disbelief.

"David will send the jet for you first thing in the morning. Plan on meeting Steve at Tetorborough at 10 a.m. Yes, Nan, we will be very careful with the painting. Thank you, Nan."

Ending the call, Abby slowly settled onto the sofa in David's office. Her eyes glazed over at what Nan had just shared with her.

"Well?" David questioned.

"Nan thinks it's an authentic Bodmer. She wants to see it right away, oh, and she says be very careful with the painting."

"Go on," he said.

Abby answered in stunned disbelief. "If it's what she thinks it is, and can verify its authenticity, this painting could possibly be worth millions of dollars."

The Following Afternoon

Nan Chisholm sat in the beautiful little breakfast nook overlooking the San Saba river.

She had thoroughly examined the Bodmer painting. It was the original... that had been missing for over a century. She shared the research and history of the painting with David and Abby.

"David, the Upper Missouri River Expedition was a huge success. The group was led by one Prince Maximilian of Wied. That party had spent two years in the American West in the 1830s. The expedition compiled one of the earliest records of the life and history of the indigenous populations of the American Plains," Nan said. "Their route followed in the footsteps of the Lewis and Clark expedition. What the group did differently was to combine a team of a trained scientists and record in pictorial and scientific written detail the entire two-year expedition."

"Fascinating," David said.

"The team included botanist David Dreidoppel, an expert in plant and animal life, and Karl Bodmer, a Swiss born artist who created these wonderful field drawings and sketches. He recorded a complete pictorial history of the expedition. Once back in Paris, Bodmer painted several works from his sketch books. His friend Claude Monet loved the works so much Monet himself recreated a few paintings from Bodmer's field studies," Nan continued.

"Maximilian of Wied wrote and published the data and sketches in book form. Three volumes were published as *The North American Journals of Prince Maximilian of Wied.*

"Karl Bodmer filled his sketch books with wildlife, depictions of native plants, drawings of Native American camps, including many sketches of chiefs and warriors alike. It was the most detailed study of the North America Plains, plant life, wildlife, and indigenous peoples ever undertaken. The body of work at the time was the most accurate and valuable record of those cultures ever created.

"What contributes tremendous value to your piece is…Well, history. What actually happened to the Plains tribes."

"You mean their ultimate demise," David said.

"Well, yes," Nan replied. "The lifestyle and livelihood, their way of life… ultimately disappeared from the plains within a few decades of the research.

"Although we do have a few examples, like 'Mother and Daughter,' that reflect very intimately those cultures that were forever lost."

"So, what do we do with such a valuable painting?" Abby asked.

"Of course, it needs proper framing and insuring…but I would say simply enjoy it. That is my recommendation. It will only appreciate in value," Nan said.

"And your estimation of that value?" David asked.

"At auction it's hard to say exactly, but conservatively $8 to $10 million, possibly more."

Chapter 29

The buffalo appeared to be adjusting well to their new surroundings. David knew transporting them by tractor-trailer could possibly weaken some of the animals; however, after three days, all of them seemed healthy and well. Magnificent, he thought. The herd slowly grazed around the small lake. Some of the bulls had wandered as far away as two or three miles from where they were unloaded. For now, with the abundant grass and the lake water, they had no reason to roam very far from here.

The fencing project was almost complete—the cost astronomical. But David knew that pipe and steel mesh was the only type of structure that could keep the buffalo contained. The sheer size of the project was immense. He had decided to run a cross fence right down the middle of the one hundred sections he had dedicated to the recovery project. This would allow moving the herd into separate 32,000-acre tracts in the event rotating grazing became necessary. The outer fencing of the adjacent 32,000 acres should be completed within the month.

Sixty-four thousand acres, a total of one hundred sections, one hundred square miles, would soon be available for the buffalo to roam free.

Four hundred animals had been purchased, transported from Wyoming, and released onto the ranch. Many of the females were pregnant. David hoped by spring the herd would grow upwards of six to seven hundred animals, as many of the cows would give birth to two calves. His goal for the one hundred sections would be a herd totaling five thousand animals. With a little luck, and good rain, that goal could possibly be achieved within a few years.

David knew the market for buffalo meat was strong, the price commanding three times that of beef cattle. He would selectively sell a small amount each fall to cover expenses.

The research he had done, however, led him to a completely different direction concerning return on investment.

Buffalo hunting.

He knew there were no longer any predators large enough to create a balance of the ecology in Texas. That balance was in fact necessary to maintain a healthy herd. So, as in many ecosystems…man would become the predator.

The plans for the hunting lodge were also complete. The contract signed, construction would begin on the facility next week, with twenty bunk rooms, kitchen facilities, even a large banquet room. The structure would also contain refrigeration, freezer rooms, and a meat processing facility. It would be a hunting enthusiasts dream. David, ever the prudent businessman, had calculated out the costs; the lodge would pay for itself within the first five years.

The outdoorsmen of Texas were flush with cash from the solid Texas economy. The other ranches in Wyoming and Montana that allowed hunting of their herds averaged $20,000 for a bull buffalo tag. David knew the mild Texas weather would attract the wealthy hunting enthusiasts. His plan was to eventually offer fifty bull hunts per season, initially at $20,000 per hunt, and possibly one hundred cow hunts each year, at a cost of $10,000 each. The estimated income would be $2 million per season for years to come.

The herd was in place. Within the next thirty days, the fencing would be complete. His ranch was large enough to support the animals without any supplemental feeding.

Now all he had to do was be patient and let nature take its course.

What was most pleasing and deeply satisfying to David J. Ross about the project—his *New Dream*—was returning a large portion of the land to its original once native species. Allowing the creation and the Creator to take control.

David paused a moment, acknowledging again his Creator, in a silent prayer.

He was not a church goer, as he would say, but a true believer in the God of Creation. Being a man who spent so many days and nights in the outdoors, he thought it all too spectacular. The creation seemed to David so perfectly designed for human life. The obvious intelligence and purposeful design of the planet revealed much about the Creator behind creation, if one cared to look.

"We are not an accident," he said aloud. The wind carried his words away across the prairie.

David, seated on his mount, was moved deep within his spirit as he observed the scene before him.

Sun, rain, wind, grasslands, springs of water would all together produce in harmony, the animals and the plant life that were native to this beautiful blessed landscape.

As he gazed across the striking scenery, admiring the buffalo herd, Nan Chisholm's words came to the forefront of his mind. "Yes, David, their way of life, their culture, the lifestyle of the Comanche…ultimately would disappear from the plains."

Chapter 30

December
Three Months Later

The time seemed to fly by...weeks had stretched into months as Abby and Sana continued their English lessons. However, friendship was what had developed, as much as Sana's ability to communicate and understand. It had now been six months since Sana awakened in the cavern. Her story was finally becoming clear to Abby and David. Topusana had slept one hundred seventy-four years in her little cavern above the Ross ranch.

Abby and David sat in the shade of the porch, speaking with Sana. The trees along the river below them golden, gently swaying in the light breeze. The beautiful late fall weather still quite warm.

The story had been slowly coming forth. How much of it to tell was Sana's immediate concern. She had no misgivings about relaying the events leading up to the Dream Time. Indeed David, as she had come to call him, mimicking Abby, investigating in his history books, discovered a complete record of the Battle on the San Saba, as it was referenced in the history books. No matter the record of any war, let alone Sana's, the pain it caused could never be communicated to the reader, thought Sana. It seemed so factual and impersonal as David read through the narrative. Sana had experienced the death, the suffering of real families, real children had died. Something the books seemed to miss...or dismiss.

As they discussed the long-ago history, Sana thought she would not share the information that Tabba was still in the Dream Time in the cavern. Neither would she share or reveal what she knew about Tosahwi and the others. She had found the sign just two day ago…the tortoise shell. Tosahwi had wakened.

She needed desperately to find him.

David seemed particularly interested in the Dream Time. While Sana attempted to explain what she knew, there was simply not a way for David to understand. She tried explaining that it was a belief, or faith even. The spiritual giftings that some people like Tosahwi were graced with…those gifts were not a science.

She gently explained to David that being a white man, there were things he simply would not understand through—how to say it—"studying books."

"David," Sana said, "there is an old Comanche proverb that says, let me think, the translation to English would be: *It is to the glory of the Great Spirit for the Numunuu (The People) to seek out and discover the mysteries of His creation.*"

David was startled at the truth of the proverb. Where had he heard that saying before?

"A person simply needed to believe, have faith, and then all things were possible… though not explainable," Sana said. Abby understood perfectly.

The question before them this fine morning was Sana's future. What would she desire to do now? Did she have dreams or ambitions? She could hardly imagine how to answer such questions.

"You know we would love to have you move in and stay with us permanently, Sana." Abby said.

"Yes, I understand," Sana replied. Indeed, the time for a change was coming, and Topusana knew it. She had many questions of her own. She would not ask those questions openly at this time.

Sana was, however, quietly discovering through conversations with Abby, the complicated process of acquiring and owning land.

Acquiring land was indeed a much different process than how their Homeland had been taken, which had been by military force. Her primary purpose and mission continued to be central in her thoughts. Her future and the future of her people was at stake.

She wondered how many had escaped the attack on her Home Camp?

Daily, she was gaining the knowledge she needed to lead *The People*. She would be very careful in answering the kinds of questions being posed to her. She wanted to trust her new friends completely. It seemed to do so would require her to totally forget the past. No matter how hard she tried to forgive and forget, Prairie Song's life called out to her over the years.

Deep in her soul she was conflicted. What to reveal? How to proceed? She needed to find Tosahwi. Sana needed counsel.

Sitting here in the beautiful setting, overlooking all that was formerly her Homeland, in the presence of the most sincere, helpful people she had ever met in her life, Topusana felt very much alone. She needed her husband desperately.

It was becoming much harder to return to the cavern. Day after day, she would return, speaking softly with Tabba, but something was wrong. He was caught. Caught in some time or space that she could not comprehend. Perhaps he would not survive. Indeed, his body seemed to be becoming weaker as the days ebbed by. Each time she made the trip, he would be in a different position. On a few occasions she had even heard him moan. Sana, having experienced the Dream Time personally, now understood more clearly the process and the gifting of Tosahwi.

Tosahwi had used the medicine on several occasions. What he described to her prior to her own experience, was that once one entered the Dream Time, the person's body and spirit moved into another time. That person would awaken after apparently only a few days of actual sleep. However, great pieces of time may have passed by on Earth. This was what Sana had experienced. Tabba had not.

He should have awakened by now.

Sana had begun to spend a few nights in the log shelter, at the invitation of Abby and David. The life the Texans lived astounded her. Soft feather beds, dreamier and more comfortable than anything she could ever have imagined, with soft soothing linens, feathery pillows, and warm down comforters to wrap oneself into and snuggle. Within that comfort Sana simply became lost. Light was everywhere, at the touch of a switch. Electricity, as David had explained it to her, was amazing. Food, refrigeration, air conditioning, heating that tumbled warm air from little boxes into each room, all of it unbelievable. Her favorite, though, was hot water.

The tub, as it was called, could be filled with the hot water, and a person could rest and soak, invigorating the body and soul. She would often take long soothing baths; it was a time for her to think, plan, escape even. There, soaking in the lovely ambiance of the oversized tub, the warm water caressing her body, Sana became lost in the quiet and dream of what her life could become. She would think and dream of what was to come for *The People*. Her People.

She had even taken to dressing in modern clothing. She and Abby had spent many wonderful days playing dress up, finding what Abby referred to as the perfect "look" for Sana. She was having a splendid time adjusting to all the fashion accessories that a modern woman required. She loved the different styles and feel of the clothing.

She now dressed like a young, "modern hip woman," Abby would say, although Sana did not understand the term. There was, however, the one exception, Sana could not quite adjust to the shoes. No matter what she tried, running shoes, heels, sandals, none could compare to her moccasins for comfort and agility. For now, she wore the moccasins only. Abby thought the moccasins did not complete some of the chosen ensembles too well. "But what did it matter," Abby would say.

Yes, Sana knew it was time to move on, time to live. This new world she had entered was now her home. She needed to continue to learn, to prepare, to not just live, but live a full life. A life filled with goodness and blessings.

Sana needed to make one final trip into the cavern. She needed to place the sign. Perhaps one day Tabba would awaken…

"I'm not sure what to do about my future, David. I know I need to continue to learn. I have been thinking of one thing I would like to try," Sana confided.

"Of course, Sana, anything. What are you thinking?" David asked, anxious to help.

"I would like to learn to drive an automobile," she said. Abby and David looked at one another, David lost in thought.

Abby replied. "What a wonderful idea!"

David did not reply, a look of concern spreading across his face.

The truth gnawing within Sana's mind slipped forth from her lips.

"David," Sana asked, "how can an individual person own the land?"

Seeing the sincerity in her face and her tone, David attempted to explain. "Well, Sana, land can be purchased now, anywhere it is offered for sale. Whoever owns it simply puts a price on it in dollars, then it may be bought on the open market or negotiated for."

Sana, looking confused, said, "The paper dollars? This is how land is owned?"

"Yes," David said.

"It seems such a strange thing for one person to own what the Great Spirit has given to all his children. The Comanche has never thought in this way. Can a single person own the river?"

David thought for a moment. "Well, yes, as it flows through that person's land, they do own it until it reaches the boundary of the owned land."

"But, David, the water does not know the boundary. The water will not stop and say I will travel no further. Does the person who owns the land and the river also own the water within the river?"

David paused, thinking to himself how to explain a concept to Sana she had never known.

Sana continued her questioning. "Can a person own the air above the land? Or the animals that live upon the land?"

David thought about the absurd lawsuits that had been fought about that very thing, airspace above a given property. How to explain to her, the Texas Game and Fish Department issuing deer and turkey permits to him as a landowner, and the complicated process it had all become. He had no easy answers to the sincere questions Sana was asking of him.

Still deep in thought, Sana continued. "Did you have to pay many dollars for this land, David?

"Well, no Sana," he answered. "This land was given to me by my father."

"Did your father pay the paper dollars for the land?"

"No, his father, my grandfather gave it to him."

"So, the land was paid for by many of the paper dollars by your grandfather?"

David, seeing where the reasoning was leading, attempted to answer as honestly as he could.

"Sana, my great-great-grandfather actually gave the land to my grandfather."

"I do not understand this giving of lands. Or sometimes giving the paper dollars for the land. My grandfather's name was Buffalo Hump."

David paused, knowing the history of the great Comanche Chief.

"Buffalo Hump's grandfathers lived here in this very place for hundreds of years. These people, my people, never owned the land. We simply lived upon it. We knew it was a gift. A gift designed perfectly for us to live within, pursue happiness and blessings. We always knew...that we all...as children of the Great Spirit, possessed the land equally."

Sana paused a moment, thinking inwardly. "I do not understand, David. I do have one more question. What was the name of your great-great grandfather?"

"His name was Sullivan Ross."

Sana felt as if she had been struck by a fist. She reached for her side as a searing pain shot through her body at the words David had spoken. Her eyes seemed to lose focus as her mind moved into a different place and time. Remembering...

San Saba River Valley
1844

Sana ran as fast as humanly possible. Scanning the horizon, she continued to scream her War Cry. She saw the flanking movement from the east; dozens of white soldiers poured forth from the brush to the east of the Home Camp. Then she saw him. Sullivan Ross astride his horse, the rifle trained on the camp. Fear resonated within her soul. This was the leader of the Texas Rangers, the man who had caused so many losses. *The People* feared this man more than any other. Something struck her in the side. She stumbled, feeling no pain, not understanding...

Present Time

Abby quickly moved to Sana's side. "Are you alright, Sana?" Abby touched the side of Sana's abdomen where she seemed to be holding herself. Abby could feel the scar through Sana's light shirt.

"Sullivan Ross, the Texas Ranger," she spoke softly.

The hurt in her eyes was obvious. The heartache on the face of David showing.

"Did you know him, Sana?" David asked softly.

"Yes," was all Sana could say.

A knowing now shown on both David's and Sana's faces.

David's heart ached deep within his soul at the understanding on the face of Sana.

"So sometimes lands can be taken without the paper dollars, without the giving of them by a father. Sometimes lands can be taken with bullets."

David J. Ross fought back the tears, a painful knot forming in his throat. "Sana, I am very sorry for what my grandfathers have done to *The People*."

"I can see in your eyes, David...that this is a true thing," Sana replied.

David rose from his chair, turned, and walked away, the tears flowing freely.

The inner turmoil, the thoughts, the guilt. He had always told himself he was simply a steward. He had tried his entire life to rationalize his station in life.

He thought of his son. Jonathan had died fighting a war of bullets over land he would never own. He had died over an ideal. Prairie Song, Sana's daughter, had died most likely at the hands of the Texas Rangers and his great-great-grandfather's men. For what? David thought. So, he himself could become rich.

David believed every man must eventually have a poignant moment like this in his life. A realization, a course-altering encounter with truth. He breathed in deeply, resolve settling in his heart. Somehow he would do everything in his power to correct the injustice imposed on Topusana and her people.

Standing in his office, surrounded by wealth, he stared at Sullivan Ross's Colt Peacemaker revolver that he kept on display. Even knowing how valuable the weapon was, David raised his fist in disgust and smashed the glass encasement. *Peacemaker?*

He removed the pistol from the display and threw it across the room, shattering the glass encased frame that displayed his great-great-grandfather's sword and scabbard. He dropped to his knees; something within David J. Ross was also completely and utterly shattered and broken.

Chapter 31

3 Days Later

Sana removed the broken deer antler from the upper room in the cavern. Lingering in the presence of Tabba, Voice of the Sun, she was uncertain her man would ever awaken. His body had continued to become drawn, his once strong arms now appearing thin, even skeletal. Sana lay beside her husband and prayed. She knew her prayers were always heard. She also knew they were not always answered in the way she would desire. The Great Spirit had a purpose in all things…that purpose was not always immediately evident to His Children.

Sana gently kissed Tabba, covered him with the buffalo robe, and said goodbye. Her thoughts floated across the years. From their first attraction to one another as children, to their beautiful marriage ceremony. Memories drifted through her mind. The birth of Prairie Song. The movements of *The People* through the seasons and times with Tabbananica, her man, she always by his side. The battles, the struggle to survive, the death of their daughter. Sana thought her life with Tabba may now be at an end. The tears began to flow. She thought to herself, how many tears could a person possibly cry in one lifetime? She paused here in this other worldly place here by her man. The sounds of the cavern awakened her senses again. The sound of running water, the feel of the air current against her skin. The smell from the cave fires brought her awareness alive. Once again, she knelt before Tabba, kissed his face, and whispered, "I will love you forever."

Although undetected by Topusana, something within Tabbananica was stirred. Deep within his spirit…Tabba attempted to reach for her.

Rising, she turned to leave. She needed to set her mind on the future and remove her mind from the hurts of the past. Even from her love…of her past life with Tabba.

Sana knew in her heart that her focus must change. Her focus *was* changing. She was beginning to understand letting go of the past—the things Tosahwi had taught her about, including forgiveness.

She began her ascent out of the cavern.

Exiting the cavern, she placed the broken deer horn in the pre-arranged hiding place, the small cleft in the large rock just below the cavern entrance. Reaching deep into the cleft, the horn was completely out of sight of anyone who might pass by. She would return periodically to check for its presence. She would know that if one day it were no longer there in its hiding place, it would mean Tabba had awakened. She prayed again that the special awakening day would come soon. Her prayers felt empty and impossible. Sana began the walk down the little canyon. She paused for a moment, gazing across the highway at her former Camp.

One hundred seventy-four years had gone by on Earth since she entered the Dream Time. Her old life with the Comanche was now coming to an end.

Looking down at her jeans, light blue pull-over sweater, and tennis shoes, she thought her previous life actually seemed more like a dream. It seemed like a different life…that someone else had lived.

Sana would begin college in the spring semester. Her driving lessons would begin next week. Her new job at the downtown coffee shop she had just started the day before. David and his friend William Travis had somehow obtained what they called a Social Security number for her. The men were also in possession of what the two referred to as a birth certificate, and other papers she did not understand, even some type of diploma had been printed with her name upon it. She had no idea why or what all the papers meant. David and Abby seemed secretive about how the papers had been obtained.

That fact made no difference to Sana or to any of the people she had met in the modern world. Those interested in the papers seemed to scarcely glance at them when she was asked to present such.

Sana set out, determined once again. She must find Tosahwi. She would await the darkness and make the trek to the large cavern. She had delayed for several days now since finding the shell, hoping he would come to her. Sana knew she must never risk giving away the Dream Time location of Tosahwi and the others. Perhaps tonight.

Chapter 32

Later that Evening

Tabbananica (Voice of the Sun) awakened much slower than Topusana. The grogginess of coming awake, but not fully, then falling asleep again for a few moments, then partially awakening, only to drift off repeatedly, put him in a state of confusion. What was happening? Where was he? Finally forcing himself awake, surrounded by darkness, his memories began to spring forth. The cavern!

Where was Topusana? Had she awakened? Feeling his way to the edge of his elevated room he located a torch they had prepared from the tar pits, quickly striking flint and stone as the light brightened the cavern. Searching the elevated rooms, he soon discovered he was alone. Sana was gone!

Panic setting in, Tabba knew he must find her. How long had they slept? Had the soldiers left the area? Were the rangers still out there? So many questions. He had feared her awakening first and not being able to survive without his protection. Tabbananica was a Warrior. It was his greatest responsibility to protect his wife and…the memories came flooding in, his daughter.

The greatest loss this Warrior could ever suffer, his daughter, Prairie Song, was gone.

A deluge of thought and memories began washing over his mind all at once. Awareness of the past, the reason for the Dream Time, the attack on the Home Camp, the death of…all of them.

Voice of the Sun felt the loss and brokenness that only death, death of a loved one can bring. He felt the pain all over again, deep in his soul.

126

Closing his eyes, he could see clearly the body of his daughter, Prairie Song. He felt the weight of her light frame in his arms as he carried her away from the Camp.

He had returned to the Camp the night of the attack. He and Tosahwi had located the survivors and escorted all of them into the large cavern, prepared them for their escape into the Dream Time. However, Tabba could not escape or enter the Dream Time until he recovered her body. He remembered well laying her in the prepared grave. The smell of her skin as fresh as a prairie spring. The beauty of her gentle spirit, still present, although not in her little body, rather in the light wind as it brushed across his skin. Tabba knew this had been Prairie Song's goodbye to him…that he had felt in his soul that dark night. He would never be the same man.

Wounded by the scars of war, the loss of his tribe and his Homelands. He had awakened again…a tortured soul.

He would use this brokenness, this heartache, as a tool, as a reason to carry on. The fire of revenge would burn in his heart forever.

The thirst hit him instantly. Working his way down the steps, he stumbled, falling to the cavern floor. He was suddenly aware of how weak his body seemed. He rested a moment, then climbed a few yards up the cavern. The water was running pure and cold. Drinking deeply, with the water reviving him, he began to remember more, the food.

He carefully returned, searching the sleeping rooms and the large main cavern floor. There was a small skin of dried meat. Eating slowly as instructed by Tosahwi, the meat was fresh rabbit, none of the deer they had prepared was there. How long had Sana been awake? Noticing another small skin at the edge of the old fire pit, he opened it.

Vegetables? Fresh corn, squash, beans. He now knew Sana had left these for him perhaps within the last few days.

As he stood to kindle a fire from the wood left to him by his faithful wife, gratefulness overcame him. Then dizziness struck him. Kneeling, steadying himself against the cave wall, breathing deeply, the dizzy feeling drifted away. He would need to eat and drink as instructed. It would take time for his entire body to awaken, but how could he rest now? His only love was out there in this new world. He needed to find her. He needed to know she was safe.

Tabba placed the vegetables and a portion of the meat with some water in the small cooking pot over the fire. He felt deep within his bones the weakness of his arms and legs, the shortness of breath, at the simplest task.

He knew his body needed nutrition as Tosahwi had explained. He would eat slowly for a few hours.

Several hours later, having consumed the stewed vegetables and rabbit meat, Tabba located his war club, knife, and bow. He quickly readied the small pack Sana had left for him with the remaining dried rabbit.

He would hunt and prepare additional meat quickly once outside the cavern. That would be an easy thing for him. Finding Prairie Flower could be another matter. There were too many questions for his mind. Breathing in, feeling the pain, touching the scars in his heart…the scars and pain would become his friends, and he would use them to his advantage.

Voice of the Sun, Tabba, began his ascent out of the cavern.

Nearing the opening, he paused to listen and wait. Extinguishing his torch, he sat in the darkness, the smells of the outside world coming to him. He smelled wood smoke and could feel the cold air as it entered the cavern opening.

It was now winter.

As his vision adjusted to the darkness, he could now see that it was fully dark outside, well past sundown. The stars would tell him how much of the night remained. It had been harvest when they entered the cavern, so some time had gone by. Climbing the last and steepest part of the cavern, he paused again at the entrance, wondering what would await him just a few more feet away in the world to which he had awakened.

Tabba exited the small opening. Standing beside the cavern entrance, he could make out a huge log shelter below him. He could also see a barn and garden. He had viewed many scenes just like this farther to the west, near San Antonio. As the white settlers had begun to occupy the Comanche Homelands, they would build structures much like what were below him. But this structure was right here before him on his old Home Camp on the San Saba.

How much time could have gone by?

Tabba clearly recognized the familiar bend in the river, the rise of land where the Camp had been, and a mysterious long dark trail running as far as he could see out toward the west. What had made this new trail? Many changes had taken place and much time had passed since they had entered the cavern.

He began to search the hillside above the cavern. Not finding the grinding bowl in the dim starlight, he decided to look for the other sign. Locating the large boulder below the entrance, Tabba reached into the cleft and removed the broken deer horn. Lowering it gently into the entrance to the cavern, he heard it slide part way down the slope. Now if she were able to return here, Sana would know he had awakened.

He turned, gazing down the small canyon, feeling again the pain as he viewed his former Homeland. Tabba pressed on into the darkness. The love of his wife was driving him, along with his other friends, Scars and Pain.

Chapter 33

Sana cleaned the last of the tables and swept the floor as the last few customers lingered over their coffee. Outside, the cold air had frosted over the windows of the coffee shop. The deep blue cold of the Texas winter was settling firmly into place. Sleet and ice were forecast to begin before morning. She was anxious to return home. Abby would be waiting up.

Starting her car, she allowed a few minutes for it to warm up as instructed by David. Sana circled the square once, in awe again at the beautiful Christmas lights and decorations. They brought such a warm, happy feeling to her heart each time she drove past them. She stared in wonder at the big fir tree with the brightly lit star atop its crown in the center of the square. The multi-colored lights glowed brightly, adorning the boughs of the tree. Christmas songs played on her radio. She began to hum along softly...*it's the most wonderful time...of the year.*

Driving away from the square and turning out toward the west on the highway, the sleet began to fall. Her cell phone rang. Quickly pushing the button on the steering wheel, Sana answered.

"Hi, Abby, yes I'm on my way. I should be home in fifteen minutes or so. Yes, it is sleeting here, too. I will be careful. I'll see you in a few minutes."

Sana, observing the weather in her headlights, thought it would be impossible to make the one-mile trek to the large cavern tonight. Although she was extremely anxious to discover who else might have survived and awakened, it was simply too dangerous. She knew she would have to wait for better weather.

****

After thirty minutes had gone by, Abby dialed Sana's number again. There was still no answer. David gathered his winter jacket and gloves and headed out into the growing storm.

Starting his truck and allowing just a moment for a quick warm up, he slowly began the treacherous drive toward town.

****

The deer seemed to come from nowhere. Sana instinctively hit the brakes. The animal collided with her car with a loud bang. The car skidded momentarily, but she quickly regained control. The deer had struck the right front of her car, and even at the relatively slow speed she was traveling, the impact killed the small buck instantly.

She stopped her car on the side of the road and allowed the adrenaline to slowly dissipate from her body and her breathing to return normal. She knew what she must do. Exiting the car, she opened the trunk and removed her long knife from its sheath.

The buck was lying on the side of the road with the sleet already collecting on its hide. Sana knelt beside the animal. Closing her eyes, she offered the prayer of thanks for the animal's life. Then positioning its head slightly in a downward angle aligned with the slope of the road, she opened the deer's neck. The warm blood began to drain from the animal's body, causing a little cloud of steam to rise in the cold air. She went to work opening the deer's belly and removing the gut sack, then she began the skinning process.

Across from the main highway, parked on one of the many side roads, Warden Reuter watched through his binoculars. It was hard to make out her appearance in the darkness. However, it was a woman, and she was alone. The key elements were in place. He wondered what her fear might taste like this cold dark night. Was the woman cleaning the illegal roadkill?

This was a perfect setup for having his way, exerting his power over another little innocent victim. He was just about to activate his emergency lights, when he saw the truck lights approaching from the west. Reuter stood down, sinking low in his seat. Perhaps another day, he would be watching this one.

Within twenty minutes Sana had the deer gutted, skinned, and quartered.

She was about to remove the back straps when she suddenly had a familiar distinct impression in her spirit.

Someone was watching her.

Leaving the small amount of meat remaining on the carcass, she quickly began loading the meat quarters into the trunk of her car. Sana noticed the bright lights of a truck approaching from the west. She was relieved to see David at the wheel as the vehicle came to a stop on the frozen surface of the highway.

At first glance David thought Sana was hurt. Coming to a stop in the road, he leapt from the truck and ran to her.

"Are you alright, Sana?"

Sana stood beside her damaged car, her clothing covered in blood, thinking nothing of her arms and hands being coated in the drying blood of the deer. There were even some blood smears on her face and forehead where she had wiped her brow.

She simply said, "Yes, David, I'm fine. The deer came from nowhere."

"I understand. I've hit many of them over the years." he said

There was but a momentary pause as the two observed the scene, both glancing at the deer carcass on the shoulder of the road.

"David, you know that I cannot harvest an animal in any fashion and simply leave its flesh to rot."

"Yes, Sana, I understand that completely."

"There is something else, David."

David looked questioningly at Sana. "What else is going on?"

"We are being watched. We should leave. Now."

Glancing around the darkened roadsides and terrain, David saw nothing. However, he knew Sana's awareness would be true and correct.

"I understand. Let's go."

"Looks like I'll be preparing dinner tonight. I hope you are hungry. I'll see you at home," Sana said, as she turned abruptly, opened her car door, lowered herself into the driver's seat, and drove away.

David walked to his truck and stood a moment, scanning the highway, and what he could see of the hillsides around him. He still could see nothing.

He was in wonder of Topusana, this little "Prairie Flower" that had wandered into his and Abby's life.

The sleet glistened in the lights of his truck, falling heavier now while coating the carcass of the deer on the side of the road. But the pool of blood was still warm enough to melt the frozen crystals on contact. The sleet was now adhering even to the surface of the road and the grass along the bar-ditch. The entire scene now glowing crystal white in the reflection of the high beams.

"Looks like a white Christmas," he said aloud to himself. It was a beautiful moment, although he wondered who could possibly be watching?

David thought about Sana. She would forever be caught between the two worlds in which she lived. She was becoming part modern woman, but she was also a Native American Comanche woman. A wife, a mother, a provider, even a protector of Earth and its bounty. He admired everything about the young woman.

He opened the door of his truck and climbed in. Turning around on the highway, allowing his high beams to scan the surrounding area, the truck lights caught the reflection of the reflector lights of a vehicle parked along a side road.

Who could be out here? He wondered. He inched forward a few hundred yards down the road. The sign of the Texas Department of Game and Fish reflected along the side of the vehicle. The truck appeared unoccupied.

David swore under his breath. He absolutely loathed the Game Department wardens, as did many landowners in Texas. The state of Texas over the years had given an excessive level of power to these men. David had seen the abuse of that power repeatedly. Trespassing, harassment of hunters and fisherman alike was the status quo for these overbearing, out of control wardens. David had attempted unsuccessfully to remove these men from his land on several occasions. Their tactics, confiscation of guns, automobiles, even boats, trailers, and RVs occurred daily across Texas. A simple suspicion of the most minor game violation allowed them to trespass on any land and detain any person. David Ross had experienced the abuse of power many times and even lobbied the Texas Legislature repeatedly to curtail the power the Game Department wielded. However, the good-old-boy network was alive and well in the halls of the state legislature. It seemed these men were untouchable and above any other law enforcement agencies in the state of Texas. David and his friend attorney William Travis had actually discovered many of these wardens had ties to some type of secret modern-day militia.

The simple fact of a game department unit being parked along the road adjoining his land was cause for great concern. David reached for the 9mm he kept close at all times. He drew the weapon from its holster and chambered a round. Warily, he continued his drive. He also sensed someone or something, some presence. And that presence felt dark and evil.

David completed the turn around and headed his truck back toward the west. Seeing no one, he unchambered the round from the Glock.

David truly felt he and Abby had been blessed with a new daughter. Protecting Topusana would be David's priority for the remainder of his days. He would make certain she was safe and well cared for. He thought for a moment how the Comanche might deal with a game warden attempting to harass a hunting party. Considering that thought, David's resolve to correct the history of this small piece of land he owned was growing. His plan was beginning to take shape in his heart and mind. Yes, he thought it was a strange series of events that had led them all to this place and time.

But God did work in mysterious ways.

As the truck departed to the west, Warden Reuter rose from his seat, started his engine, and drove east. What the hell was going on with Ross, he wondered. The man was an enemy of the Department. The next time there was a game violation, he would make certain the dashcam was running and some militia personnel were on duty.

Chapter 34

Tabba worked his way down the canyon, feeling the cold of the winter enter his lungs, invigorating his senses. He was indeed alive. Giving the log shelter and barn a wide berth, he moved up and over the ridge to the west out of sight of the possible Texans who may be living here now. Crossing what he recognized as a fence, he approached the surface of the black trail, it seemed nearly perfectly level. How could this have been built? How much effort it would take to level such a huge wide trail running as far as he could see to the west and the east? Many questions were running through his mind.

In the darkness while moving across the black trail, Tabba negotiated another fence that was also built on the south side of the black trail above the river. Working his way toward the river and his former Camp, he found the place that was the approximate center of his old Home Camp.

Tabba stood in the darkness, observing, his heart filled with a strange heavy weight. There was nothing left, no council lodges, no fire pits, no poles for the teepees. The small corrals where they had kept the ponies were also gone. Everything he remembered about his home had vanished. There was simply no evidence that the Camp ever existed. He did not understand. Surely something would have been identifiable, something left, some indication of their former life here...there was no trace.

How could this be? His people had occupied these lands for centuries. Their Home Camp here along the San Saba had been a safe haven for his entire life. How could any evidence of his *People's* existence be completely erased? The whites had invaded this last remaining stronghold, taken this land by force. The whites had killed his daughter and many of his friends and family. It appeared the rangers, the Cavalry, the United States Government had achieved what they had set out to accomplish, the removal and complete extermination of *The People*.

Much time had to have passed upon the earth since he entered the Dream Time.

Perhaps, thought Tabba, he could bring a reminder to the whites that this was the land of the Comanche!

The storm continued to press down on and around him. Now the starlight faded away as the cloud cover moved in rapidly from the north. Tabba pressed on in the darkness. He needed food. Knowing the deer would be bedded down, he thought it unlikely he would encounter any on his nighttime foray. Moving down stream with the river, there was a possibility of "jumping" a deer herd, alarming them into moving. After an hour of walking, he had no such success.

It was becoming much colder now, the sleet beginning to accumulate on all surfaces. He decided he would move back toward the shelter of his cavern. Hunger was a thing the Comanche could endure. Perhaps tomorrow the deer would move; the sleet and snow would show their trails. Hunting would be much easier in the morning light.

Tabba crossed the black trail again, now on the north side of the long ribbon that was being transformed into a gleaming white surface. Carefully he moved along in the darkness.

He smelled the blood first. How could this be? He moved toward the scent nearer the edge of the wide trail. There in the darkness, he spotted the fresh deer kill. The carcass was still slightly warm. The skin, expertly removed, was still gleaming in the dim light. Examining the carcass, he saw that all quarters had been removed, but the tender loins and backstrap were still in place along the inside and back of the animal. Tabba knelt in the storm, whispering a thank you to the Great Spirit over this incredible find.

Working expertly, Tabba removed the inner tenderloins, then the backstraps along the spine of the deer. Placing them across his shoulders, he also gathered the deer skin, and carrying it in one hand, he began the long walk back to the cavern. Gratefulness overcame him in the discovery of this unexpected blessing.

Arriving back at the cavern entrance, Tabba once again observed the log shelter from above. Bright lights were glowing from within, illuminating the sleet as it fell around the structure. Smoke curled from the huge fire vent on the roof top. The scene before him had a sense of serenity and comfort. He could imagine the Texans inside enjoying the warmth of the fire, perhaps sharing a meal together. He would soon find out more about the Texans living in such great comfort on his Homelands.

Tabba could disrupt their peace-filled little setting soon enough. This was *his* land, *his* home.

Once inside the comfort of the cavern's large room, Tabba struck a warm fire of his own. Thinking through the events of the evening, he determined the Texans would have to wait to feel his arrows. For now, finding Sana would be his priority.

The meat sizzled as it roasted over the open fire, the aroma permeating the entire room. His stomach grumbled; his mouth watered. He knifed the first piece. It was only partially cooked; however, the warm moist pure venison was delicious. He smiled with approval. It seemed as if the nutritious pure meat instantly strengthened his mind and body. Tabba thought the gift of the deer carcass and the warm meal also strengthened his inner Warrior, perhaps even more than his physical body. Normally ten pounds of meat would have been enough food for two or three days. However, on this cold winter night, he was simply famished. He consumed the entire delicious, miraculous find.

Tabba lay in the dim light of the fire sharpening his arrow heads. The warmth of the huge buffalo robe and a belly full of venison lulled him into a sound sleep.

Tabbananica would dream of his beautiful wife, Topusana.

Perhaps tomorrow…he thought as he drifted off. He would sleep soundly and motionless for hours.

Chapter 35

Tabba awakened feeling strong. The pure natural venison meal from the previous evening had instantly given him back much of his strength. His body was beginning to recover. Drinking deeply from the cavern water, it, too, invigorated his mind and body. He readied his weapons for the day.

He could tell from the smoke hole it was still a wintry sky as an occasional piece of frozen rain would make its through the smoke opening all the way to the cavern floor before quickly melting on impact. Taking stock of his meager supplies, he needed food, more firewood, and more than anything he needed to find Topusana.

Exiting the cavern, the world outside was a frozen wonderland. The quietness was unbroken, no sounds came forth from the log shelter, nothing stirred whatsoever. Gazing across the once dark trail, which was now completely covered in white ice, he again looked upon his Home Camp with longing. How long had it been? So many years spent in constant struggle with the white soldiers. He tried to remember a time before the invasion of his Homeland when *The People* were simply existing, living without war. It must have been when he was a young boy…the last time he had experienced living in peace at least twenty-five seasons, he thought. An entire lifetime in constant conflict and struggle.

He wondered was there a chance that the struggle, the conflict, the war, could end? He and Sana had discussed at length prior to entering the Dream Time the possibility that in the new and different time in which they would awaken whether peace would be a possibility.

Tosahwi's medicine was indeed powerful. The Dream Time was successful. They had escaped. Tabba set out, attempting to not think quite so much of the past, but to set his mind and hopes on the future.

The deer herd moved slowly this cold frozen day. They had been easy to track on the snow and ice-covered ground as they worked their way along the riverbank, watering.

His bow shot was perfect. The arrow sliced through the flesh in the center of the kill zone. The arrow pierced the skin and first lung, hardly slowing as it traveled completely through the deer's body, piercing the second lung and exiting the skin between ribs on the opposite side of the entrance wound. The kill was a clean pass through. The animal ran only a few feet before tumbling head over heels, death coming quickly, humanely.

Tabba, in no hurry, walked silently toward the fallen animal, praying as he walked, grateful for the bounty Earth had provided. Using his long knife, he quickly severed the arteries in the neck of the buck, the animal rapidly bleeding out. Tabba decided he would gut and skin the deer, then carry the entire carcass into the back of the cavern. There he could take his time processing all usable parts, feasting for several days and gaining much needed strength. In the tradition of his people, after removing the gut sack, he located the liver in the upper rear of the carcass. The organ was complete and intact. Tabba sliced through the connecting tissue and removed it. Holding the warm organ in his hands, he gave thanks again and took in a huge mouthful. The warmth of the meat and blood coated his mouth, tongue, and throat. It was delicious.

Consuming most of the liver ravenously, Tabba felt the spirit of the deer. The strength the animal possessed with its agility, its wisdom, its very life… revived him.

****

As Tabba carried the body of the deer over his shoulders, he crossed the first fence on the south side of the dark trail, just below a rise in its surface. Suddenly, while crossing in the middle of the dark trail, he heard a strange sound moving toward him. Pausing in the center of the ice-covered trail, he listened trying to make out the sound. It was clear that sound was moving toward him quickly. Pausing, he could see the outline of a bright light silhouetting the ice-covered surface, just over the rise in the trail. He began to run the remaining distance across the wide trail. As he entered the grass on the edge of the smooth surface, a huge stagecoach with no horses, as he would describe it, came into clear view. Continuing to run, Tabba threw the deer to the ground, leapt across the fence on the north side of the trail and turned to observe the large stagecoach coming to a complete stop.

Bright red and blue lights from atop the stagecoach began flashing, a loud whining noise coming also from the front of the stagecoach. Tabba then saw the sign of the Texas Rangers on the side of the great stagecoach, a bright gold star.

The Texas Ranger exited the stagecoach with his weapon drawn, calling out words Tabba did not understand. Tabba dropped to the ground instantly, rolling into the deep grass, expertly concealing his location. While continuing to crawl through the underbrush, he moved away from the Ranger with the weapon. Tabba could hear the Ranger shouting loudly. Tabba paused and peered through the cover. The man was speaking into a black box on his shoulder. Almost instantly came a similar high-pitched whining sound from far down the surface of the dark trail. Tabba sensed there must be other Rangers coming. Instinctively, he readied an arrow.

Tabba stood, showing himself to the Ranger. Leaping the fence, he climbed the shallow grade and stepped onto the ice-covered surface of the wide trail.

The dashcam recording the scene would show Warden Reuter fired without warning, the shot missing its mark badly. Tabba, under attack, having been fired upon, did not hesitate. He knocked an arrow and loosed it.

The arrow found its mark, penetrating deeply into the chest of Warden Reuter. The man dropped to the ground in a shower of blood. Tabba calmly and defiantly walked toward the man.

Tabbananica, Voice of the Sun, began screaming at the Ranger. His voice was booming and powerful. Warden Reuter had never heard such fierceness in a voice coming from any man. The voice was that of power and strength, like that of thunder even.

What had happened? the warden thought, looking down at the blood flowing freely from his body, the arrow protruding from his chest. He attempted to raise his weapon again as the *Indian?* approached him.

Reuter knew he would bleed to death before help arrived. *But an Indian, wearing full dress, with a bow for his weapon?*

Tabba, his voice resplendent, daring, began to mock and interrogate the wounded Ranger.

"Will you never cease? Are you the one who killed my daughter? This is Comanche land! This is our land! Do you feel my arrow in your belly? I am

Tabbananica. Voice of the Sun!" His thunderous voice boomed across the scene.

Tabbananica approached the Ranger, his war club raised.

The wounded game warden fired his weapon several times, missing repeatedly.

In a controlled rage, seething vengeance, and deep anger, Tabbananica let out his War Cry.

The warden's bladder released. He cowered in fear at the sound, a sound unlike anything he had ever heard before. Chilling, primeval, guttural, and powerful.

It would be the last sound he would ever hear. The war club met its target. The blow was fierce. The skull of the warden caving at the force of the weapon, blood and brain matter spattering on the layer of ice beneath him. Warden Reuter died instantly.

A few moments later, Tabba observed a second stagecoach approaching the scene cautiously. Bright blood-red light again flashing atop the stagecoach. Warden Bryant stopped his vehicle and observed from 100 yards away. Bryant could make out the body of Reuter lying on the highway. Cursing under his breath, he and his colleges knew this day would come…for Reuter.

Warden Bryant radioed dispatch.

"Ten twenty-four…ten twenty-four…officer down. Unit Three-Twenty request immediate assistance."

While exiting the truck with his own weapon drawn. Warden Bryant cautiously approached the man with the bow and club. Bryant identified himself and directed the suspect to lower his…*bow?*

Tabba turned to face the Ranger, his bow drawn. Walking directly toward the Ranger and closing ground steadily, Tabba loosed another arrow. It struck the man in the shoulder, the arrow burying deep into bone. He quickly knocked another arrow and loosed it. This arrow also struck the Ranger, this time in the leg, with a loud crack, the sound of bone breaking and shattering.

Warden Bryant fell to the ground, rolled into a firing stance, and returned fire, striking *The Indian* in the left side. Warden Bryant then slowly crumpled flat to the ground and lost consciousness.

Tabba continued to walk toward the Ranger and readied his war club. The world suddenly began spinning out of control. He stumbled and fell, then slowly regained his footing. Looking down, the blood was flowing profusely from the bullet wound in his side. The bright red blood was a stark contrast as it fell in great drops onto the white ice-covered trail.

His vision blurred as he fell again onto the frozen surface. As he attempted to crawl toward the Ranger, the white sky suddenly began to turn grey, then darkened to black, then there was nothing.

The scene became eerily quiet. One man was dead, the other two clinging to life. The sleet had turned to a light snow now drifting gently down, covering some of the blood drops along the sleet covered highway. Many of the crystal-like snowflakes landed on Tabba, clinging to his eyebrows, eyelashes, and thick black hair of his braids.

The dash cameras on both the wardens' vehicles continued to run. The camera from Warden Bryant's vehicle recorded the motion first, as it pointed directly down the highway to the west.

In the first few frames, the object appeared to be a large black animal. Crossing the fence on the north side of the road, it stood upright, walking like a man. As the image came into better focus, it appeared to be a dark figure robed in a hide or skin of some kind. As the figure continued to move closer into view, it became clear the head of the creature had horns and large ears. Now within clear focus and view of the camera, the figure clearly was that of a man.

A heavy buffalo robe was draped across his body from the shoulders down. The man was wearing a deer headpiece—the full head of the deer—its eyes, horns, and ears sitting atop the man's head. The deer cape flowed across his shoulders and back, the hide reaching midway across his torso. The headpiece was partially covered in snow. As the man approached Warden Reuter's vehicle, which pointed to the east down the highway, it also recorded the movement of the man. When the man was within ten feet of Reuter's vehicle the sound of muffled words or singing could be heard on the recording.

The man then paused a moment over the body of Warden Reuter, and in a slow gliding motion waved his hands across and above the corpse. Rising, the man continued down the highway toward Warden Bryant's vehicle, both dashcams recording his movements. As he moved between the two vehicles, the man's singing became clearly audible now. The songs were not sung in English but were some kind of Native chant.

Now standing over Tabbananica, who was lying on the highway surface between the two vehicles, the man knelt over the body. He appeared to reach into a small pouch strung across his chest and applied some substance to the wound on Tabba's left side. Then rolling him over to his side, the man again reached into his pouch, sprinkled the powdery substance in and over the exit wound in Tabba's back. What the cameras could not detect was the instant coagulation of the bleeding wound.

Rising again, the songs could be heard clearly, as the man lifted his hands toward the sky. He then continued down the road toward Warden Bryant's vehicle.

Upon reaching Bryant, again the man knelt, tearing open the man's shirt, and applying what appeared to be some type of dust to the shoulder wound of Warden Bryant. The arrow was buried deep into bone; the man knew it could not be removed. Examining the wound in Bryant's leg, the man reached down and snapped the arrow in half that was protruding from the front of his leg, discarding the back half of the arrow. The man then pushed the arrow the rest of the way through the wound, breaking the skin behind the Warden's kneecap, and extracting the front half of the arrow from the rear of Warden Bryant's leg. Reaching again into his pouch, the man applied the material to the front and rear of the leg wound.

Rising and raising his hands, the man appeared to do a kind of dance. His voice becoming clearer, his song was mesmerizing, even on the poor audio of the dashcams. The song was clearly some kind of worship.

The sound of emergency vehicles could now be heard on the dashcam recording. The man turned and slowly moved toward the north side of the road, leaping, in a single stride, the five-foot fence that aligned the highway. The video began to blur. It seemed the man knelt to his hands and knees, lifting the carcass of the deer Tabba had killed. He placed the carcass over his shoulders. Once again from a distance, the dark figure now resembled a large animal. He then walked away through the brush and out of sight.

Tosahwi knew he could not move Tabba without causing further injury. He would go for help, perhaps there was time.

****

Tabbananica awakened, bound with iron shackles, tied to some type of sleeping mat. Rangers were present, watching his every move. Bright light shone into his vision; the pain was intense. His head ached as his body contorted from the pain in his side. A man in white poked something into his arm, his vision blurred...

But she was there! He saw her...Topusana was reaching for him. Then once again the darkness overcame him and she was gone.

Chapter 36

Earlier the Same Morning

Sana had risen early, enjoying a long hot soothing bath. The water mesmerized her. Still in awe that at the turn of a handle, hot watered poured forth, easily filling the over-sized tub. She added a drop or two of the fragrant bath oil as Abby had instructed, then spent half an hour soaking, meditating, thinking of her future. Enjoying her quiet time until the sky began to lighten in the east.

She dressed in a warm winter outfit: jeans, a cashmere sweater, thermal socks, a down jacket, and today her moccasins were a good choice. She needed to be at work for the late morning shift. It would be her last workday prior to the big Christmas celebration Abby had been planning. Abby's daughter, Grace, would arrive later in the day. Preparing coffee for the three of them, Sana seated herself in the cozy breakfast nook, the fragrant warm coffee steaming in her cup. Glancing outside, the sleet was still lightly falling. It was a beautiful scene. From where she was seated, she could see across the highway into the center of her old Camp. Sana thought what a contrast to her former life on the San Saba.

She thought of Tabba. It had been several days since she had ventured up the canyon to check for the sign. It was always such a disappointment to find the horn undisturbed.

With all the activities Abby was planning, Sana thought it may be several days before she had an opportunity to the trek up the canyon and check the cleft in the rock again.

With no sound from Abby and David's bedroom, she decided this morning might be her only opportunity to do so for several days. Donning a wool hat and winter gloves, she exited the kitchen door and silently walked up the little canyon to the cavern entrance.

The walk was invigorating. The falling sleet was accumulating and made a light crunching sound underfoot. The depth of the ice crystals caused the sleet to compress with each step, giving her just enough foothold to move easily without slipping. The wind had died down overnight. The stillness and frozen beauty of the morning, she thought, *surreal*, a vocabulary word from her study yesterday with Abby.

Reaching the entrance to the cavern, Sana paused a moment and whispered a prayer for Tabba. She reached into the cleft in the large boulder. She could not feel the horn.

With a momentary panic setting in, she lowered herself onto a knee, reached into the cleft as far as she could possibly stretch her arm, and touched the back of the opening.

The deer horn was not there! Tabba had awakened!

Her heart racing, Sana moved the few steps toward the entrance and started to enter the cavern, but quickly noticed the tracks leading away from the entrance. One set of moccasin tracks shown moving one direction up and away from the house, over the ridge to the west.

Tabba had exited the cavern this morning. Even with the sleet continuing to fall, it had not obscured the moccasin prints he had left behind. He had walked here probably less than an hour ago. There were no tracks returning. Sana knew he had awakened, he had ventured out of the cavern, and he had not returned.

Turning, Sana raced down the hill toward the house.

What to say to David and Abby? The truth? Why had she felt the need to keep his presence from them?

The sound of a gunshot could be distinctly heard from the highway out toward the west and below her, followed by a siren far down the highway toward the east. Sana began to pray as she hurried down the canyon toward the house.

Chapter 37

David was reheating his coffee in the microwave as Sana entered through the kitchen door.

"I thought I heard a gunshot a few minutes ago. Hunters, I suppose," David said without looking up. "The last rifle hunt started yesterday, although that seemed pretty close to the house."

Sana did not reply. David turned toward her, greeting her with a cheerful, "Good morning."

They both heard four more gunshots in the distance out toward the west, all within a few seconds. The volley of gunfire echoed through the countryside.

Then David saw the frightened, panicked look on her face.

At that moment Abby entered the kitchen with a cheerful, "Good morning."

The greeting was met with the eerie quiet of the moment. Seeing the concern on Sana's face, Abby moved to her, gently taking her hand.

"What's wrong, Sana?" Abby asked.

"I need to talk with you both. Please sit," answered Sana.

The three seated themselves around the quaint, beautiful little breakfast nook Sana so loved.

"Abby, David, as you know, I have a husband. His name is Tabbananica, which means Voice of the Sun. I don't know what to say, umm, or how to say it."

"Go on, Sana," Abby spoke gently.

Sana continued quietly, "He entered the Dream Time with me, after the attack on our Camp."

"Yes, go on," Abby said, coaxing Sana along.

146

"He never awakened," Sana spoke quietly. Abby and David, wide eyed, an expression of disbelief on their faces, looked into one another's eyes.

"Where is he now, Sana?" David asked.

"Well, he was in the cavern."

"Your cavern?" David asked.

"Yes, I don't know why I didn't tell you. I think because I am still so afraid."

Abby moved toward her, wrapping her arms around Sana and embracing her, feeling the fear, comforting her like a mother.

"I'm very sorry I did not share this. It is all…was all so confusing. I was trying to protect him. Something was wrong; he was becoming so weak. Abby, I did not think he was going to survive."

Tears began to gently roll down Sana's cheeks. She was becoming more upset by the moment as she began to let out the inner secrets, the truth.

"Abby, David, most of my tribe and family were slaughtered…right here outside this window." Sana gazed outside the serene little breakfast nook in the direction of the river. "From my perspective, that loss, of all I know and loved, happened only a few months ago. Please understand I was attempting to protect him."

Abby and David sat in silence a moment, stunned at the perspective they had gained from Sana's heartfelt reasoning. David gazed out the window, imagining the battle, the loss, a new resolve taking shape within him.

"So, what has happened, Sana?" David asked, a look of concern on his face. "Is your husband all right now? Is he alive?"

"I left a sign for him. It was hidden in a better place than the metate."

Realization dawned on David's face.

"The metate was a sign? Left for your…his…your Tabbamaca?" David asked, stunned.

"Yes, David. His name is Tabbananica, or Tabba. I have been checking for the new sign, although not as frequently in the last few weeks. This morning I walked the canyon to the cavern entrance to check the sign I left."

"And?" David asked gently.

"The sign is gone."

"What does this mean?" David asked.

"It means Tabba has awakened."

Abby and David looked at one another simultaneously.

"I found his tracks in the ice; he exited the cavern this morning possibly only an hour or so ago. Then on my way back down the canyon I heard a gunshot. It came from the direction of the black ribbon. I'm sorry, I mean the highway." Sana brushed away her tears.

The sound of sirens could now be heard even inside the ranch house, faint at first, but growing louder as the emergency vehicles, and sheriff deputy units sped toward the "officer down" call.

"You think something has happened to Tabba?" Abby asked.

"Yes," Sana replied. "Please understand, my husband is a Warrior."

David, his brow raised, peered toward Abby. Recognizing the look of concern on David's face, Abby asked, "What does that mean, Sana?"

"It means," David said, "if Tabba has any form of confrontation it will not end well for whoever confronts him."

Sana looked directly into David's eyes and with understanding said, "Yes, David, that is exactly what it means, and I fear the confrontation may have already occurred."

As the three considered all that had just been revealed, the sound of the house telephone ringing broke the silence of the moment. David answered and after listening a few moments said, "I see." How should he respond? "Yes, Sheriff, we will stay put here for now."

David had grown up with Fred Mason, the sheriff of Grove County. Although the two were cordial to one another publicly, David despised the man. He had been a bully since grade school and continued to be one in his dealings with criminals and the public alike. Guilty until proven innocent was the rule of law in much of Texas. Fred Mason held no exception to that rule. Over the years David was amazed that the man continued to be re-elected. However, Fred Mason's tough-on-crime stance resonated with most folks, although most did not know what David knew. Intimidation, jailing of suspects under suspicious circumstances. Circumstances that if they occurred in other counties, said suspects would not even receive a traffic citation. Beatings had been reported by many illegals that were detained. All of these actions were ignored by Border Patrol agents, judges, other officials, and in particular voters, who evidently were more in favor of low crime rates than injustice.

David turned away from the two women and lowered his voice. "Yes, we all heard shots this morning, Fred. I'm sure we can answer any questions you may have. ...You're welcome, Fred."

David slowly placed the phone back onto its cradle. He wondered how much to say, what to reveal, now understanding completely Sana's concern.

The two huddled together, awaiting the news David might have.

"Well?" Abby asked.

"That was Fred...um, he asked us to stay put. There has been a shooting out on the highway. Well, a shooting might not be the correct word." What should he say and how to say it?

"David!" Abby spoke in her sternest possible voice. "Tell us what's happening!"

"They are processing the scene, but it appears a game warden was killed, and another seriously injured."

"Oh my, right here on our highway?" Abby exclaimed.

"Yes, and uh, the suspect is in custody, although he was also wounded, but by gunfire," David added.

"David Ross, what the hell are you saying?" Abby demanded.

"The wardens, both the one that was killed and the officer that shot the suspect, were not shot with a gun. They were shot with arrows."

"Where is Tabba?" Sana asked rising, knowing full well that Tabba was whom David was referring to as "the suspect."

"Sana, Tabba is in custody, although he is being transported to the hospital as we speak."

"I must go to him. What is this word, *suspect*?" she asked.

David hesitating, replied. "It means they think Tabba is the man who shot the arrows."

"I understand," said Sana.

"David, she must go," Abby said. "Tabba can't communicate with anyone. Sana needs to be there."

Thinking through the process Tabba would be faced with, David said. "I agree, let's go."

Picking up his cell phone, he dialed his attorney's number.

"What's up friend?" William Travis answered. "Calling to wish me a Merry Christmas, I hope?"

"We need you now, Will, how soon can you get here?" David asked.

"Well, the roads are terrible, so is the forecast. More snow and ice all day. It can't wait?" Will asked.

"I'll send the jet; it's fully weather capable. Steve will meet you at Austin Executive within the hour. When you land, take my airport truck," David barked out instructions.

"OK, meet you at the ranch house?" Will asked.

"No, go directly to the hospital. We will meet you there. I'll explain later."

"David, What's going on, are you guys alright?"

"Yes, we're all fine. Call me from the plane, and I'll explain more. I'm sorry I can't explain more now, Will, but we need to go. Oh, and identify yourself at the hospital as the counsel for the suspect, then they'll let you in," instructed David.

The line went dead as David hung up, the women already awaiting him in the truck.

Steve had just landed the Citation CJ3, delivering Grace from Santa Monica. Abby, ending her own phone call, said, "Steve will be taking off for Austin within ten minutes. He says it's only a twenty-minute flight. They should be back here within the hour. Grace is taking Steve's car. I've asked her to meet us at the hospital."

"OK. Will is en route to Austin Executive."

"You know you should be grateful for that man being in your life?" Abby said.

David, looking confused, said, "Which one?"

"Well, I was talking about Steve, but actually both of them, Steve and William."

David thought to himself that was true enough.

Chapter 38

December 23, 11:00 A.M.

David, along with Sana and Abby, arrived at the normally quiet small-town hospital to the confusion of a dozen or more emergency, police, and sheriff vehicles. Making their way through the turbulent scene, the three gathered at the Admissions desk where the nurse was busily giving orders concerning the arriving airlift helicopter. David started to speak; the woman silenced him with a stern look, then raised an index finger to her lips indicating for him to be quiet for now.

As the three stood listening, they could hear the helicopter landing on the roof. Moments later, a gurney with several doctors and nurses surrounding it, concealing the possible identity of the patient, was rapidly rolled by them and loaded into the elevator. David looked questioningly toward the admitting nurse. She responded by motioning him toward her.

"Hi, sorry, Mr. Ross, that was Warden Bryant. He's being transported to Houston. It looks like they'll have to amputate his leg. It was more than we could handle here in our facility."

"Thank you for the information, um, Miss?"

"It's Christi Hall. I'm sorry. Mrs. Ross was my first-grade teacher. I feel like we have known each other a long time."

Abby, hearing the exchange, moved forward and embraced her former student with a warm greeting. Abby was always surprised to see her former students in all walks of life all grown up with families of their own. They exchanged pleasantries and a few fond memories. Abby quickly changed the subject to the present circumstances.

"So, Christie, what about the other injured men?" Abby asked.

Rising from her seat, Christie pulled Abby aside, confiding in her, whispering like she possessed the latest gossip the entire town was desperately trying to find out.

"Well, Mrs. Ross, the other warden, as you may know, died at the scene. And can you believe it, he was shot full of arrows by a real live Indian! I just can't quite believe this. The Indian man is here! I'm not normally afraid, Mrs. Ross, but this just plain scares me."

Abby listening intently to the information, then asked under her breath, "So, the Indian man is, you mean here, in our hospital?"

Christie, again whispering, said, "I'm not supposed to say…but yes, he is right down the hall here. Can you believe it? They have him under guard and all, but Lord Jesus, I thought I had seen it all!"

A look of disbelief crossed the young woman's face momentarily. "They say he was shot also, but he's fine." Again, lowering her voice, "He's in stable condition; his surgery to close the wound was only thirty minutes or so. They're not allowing any visitors. I hear he will be charged with the murder shortly, as soon as the sheriff gets here…at least that's what they say." A look of satisfaction crossed the young woman's face as she revealed all the insider information of which only she was in possession.

"Thank you for letting us know what's happening, Christie, you take care now," Abby said softly, playing along. The two hugged again as Abby motioned for David and Sana to join her in the small waiting area.

"He is here?" Sana's eyes widened the look of concern on her face. "Tabba is here in this place?"

"Yes, his condition is stable. From what Christie told me, he is under guard. I mean I think he is under arrest, and the deputies are guarding his room. He had surgery already. Evidently, he was shot, but he's all right, Sana. Tabba will recover."

"This is good news?" Sana asked, not understanding the word *recover*.

"Yes, it's very good news. Sana, I suppose Tabba could have easily been killed," Abby said.

"But there is trouble for him?" Sana asked.

"Yes, Sana," David said. "There is much trouble ahead for Tabba."

"What does this mean for him?" Sana looked quite troubled.

"My friend and attorney, William, will be here in a few minutes. He can explain better than I can, but Tabba will be," David thought about how to reply, "held prisoner. He will go before a court or a judge. They will hear the entire story."

"And then?" Sana interrupted.

"Well, there is no way to say what the court will find. William will defend Tabba throughout the entire process," David said.

"David, will they kill Tabba for what he has done?" Sana asked, getting directly to the point of her questioning.

"I don't know, Sana. It is a possibility in Texas."

The three stood in silence as the reality of what had occurred and what lay ahead for all of them permeated the moment.

Sana turning to Abby and embraced her. The two wrapped their arms tightly around one another, Abby giving her entire being and emotion into the embrace. Sana returned the embrace completely and melted into the arms of her only friend. No, she thought, it was more than friendship.

"I need you, Abby. I trust you," Sana whispered into Abby's ear.

"I know, Little One, it will be alright; I will be right here with you. You will be safe with me," Abby said.

Chapter 39

Grove County Hospital
December 23, 12:30 P.M.

William Travis, attorney at law, entered the front doors of the hospital in Little Grove, Texas, after his short flight from Austin. David had talked with William during the flight, giving Will the basics of the story. He was met by David and Grove County Sheriff Fred Mason. Also present was Grove County District Attorney JD Sneed. The four men made their way to the small chapel located in the rear of the building. It seemed to be the only room available for the immediate conference requested by the counsel for the defendant, William Travis.

"Mr. Travis, as I understand you will soon be designated as counsel for the defendant?" JD Sneed asked.

"Yes, that is correct. However, I suggest we dispense with the formalities, you may call me William, please."

JD, with a friendly Texas wave, said, "I agree, call me JD. I think you have already met Fred," nodding toward the sheriff, "and of course you two know one another well."

Again, the man nodded in the direction of David. "So, may I be upfront here, William? The investigation and crime scene are still being processed. However, at this time your client is under arrest and being held on first degree murder charges, along with a long list of other felonies, which are being prepared as we speak. Now considering your client's medical condition and the fact that we have not been able to communicate the arrest status, nor read him

154

his rights, the defendant will remain in custody until such time as that can be accomplished. Do you have any objections to our planned course of action?"

"Do we have any information as to his medical condition, specifically the prognosis?" William asked.

"The doctors tell us he will recover fully and will in all likelihood be able to communicate with us in the next twenty-four to forty-eight hours," JD replied.

"I will need to speak with the doctor myself to verify that, of course; however, I have no objections to your plan, nor could I stop them if I did, wouldn't you agree, JD?" William said.

Sneed, ignoring the reply from William, continued. "I'm thinking due to the holiday, that we set an arraignment hearing for Friday the 28th. I think I can get the judge to come in. It should be a relatively short process. Then we will get the ball rolling, so to speak, after the first of the year as far as a trial schedule."

"It seems you're in a bit of a rush, Mr. Sneed, don't you think?" replied William.

The district attorney's demeanor changed instantly, his eyes narrowing.

"So, we are back to a little more formality now, Mr. Travis?" His posture seemed stiff and commanding.

"I just think you might want to make certain that all the procedural rules are followed, so as to avoid any grounds for appeal."

The statement from Mr. Travis was, in fact, a veiled threat, William feigning innocence.

"Mr. Travis, we will release our evidence to you soon. As of now that consists of the murder weapon, the, um, arrows that were fired, and even complete video of the entire crime scene as the murder and assault occurred.

"I frankly have never viewed a more complete record of what happened in any case I have ever brought to trial. I see no need to attempt to withhold anything from you. Let's face it, Mr. Travis, this is pretty much a slam dunk on our side. I'm not sure where you are going with this procedural bullshit. So, I'm suggesting for the benefit of the taxpayers of Grove County and the State of Texas, we simply move forward as expeditiously as possible."

"Very well, Mr. Sneed. Just a question or two for you. You say you have not spoken to or questioned my client?" William asked.

"That is correct," JD Sneed replied.

"And just to verify, procedurally, the hearing you are requesting for arraignment is four days from today? Correct?" asked William.

"That is correct, sir," the district attorney said.

"And forgive me, but let me verify, my client will need to understand completely the charges being brought against him at that hearing, correct?" asked William.

"Yes, that is correct." The impatience of Mr. Sneed was beginning to show. "As any first-year law student would know." he said

Taking the insult in stride, William continued. "So, you have made arrangements to have a translator represent your office for the hearing next Friday?"

"What the hell are you talking about?" Sneed fired back.

"I assumed you knew, given the expeditious scheduling, my client speaks absolutely no English. Not one word. So again, procedurally we may not be in quite such a rush, as the prosecution seems to be."

"Alright, Mr. Travis, just where the hell is your client from, and what language does he speak and understand? As a matter of fact, we have not been able to locate any ID on the suspect. So naturally we will need you to fill in some blanks for us. Or the Sheriff's Department needs the information for detaining purposes." As his voice rose, the temper of one JD Sneed clearly was seen by all the men in the room.

"Well, as soon as I can determine that information, I will be glad to let your office know. However, as of this time, I am not quite certain of the dialect myself," William said.

"Dialect? What the hell are you talking about?" JD Sneed yelled across the small chapel. "This meeting is over."

JD Sneed rose from the conference table that had been hastily set up and stormed out. The other three men sat in stunned silence as the door to the chapel slammed shut. JD Sneed could be heard berating a colleague as he walked away in anger. Sheriff Mason broke the silence. "David, is there any information you might share with me that can assist my investigation?"

"Yes, Fred, well, I would need to give that some thought." David paused a moment and glanced at William, seeing and understanding instantly the communication from Will. Do not say one word, was clearly evident on Will's face.

"Fred, it seems like with the video and all, there's not much I can add."

"That's fine. David, I'm not sure where you are on all of this. But please remember an officer was killed today. This is our hometown, our county. We all need to do the right thing here."

"Have you ever known me to not do the right thing, Fred?" David replied.

Thinking of the question and David Ross's character, the answer was an easy one.

"No, I haven't." Placing his grey Stetson cowboy hat on his head, Sheriff Fred Mason rose from the table and nodded toward William and exited the little chapel.

"Well, you handled the DA pretty well, don't you think?" asked David.

"I simply bought us some much-needed time, David. But I also learned of his short temper, which believe me, I can use to our advantage."

Seeing the concern on Will's face and his demeanor, David said, "You don't seem too encouraged by this meeting in spite of winning round one."

"They are in possession of the murder weapon, a video, and, I'm sure, DNA from the scene. And don't think for a second, he wasn't holding back. The charge will not be first degree murder, David. They will charge Tabbananica with capital murder, making this a death penalty case. This situation is probably exactly what he stated. A slam dunk."

William and David sat in the quiet atmosphere of the little chapel lost in thought for a moment, contemplating all that was ahead. Will spoke after a few moments.

"You know, I had a professor in law school, a brilliant man and legal scholar. He taught us all something that I need to consider here."

"You have my attention. Go on."

"He taught us to open our minds, to seek out and find the truth. Especially when it seems the case appears to be a 'slam dunk.' His thinking was that when everything seems too obvious, and the verdict a forgone conclusion, as our new friend the DA believes, that is when we as lawyers might very well be missing the truth. David, there is more than likely something hidden here, some fact, some truth that is not so obvious. We have to find out what really happened out there on the highway."

"By *we*, you are obviously including yours truly?" David said.

"Yes I am."

Chapter 40

Later That Afternoon

Tosahwi carried the deer carcass that had already been skinned and cleaned by Tabba across the small canyon through the ice and snow-covered ground. *The People* were hungry, those who had awakened. He was the only one allowed to leave the safety of the cavern. The others would be compliant. They carefully followed his instructions. All were recovering from the Dream Time.

The food would last another two or three days. Then he would venture out again. Tosahwi had explored the area north of the cavern and was surprised to find the buffalo this far south during the winter months. He knew the locating of the buffalo was without a doubt a gift from the Great Spirit. As soon as his sons Neeko and Tosa recovered, perhaps in only a few more days, they would exit the cavern together for a buffalo hunt. One animal would keep his people fed for over a month. It would be an easy thing for the strong young Warriors.

Tosahwi had tracked Tabba and watched the conflict with the Texas Ranger from the ridge above the wide trail. The Ranger had made a fatal mistake firing upon Tabba. It was a brave thing Tabba had done this day. He knew stopping the bleeding would save his life. Tosahwi also knew these kinds of wounds often resulted in death if the injured were moved to hastily. They had taken Tabba away in the great flashing stagecoach.

There was no doubt Tabbananica, Voice of the Sun, was now a prisoner.

Tosahwi was well aware of the trail Tabba must walk. As he turned and moved away from the black ribbon, he began to pray that Tabbananica would have the strength to endure his walk.

Chapter 41

The Texas Gulf Coast
August 1840

Buffalo Hump raised his War Cry as six hundred Comanche Warriors descended on the Texas port city of Linnville. The raiding party encircled the town on three sides. Raising his lance high, he gave the signal. The fire arrows were launched. The town began to burn.

Buffalo Hump observed the town burning from a small rise of land, a flame burning within his own heart for those who had been massacred at the Council House. He would allow the Warriors to pilfer the town for two full days.

This would be the largest attack ever, both in sheer numbers of Comanche and the amount of loot and treasure carried away by any Indian Nation in the history of the United States. Although, some history books would never acknowledge that fact due to Texas still being a republic and not part of the United States at the time of the "Great Raid." This fact made no difference whatsoever to Buffalo Hump.

Word had come to him in the Llano from the survivors of the Council House massacre. It had taken him several months to raise the Comanche bands to action.

Buffalo Hump led the huge war party on their movement out of far west Texas, giving specific direction to his Warriors. Burn any settlement. Take many scalps. The Comanche Warriors willingly complied.

The war party skirted to the northwest of San Antonio undetected. Buffalo Hump had observed just yesterday the town of Victoria being decimated by his Warriors. They had taken one-thousand head of horses. Dozens of whites were killed. Today, he again observed this town of Linnville aflame. He thought the leaders of the Republic of Texas would rue the day they had murdered the twelve chiefs and the women and children at the Peace Conference.

Buffalo Hump could smell the distinct scent of revenge in the air.

The total number of the raiding party, including the supporting women and children, numbered over one thousand Comanche.

Sitting astride his war pony, Buffalo Hump noticed some of the inhabitants of Linnville escaping by small boats, or anything that would float, paddling toward the large shipping vessels anchored in the harbor. Motioning to a group of his Warriors, the attackers raced their mounts along the shoreline firing flaming arrows into the escaping boats and small vessels. Several of the small craft caught fire. The escapees dove into the water, attempting to swim for the large ships at anchor. Many whites drowned in the sea after entering the water.

Buffalo Hump rode through the streets of Linnville, surrounded by whooping Warriors. The town was virtually abandoned. This left Linnville to the whims of the raiding party. For two days the Warriors scoured the township, any whites found in hiding were killed and scalped. Storehouses were systematically sacked and burned. The Comanches took anything of value. Another two thousand head of horses would be rounded up and led away from the town. The Comanche had no use for the hundreds of cattle in stock pens surrounding the town, so they were slaughtered in the pens and streets of Linnville.

The real treasure, however, was discovered in the local bank vault. Freshly minted silver coins. Thousands of silver coins meant as payment for cattle, warehouses full of goods, and building materials. Buffalo Hump ordered the silver coins to be loaded onto hundreds of stolen donkeys and readied for the return trip to the Llano. Furnishings, clothing, cookware and the like were also pilfered.

Buffalo Hump watched the town burn from his vantage point on the small rise of land. The destruction would be so complete the townsite would be abandoned permanently and never rebuilt.

Buffalo Hump was proud of his people. The Texans would feel the loss for years to come. This was Comanche Land. Perhaps the Texans would now show proper respect to the Numunuu.

The return to far West Texas, however, was proving quite difficult. The Comanche were used to raiding and then quickly evading any followers. The sheer size of the loot, three thousand horses, hundreds of donkeys loaded with silver, bounty of all kinds was hindering the escape of the Comanches. The one-thousand member Comanche raiding party traveled a full day toward the northwest. Stopping for the night, the group camped a mere ten miles inland of the Texas coast. The celebration fires were lit. The People relished in the victory. The songs began around the sacred fires.

As the sun set on the celebration, Buffalo Hump called his leading Warriors to his teepee lodge. The sacred pipe was passed among the men. The Warriors present were overflowing with pride and the satisfaction that only retaliation and restitution can bring within a man. Buffalo Hump sat in silence, absorbing the sense of victory that permeated the atmosphere within the lodge. *"We still have far to go my friends,"* he said. All encircling the lodge fire nodded in agreement. He paused a moment, enjoying the sense of victory deep within his own heart.

"What route shall we take in returning to the Llano?" he inquired of his Shaman Tosahwi.

"Lead the people along the same route by which we came to this place. Although, the Texans will be awaiting. The Great Spirit has revealed this to me. We will be too many for them. More Texans will die on this raid, as may some of our Warriors," Tosahwi said.

Buffalo Hump acknowledged this advice with a slight nod, as did the other Warriors gathered in the war council. Tabbananica listened quietly and relished in his heart that more Texans would feel his arrows.

August 1840
Three days later

The Texas Rangers had discovered the trail left by the huge War Party as it skirted to the north and west of San Antonio on its foray toward the Texas coast. Knowing the War Party might well return on the same route, the rangers prepared an ambush. The three days the Comanches had spent on the coast gave the rangers time to gather volunteers from the Texas Militia. Volunteers from the towns of Bastrop, Gonzales, and Lockhart moved to intercept the raiding party along the banks of Plum Creek.

The Texans had several opportunities to attack prior to that location, but the Texan commanders were simply too outnumbered by the Comanches. Several times they delayed initiating an attack.

Finally, a battle charge was ordered, and a running gun battle was commenced along the banks of Plum Creek near Lockhart, Texas. The bounty proved too cumbersome for the Comanche tactics. The Warriors simply could not outrun the Texans with the heavily loaded pack animals.

The losses on both sides were light. The Texans reported killing at least eighty Comanches. The number was, in fact, much lower, as only twelve bodies were recovered.

More than a dozen Texas Militia lost their lives in the pursuit. The War Party could have suffered much greater casualties, except for one ingenious tactic devised by Buffalo Hump. He ordered several of the bags loaded with silver coins to be cut open.

As the Texans pursued the Comanches, many of the rangers and militia alike stopped to collect the silver coins left along the trail. Some of the leaders of the Texans were furious at the actions of the militia, as they began to line their pockets with the stolen loot. Many abandoned the fight to return to their homes…quite wealthy.

This action by Buffalo Hump effectively ended the battle and any further pursuit as the number of Texans pursuing the War Party shrank to less than twenty men. The remainder of those men also began to follow at a distance, lining their saddlebags with silver coins that had been falling along the trail.

The Comanche War Party under the leadership of Buffalo Hump would escape into the vastness of the Llano Estacado.

Present Day

David Ross sat at his desk and read late into the night from his history books. The story of Topusana's Grandfather Buffalo Hump was both captivating and heartbreaking. Not a single Comanche tribe, band, or individual had survived the onslaught and outright war perpetrated against *The People*.

David read the conclusion of the research: Thirty-five years after the "Great Raid" and the following years of pursuit, the remaining Comanches were starving, the result of the whites killing immense numbers of buffalo. The last free band of Comanches, under the leadership of Chief Quahadis, surrendered to Colonel Mackenzie and the United States Fourth Cavalry in the canyon country east of what is now Lubbock, Texas.

Had it been for not one, but two devastating smallpox outbreaks (that many believed had been spread intentionally) that killed seventy-five percent of the Comanche Nation in Texas, and the development of repeating fire rifles of which the Comanche had none, then perhaps *The People* could have survived. However, they were outgunned, starving, and an obstacle to the completion of the transcontinental railroad system. Texas made a halfhearted effort to provide a reservation along the Brazos River. A mere twelve hundred acres was set aside for the reservation. The surviving Comanche were effectively jailed within the confines of that small reservation.

The surrounding white settlers were quite uncomfortable with the presence of the Comanche. Vigilante groups made certain the few survivors, including Chief Buffalo Hump, were harassed and accosted on a regular basis. Several Comanche were murdered, shot on sight. The perpetrators of the murders claimed the Comanche were caught "off the reservation." The killings ruled justifiable by that fact. Any crime committed within one hundred miles of the reservation was quickly blamed on the Comanche living in the area. Many of those alleged crimes were designed and orchestrated by the vigilante groups, intended to show the Comanche had no ability to co-exist with the white settlers. The few remaining Comanches led by Buffalo Hump signed one final peace treaty.

The treaty promised, on the complete movement of the tribe from Texas to the Fort Sill, Lawton area of Oklahoma, a reservation, a guaranteed Homeland. That area at that time was known as *Indian Territory*.

During the movement of the surviving Comanche from Texas to Oklahoma, the tribe was attacked yet again while camped in the Wichita Mountains. United States troops led by Major Earl Van Dorn slaughtered more than eighty warriors during the attack. Van Dorn later claimed he had no knowledge of the newly signed treaty. The reservation land on the Brazos was sold to the neighboring landowners. Many of those landowners were members of the vigilante groups.

The Texans would have their way. Not a single Comanche survived the extermination of *The People*, the culture, the buffalo, or their sacred way of life in the entire state of Texas. The small reservation in Oklahoma would be all that remained of the once great and proud *People*. The Numunuu were no more and would never again roam the wide-open plains of Texas, or the *Comancheria*, as it was called before the Texans arrived.

The great Comanche Chief Buffalo Hump, grandfather of Topusana, would live out his last days in a small clapboard house on the reservation near Lawton, Oklahoma. He attempted to set an example to his surviving people, becoming a farmer, understanding the only hope *The People* had for survival was to adapt to the ways of the white man. Buffalo Hump died in 1870 at the age of eighty, a broken man. His generation being the last of *The People* to live free upon the earth.

David closed the book, deep in thought. The history books had a small error in their content. There were in fact three survivors of this attempted extermination. He wondered aloud, "What will Texas do differently this time?"

Knowing how governments operate and react when faced with the unknown, he feared inwardly for the survivors.

PART TWO

Chapter 42

Christmas Eve

Abby, Sana, and Grace sat together in the cozy breakfast nook adjoining Abby's kitchen. Sana occasionally peered out the window in the direction of the San Saba River. The storm had continued to intensify, and huge snowflakes drifted to Earth from the heavens, dancing in the soft glow of the porch light before gently settling on the trees and flowerpots in view of the little nook. The three talked and enjoyed the hot tea Abby had prepared.

Sana and Grace had taken to one another instantly. Even in the difficult circumstances the day had brought, friendship was at the forefront of the quiet evening that was developing.

They had talked of all that had occurred over the last few months, the entire story. The Dream Time, the awakening, the garden adventures. Grace was astounded by the story. Catching her mother's eye occasionally, an expression of wonder and disbelief on her face as the story unfolded.

"Mom, I can't believe you didn't share this with me. This is simply fascinating."

It was hard to comprehend that laughter would occasionally erupt from the three, considering the present situation. But all three of these beautiful women seemed to bond and know a deep spiritual truth. They were consciously, or perhaps subconsciously, putting that truth into practice. "Laughter was indeed a good medicine."

The evening reminded Sana of many such evenings she had spent with her own family and the women of her tribe around the fires of her old Camp. There was a closeness, a bonding that only seemed to take place in this kind of setting.

Sana observed as David and William Travis had excused themselves to visit privately in David's study, just as the men and Warriors always had done.

Why was that, Sana wondered and then asked aloud, "Why is it the men always separate to go and discuss manly issues, leaving the women to their girl talk?"

Grace smiled broadly and replied to Sana's embarrassment, "They can't discuss the size of their manhood in front of the women!"

Abby laughed out loud, Grace rolled over giggling as Sana smiled at the lighthearted talk. Sana blushed, which was instantly noticed by Grace, causing more laughter.

Grace was enthralled with Sana's natural beauty, touching her hair and face. "My goodness, Sana, you are the most beautiful woman I think I have ever seen! You know you should come out to Malibu, we could go shopping, get you a modeling contract, movies, the whole enchilada!"

Sana smiled; she didn't know quite how to respond.

"I'm serious, you would love the ocean."

Sana nodded while thinking what and where exactly was Malibu? Abby sensed the confusion and opened her map application on her phone and began to show Sana where California was. Grace opened her phone and began to go through picture after picture of Malibu, her house and the ocean, even her dad's sailboat and airplane.

"Mom, when can you guys come out for another sail?" Grace asked.

"Well, we do have some issues here but perhaps it might be a good idea," Abby pondered.

"So, you would like to go, Abby?" Sana asked.

"Come on, Sana. I call her Mom. Stop calling her Abby; she's your mom, too. Call her Mom!" Grace said.

Abby smiled, her heart warming at the thought.

Sana hesitated then replied, "Ok, Mom, you want to go to Malibu with me and sister?" The three roared with laughter.

As the three women continued their talk, Grace motioned for Sana to move around and sit in front of her. Grace began to weave Sana's beautiful hair into a lovely braid. Just as her mother, Kwanita (God is Gracious), used to do so many years ago…in another time.

Sana thought again how much this was just like the evenings the women of her family and tribe would sometimes spend together. The quaint little breakfast nook glowed with the lighthearted laughter and love of the kind hearts that filled the room.

Sana was in awe. So many things to comprehend. A boat for sailing on the ocean, an airplane for flying across the earth. Sana imagined seeing the vast ocean for the first time. Taking it all in, it was a bit overwhelming, but she had never felt such love and acceptance ever in her entire life. Sana knew she would be safe here, with Mrs. Abby Ross.

Then Tabba came to her mind again. She hesitated to change the light cheerful conversation but decided to confide in these kind, compassionate friends. Fighting back the tears, Sana asked, "Will Tabba recover soon? Will he ever be set free?"

Chapter 43

December 24
8:00 P.M.

William Travis sat in the study of his best friend and client David Ross. The fire softly burned, giving off the fresh odor of mesquite wood as it smoldered and crackled. The dark paneling and subdued light gave the two men a sense of calm during the storm that was certainly about to boil out of control. William sat quietly digesting the entire story that had just been shared with him. Both men seemed to be lost in thought, each awaiting the other's next words. William stood and peered out the window at the heavy snow now falling. He took in a deep breath, exhaled, then drank sparingly from his whiskey glass. The aged blend, he thought, perfect. Both men enjoyed the quiet moment.

William Travis was as honest and truthful as a man could be. He had always been a leader. He was an exceptional student and athlete in high school. "Will," as David referred to him, was the "All American Boy." With rugged good looks, blond hair, blue eyes, he was the young man all the girls in school wanted. However, Will had one girl through his entire high school days and even into college. Shelly would later become Mrs. William Travis.

Who would know her life would be so short? In hindsight it was such a blessing the two had spent all those school years together, as the years after school were very few indeed. The cancer was aggressive, the suffering minimal. A picture of mercy...David had always thought.

One never knows the number of days he or she might be granted, so live them well. The words David would never forget as he had read what Shelly had prepared for the day of her memorial. David knew those words were quite similar in the wisdom they contained to those of the great teacher King Solomon.

David had known Will since the first day of kindergarten. They had literally grown up together. The two possessed a rare friendship, a friendship founded on trust and honesty. The two had been inseparable during their growing up years.

But life had happened. After graduation from high school, David departed for the coast. Will was offered and accepted an academic scholarship to Harvard. Graduation night the two joked together and promised to "catch up" during the holidays and summers. Those days never came about. They would not see one another again until Will's wedding four years later. David remembered thinking at the wedding, what happened to the time?

Now it had been forty-five years since they had graduated from high school together. David wondered again, not where goes the time, but rather... where go the years?

David admired Will and his moral character more than any other person on the planet. After the death of his wife, Shelly, Will chose to remain single. He felt he could never again replace the soul mate he had loved and lost. He felt blessed to have had the years granted to him with his wife. Yes, his plan would have been for more time and children and the richness of life that came with children. Those things Will knew were not his to grant. He was, despite the loss, a grateful man. "Better to have loved and lost, than to never have loved at all," was a mantra by which William Travis lived.

Will had many attractive offers after Harvard Law School but declined all. He had been reading of the plight of many of the nation's military veterans.

William Travis, a descendant of one William B. Travis, the twenty-six-year-old lawyer and commander of the Texas forces who was killed in action at the Battle of the Alamo, applied to and was accepted to the United States Navy. He would become a JAG Officer and a leading advocate for the military veterans and personnel as they returned to civilian life after years of active duty. Later in his career, Will would represent the young men and women of the US Navy as they returned from the war in Iraq and Afghanistan.

He would eventually represent Lieutenant Jonathan Ross. Jonathan, very deservedly so, was recommended for the Medal of Honor by his superiors and commanders. His fellow soldiers also received recommendations for the medal, Chief Petty Officer David Toons and Master Chief Petty Officer Mickey Sanders. The process was long and arduous and highly political.

Will fought every step of the way for the three brave young men who risked everything in their attempt to save their wounded and dying fellow soldiers. They deserved the medal. They were qualified in every way to receive the honor. However, the administration in power at the time did not want to draw unneeded attention to the ongoing protruded political struggle the country was experiencing.

Will thought the bureaucrats and appointees simply didn't care about the actions of the three brave young men. The politicians were much more concerned about posturing and appearance. Those in power at the time simply did not need any war heroes. The administration would use party lines to prevent the required vote from ever occurring.

Will thought the politicians had taken the gutless way out. The leadership in Congress would allow the time of action required, which was a vote within eighteen months of recommendation, to expire. The vote required in Congress for approval to award the Medal of Honor to the three brave young men would never occur.

After a twenty-nine-year naval career, Will resigned over the debacle. He returned to his home state of Texas and opened a small firm in Austin. He still represented many of the young men and women who were returning home from Iraq and Afghanistan. These brave young soldiers deserved better, better than they were receiving from their government. He would see to it that many received the medical care, mental and physical therapy, and the pensions they deserved. He loved his work and was completely content in what he was doing.

A murder case was not quite on his radar.

Will spoke first, breaking the serene moment the two were sharing.

"That same cavern we ventured into back in high school?" Will asked.

"Yes, it is," David replied.

"Wow, I remember that trip like it was yesterday. You know if I have to go back into the cavern as any part of my representation, I'm out." The two shared a brief smile of which only they could understand the meaning.

"So how do we explain this to, well, everyone? The press, the court, even the investigating officers?" Will asked.

"That's why I hired you, Will. You go and do what you do. Tell them the truth."

"Hm, you know they will not be able to deal with the truth, don't you?" Will said.

"By *they* you mean all the above, the press, the prosecution, the public?"

"Yes, that's what I mean."

"I may become the *crazy* in this trial, David. I do have a firm and a reputation."

"It's your call, Will. I understand completely your concerns," David said, thinking that he also could become labeled as a *crazy*. "You will not be the only person that gets that label."

"That's probably true," Will replied.

"Do you believe the story, Will?"

William paused a few moments, picked up the metate and pestle. Holding them carefully, a feeling of something extraordinary dawned in his mind. This was a breakthrough. A breakthrough in science, faith, and history. William Travis had spent his life's work defending the less fortunate, those run over and taken advantage of by the "system," whether that was due to corruption or simply lack of care by those who were supposed to administer relief and justice. His life was defending the downcast, the deserving. It was what he did. William Travis considered his work a calling.

What better way to use that calling than defending the Texas Comanches? They had been nearly obliterated from the face of the earth and for what purpose? They were an inconvenience. The Comanche Nation had been a difficult enemy; they should not have lasted as long as they did. Texas, and later the United States, failed terribly, this *People* time and again.

The thought that this opportunity was something more, something extraordinary, wouldn't leave him. This was not about the murder trial, but much more. This situation, he thought, might turn out to be about a long overdue restitution.

He pondered the question asked of him by his lifelong friend and supporter. Although he had many doubts about the validity of this incredible story, the facts before him were, it seemed, irrefutable. Tabba, the Warrior, seemed quite authentic. He had killed a man at one hundred yards with a primitive bow. Topusana, his wife, was clearly not some imposter or actor. The metate he held in his hands, imagining…something deep within his own spirit wanted to believe, hope even, that it all was impossibly true.

William Travis answered. "Yes, David, I do believe the entire story, and yes, I will help Topusana and Tabbananica."

Chapter 44

Christmas Day dawned, the Ross home decorated in beautiful Christmas array. Abby always went all out for the holidays. The spruce tree in the center of the great room was over twenty feet tall. It glowed brightly, illuminating the entire room with its tiny colored lights. Surrounding the tree were brightly wrapped packages of all sizes and shapes. As Sana entered the room, she did not recall the packages from the prior evening. Outside, the dim light of early morning was aglow. The eastern sky was just beginning to lighten, revealing eight inches of fresh snow, a few small flakes continuing to drift about. The snow blanketed everything in sight, the trees along the river, the highway, and even the cars were shaped into strange great humped figures. Decorations adorned the room: holly, red bows, reindeer, even a beautiful antique sleigh displayed in the big front window. It was filled with beautiful red flowers, "poinsettias," Abby had explained, ever teaching Sana new words and phrases.

Sana sat alone on the sofa in the beautiful room. The nativity figures Abby had explained to Sana shown with a small dim light. Sana studied the face of Mary in the scene, imagining how the young girl must have felt becoming the mother of a God. Sana could not imagine such a burden for a young woman.

She arose from the sofa and opened the large book she had read from each day. The Bible was displayed on a high platform. Sana continued to read the story of the child sent to Earth to die for other's mistakes. It seemed such an unbelievable sacrifice. She was fascinated by the story and the similarities it contained to that of the Great Spirit. The book referred to "God the Father," who seemed to Sana to be very much like the Great Spirit. The "God the Father" in this book lost his only Son.

Sana thought she could believe in and relate to a God who knew her own level of suffering and loss. This "God the Father" seemed to be very much a Father of love and compassion. Just like the Great Spirit.

Sana finished a chapter of torture and suffering and the hanging of the Savior on a cross, while his mother, Mary, as told in the story watched the events unfold before her very eyes. Sana was stunned. Like her, Mary also had watched her own child die.

Sana again gazed at the little carved figures. Lost in her own memories, she recalled the terrible day she had watched her own daughter be tortured, violated, and murdered. She knew there was no greater pain or heartache conceivable. The tears that lay just beneath the surface began to flow freely. She decided she would need to ask Abby more about this awful, sad story.

She again seated herself on the sofa. The tears ebbed now. The painting of her and Prairie Song had been removed from above the fire pit. However, she truly wished it was back. She wanted more than anything this morning to be reminded of the love of her daughter. The brief life they had shared together seemed so long ago now.

She began to recall the scene from yesterday in Tabba's hospital room.

Sana had eventually gained approval to enter Tabba's room the previous afternoon. Seeing his face thin and drawn, his eyes tightly shut. He seemed to rest peacefully except that one moment when he had stirred. She knew he had recognized her; she had seen the awareness and recognition in his eyes, ever so briefly. Tabba now knew she was with him.

She wondered how long Tabba's life would continue.

The nurses had promised to call the moment he awakened. If only she had been there when he had awakened in the cavern. Maybe she could have intervened. Her mind wandered…perhaps she knew better. The plan of life, the beginning and ending of our days was not in our hands. Those days of beginning and ending belonged only to the Great Spirit, or perhaps "God the Father" referred to in the Book.

Sana wondered if the two could possibly be the same God. She knew the creation story of her own people. The Comanche believed they had been created from swirls of dust. She had recently read in the Book of Faith how God the Father had shaped a man from the dust of the earth. The similarities were remarkable, she thought.

Sana was drawn back in the moment as Abby entered the room quietly. Sana sensed her presence and turned to her. Abby moved across the room, embracing Sana. Abby spoke softly, "How are you this morning, Little One?"

"Oh, I'm fine...Mom," Sana replied, the warmth of the moment causing a smile to grow across Sana's face.

Abby smiled. "May I fix you some coffee or hot chocolate?"

"Hot chocolate!" came the loud reply from the top of the stairs as Grace bounded down the stairs.

"Did Santa come?" Grace moved toward Sana, directing her and pointing to the presents under and surrounding the tree. "Looks like he did! Yep that fat man came right down the chimney, what a guy!"

The three women picked up the laughter again this morning, just as they had the evening before. David and William both entered the room at the same time.

"Merry Christmas!" David exclaimed.

"Merry Christmas!" came the replies from across the room.

"While I have everyone's attention, and since I'm a lawyer, let's make a deal for the day," Will said.

"You have the floor, counselor," Abby said.

"It's Christmas. Let's all agree to celebrate. Considering what may go on here the rest of the week or the rest of the year. Today I hereby declare 'Christmas Day.' It shall be treated as such. Celebration, giving of gifts, eating, and generally being merry are the only activities allowed to take place in this home this fine snowy day! Agreed?"

With the nodding of heads, the five agreed and began the celebration. Tomorrow would have enough trouble of its own. Each would do their very best this day to not worry about tomorrow.

However, Sana remained quiet and thoughtful, while wondering how a person might completely block out those troubles of tomorrow.

Chapter 45

December 25
4:00 P.M.

David, we need a translator ourselves," Will said, as the two men were again meeting in David's study.

"And where are we supposed to find a translator that speaks Comanche and English?" David asked.

"I am going to leave that to you. The DA has objected to Sana acting as translator for the defense. After thinking it through, I believe it would simply be too difficult for her to do so anyway. I will need all the help I can get in preparation for the upcoming trial. I have already sent for two of my paralegals to join us here for the duration. Believe me, I will be bogged down with details. So, can you help?" asked William.

"Yes, of course, I'll get right on it."

"Good. I also have located some office space on the square. I'm going there now to sign a six-month lease. I'll need the space, and you and Abby will need your privacy."

"I understand. I suppose I need to post some funds to your account?"

"That would be wonderful. Send more than you think I'll need."

"Done," David said. Later that afternoon, he transferred $300,000 to William Travis's corporate account. That should cover him for a while, he thought.

As William departed for town, David turned to his computer to research the modern-day Comanche Nation.

He was quite surprised to discover the Comanche Nation based in Lawton, Oklahoma, was a vibrant, thriving enterprise. The tribe operated casinos, hotels, a school system, a home construction industry, an agricultural division, and even a recreational water park.

David also sadly discovered there were an estimated fewer than thirty elder tribal members who still spoke and understood the native language. Although, a program had been put into place for those elders to mentor and teach the younger tribal members the language and history of the *Numunuu*. The program, David thought, did not have the appearance of being very successful. The language had been classified as endangered by the United Nations, which had a protocol for such a designation. Of the utmost consideration for such a designation was a simple question. Was the language of the once great Comanche Nation being taught to the present generation of children? It, in fact, was not. The language was indeed in danger of becoming a forgotten one.

David decided he would travel to Lawton and visit with the leaders of the Tribe. Perhaps he might be able to better communicate his needs in person. And perhaps he could also communicate some of what was happening in Texas with Topusana and Tabbananica. How to broach that subject and just what to reveal began running through his mind.

He wondered if Sana might be interested in the trip to Lawton.

A visit with the Elders of her people could be quite enlightening for Sana. He pondered how she might react to what they could and would discover there. She could certainly assist him in locating the right person for the job. He would need wisdom to consider this decision. He thought he should inquire of Sana and Abby before deciding.

David rose from his study. Calling out for Abby, she answered him from up the stairs. Climbing the stairs, he could hear the girls talking from Sana's room. Knocking on the door, Grace answered, "Come on in, Dad, we were just hanging Sana's Christmas gift."

There in the large dormered guest room, Abby was just straightening the masterpiece centered over Sana's bed. "Mother and Daughter" hung in the perfect light.

Abby and David had discussed at length what to do with the piece after the visit with Nan Chisholm. The value they all knew was astronomical. But to David and Abby, the painting's value was not the issue. This was Topusana's portrait. No other person on Earth could ever appreciate it more than she did. David, ever the pragmatist, looked at the gift of the painting as perhaps an inheritance. He was doing everything in his power to adopt Topusana and that included setting her new life journey on a steady financial foundation. He and Abby had more money than they could ever spend. The gifting fit well into his financial plan. That plan was simply to give, identifying worthy projects and funding those projects silently. If Sana ever needed the funds, she would be financially set for life from the proceeds of a sale.

"Ten million dollars is the most expensive Christmas gift I have ever given," Abby said as she and David had discussed the gift. David, smiling at his lovely wife, looked at her questioningly.

"Abby, sweetheart, what did you pay for the painting?"

"Well, if I remember correctly, I paid eight hundred fifty dollars for it."

"Forgive me, dear, but that's not that much to spend on your new daughter, is it?"

"I see your point, David. I need to always look at it like that, don't I?"

"Whichever makes you feel the best about it."

"David, it all makes me feel wonderful, the entire story of how this painting was born and traveled the world, finding its way here to us, and Sana being out there on that frozen plain starving…it is simply an incredible coincidence, isn't it?"

"I don't believe this is a coincidence at all Abby," David said. "Only supernatural intervention could ever paint a story such as this one. Let me ask you a question, though, about giving such a generous gift. Do you feel blessed in your heart to give this painting to Sana?"

"Of course," Abby answered honestly. "My heart is overflowing with blessings, imagining what this might mean for Sana in the future and even now. And yes, my heart is filled with blessings, to answer your question. It makes me feel just wonderful!"

"I just always like to verify these truths I know in my own heart, Abby… about giving. It is indeed more blessed to give than to receive, is it not?"

"Yes, David, absolutely without a doubt, it is," Abby said resolutely.

Now David and Abby observed as Sana stood gazing at the amazing scene, her eyes clearly filling with tears. However, David could tell they were not tears of sadness but rather tears that come from a full heart. Sana crossed the room and embraced him.

"Thank you, David. It is such a beautiful gift," she whispered.

David seemed content to just smile as Sana embraced him.

"I'm sorry to interrupt such a wonderful moment," David said. "But we have some pressing issues to discuss." Just then the house phone rang. David picked up the nearest extension. It was the hospital calling; the nurse on the other end of the line speaking frantically.

"Mr. Ross, Tabba has awakened. It is not going well. Could you please come quickly? None of us can understand what he wants. He just keeps yelling in this *voice*, this incredible voice."

"What is he saying? "David asked.

"He just keeps repeating one word. Listen." The nurse held up the phone, and David could clearly hear a thunderous voice, "*Topusana, Topusana, Topusannaaaa.*"

"We're on the way," he said.

Chapter 46

Grove County Hospital

The two embraced one another, Tabba stroking Sana's beautiful long hair, breathing in her scent. They locked into an embrace so tightly, he never wanted to let her go. She felt there was no safer place in the world than in his arms.

"*Are you being held by the white soldiers?*" he whispered in her ear.

Hearing her native tongue for the first time in many months, Sana replied, "*No Tabba, the Texans in the log shelter…are my friends.*" She felt him tense as her words sank in.

"*What has happened to your skins? I thought surely they had forced you to dress as they are,*" Tabba spoke quietly to Sana.

"*Tabba, my friends Abby, David, and William are helping you. They have been helping me since I awakened. You have been asleep a very long time, several moons. It was difficult for me without you. But please listen, they are your friends also, Tabba.*"

She rose from his bedside, pulling a chair next to him, staring directly into his eyes.

"*Tabba, we made it…the Dream Time was successful. Do you understand, Tabba? We may have a…new beginning now.*"

"*I understand, Sana…A new beginning, the reason for all of it.*" The two sat in stillness for a moment, the only sound coming from the rhythmic beat of the heart rate monitor.

"*However, I am a prisoner. Is that not true?*"

"Yes," she said. "*The thing that happened on the black ribbon, the ranger you killed, the whites are angry. But it is not as in the past. You may be a prisoner for some time. They will hold what the whites call a court.*"

Tabba's eyes darkened at her words.

"*Sana, have you seen anything of the future concerning this court?*" Tabba knew Sana had the gift of visions, even though she denied its strength in her. Tosahwi and Tabba knew it was hers to possess. She would one day realize how gifted she truly was, he thought.

"*I have sought out the Great Spirit, Tabba. I have asked continuously of the Great Spirit; however, I have seen nothing clearly.*"

Sana closed her eyes and lowered her head in disappointment. Tabba reached for her chin, raising her head gently.

"*My love, you will hear from the Great Spirit soon. You are his chosen vessel, Sana. Understand, my wife, we never could have come this far without his help. The Great Spirit will speak when the time is perfect...and you will hear clearly, my Prairie Flower.*"

Sana's heart rose at his words; she knew the truth of what Tabba had spoken. Resolve again settled in her mind at his encouragement and gentle reminder.

"*For now, I must endure this treatment from the rangers,*" he said, raising his shackled wrists.

"*Be patient, my love, it may take the full seasons...maybe six moons our friends tell me. Is that too long to wait for me?*"

Tabba saw the light glimmering in the eyes of his beautiful wife as she reassured him. "*I could wait a thousand years if you are at the end of the waiting,*" he said, his eyes peering into her soul.

Sana, a longing in her heart for her husband, moved again to embrace him.

"*What do you know of the others?*" he whispered quietly.

"*Tabba, I have just recently found the sign. I have not been able to unite with any of the people nor do I even know if any survived the attack other than Tosahwi.*"

"*Sana, Tosahwi has awakened, seventeen members of the Tribe escaped with him. You must go to them soon.*"

The deputies outside the partially open door, called to Sana. "Times up, ma'am, going to have to ask you to leave now."

Sana spoke quietly, a look of shock and disbelief on her face at the news of the *others*.

180

"This is a good day, my husband. Do you know what this means? Our People…a fresh new beginning for our Tribe." Tears began to run down her face at the revelation. The eyes of the two locked into one another's soul. A knowing was present within the hospital room and within the two hearts. They would be enough.

"I will return later today, Tabba. I will be here every day to see you. I need to ask something of you, my husband."

"Yes, Sana, what is it?"

"Tabba, you are a Warrior…you are my Warrior. I know you could fight your way through these few rangers and make your way to the cavern. It would be an easy thing for you to do."

"Yes, you are correct, Sana. I have already been thinking about such a thing."

"This is my request, Tabba. Do not do such a thing. If you will be patient, you will have me soon…as your wife. It is the only way… and you must promise me," Sana pleaded.

"I will do as you say, Topusana. You may need to remind me daily, but I will do as you say. For now, these Texans are safe."

William Travis was standing at the nurse's station and overheard the deputy's request for Sana to leave Tabba's room. He turned to the nurse on duty. "Get me the doctor in charge of this floor, now!" Then he abruptly moved down the hall toward the room.

Identifying himself as the attorney for the suspect, he immediately questioned the deputies seated in two chairs outside Tabba's room.

"Excuse me, I must have heard you two incorrectly. Did you just tell this man's wife her time was up?" William spoke in a gruff voice.

The two looked at one another. The first deputy answered just as the Tabba's doctor arrived in the hallway, stopping to listen.

"We are just following orders," said one deputy.

"And whose orders were those exactly?" William asked.

"Well, the district attorney said no visitors for more than fifteen minutes."

"This is not a prison!" William stated, his voice rising. "This is, in fact, a hospital. The visitor is this man's wife; she is under no orders whatsoever that circumvent those of any other visitor to this facility. You have no right whatsoever to demand of her some time limitation imposed by any outside authority. You will retract that order now!"

As the deputies stood stunned, William Travis paused. "Immediately!" The two looked at one another in disbelief that they would be challenged. Both deputies rose from the chairs. The first deputy spoke. "Well, we think the DA has some authority in this situation."

Tabba's doctor, Dr. Blake Tower, interrupted.

"No, sir, I can assure you he does not. Your job here is to make sure the suspect, who is under my care and my orders, does not leave his room. Period! That is your sole purpose in being here. You may sit down and resume your one duty. If I hear anything of this nature again, I will have you removed. You can watch just as easily from the nurse's station," Dr. Tower spoke emphatically. William Travis turned to the doctor and introduced himself.

"William Travis, I'm counsel for your patient." William extended his hand.

"Please call me Dr. Blake." The doctor offered his hand in a firm handshake.

"Thank you, Dr. Blake. Please call me William. I know there is some confusion and information coming forth that seems quite unbelievable." The men gazed into one another's eyes. Mutual respect and understanding was on each man's face.

Entering the room, William was surprised to see Sana and Tabba wide-eyed, holding one another's hands.

"It's OK, Sana, you do not have to leave," William said.

"I heard. Thank you, William," Sana replied.

"*What? Has this man helped us in some way?*" asked Tabba.

"*Yes, Tabba, this is the man who will help you before the court. His name is William Travis.*"

Tabba straightened himself on the pillow as much as he could and offered his shackled hand to William. Then he spoke perfectly a few of the only words he knew in English.

"I am Tabbananica, Voice of the Sun."

William was taken aback at the purity and power in the man's voice. The intensity and fierceness in his eyes and the obvious intellect were... astonishing.

****

Two hours later Tabba was sleeping soundly. Sana exited the room to the stares of the deputies. Abby, David, and William met her in the waiting room.

"How is he doing, Sana?" David asked.

"I think quite well, considering. Dr. Blake is a good man. He says Tabba will most likely sleep through the night. He promised to call my phone as soon as Tabba awakens. He plans on keeping him here for a few more days. He said something about this being the best place for him…in light of the situation?"

As William listened to the exchange between David and Sana, he understood perfectly the doctor's actions. He was grateful for the compassionate decision and made note to contact Dr. Blake soon.

"So how was your visit? Tell us more, Sana. You have not seen one another for a long time," Abby queried.

"Well, I have convinced him not to kill any other Texans for the time being," Sana said to the raised brows and surprised looks from of all three of her friends.

Chapter 47

Lawton, Oklahoma
December 27

The jet touched down smoothly, kissing the runway with its main tires first, then Steve gently lowered the nose onto the runway, slowly decelerating. The landing was textbook perfect. In the rear cabin of the jet, Sana held tightly to the arm rest with one hand and gripped Abby's hands with her other. She was in awe again; this was indeed powerful medicine.

They had crossed a large part of Texas in only thirty minutes. Sana watched the moving map as the flight path took them across the center of what was formerly the Llano Estacado. Daring to peer out the window, she could see below many small towns and settlements.

This is what it's like to be an eagle, she thought. Soaring on the heights, searching the land below. She often thought in wonder in her former life as she would watch the eagle soar so high it would eventually disappear...what it might be like to ride the wind across the sky.

It was hard for her to comprehend the speed at which they traveled. Studying the map and the distance, she compared it to the only way she knew of traveling...walking. The way she had always traveled. Two hundred and forty miles, as Abby helped her with the math equation, twelve to fifteen miles per day; it would have taken her eighteen days to walk the distance they had just traveled in less than one half of an hour. Topusana was in awe.

They drove to the building, following the directions given from David's phone, where the program for language studies was located on the Tribal lands of the Comanche Nation. The woman behind the desk was obviously Comanche. Sana greeted her in their native tongue.

"Good morning, my sister, I am Topusana."

The young woman did not understand a word Sana had spoken. An awkward moment passed before the woman replied, "I'm sorry I do not speak our native language, but Mrs. Running Deer is awaiting you in her office. I'll let her know you are here." Smiling, the young woman extended her hand. "My name is Brenda; it's nice to meet you."

"My name is Sana. It's a pleasure to meet you, Brenda. These are my friends David and Abby." Polite smiles were exchanged, then Brenda departed down the hall and into a side office.

Sana was surprised to meet and encounter her first Comanche descendant in this modern world. Even more surprised that the woman did not speak or understand one word of the basic language of her people.

Mrs. Running Deer met the three in the lobby of the office with a warm greeting. David and Mrs. Running Deer had spoken at length over the phone the day before. David only relayed the fact of their need for a translator and the truth that the translator was needed for a murder trial. That was basically all she knew.

"Well, it's a pleasure to meet you all, and welcome to our Homelands," Mary Running Deer said. Topusana spoke first in her native tongue again.

"Thank you for agreeing to see us. My name is Topusana. These are my friends David and Abby Ross."

Mrs. Running Deer replied in Comanche. *"I am Mary Running Deer. It is good to meet you, Topusana. You may call me Mary. Perhaps we should use English, so your white friends will understand."*

"Yes, I agree. Thank you again, Mary."

"So, I understand the request you have made. Sana, can you tell me more of your story?" Mary asked. Sana looked toward David, who nodded approval.

"I have just recently arrived in this *time*. My husband, Tabbananica, and the Shaman Tosahwi and I entered the Dream Time in the year 1844, after a battle in which most of my tribe and family were killed." Sana continued, "I recently awakened, and if not for the kindness shown by my new father and mother, I would not have survived. My new mother, Abby, has taught me English. My husband had an encounter with the rangers upon his awakening a few months after I awoke. The altercation was just three days ago. The ranger was killed. Now Tabba is held prisoner, awaiting a trial. I could easily translate at this trial;

however, on the advice of my new mother and father and our attorney, we are seeking another person for this assistance. I have prayed fervently for this person to come forth this day. Might you be the person to help us in our time of need, my sister?"

Abby and David sat in suspenseful silence not knowing whether the woman would laugh out loud at the story…or call security.

Mrs. Running Deer sat in silence for a moment, closing her eyes as if praying herself. Taking in the incredible story, she nodded toward David and Abby. The moment now seemed to take on a different reality as Mary began to speak.

"I am not the woman you seek, Topusana. However, I know who it is that will assist you and Tabbananica. We will go to her now." Rising from her desk, Mary Running Deer asked, "May I ride in your vehicle with you?"

"Yes, of course," David said.

"And may I say thank you for helping this daughter of ours. Her journey has been long and difficult," Mrs. Running Deer said.

"Um, you're welcome," Abby replied.

The drive through the reservation was somewhat depressing, David thought. The roads were in extremely poor condition and the homes dotted along the small highway in ill-repair. Broken down cars and trucks, unpainted barns and houses alike lined the highway. Trash burned in barrels, and that which was not burned was spread over most of the overgrown yards of the home sites. After a forty-five-minute drive, Mary, as she insisted she be addressed, directed a turn off the small semi-paved road onto an even rougher red dirt road leading farther away from development. The snow had partially melted and the mud began to coat the vehicle as David shifted into four-wheel drive.

"Mary," David asked, "don't the casinos generate income for the people?"

"David, the men who loan money to the tribes across North America seem to receive all the revenues of the casinos. The debt is so heavy a burden and loaned at such high interest rates, many tribes see nothing of the profits. It has become another broken promise, another great lie imposed upon our people. The answer to your question is no. *The People* are not benefiting from these casinos."

Along this single lane road, the houses appeared to be in even worse condition. Several large groups of teenagers were gathered around the burning barrels along the dirt road. David spotted more than one whiskey bottle among the teens. The group observed the teenagers from the SUV, traveling slowly as they made their way deeper into the reservation.

"You can see the plight of my people, can you not, David?" Mary noticed David observing from behind the wheel.

"Well, Mary…honestly it seems *The People* are quite poor."

"Our young people struggle the most. We have many government-run programs. But what you are seeing is despair," Mary said. "There is no government program for despair, David.

"The white Texans sent us here many generations ago. My observation is this: when a once free, happy people as we the *Numunuu* were, are imprisoned on a small piece of land there is a brokenness that occurs. The spirit of the people has been broken, David. Poverty is rampant, as is drug and alcohol use. We Native Americans statistically have one of the highest fetal alcohol syndrome rates in the world. Some of the people are beginning to succeed. Some are recovering from the loss of who we were. But many, as you can see, are not."

David, Abby, and Sana sat in silence, observing from the red dirt road the truth of what Mrs. Mary Running Deer spoke.

"Perhaps in your new beginning you will have the opportunity to change the story of the Numunuu, Topusana," Mary said.

"It is my dream to do so, sister," Sana said.

Taking another sharp turn onto another muddy, rutted road, the four bounced along as the rented SUV struggled to maintain itself in the center surface. As they rode along, Sana observed there were no longer any houses, just a few abandoned single wide trailers. She spotted several horses inside a broken-down barbed wire fence. The animals looked pitiful, ribs showing along bent backbones, hooves and legs covered in mud. The small pasture the animals occupied had not a blade of grass. The road suddenly just ended.

David stopped the vehicle.

"We will walk from here," Mary said.

As the four exited the SUV, the smell of wood smoke drifting through the air met their noses. The wind whistled through the small trees, the temperature a biting cold that ran right through a person, Abby thought.

David followed Mary as she made her way through the low brush. Abby and Sana followed closely behind.

As the terrain opened, a small home, or a structure resembling that of a traditional Comanche lodge, David thought, was nestled against a shallow hill. Smoke rose from a small metal chimney along one side. A tiny creek gurgled along the opposite side.

The view across the open plain from their vantage point was absolutely stunning, Sana thought. It reminded her of many scenes she had witnessed personally when moving with *The People* across the plains.

The old woman stood in the doorway, watching the foursome approach.

"Welcome, my children," the old woman spoke to the group in her native tongue.

Mary greeted the woman with a light kiss on the cheek and said something inaudible to her. *"Come inside, out of the cold, my children, our meal is just about ready."*

Mary entered the lodge first and seated herself on the floor on a huge buffalo hide. Topusana followed, seating herself next to Mary. Abby sat next, followed by David. Lastly the old woman feebly crossed the room and sat on the buffalo hide by the wood burning stove.

"Grandmother, these are the people who have come to see you this day. They are the ones Tosahwi told you about…Topusana and her new mother and father, Abby and David," Mary said.

The woman looked to be at least ninety years old. Her eyes were colored over a pale grey and were filled with what appeared to be large cataracts. She wore a beautiful dress adorned with bead work David recognized immediately as authentic. A medicine bag hung around her neck and was full of something. The something caused the sides to bulge outward. Brightly shining silver jewelry graced both hands and wrists, along with a huge silver squash blossom necklace. Her teeth were mostly missing; the few visible were dull and crooked. Her hair was a pure grey, braided and long in the tradition of her ancestors.

The old woman, nodding and now speaking in English, addressed Sana, "Welcome. You have traveled far, over many years to come to me, my child."

"Yes, Grandmother, it has been a long journey."

"My name is Hantaywee, the meaning is Faithful One. Most from the tribe refer to me as Old Grandmother. It is an honor to me…for you to do so also. Tosahwi said you would be coming to me soon."

David and Abby were taken aback at the statement, remembering he was the shaman that had sent Tabba and Sana into the Dream Time. The other two women simply nodded in agreement.

"How long will the trial go on?" Grandmother asked, turning to David.

"I am not certain, Grandmother, perhaps six months," David said.

"And the two of you will take care of me during this time?" Grandmother asked, addressing Abby.

"Yes, of course, Grandmother," Abby said.

"Good, this thing is settled now. Let us eat."

The old woman bowed her head and began to sing. Sana joined in, as did Mary Running Deer. The tune was broken and lamenting. The sound filled the small lodge with thankfulness.

Abby and David, while forgetting to bow their heads, watched in fascination and wonder at the purest form of giving thanks and worship either had ever witnessed.

As lunch was served from a large pot on the wood-burning stove into small hand-carved wooden bowls, the three Native women began to converse in their native tongue.

David and Abby listened to the dialogue, enthralled with the sound and rhythm of the language.

The stew was delicious, unlike anything they had ever eaten. Abby wanted to ask what it was, but decided it better left unknown.

When everyone had finished the meal, Grandmother turned to David. "The big bird will now deliver us across the sky to Sana's home?"

"Um, yes, Grandmother," David said.

"It is a good thing...I am becoming much too old to walk to Texas."

Chapter 48

December 27
The Ross Ranch

David was overseeing the workers as they were finishing up the installation of the wood burning stove. Hantaywee, or Grandmother as she preferred, had not taken to the luxuries of the ranch house. Abby thought the downstairs guest room would be perfect for her. But upon inspection, Grandmother refused the comfort of the luxurious room.

"What else is there? I need to have my fires. I also need to see the old Camp of my people. …There is too much comfort here."

David thought a moment. "We have the bunk room in the barn. We keep it for the ranch hands." A questioning look shown on his face.

"David, we can't permit Grandmother to live in the barn, can we?" Abby said, wondering herself if it might not be a better fit.

"Let's go to this barn." Grandmother turned and reached for Abby to lead the way. They had discovered quickly that Grandmother's eyesight was extremely poor, due to the large cataracts. With her hand on Abby's shoulder, the two made their way across the driveway toward the barn. Pausing before they entered, Grandmother could smell the scent of horses and alfalfa feed.

"This is much better already," she said.

"Here in the end of the barn is a room for sleeping, Grandmother. It has a small kitchen and a bathroom. If you only step outside, you can see across to the river," Abby said.

"Yes, this will do fine, where is the wood stove?"

"Grandmother, it will be installed before sunset, and I will bring the firewood for you also," David said.

"Thank you, David. You are a good man."

David straightened at the compliment, smiling at Abby.

"Well, I'm glad to help, Grandmother."

Hantaywee nodded toward David and spoke in her native language, "*You are not like your great-great-grandfather. He was a dangerous man. The time of the generations has helped you, David J. Ross.*"

David, not understanding, simply nodded. He decided to head to town for the stove and supplies needed. He dialed Jason, his ranch foreman, asking him to bring a helper and his tools.

Two hours later, smoke poured out of the little chimney top as the fire David had kindled began to give off a wonderful fragrance and a comfortable warming heat. He had to admit it added a coziness and comfort to the little room at the end of the barn. Grandmother settled on the blankets Abby had piled one on top of another. It wasn't a buffalo hide as she had requested, but it would do for now.

David would do his best to find a buffalo hide and have it expressed to the ranch tomorrow.

Grandmother seemed happy and content.

Abby sensed the time to leave Grandmother had come. "Just pick up the little phone there and dial this number if you need me, Grandmother."

The old women nodded and closed her eyes. "It is now time to bless this new home."

She began a quiet song, humming at first. The song was beautiful, Abby thought. Not knowing whether to stay, Abby silently backed out of the room and turned toward the house. As she met David in the drive, the song grew louder, rhythmic, and worshipful.

"Well, she seems right at home now, don't you think?" David asked.

"Yes, she does. I have a few things I need to take her for her cooking, and a grocery list. She said she would cook the delicious stew for me again because she noticed how much I liked it. Isn't that curious, too?" Abby said.

"Does that mean you know what it was?" David asked.

"Yes, it's funny. She said just bring me a fat roast from the butcher shop."

David laughed. "Quite a mysterious ingredient." The two smiled at one another.

"I suppose her directness is better than not knowing she needs something.

I actually admire the honesty of her…um…requests. It's so genuine and authentic," David said.

"She seems so wise; don't you think, David?"

"Yes, she does, Abby, I suppose if you have lived as long as she has, you would gain much wisdom about life and people. You know, she told me she was more than one hundred years old."

"Wow, I thought maybe she was in her nineties. She doesn't know her exact age?"

"No, however, that's not unusual in her culture. The reservation agents did not keep very good records, especially of the older Tribal members," David explained.

The two stood in the drive between the house and barn. The singing could be heard faintly coming from Grandmother's little room in the barn.

"You know, I think we could learn a lot from Old Grandmother, if we just listen and observe. There is a reverence about her I wish I had more of."

"I agree completely."

David took her hand and the two crossed the melting snow on the drive and entered their beautiful home. They immediately heard the lighthearted laughter of Grace and Sana coming from Sana's room at the top of the stairway.

There had been a time, Abby thought, she would never again feel the contentment and peace that warmed her heart as this present time now was doing.

Even in the midst of the brewing storm, Abby possessed a peace that really was beyond understanding. She, like Grandmother in her little room, whispered a prayer of gratefulness. Abby wished she knew better how to express her heart.

She wished she knew the songs…

Chapter 49

December 28
Grove County Courthouse

J D Sneed sat in the judge's chamber listening to William Travis, counsel for the defendant. The man must have a screw loose, he thought. The story of Comanches traveling through time, awakening in a cave, and encountering the game wardens was as bizarre a story as he had ever heard. And after twenty years as a prosecutor he thought he had heard it all. Until now.

Judge David Connelly sat in silence as he listened to the story in wonderment. The judge himself was a native Texan and history buff. He knew well the story of the Comanche Nation.

Judge Connelly had majored in Texas history in his undergraduate years at Baylor University. On his acceptance to Baylor Law, David Connelly had graduated at the top of his class. He had spent a few short years as a prosecutor himself. With a stellar judicial record, he quickly advanced through the ranks of the Texas attorney general's office, eventually serving as Attorney General of Texas under two separate governorships.

Judge Connelly had the law in his blood. After his retirement, he was just not ready to give up on his love of the courtroom, the law, and the status and fulfillment that being a lawyer brought. Judge Connelly, upon his retirement and moving back to his family ranch in Grove County, ran for District Judge of the county and had decidedly won three consecutive elections for the position. He was now serving his third four-year term. He was highly overqualified for the position he now served, but David Connelly was happy and content in his position, both in the community of his hometown and in the legal community in which he ruled. He had a reputation of fairness and firmness in dealing with criminal cases that came before his court.

The workload of his docket he kept uncluttered and efficient. In fact, he had quite an easy schedule, as the crime rate in Grove County was one of the lowest in the state. For all practical purposes, his job was full-time pay for a part-time schedule. One of the factors that allowed him at his age of seventy-seven to continue to serve.

His record was without blemish. The judge had never had a conviction overturned. Any appeals were sooner or later found to have no basis. The man was excellent at what he did.

As he sat listening to the short summation from William Travis, he was secretly captivated by the story and the possibility of it being true. He thought this would be an interesting case to say the least.

"Your Honor, my client has absolutely no way of understanding the charges the prosecution has put forth and is contemplating filing against him. I have no ability to communicate to him what he is facing. We are simply making a motion that the prosecution provide the translator—at their expense—to proceed with arraignment and trial. It is required by law that the defendant completely understand any and all charges being brought against him. Unless the prosecution is considering not bringing charges at this time and releasing my client." William directed a questioning look toward the DA.

"Just hold your nonsense there, Mr. Travis," said JD Sneed. "I have no intentions whatsoever in not bringing your client to justice. However, isn't this suspect married? And doesn't his wife speak and understand both English and Comanche?"

Not knowing how the DA had come by this information, William decided he needed to have the hospital room swept for bugs. "Is it lawful for your office to eavesdrop on my client's private conversations?" William asked loudly.

"Your Honor, I won't have false accusations about my office spoken even in this pre-trial setting," JD Sneed replied, quickly losing his composure. William was learning quite easily how to push the man's buttons.

Judge Connelly never put up with pre-trial sparring from any attorney, especially in his quarters. "That's enough from you both. This is not complicated, counselor," he said, addressing the DA. "Go get yourself an interpreter if you wish to proceed. Mr. Travis, will you also be retaining your own consultant for your defense?"

"Yes, Your Honor, I have already done so. Mrs. Hantaywee of the Comanche Nation will translate and be a part of the defense team, with your approval."

"Approved," the judge ordered.

"Well," said Judge Connelly, glaring at the DA, "looks like the defense is way ahead of you on this again, JD. I suggest you get your act together. As for your suggestion that the defense is dragging its feet with, how did you put it… this interpreter bullshit, was it? That is clearly not the case. The arraignment schedule is still waiting on your office.

"As for the request to allow the suspect to either be charged within the time limits allowed or be set free," Judge Connelly continued, "I find the extenuating circumstances within my authority to hereby extend the detaining of the suspect. There is obviously enough evidence presented to hold the suspect over for trial. Tabbananica shall remain in custody; however, based on the note from the overseeing physician, Dr. Blake Tower, for now the defendant will remain confined to his room at the hospital. Furthermore, I have become aware of your attempt to circumvent hospital policy and the rights of the accused… and understand me clearly, Mr. District Attorney. Do you understand you have established grounds for appeal, or mistrial, by not allowing the suspect access to his attorney?"

JD Sneed was fuming. This judge was lecturing him? He swallowed his pride for the moment. "I apologize, Your Honor, it won't happen again."

What JD Sneed wanted to say was, don't you understand I am up for the appointment to the Court of Appeals that oversees your district? Instead JD Sneed remained silent. He would soon have the power to overturn every decision this judge sent down. However, he knew this case was important to that appointment. He would abide with this seemingly unfair treatment…for now.

"Alright then, how much time do you need, Mr. Sneed?" the judge asked, looking at his calendar.

"I would think we can secure an interpreter within the next forty-eight hours."

"Fine, I will set the arraignment hearing for next Monday, January 1 at ten a.m."

"That's New Year's Day, Your Honor?" JD Sneed questioned.

"That's correct," the judge said. "You get an extra twenty-four hours by my count. Better get busy, don't you think? And if you cannot proceed with the scheduled arraignment hearing you will leave me no choice but to release your suspect until such time as you are prepared to bring charges against him."

Judge David Connelly always made his best effort to be as fair and impartial as possible. However, the fact was he simply did not care for DA Sneed. The man had fumbled through several victories in his courtroom simply due to the fact that the judge himself had coached the man through the process of convicting easily winnable cases. He did so for the pure motive of convicting the guilty. Over the last several years, the judge had seen clear evidence of witness tampering and misconduct by the DA and his assistants. In short, Judge Connelly knew JD Sneed considered himself above the law and willing to break the law in order to win a case.

How to manage this case and this DA would prove difficult indeed. One thing was certain, Judge Connelly would do his best to make sure the truth came out during this trial.

Connelly knew JD Sneed was being considered by the judge's own friends and colleges for the Court of Appeals position. When the calls came, as they would soon, his report would not be favorable.

"That is all, counselors." The judge rose but paused for a moment. "Mr. Travis, could you please stay a moment?"

"Yes, Your Honor," William said.

JD Sneed turned and exited the chambers, fuming...again.

"Mr. Travis, if I were to do some research concerning the Comanche Nation in Texas to prepare me for this trial, where would you direct my reading?"

"The Council House Fight, The Great Raid, and The Battle on the San Saba would be a good start."

"Thank you, Mr. Travis. I have not studied on those accounts in years but have heard of them all. May I ask why those?"

"They all involved my client, either directly or his immediate family members."

The judge looked inquisitively at William. "By that, you mean he was present?"

William replied simply and directly. "Yes...evidently so, your Honor. The attack on his Camp on the San Saba occurred in late October of 1844, if I recall. According to my client, he and his wife entered the Dream Time the following day. After interviewing them both, they seemed to think they had only slept for a day or two, at the most. However, as unlikely as it may sound, upon their awakening, some 174 years had elapsed on Earth."

"Fascinating," the judge said.

"Yes, it is, isn't it?" "William said. "Your Honor, I know we can't and won't discuss the upcoming trial…but regarding that timeline and your study, from Tabbananica's, excuse me, my client's perspective…and his awareness of the time frame. His daughter was raped and murdered by the Texas Militia…just about a week ago. Again, from his perspective of time."

"This is somewhat hard to comprehend," the judge stated.

"Her name was Prairie Song. She was thirteen years old."

Chapter 50

January 1

Abby and Sana entered Tabba's hospital room for the fourth consecutive morning. The lessons were going well, Abby thought. Tabba also had a keen intellect and was quite good at sounds and mimicking the words she and Sana would speak.

"Good morning, Tabba," Abby said.

"Good morning, Abby, good morning, Sana." Tabba said, his voice strong and resplendent. Sana moved to him, embracing him tightly.

"*It is good to see you, my love. You are becoming stronger...I can see in your eyes, my husband,*" Sana said.

"*It is true. I have been up walking this room again today. The deer meat you are bringing me is helping. I am so grateful, my wife. I do not know this food the white man eats.*"

Opening her pack, Sana presented Tabba with more fresh roasted deer meat and a bowl of vegetable soup in a thermos. Tabba seemed famished again and began eating as the two settled in for a short English lesson.

Abby politely waited as Tabba quickly consumed the entire meal in less than five minutes. She began with a quick review of the alphabet sounds, then moved to the sight word cards. Tabba, while trying to please Sana, had repeated several words. It would soon be time to start putting the sight words together into phrases. Knowing that Tabba would be moved to the county jail today and discharged from the hospital, Abby whispered a silent prayer that she would indeed be given access to the prison to continue the lessons.

The knock on the door came early. The deputies entered the room and left the prison clothes for Tabba to wear to the hearing. Abby could tell what an insult it was to Tabba, as a man, in having to dress in the orange jumpsuit. It was extremely demeaning to him. Discarding his beautiful deer skins, along with the colorful beaded breastplate, the disgust on his face was obvious.

As Tabba removed his upper garments, Abby excused herself from the room, but not before noticing the perfectly sculpted muscles of Tabba's upper body. He looked, she thought, much like a trained athlete, perhaps a boxer or gymnast. She was amazed at the perfection of his physique. Sana was also admiring the beautiful body of her husband, longing for his touch.

Sana assisted Tabba with dressing in the awkward jumpsuit, then opened the door and motioned for Abby to re-enter the hospital room. Tabba sat on the edge of the bed, dressed in the orange jumpsuit.

"*I can endure this, my love. It is possibly only six moons?*" he asked staring into the eyes of his beautiful wife.

"*Yes, my husband, perhaps less…and remember I am yours forever, after.*"

The deputies knocked again and entered the room. They had a set of chains with them.

"Sorry, ma'am, following orders. He must wear these for the transport and while in the courtroom."

Tabba rose from the bed. He had seen and known shackles before. Proudly, yet somehow defiantly, Tabba held his hands out toward the deputies. They attached the shackles to his wrists. Then Tabba, without instruction, turned around and slightly spread his feet. The shackles were then attached to his ankles, the slack taken up so he could only take a partial stride.

He stared at the two deputies, knowing at any moment he could still easily take their lives. The two men were aware of the danger this man posed. Tabba could sense their fear. Good, he thought, these Texans were alive now only because of Topusana.

Sana caught her husband's eyes with a look and the knowing of his thoughts. She spoke.

"*I know it would be an easy thing for you, husband…please don't…please wait for me.*"

"*One thousand years would be an easy thing, my wife.*"

Abby and Sana exited the room behind Tabba. Tears began to flow down Sana's face, as she watched her husband struggle to walk along the hallway in the shackles. Sana remembered another time and place…so far away.

Abby, observing Sana, felt the rush of emotion also. The raw feelings that can only come from a mother as she witnesses her child struggle and suffer. The tears silently broke forth from Abby's own heart and ran down her face as Tabba was led away.

Grove County Courthouse
One Hour later

Tabba stood in the courtroom dressed in a state-issue orange jumpsuit, his hands and feet shackled, as the charges were read in his Native tongue by one Barbara Buckley, PhD.

Dr. Buckley was a specialist in Native Language Studies from the University of Kansas. While not exactly conversationally proficient at the language of the Comanche, she did understand and speak the basic dialect. She was the only person the DA's office could find on the planet who could be retained for the case. She had struck a quite lucrative deal.

After an exhaustive search of the Comanche Nation in Oklahoma, not one single tribal member would agree to assist the prosecution. JD Sneed departed the Lawton, Oklahoma, reservation at the request of the Tribal Police after losing his temper in the office of one Mary Running Deer. He would not be welcomed back on the reservation.

Tabba was, after the reading of the charges, completely confused. He had no idea what the women was speaking to him. Her words ran together and made no sense to him.

Turning to Grandmother, Tabba asked, *"What is the woman saying?"*

In her Native tongue, Grandmother attempted to question Dr. Buckley, who in turn did not understand the questions Grandmother had for her. Judge Connelly, seeing the confusion in his court room, began his own line of questioning.

"Mr. Travis, could your interpreter understand the charges read by the Prosecution?"

"Your Honor, I think it appropriate to simply question her yourself, she understands English perfectly."

"Very well. Mrs. Hantaywee, can you repeat, in English, the charges as read to the accused?"

Grandmother rose from her seat at the defense table. "Your Honor, this woman said there would be a murder charge, and then she talked about shooting a gun, and then she said there would be no time for hunting during the trial. I do not understand this woman. I think she may be drunk."

JD Sneed burst out with an objection, while Judge Connelly banged his gavel, calling for silence. "Mr. Sneed, overruled! I am questioning the defense and your expert. Now be silent while I attempt to understand what has been said."

"Dr. Buckley, could you repeat the charges?" the judge asked.

Dr. Buckley attempted again to read the charges to the defendant, finishing her statement awkwardly.

"What did you hear this time, Mrs. Hantaywee?" the judge asked.

"The same, Your Honor, I do not understand who would go hunting during a murder trial. But Tabba says he will agree not to do so."

William Travis addressed the court. "Your Honor, may counsel approach the bench?"

"I have a better idea, a ten minute recess. Mr. Sneed, Mr. Travis, in my chambers now."

Judge Connelly's Quarters

"Mr. Sneed, your expert translator has made it quite clear the accused may not go hunting during the trial," Judge Connelly said.

JD Sneed seemed quiet and smug for the moment. "It does seem she has misrepresented to me her abilities."

William Travis spoke next, and each knew what was coming. "Your Honor, as you know, my client has been held well past the ninety-six-hour limitation. I request he be immediately released, as the prosecution has not been able to bring the charges and arraignment as required by Texas law."

"I will take that request into consideration momentarily, counselor."

"Surely you can't seriously consider releasing this murderer! Your Honor, an officer has been killed! This man is a danger to our community! Not to mention a huge flight risk. I will not allow it!" JD Sneed was insolent and demanding.

"You will not allow it? Is that all, counselor?" Judge Connelly stated, staring in disbelief at the audacity of the district attorney's language.

There was a quiet pause as the judge appeared to consider his options.

"Mr. Travis, just for conversation's sake, where would the defendant reside in the event this court releases him?"

"He would be under the supervision of and residing at the Ross family home. And, Your Honor, may I disagree with the prosecution. I do not believe my client to be a flight risk whatsoever."

"And how is that?" JD Sneed rudely interrupted.

"That's enough, Mr. Sneed. Keep silent or I will find you in contempt," said the judge.

JD Sneed again bit his tongue in front of this ridiculous judge and the foolish path the man was considering.

"Go on, Mr. Travis, please explain."

"Your Honor, my client doesn't know how to drive an automobile, he has no identification, and no money for that matter. He speaks no known common language. He could never purchase a plane ticket or travel by any other means of mass transit without some type of identification, which I can assure he does not possess."

Judge David Connelly rose and said, "I'll need a few moments in my library. I trust you two can contain yourselves here for a moment?" The two attorneys nodded to one another as the judge exited the chambers to a small side study. The two men waited in silence.

Judge Connelly went straight to his reference books, although he already knew what must be done. The law was clear. Once again, this district attorney had not been prepared enough to conduct a simple arraignment hearing. The judge knew there was a way to keep Tabbananica in custody, but he would no longer assist this prosecutor in any way. On returning to his chambers, if the DA didn't know what course of action to take according to the law, the judge would release the suspect in an effort to conduct the process correctly. If he unlawfully detained the suspect, he may never face trial. As it was, he did not think the suspect Tabbananica was a flight risk by any means.

The judge had been studying. He knew where the Comanche Home Camp was located, on the property of the Ross family ranch. After his years of experience, he could read a man. He could tell this suspect wanted nothing more than to be free and return to his homeland.

He would most likely be free for a few days. The judge was certain the DA would find an adequate translator and the arraignment hearing would take place soon. Then the suspect would be incarcerated for the length of the proceeding and probably would face a lifetime sentence, or worse, after the sentencing phase.

He arose and moved through his chambers, quickly directing the two attorneys to re-adjourn in the courtroom.

"All rise," the bailiff ordered as the Honorable David Connelly entered the courtroom. The few spectators obliged, as did Tabba, Sana, Abby, David, Grace, and the prosecution team. Grandmother rose last, beginning to shuffle her feet and slightly moving rhythmically from side to side and humming softly.

"I hereby order the defendant released under the supervision of Mr. David Ross, until such time whereby, the prosecution is able to charge the defendant and those charges can be effectively communicated. Furthermore, if and when those events occur, the prosecution will need a competent translator in place to be interviewed by myself and the defense team prior to my approval. Is that understood?" The judge stared at Mrs. Buckley and JD Sneed.

"This court is now adjourned. Bailiff remove the shackles from the suspect. You are free to go for now, Mr. Tabbananica." The judge arose and exited the courtroom quickly but not before he heard the sound of singing coming from Mrs. Hantaywee, or Grandmother, as she was being referred to even in the courtroom.

Chapter 51

Tabba sat in the front of the pick-up truck, riding alongside David Ross. He was in awe of the speed at which they traveled and the smooth trail that had been carved into the earth for the purpose of driving as Sana had explained to him. He could not believe his woman actually knew how to steer one of the fast, sleek automobiles.

As the five arrived at the ranch house, David brought the truck to a stop near the barn. Grandmother exited and spoke to Tabba and Sana. *"I will have a meal prepared once you return from the cavern. I am rejoicing that you are now with us, my son."*

"Thank you, Grandmother, I am grateful for your assistance today," Tabba said. Directing his voice to David and Abby, Tabba spoke, *"And you, my new friends, I am beginning to see how you have protected and honored my wife while I was not able. With all that I am, I thank you for your kindness."* Sana quickly translated his words to English. David and Abby nodded, smiling.

"Where will you two stay, Sana?" Abby questioned.

"Mom, I do not think Tabba can stay inside your beautiful home. For the time being we may stay in the cavern or perhaps the barn."

Abby, looking concerned, started to speak, but David interrupted. "Why don't you two decide for yourselves. There is another bunk room on the opposite end of the barn. We can install another wood burning stove there if you prefer. The decision is for you and Tabba."

Sana translated for Tabba, who replied, *"I will build us a small lodge on our old Home Camp across the black ribbon. It is an easy thing for me to do.*

204

By tomorrow evening, the smoke will rise from the lodge. We will start our new beginning on our old Homeland, upon the land of our ancient Camp."

"It is a good plan, Husband."

Grandmother excused herself to prepare dinner. Abby and David were simply exhausted from the stress and activities of the last few days. The two climbed the stairs and were both sound asleep for a long afternoon nap before pulling the covers over themselves.

Grace was just entering the drive ,arriving from the courthouse. She made her way to her room to return some long overdue phone calls. She had ignored most of her correspondence from friends and business associates over the last few days. It would be a relief for her to finally have some time alone to catch up.

Tabba and Sana promised to return shortly, they needed to retrieve their buffalo robes and the few worldly possessions from the cavern. They turned and began the trek up to the little cavern above the garden, this same walk they had made hundreds of times.

****

The fire Tabba had kindled crackled softly, the dim light it gave reflecting off the cavern wall. Sana came to him. The glimmer in her eyes shone brightly, her warm supple body caressing his muscled torso in the embrace. The two undressed, observing the natural beauty of one another's bodies, desire rising, the two unashamed.

Moving beneath the buffalo robes, they kissed passionately and became one flesh. Time seemed to stand still under the warmth of the buffalo hide, in the security of one another's arms at long last. The yearning desire and longing of their bodies and souls intertwined. It seemed they had waited an eternity for one another.

New sounds once again filled the cavern. Sounds of pleasure, fulfillment, ecstasy. The sounds echoed softly through the small cavern in the Texas hills.

****

In a way that only a woman can know, Sana knew in the depths of her womb his seed had taken hold of her body and soul.

After Prairie Song's birth, Sana had prayed many times for the Great Spirit to bless her with other children. Who could know the mysteries of the Great Spirit? She knew it was the Spirit who gave direction to a woman's womb.

Topusana also knew in her heart, without a doubt, she would once again bear Tabbananica a child. Later, resting in the comfort of her husband's arms, she laughed aloud at the gift of motherhood.

"*What is it, woman? I will teach you to laugh,*" whispered Tabba.

Smiling, with the look of desire in his eyes, Tabba reached for her again. The two writhed in ecstasy under the buffalo robe as the fire burned softly in their little cavern.

Topusana was indeed…alive!

Chapter 52

January 2

Tabba, the sweat pouring from his brow, worked feverishly cutting small trees and shaping the poles for his new lodge. He had already selected and cleared the brush from the small rise of land near the edge of the San Saba River. The site was expertly concealed from view. He would make the lodge scarcely detectable from the surrounding trees along the river. Using some standing timber for part of the lodge's roof line, it would blend perfectly into the backdrop of water and vegetation.

David watched the laborious process from across the highway, finally saying to Abby he couldn't take not helping any longer. At the objection of Abby, he loaded his chainsaw into the backhoe bucket and drove the machine down the drive and across the highway.

With Tabba and Sana greeting him, he offered his assistance. Tabba was just beginning to level by hand the small embankment. He began explaining through Sana the necessity for a level floor, and the sinking of the living area below the natural surface of the ground. *"This will provide an added level of warmth, to lower the entire area."*

David, understanding the idea, started the backhoe and within ten minutes had dug the area down two feet and leveled it perfectly.

Tabba was astounded at the amount of earth the machine could lift and move effortlessly. Admiring the progress, Tabba began to take the trunks of trees he had cut with his ax and assemble a few logs into the beginnings of a circular frame.

David, understanding the process, used a tape measure to get the correct length. Then moved down river slightly and began cutting the perfectly correct size trees with the chainsaw. Loading them in the bucket, within an hour he had more than enough small logs to complete the structure.

Again, Tabba was in awe of the amount of work that could be done with the "beaver saw," as he called it. Smiling at David and patting him on the back, Tabba said in English, "Good work."

Now Tabba, directing David, with Sana translating, showed David the plan for the lean-to roof. David made the measurements, returning in another half an hour with more than enough cuttings for the roof structure. All the while, Tabba was trimming and cutting cedar boughs for placement on the roof frame.

Within another hour the structure was complete. Sana had covered the entire floor area with buffalo hides and robes. She hung a few pieces of bead work around the comfortable little lodge.

"Now we only need a fire pit," Tabba said.

David, with Sana translating, said, "I have a gift for you, if you will permit me. I'll be right back." Starting the backhoe, David returned to the barn and loaded the newly purchased wood burning stove into the front bucket. Pulling up to the site, David unloaded the stove and insulated pipe at the entrance to the lodge.

Taking the lead, Tabba moved the stove into place and ran the pipe through the cedar roof, attaching the insulated collar where the pipe penetrated the roof. Then Tabba, climbing a nearby tree, attached the chimney top piece into place. Within a few minutes, Sana had a fire crackling, the wood burning stove already warming the small structure.

"Now the woman's work," Sana said. "I will fill the cracks between the wooden poles with mud and straw from the river."

"I can use the machine to help," David said.

Tabba and Sana watched as David drove the machine into the river. Turning it around with the bucket partially filled with water, he lifted the bucket slightly higher. David then plowed into the riverbank and up, gathering mud and straw and water into the bucket.

The two were amazed as Sana sank her hands into the five hundred pounds of material the machine held. Adding a slight amount of straw here and there, within the hour she completely sealed the structure. The mixture began slowly drying in the afternoon sun.

The lodge would be warm and dry. A perfect little home for now.

David slapped Tabba on the back, smiled, and shook the man's hand. It was a good day's work. But as often happens when men work together, a bonding had taken place.

Tabba had never in his life trusted a white man. However, this man David J. Ross had shown something to Tabbananica this day. Sana, seeing the friendship forming throughout the day, whispered to her husband, "*As I told you, my husband, this man is our friend. He and his woman Abby will help us in many ways.*"

"*I heard your grandfather say to me when I was a very young boy, 'the white man cannot be trusted.' And it was true for him in his time. This man is different; this is a man I believe I can trust.*"

The songs of Old Grandmother could be heard softly. The three looked toward the highway and saw the old woman approaching along with Abby and Grace. Grandmother carried the cook pot and Abby a pitcher of lemonade. Grandmother called out, "*It is time to bless this new home and share a meal.*"

The six entered the little lodge on the San Saba, sitting in a circle on the buffalo robes. The stove glowed with warmth. The songs, the gratefulness, the worship permeated the atmosphere of the lodge and touched the hearts of those within its shelter.

After the meal, with the quiet talk of friends gracing the new home, Grandmother looked slyly at Topusana and asked in English.

"Are you thinking of any names yet for the boy child?" The comment brought an immediate silence to the dinner. Awareness of what she had spoken was slowly realized by everyone except Tabba, who looked questioningly to Sana.

Abby screamed with excitement, as did Grace, while the three hugged one another with joy at the news.

"But how... how can you know...in one day? And how can Grandmother know?" Grace asked.

"Yes, child, it is true; these things are whispered to me by the Great Spirit, and to any who care to be still and listen," Grandmother said.

Tabba rose, his awareness of the topic dawning in his mind.

"*I ask about the name for a reason, my child. There are two boys within your womb. You need not one name but two names to consider. You will soon receive a double blessing from the Great Spirit,*" Old Grandmother said.

Tabbananica, the Warrior, began to understand and realized he would soon have two sons. The Warrior, upon hearing this revelation, did not understand nor could he stop the water that came forth from his eyes.

Chapter 53

The phone in David's office rang. He picked up the receiver and listened. Fred Mason was calling as a courtesy, alerting him to the warrant that had just been issued for Tabba's arrest.

"You want to just bring him in, David?" the sheriff asked. "The DA wants a scene; he's even notified the press and attempted to get me to adhere to his schedule for the production. I'll have none of this bullshit," Fred said. "If you could bring him in, say around 10:30? Use the rear entrance to my office. I'll have my deputies waiting. The show isn't supposed to take place until 3:00, so I think we can avoid it altogether."

"Fred, thank you for the consideration."

"Well, I won't be manipulated into the circus act," the sheriff said. "And you're welcome, David."

8:15 A.M.

Tabba and Sana had spent the last two weeks together. In many ways it was the best two weeks of their entire lives. No longer did they constantly scan the brush and hillsides for the white soldiers and rangers as they went about their activities.

The two lived free and in peace, in a way they had not been able to their entire lives. Tabba continued work on the lodge, shaping the ground around the structure so water flowed away from it. Piling branches and leaves around and against the structure until it blended into the surroundings and was difficult to detect even when a person was quite close to the lodge. The two hunted together and prepared meals each night in the peaceful comfort of their little home.

The English lessons continued each morning with Abby. Tabba was learning quickly; he could already speak a few basic phrases and could identify many common objects. In the relaxed atmosphere and with no longer the danger of conflict each and every day and night, the two slept and loved and enjoyed for the first time in their lives…just living.

Living at peace.

Lying on the buffalo robes on this quiet morning, Tabba asked Sana how her heart was feeling concerning Prairie Song.

"Come, let me show you something." Rising, she led him out of the lodge and headed across the highway and onto the porch of the Ross's home.

Sana knocked gently on the door of the ranch house. Abby opened the huge front door and greeted the two.

"You don't have to knock, sweetheart." Abby gave Sana a warm hug.

"Mom, I need to show Tabba the painting," Sana spoke softly.

In the beautiful dormered room overlooking their former Home Camp, the two stood frozen, hand in hand. The Warrior again losing control of his tears.

"How is a thing such as this possible, Sana?" asked Tabba.

"It is a long and unbelievable story, my husband."

Tabba stared into the painting and spoke aloud his thoughts. *"You are the perfect mother."* He could not take his eyes off the painting. His wife. His daughter.

"Tell me, Husband, what you remember of this day."

Tabba paused. *"It will help you?"*

"Yes…I need to remember."

Tabba spoke, recalling. *"The cold. I have never been that cold in my entire lifetime. The frozen prairie was crystal white. And I remember the hunger. I remember the prayers of Tosahwi. I remember the responsibility I felt as Neeko and I set out. I remember praying myself and thinking…How can a father protect a child from such a thing as hunger?"*

Sana smiled, recalling those were her exact thoughts that day.

Tabba continued. *"When we finally caught up to the buffalo, I was so determined. Although it was an easy hunt. The wind was so severe the beasts never saw us or heard us, no chase, no challenge from the animal we killed. The buffalo was simply huddled on the prairie. I walked right up to it and drove a lance into its belly. The buffalo gave up its life easily.*

"It was an answered prayer.

"I remember wanting to ride as fast as I could back to you and Prairie Song. Neeko made me think and move slowly and cautiously. He wanted to be certain we made it back with the meat. We walked, leading the ponies, to carry as much meat as possible.

"And I remember the two white men we met. We let them go. It seemed more important to return to The People *than worry with two lost white men trying to find the soldier fort.*

"They were strange men. One stood for a long time, drawing in a book as we walked away." Tabba clearly recalled the time.

"The man you met, Tabba, was Karl Bodmer. He is the man who created this painting."

Tabba paused in awe. Remembering. Reliving that long-ago day.

"It is good to remember a story of our family with a happy ending, my husband," whispered Sana through a mist of tears.

"Yes, indeed it is, my wife. After we set up a few teepees and started the fires, we were warm and full and safe that cold winter night. Prairie Song seemed so happy." Tabba remembered the sweet smile on his daughter's face.

The two stood and held one another for a long time as they stared and remembered. A kind of healing took place. Tabba was glad in his heart this painting existed. He would plan to come here often…to remember.

However, Sana knew deep in her soul, this would be the last morning the two would spend together, possibly for many moons. The times were still not clear in her vision.

10:00 A.M.

David and William walked across the road down to the lodge on the banks of the San Saba river. Smoke curled from the little chimney, a light breeze beginning to stir. David thought the breeze slightly warm for January. The sun shone brightly, reflecting off the water. The sound of the river gurgling and the smell of the burning wood caused William Travis to pause.

"David, it could actually be 1844 or now. It is hard to tell from what is in my field of vision."

In either time, the scene would be exactly as it presented itself.

Sana answered the knock. She could tell the news was not good. Abby was just finishing up the morning's English lesson. Tabba was improving rapidly, she thought.

"I just got the call. Tabba needs to be at the Sheriff's office by 10:30," David said. "I guess the good news is there will not be an arrest. We can take him in. Fred will allow him to surrender himself to the court."

Tabba rose from his seated position. "I am ready. May I have a moment with my wife?"

David, Abby, and William exited the lodge and waited outside.

"Have they issued an arrest warrant?" Abby asked.

"Yes, however it was considerate of the sheriff to allow us to deliver him to the jail. The arraignment hearing is at 4:00 p.m.," William said.

"*I won't be long, my wife.*" Tabba embraced his wife. "*I wonder, will I see my sons born?*"

"*It is still not clear to me, Tabba.*"

"*Even in the unknown, thinking of my sons will give me strength,*" Tabba said.

The two exited the lodge and all crossed the highway. Moving slowly, enjoying the few moments together with their friends, not knowing what lay before them nor how long they would be apart, Sana could feel the separation already. She thought it strange how this feeling of separation could occur while holding her husband's hand.

Old Grandmother was awaiting them on the porch. "We must go now. Tabba needs to be delivered by 10:30. I am ready to translate."

David and Abby were becoming used to Old Grandmother knowing things that had not been communicated to her...at least not in the normal way that communication took place for most. William was amazed...again.

The group loaded into the double cab pickup and headed to town, with one unusual request.

"May I drive again, David?" Tabba asked.

Smiling, David said, "Of course. Just try and keep it under ninety this time. The girls are with us." The two friends shared a brief smile.

Later That Afternoon

District Attorney JD Sneed waited outside the sheriff's office until 3:00 p.m. The film crews also waited in the production trucks, engines running.

Entering the offices, he demanded to know why the sheriff was late for the arrest. He further questioned the exact location of the deputy units.

Following instructions from the sheriff, the dispatcher on duty said she was not allowed to disclose information on pending arrests or the location of the deputies on duty.

JD Sneed was fuming. He demanded to speak with the sheriff immediately.

"I'll let him know you're here," the dispatcher said. After a few more minutes of waiting, Sneed, with the news crews in tow, departed in a "fit," as the dispatcher described the encounter to her boss, Sheriff Mason.

JD Sneed drove out of town along the main highway at a rate of speed the news vans could not keep pace with. Arriving at the Ross ranch, he quickly discovered the gate to the home was locked. No one answered the call button as he pushed it repeatedly. It appeared no one was home. There were no sheriff units anywhere in sight. Then news crews arrived, hastily set up, and began to record.

Sneed's cell phone rang, his assistant informing him he was late for the arraignment hearing and that the suspect was already in the courtroom. In a rage, Sneed swore loudly and threw his cell phone across the highway…in a temper tantrum the news outlets film crew recorded.

The event would play on the evening news stations out of San Antonio for three consecutive evenings. Fox News and CNN also ran the clip throughout the following day.

As JD Sneed sped away toward the courthouse, the film crews in trail attempted to follow, quickly losing ground.

As the vehicles disappeared to the east, the highway became still and quiet. Tosahwi exited the cover on the south side of the black ribbon. He located the shiny box the man had thrown across the road and placed it in his day pack.

Three miles down the highway the deputy clocked the automobile driven by JD Sneed at 105 mph. The resulting pursuit took an additional ten miles before JD Sneed eventually pulled over to the side of the road.

The deputy, as instructed, took his time in issuing the speeding citation.

The news crews in trail of the district attorney eventually caught up to the scene and recorded most of the traffic stop. The producers had a difficult time editing the recording of the event for broadcast as the tirade of language from JD Sneed made most of the video unintelligible due to the bleeps required for the airing of the recording.

Sheriff Mason, and his entire staff, enjoyed reviewing the dashcam footage of the event over coffee and donuts the following morning.

Chapter 54

4:45 PM
Grove County Courthouse

We are all glad you could join us, Mr. Sneed." Judge Connelly, glancing at his watch, was clearly irritated.

"I apologize, Your Honor, I, uh, well, I was—"

"Save it, Mr. Sneed. Are you prepared to proceed?"

"Yes, Your Honor."

Tabba stood before the judge as the charges of capital murder and attempted capital murder were read. He understood every word spoken from the translator. Grandmother repeated the charges to Tabba in Comanche and then translated to William what she had heard in English. Dr. Rainwater also translating for the prosecution table.

Judge Connelly asked for confirmation from the defense. "Is the reading clear and correct, Grandmother?"

"Yes, Your Honor, this thing is understood."

"Dr. Rainwater?"

"Yes, Your Honor, the translation is correct," she said.

JD Sneed had done his homework. He had discovered that the dialect was an Uto-Aztecan language that was also spoken by the Shoshone Tribe. He had located a translator from Utah who even understood the subtle differences in the two dialects. After the interview with Grandmother, the judge and the defense had approved Dr. Rainwater's inclusion for the prosecution as a translator.

Dr Rainwater was expensive but proved her worth and necessity. She sat quietly, regally even, William Travis thought. She indeed looked very much the modern Native American woman she was. She was dressed in a beautiful black lace dress and knee-high black leather moccasins. Her high cheek bones and jet-black hair, which was pulled back at the nape of her neck and tied with a turquoise ribbon, were striking. To William, her appearance was simply stunning. She was adorned in beautiful turquoise bracelets with matching earrings and the most striking color William had ever seen in the squash blossom necklace that hung around her neck.

This was the second time William had admired the woman's presence. He was enthralled at her natural beauty.

He had not been attracted to any woman in the way he was now thinking, in a very long time. "Get a hold of yourself, counselor," he said to himself. "Stop acting like a schoolboy…you have a serious job to do here."

Dr. Rainwater was thrilled to be here. From her studies in Native American History and Faith, she knew of the medicine of the Dream Time. It was an honor for her to meet Tabbananica. She was fascinated by his story and that of his woman, Topusana.

The judge, while directing his inquiry to William, asked, "And how does the defendant plead to the stated charges?"

William rose from his seat at the defense table. "Not guilty, Your Honor."

"And will you be requesting a bail hearing, Mr. Travis?"

"Yes, we will, Your Honor," answered William on behalf of the defense.

"I'll save us all some time. That will not be permitted. There will be no bail allowed in this case. Is that understood?" said the judge.

William had known it would never be allowed, but it never hurt to try.

"Yes, Your Honor." William said.

"I hereby order the defendant remanded into custody immediately, awaiting trial for the stated charges. Sheriff, you may now take custody."

The two deputies moved alongside Tabba, who had already been dressed in the prison clothing and shackled in the chains.

"Just to tidy up a few issues. We will hold a hearing at 10:00 a.m. tomorrow to determine if the prosecution intends to seek the death penalty. Are there any objections to moving forward on this issue?" spoke Judge Connelly.

"None from the prosecution, Your Honor." JD Sneed answered. "It is my intention to seek the death penalty."

"Is there any objection from the defense?" repeated Judge Connelly.

"Yes, I object vehemently, Your Honor." William stated.

"Fine then, 10:00 a.m. tomorrow it is," the judge stated. "We are well ahead of the ballgame here. We will impanel a jury this week. Let's talk trial date, gentleman, shall we?"

The judge wasn't asking but ordering the respective counsels. This would be quick and efficient, William thought.

"I suggest one week from today. Thoughts?" continued the judge.

"We are prepared to begin prosecution on that date, Your Honor," JD Sneed said, addressing the judge and defense.

The judge peered toward William and awaited an answer.

"I don't see how we could be ready, Your Honor. The prosecution has not released its witness and evidentiary statements of discovery to the defense. We will need time to prepare based on that information," William said.

"OK, how much time do you need?" asked the judge.

"Well, more than a week, Your Honor," spoke William.

"Fine, I'll double your time needed. I hereby order trial to commence on January 30, two plus weeks from today. Mr. Sneed, you will notify the jury, once selected, there will be a pretrial meeting the day before with the assembled jurors."

"Understood, Your Honor," Sneed said.

"Are you with me, Mr. Travis? You look confused," spoke Judge Connelly.

"Um, yes, Your Honor, we will be prepared. I respectfully request the documents be turned over to me today," William said.

"So, ordered…Mr. Sneed?" said the judge.

"Yes, Your Honor, I will see to it."

The judge banged his gavel. "This court is now adjourned. Sheriff."

Fred Mason rose and moved across the room. Taking Tabba by the arm, he led him away to his jail cell.

Chapter 55

January 18

The jury selection had taken place over the last two days. William Travis and the defense team had studied the potential list. They were at a distinct disadvantage, as DA JD Sneed had polled most of the possible jurors many times over in his tenure as district attorney. He knew most of the jury pool personally.

William had hired a local attorney to assist him in the process. David's and Abby's input, though limited, also helped tremendously, as they also were familiar with many from the pool of prospective jurors. William knew nothing about any of them.

The list was being narrowed rapidly as the DA seemed to instantly know he had no need to question several of the potential jurors.

William was looking for one thing in a potential juror: sympathy. Having only six strikes, he used all six for each juror to which the DA had no objections. William knew without a doubt he had used the strikes successfully as he watched the temperament and demeanor of JD Sneed change with each strike the defense used. All those struck from the pool were older white males.

The jury makeup, William knew, was very much now up to the prosecution. JD Sneed would determine the remaining participants of the jury panel. In a huge gamble, William began harsh questioning of the jurors he himself wanted to serve. JD Sneed took the bait, allowing these prospective jurors to be chosen.

Judge David Connelly saw through the strategy of the defense immediately, admiring the tactic from William Travis. JD Sneed saw none of the gamble and tactic. He unknowingly allowed a sympathetic jury of five men, one of whom was Hispanic, and seven women—one of African American descent, two Hispanic, and the remaining four older white women.

The jury was impaneled and seated. A foreman was elected. The alternate also being a Hispanic American, once illegal, but now a legal citizen. Lupe, as she was known, had five children all one year apart. All five children were raised speaking Spanish only at home. All five had learned to read and write English, solely due to the concerted effort of their first-grade teacher Mrs. Abigail Ross.

David hoped someone might possibly be unable to serve, allowing Lupe a seat.

William was elated as he and David sat once again in David's study going over each juror and what David knew of their respective back grounds.

"Your foreman is my greatest concern," David said, pondering his history with the man. "Jim Bob Skaggs is a crook."

Jim Bob Skaggs owned and operated the local funeral home in Little Grove, Texas. David knew of several accusations against the man, all by innocent family members who were quite simply, as David put it… "screwed over royally." The man had no ethics whatsoever when it came to charging the exorbitant fees for his "services." Wealthy and poor families alike were taken advantage of, at the most difficult times of their lives—upon the death of a family member.

David despised the man. He knew several former employees who over the years had confided in David or Abby about the mistreatment the man administered to those under his employment. Verbal abuse, intimidation, and bullying, including the most unimaginable assortment of swear words any sailor could contrive, was how the man managed his employees. Demeaning and immoral behavior was a daily tactic for Jim Bob Skaggs. Several individuals had left his employment with stories of intimidation and threats of blackmail were they to reveal any of the secrets of his business "billing and collection policies."

Knowing how ruthless Jim Bob Skaggs was behind the scenes, it made David's stomach turn when attending a funeral. He would see Jim Bob Skaggs switch personalities instantaneously. The man could put on such a sincere voice and persona, becoming the meek and mild funeral director. David saw through the act, Jim Bob Skaggs behaving as if he cared about the loss of a loved one. David knew he did not care one iota. David thought the display bordered on bi-polar behavior.

"So how does a man of that character succeed in any business?" William asked.

"The way many that have come before him do. Firstly, he has a monopoly," David said.

"And?"

"Secondly, he is a deacon in the biggest church in town and also the Sunday morning organist," David said. William looked shocked.

"Yep, the sheep are often the most easily deceived," David said. "And once you make that club, evidently, you're in for life, no matter your behavior toward the public That man will not be supportive of your cause."

William Travis, ever the attorney, wondered how he might use this man's ethics, or lack of, to his advantage.

Chapter 56

There was something *off* on the dashcam video. William continued to run the clip over and over again. He could not quite put his finger on what was wrong, but something was not right. The video was smooth and unbroken as he viewed it, but there was something. He decided to call an old friend from Naval Intelligence.

Commander Bryce Houston (United States Navy Retired) had arrived via the CJ 3 business jet just this morning. Steve, David's pilot, delivered him to William's new office on the square in Little Grove, Texas. David had agreed to meet with the two. David Ross was not easily impressed; however, Commander Bryce Houston was an impressive individual.

"Mr. Ross, may I say I'm deeply sorry for your loss, sir, belated as it is."

David peered directly into the man's eyes.

"I knew Jonathan personally. He was one of the best. We often worked together…on his missions. I never knew a braver soul," Commander Houston said.

"Please call me David, and thank you, sir, for what you've done, and are doing now."

Commander Houston, David recalled, was a computer espionage specialist. The man knew more about computers than most any person on the planet. He had spent his life defending the nation from cyber attacks, uncovering terrorists' plots, and tracking criminals across the globe. All from a small office in Maryland that housed Naval Intelligence.

After a little catching up, William and Commander Houston went right to work on the dashcam video.

Commander Houston, or Bryce, as William called him, watched in awe as the story unfolded before them.

With his first viewing, Bryce was so enthralled with the activity itself he didn't notice much about the clip technically. The video clearly showed a man running in front of Officer Reuter's patrol truck, carrying a deer over his shoulders. The man was obviously Native American and dressed as such. The next scenes were of the empty highway in front of the vehicle. The audio portion of the digital clip recorded a call for backup to another warden who was less than ten minutes from the scene. There were several unintelligible sounds for a few seconds. Officer Reuter then shouted instructions directed toward the suspect.

"Stop! Dammit…I said stop!" The commands were distinctly audible on the recording. Then the suspect appeared clearly in the camera's view, climbing the embankment on the highway. The Native American man turned and faced directly toward the vehicle.

The audio portion of the clip seemed to have some type of glitch or error in it at this point on the recording. The digital video data continued to run; however, the sound on the recording simply disappeared. Bryce leaned forward, his interest piqued by not what he saw, but what he heard…or more precisely, did not hear.

Running the clip back again he began to take notes on a legal pad. The siren from Officer Reuter's vehicle could be heard, and then silenced as it appeared the siren was turned off. Then the sound of the vehicle door opening. At exactly 6:01:45 on the digital timer—this time stamp reflected the time Officer Reuter had been on duty—the audio portion of the clip went silent. At the time stamp 6:01:47.3 the audio data again was heard perfectly. At 6:01:49.5 Officer Reuter came into view of the camera; the sound now clearly heard again on the audio portion as he moved forward a few steps toward the suspect with his weapon drawn. At precisely 6:01:50.5 the suspect could be seen knocking an arrow and firing it from his bow at the officer. Officer Reuter was standing near the left front bumper of the Game Department vehicle, in full view of the camera.

The impact was audible; however, the flight path and projection of the arrow as it flew through the air could not be seen. The sound of grunting was heard as the officer fell to the ground. Blood could be seen spattered across the hood of the vehicle. The suspect came into full view now as he approached the officer's vehicle. The man slowly drew what appeared to be a hatchet, or some type of club, from his belt. The audio portion clearly recorded the man

222

shouting at the officer in some unknown language, Bryce assuming correctly from the story it was Comanche.

The voice was loud and clear and echoed slightly on the recording. As the man approached, Officer Reuter fired four consecutive shots at time stamp 6:03:30. All the pistol shots missing badly as he did not, from what could be seen, appear to even take aim. It was obvious the officer was losing strength from the blood loss. The suspect let out some type of cry or call that sent shivers up the spine of one Commander Bryce Houston.

As the suspect raised his weapon, a fierceness could be seen on the man's face and in his eyes even, Commander Houston thought. The video captured the impact of the weapon, the sound of Officer Reuter's skull cracking could be heard. The blood spattering across the front of the vehicle and even on the windshield in front of the camera was clearly seen on the recording.

The video ran for another thirty-two minutes until the sheriff deputies investigating the scene turned off the vehicle's engine and stopped the recording.

Commander Houston sat in silence a few moments as he reflected on what he had seen and heard.

The brutality of the attack was sickening, although, having worked in Iraq and Afghanistan, it was nothing he hadn't seen before. He was more impressed with the accuracy and skill of the suspect's bow shot, the fierceness of the attack, and the voice the man possessed.

Breaking the silence, William asked, "What do you think, Bryce?"

"I think I don't want to piss this guy off....That voice?" he said.

"Impressive, is it not?" William said. "I've heard the warden was found, um, having urinated on himself." The three men sat in silence again for a few seconds, pondering exactly how that could certainly happen.

"I have the dashcam video from the second vehicle also. If you're ready?" William said.

"Let's talk about this one for a minute first. I suppose you have had the audio translated?" Bryce asked.

"Yes, what I have here is a transcript if you want to read it along with the video running; it helped me." William said.

"Let's do it," Bryce said, as the two watched again.

Commander Houston was able to fill in what he thought was the correct timing for the first phrase.

"Will you never cease?" followed by, "Are you the one who killed my daughter?"

"Wow, he's actually questioning him?" Bryce said.

"Taunting him might be a better word," William said.

Then the translation said, "This is Comanche land! This is my Land!" Followed by, "Do you feel my arrow in your belly!" The final taunt or statement, "I am Tabbananica, Voice of the Sun!"

Commander Houston played the clip again, reading the translation aloud as it played. Taking his pen and legal pad again, he began to take a few notes. William sat patiently as his friend paused several times and continued to write. Finishing his thoughts, Commander Houston said, "Let's see the other video now."

The three sat enthralled again as the second video played. The dashcam from Warden Bryant's vehicle showed the entire event from the time he arrived on the scene with the dashcam in his own vehicle running. The officer undoubtedly could be heard identifying himself as he exited the vehicle and requested the suspect to lower his…bow. The call for backup and the officer down call were also clearly recorded.

Both the bow shots at Officer Bryant fired from the suspect were clearly seen, along with the gruesome audio of both arrows loudly cracking bones. The shot from Warden Bryant's service weapon was distinctly audible. The impact of the bullet and its effect on the suspect was also clearly seen, the suspect falling on the ice-covered road twice, not rising the second time.

William stopped the recording at that point.

"Is there more?" Bryce asked.

"Yes, there is. But let's think through what you have seen," said William.

"What did your translator say about the loud cry, prior to the attack with the club?" Bryce asked.

"She said it was a War Cry, the weapon a war club, an item evidently carried by all Comanche Warriors. She also said something very interesting about Warden Reuter after watching the tape. Bryce, I believe this woman has some kind of spiritual insight."

"So, is she a Medicine Woman?" Bryce asked.

"Well, yes, she is. I would like for you to meet her. Doing so may explain a lot," William said.

"OK. What did she have to say?" asked Bryce.

"She said, while pointing to Warden Reuter on the video screen, 'This was a bad man!'"

"Do you believe what she said?" Bryce asked his friend.

"I have one of my paralegals researching his background now. So far, the DA and the Game Department won't release any records to us, which raises my suspicions," William said.

"Good point. What is there to hide?" Bryce asked.

"Obviously something," William said, quietly thinking to himself.

"Do you notice the difference in responses from each of the wardens, William?" asked Bryce.

"Yes, clearly Officer Reuter did not identify himself in any fashion as a law enforcement officer."

"I noticed that also."

"So, anything else *off* from your expertise?" William asked.

"Yes, there is, Will. I'm glad you called me. This data has clearly been tampered with," he stated very matter-of-factly. "Our job will be to determine who did so, when it was changed, and on who's device." Commander Bryce Houston replied.

David Ross sat in silence the entire meeting. Listening, observing. The four shots that came from Officer Reuter's gun he remembered. He sat concentrating on what he remembered from the morning of the attack. Suddenly, it dawned on him what was not on the tape.

The first shot. A single shot.

He had heard it coming from the west, just down the highway, thinking it was a hunter. He had commented to Topusana about the gunshot; she had heard it also while returning from the cavern. Abby had also heard the initial single shot.

There had been six gunshots the morning of the attack. One single shot that he and Abby and Topusana had heard. A few minutes later they all heard the four shots that were on the recorded dashcam. And a few minutes after that they heard the one shot from Officer Bryant's weapon, as recorded on the dashcam in his unit.

David knew what Commander Houston was so matter-of-factly stating about the evidence. It had been altered. The first shot evidently from Officer Reuter's gun had been erased from the dashcam audio. By someone.

Chapter 57

Why? Why would the DA or Sheriff's Department or the Game Department risk altering the video from a murder scene? The sheriff's reports would also need to be altered to match the video. How many people could be in on this cover-up, William wondered. He was quickly making a list of the possible individuals or departments that could have had access to do so. It was not a very long list.

"The most important question is, Why?" Commander Houston stated.

"The obvious answer is there's something they don't want heard," replied William.

"That could only be a gunshot… the first gunshot I heard," David said.

"David, having three witnesses corroborate the number of shots fired that morning will be powerful testimony. But we need more," William said.

"Tabba still has no recollection of the number of shots fired at him?" Bryce asked.

"None whatsoever." William said, deep in thought. "Perhaps that can help us in some way."

"Let's look at what we do know, and if this first shot is possible. The sound on the audio stops at 6:01:45.0. It picks up again at 6:01:47.3. We're missing 2.3 seconds of audio," Commander Houston said, reviewing his notes. "Then we see Officer Reuter at 6:01:48.8 with his weapon drawn, 1.5 seconds after the audio has begun recording again. A total of 3.8 seconds he is out of sight of the camera. For 2.3 of those seconds there is no audio. What can happen in 2.3 plus 1.5 seconds before we see Officer Reuter?"

"That's 3.8 seconds total," William said, acting out the motion of stepping out of a truck door, drawing a weapon, and firing, then moving forward three steps.

David began timing the movement. "Four seconds exactly," David said.

The three men thought through the enactment. "Of course, we need to be much more precise. Measure the distance from the truck door to the camera view. We can have a specialist recreate a recording of the movement," Commander Houston said.

"Will, what is the significance if Tabba was fired on first?" David asked.

William thought through the scenario. "If that were so and there was no warning issued, then this entire event is, to put it simply, an act of self-defense."

"Let me show you the rest of the video," William said. He started the video of the dashcam from Officer Reuter's vehicle again.

There was no sound, and the lack of sound this time was accurate. The view down the highway showed through the blood-spattered windshield of Officer Reuter's truck. In the distance three men were lying on the ice-covered road. They noted the reflection of Officer Bryant's emergency lights flashing colorfully and brightly in the distance.

A figure appeared; at first it resembled a large animal moving down the hill on the north side of the highway. As the figure moved closer, leaping over the fence, it was apparent now that whatever it was it was walking upright… like a man. As the figure drew nearer, singing could be heard. A few moments later the figure appeared close enough to be identified as a man. The man was wearing a huge buffalo robe and some kind of deer hat or cape across his upper torso, complete with head, horns, and eyes.

The singing was clearly heard on the recording as the man appeared to wave his hands over the dead body of Officer Reuter.

The three men were captivated by what they were seeing on the video. All remained speechless as the recorded data continued to play. The video continued to record the sound of the singing, the words clearly not in English. Commander Houston and David knew it had to be Comanche.

The man moved down the road, kneeling over Tabba's body. He reached into a bag strung around his neck, evidently applying some type of treatment to Tabba's gunshot wound.

William stopped the video and switched to the dashcam video from Officer Bryant's truck.

Again, the singing, or chanting perhaps was a better description, could be heard. The man kneeled before Officer Bryant, again applying some type of powder to his wounds from what David recognized now as a medicine bag dangling from around his neck. Then the man broke the arrow in half and removed it from Officer Bryant's leg. David thought the process much like what he had seen in several western movies. The necessity of breaking the arrow and forcing it through the back of Officer Bryant's leg was gruesome, but effective.

The doctors would later explain this was absolutely what they would have done, albeit in an emergency room with proper equipment.

Then the man performed a dance of some kind, the raising of arms and hands, the clear song the man sang, appeared to be some type of worship.

The man moved away from the scene as the sound of emergency vehicles could be heard approaching. Officer Bryant's camera showed the man bounding over the fence again on the north side of the highway. He lifted the carcass of the deer, carrying it over his shoulders, as he disappeared from view, moving out of the field of view of both cameras.

The three men again sat in deep thought, pondering what they had witnessed.

Commander Houston spoke first. "Who the hell is that? You boys have another Comanche out there somewhere?"

David spoke next. "Old Grandmother, our translator says this is Tosahwi, the Medicine Man who sent Tabba and Sana into the Dream Time. Evidently he has also awakened here in our time."

"Do you realize you may have an eyewitness to what occurred out there on the highway?" Commander Houston said. William and David looked at one another simultaneously, the awareness and possibilities racing through their minds.

"Grandmother, our translator, said the song sung over Officer Reuter was a curse," William said. "The request in the song is to not allow the man to escape from the grip that death had on him. The songs sung over Tabba were of healing and victory, the song reserved for a Warrior, only to be sung when an enemy has been destroyed. The song and dance sung over officer Bryant was... the translation a bit difficult to understand. Basically, that he be allowed to live if he repented of his evil. If he did not, he was awaiting the curse of death. This was Grandmother's translation. I trust it to be completely accurate. She also identified the man in the video. His name, again, is Tosahwi."

"So how can I help you further, William?" Bryce asked.

"It would take us weeks to go through the discovery process and attempt to obtain the personnel records from the Game Department on Reuter. Not to mention seeking the information from the DA tips our hand a bit," William said.

"You know there is also the ammunition dispensary," Bryce added.

"I had thought of that," William said.

"What does that mean?" David asked.

"All law enforcement agencies keep an exact record of ammunition dispensed to each officer. It is signed for and each bullet accounted for," William explained.

"You can also be assured that whoever has attempted to cover up an extra shot being fired has already been reviewing those records," Bryce said.

"And altering them, I would think," William said, following the logic. "I think I can request that information without alarming the prosecution. It would be a standard request in a law enforcement shooting."

"Then we would at least have the record; it will look perfect I can guarantee you. But if we prove another shot was fired, then there is even more evidence that records have been tampered with and altered," Bryce added.

"So how do we prove any of this? How do we find out who might have altered the dashcam, the ammunition logs, and who is withholding the information on Officer Reuter, without the prosecution knowing we are onto them?" William asked, thinking aloud.

"Counselor," Bryce spoke, "you may have a decision to make." David and William pondered what his plan might be. "You're dealing with a very unscrupulous prosecutor. In my view, Sneed is the only individual in this story who has both the motivation and possibly the access to alter the evidence and the influence to withhold the personnel records."

"So, what do I have to decide?" William asked.

"It's a decision I made long ago, gentlemen," Bryce responded. "When protecting a nation or an individual from evil unscrupulous villains, both my country, the United States Navy, and myself as an officer of such, determined our course of action. Those honorable institutions and I would use any and all means necessary to stop such unscrupulous evil men from harming our troops or innocent civilians. Much of what was necessary was made legal by Congress passing the Patriot Act. I committed to do anything within my abilities to discover the truth and stop those evil forces from their planned plots and schemes. This situation, in my mind, is no different. Someone thinks they are above the law, and that someone will go to any length to have what they want in spite of the law.

"What you need to decide, William, is are you willing to do whatever it takes to discover the truth? Because I can have all the data you need in about an hour, including the personnel file on Officer Reuter and the phone and email records from the DA. I can assure you that information will lead you to the person who altered the dashcam video. I can also access the ammunition records from the Game Department."

The three men sat in silence for a moment. "But all those computer systems have firewalls and security systems, don't they?" William asked.

"Please, my friend, it's what I do. Those supposed safeguards are no match for the technology to which I have access. Five minutes and I'm in, and they will never know."

Again, a pause as William and David thought about how to proceed.

David spoke. "I have been rather quiet, just listening, but if I may interject. I was just thinking of, well, a truth I have always put into practice in my business dealings."

"Go on," William said.

"It's actually an old proverb," David said. "When dealing with the people of the world... you should be as wise as a serpent, yet as innocent as a dove."

"I think I understand," William said.

Looking directly into the eyes of his friend, Bryce said, "Listen, Will, you may not choose to use the information I can obtain, that is up to you. However, as any warrior knows, having the truth of what your adversary or enemy is planning gives you an immeasurable advantage."

"Even if that means becoming as unscrupulous as they are?" William asked.

David stood. "A man's life is in the balance. When that is the case there should be no boundaries to knowing the truth," David interjected. "Believe me, I wish Jonathan had known what he was walking into."

The other two men were stunned at the directness and raw truth of the statement. William thought for a moment and understood completely what David was saying.

The "enemy" would attempt to execute Tabba.

William made his decision. "Is this where I say we never had this conversation?"

"What conversation?" Bryce said.

Chapter 58

Sana and Abby sat in the little kitchen nook, enjoying the beautiful early morning sun.

The sun beams reflected off the beveled glass picture window, projecting colorful little rainbows across the breakfast table. Sana touched them with her hand, the rainbows then glowing on her skin. A wonder, she thought. The hot tea with honey, warm muffins, and light-hearted chat warmed Sana's heart and soul.

It had only been a few weeks, but Sana could feel the little pouch of growth in her womb, along with the occasional movement from within. Her mind in disbelief still…two sons.

Abby, seeing the expression on Sana's face, smiled. "Only eight more months, Little One. Sana, I am proud of you for being so strong and positive. Many women I have known would be deeply troubled at your circumstance. Your faith is so strong. Do you know how much I admire you?" Abby asked.

"Mom, I don't know if I am so strong. Many days I feel weak and helpless."

Abby looked questioningly at Sana.

"Do you believe in visions, Mother?"

"Well, I'm not sure I understand; do you mean like you saw something in the future?" Abby questioned.

"Yes, that's exactly what I mean."

"You know after all that has occurred, I'm really open to your faith and beliefs or truths. Grandmother certainly seems to have foreknowledge of many things that happen."

"I read in your Book of Faith today about young men having visions and old men dreaming dreams. The Book said those things would come from the Spirit. So, in your faith also the same gifting is available, is it not?"

Abby was surprised that Sana had been reading and comprehending and even contemplating these great mysteries.

"Yes, Sana, I do remember that verse, so to answer your question, yes, I do believe in visions. Where we need to have discernment is in what someone claims to know or has seen. I mean, it cannot conflict with what is otherwise known to be truth," Abby said.

"Mother, I have the gift of visions, of seeing the future," Sana stated. Abby listened intently.

"I have now had two visions in my lifetime. Both have proven to be true. They have been given me as a comfort, from the Great Spirit.

"The first time I had a vision was on the frozen prairie. The day Prairie Song had stumbled. She was hurt and cold and starving, as was I," Sana said.

"I remember you telling me the story, the reason for your embrace."

"What I told Prairie Song that day also gave her comfort. The vision gave me comfort. I knew Tabba would find the buffalo that day. I had seen it. Not as we see things in this world with our eyes. But I had seen it with my eyes closed. I knew in my heart what I told my child was true. She would be warm and safe and full that very night…with me."

"That is indeed the absolute best comfort we could ever give a child, isn't it?" Abby said, reflecting on her own memories.

"The second time I had a vision was the night before I knocked on your door." Sana continued. "I had lost my family and daughter to the white soldiers and rangers. I thought you might call the rangers. Every day fear was my world. But again, the vision I saw with my eyes closed tightly was a kind, beautiful, loving woman welcoming me in. That woman was you, Mother."

Abby just listened, the tears welling up in her heart.

"So again, the vision I saw gave me some inner strength. A comfort and hope I could never have on my own. I knew I had…a Helper. Tabba has attempted to tell me I have always had this gift. At first, I doubted him. I doubted the Spirit. It was wrong to doubt. But now I think I know without any doubt. It is a true gifting."

"So, Little One, have you seen something new?" Abby gently asked.

"I have been seeking the Great Spirit for a new vision. As of this day I have seen nothing. When the time is right, I know He will show me our future. He will show me Tabba's future. Knowing this relieves my heart in many ways. Knowing He has guided us this far and remembering what He has done for us in the past also gives me strength.

"Please understand this gifting has been given to me as a comfort. In both of those instances the visions seem to have the same purpose, that of comfort to the troubled. Is that consistent with what you know as the Truth, from your Book of Faith?"

Abby thought a moment. "Yes, very consistent. God the Father is referred to as the Comforter; it is one of His names. In another place He is called the God of all comfort. There is more, though, to the giving of His comfort. He wants it to be shared; this comfort you receive you should use to comfort others."

"Like the first vision, what I knew also comforted Prairie Song," Sana said.

"Like now, what you are sharing is comforting me."

Sana paused and thought about that for a moment, all the pieces of faith, and gifts, and love fitting together. Like a complex lifelong puzzle being gently pieced together. The mysterious picture coming into focus as the last few pieces were fitted perfectly into place in her mind, Sana believed in her heart.

"You say that I seem strong, full of faith, unafraid," Sana said.

"Yes, you possess all of those things, Little One."

"I actually feel quite weak some days. What you say is only so because I know the Great Spirit will guide me no matter the outcome. That is why I am not afraid or distraught or troubled. I am truly grateful. I have been comforted again, this time without seeing."

Abby was amazed at the strength and faith and wisdom of this beautiful woman she was now privileged to call daughter.

"I think there is more, Little One," Abby said. "I think what you are telling me is good and true and wonderful. However, what I think you now know to be true means that no matter the outcome or any circumstance that you face in this life, good or bad, you will always be comforted. As we both have been in the loss of our children.

"You know, God the Father helped me in the loss of Jonathan. He has done so not through the gift of visions as He has with you, but in a different way."

"How so, Mother?" Sana asked.

"He has always sent a person to comfort me. Even when I thought I was completely healed of the hurt. I did not even realize I was still not whole, that I still had the void or emptiness. I didn't realize the hole was still in my heart… until He sent you to me…and that emptiness was filled."

Chapter 59

January 20

William sat at his desk digesting the 180 pages of data Bryce had delivered to him. The file was printed and resourced in a professional easy to read format. The content was unbelievable. A clear and concise timeline, implicating the district attorney and his intentional cover-up of the evidence.

The truth was found on every page of the report.

William Travis inwardly fumed. The motive was crystal clear from the email trail. Political gain was at the center of the cover-up.

JD Sneed needed to win this case to secure his appointment to the Court of Appeals.

With the beginning of the trial just days away, William Travis indeed had a decision to make. There was enough evidence to move for an immediate dismissal of the charges. However, how to explain his possession of this file…it would implicate himself as an attorney.

The personnel file on Officer Reuter was a long and sordid history of misconduct and, William thought, outright criminal conduct in the line of duty.

Sexual assault had been reported by two different women. Both of whom had been detained by Reuter while the women were hunting alone. One of the women had filed charges of rape against Reuter. Those charges were later dismissed, according to the file, after the woman was bombarded with the ugly questions from an attorney retained by the State of Texas. Said attorney accused the woman of seducing Reuter. The man used the outrageous language in a deposition.

"Didn't you really want it? Weren't you actually asking for Officer Reuter's sexual advances?"

The woman's testimony had been the exact opposite. She had viciously fought her way out of the attack. The pictures in the file showed bruising and her face bloody several hours after the incident. Like many other women, she did not think she could endure the abuse of the process; unfortunately, the victim decided to withdraw the charges and spare herself and her family the indignity.

There was more about Reuter. Charges of domestic abuse, four different counts. Each incident was followed by an eventual divorce. Both of Reuter's two ex-wives had to obtain restraining orders during the process of those divorces. Each reported fearing for their lives, the man that surveilled, followed, threatened, and harassed them, Officer CL Reuter of the Texas Department of Game and Fish.

The most compelling fact uncovered in Reuter's personnel file was, however, an incident involving the firing of his service weapon without warning at a group of hunters in far north Texas.

The men were bird hunting on their own land. They had evidently had a previous run-in with Reuter. Thinking the best way to deal with the warden's bullying, as they reported, was to simply lock all the gates to their own property, thereby locking Reuter out.

Officer Reuter, it was reported, was later identified on a trail camera, shooting the locks off the closed gates. Then as if that was not enough, while attempting to detain two of the men, Reuter drew his weapon without warning and fired three shots over the heads of the men. The other friends and family members while hearing the shots, thought the three shots the universal sign of a call for help. When the remainder of the hunting party arrived on the scene, they were shocked to see their friends on the ground held at gunpoint. There was a standoff as the men encircled Reuter with their own weapons drawn. Reuter finally backed down and the hunting party then disarmed Reuter and escorted him from their land. Reuter chose not to explain to his superiors the two black eyes he received during the incident.

Recalling now that Grandmother was surely correct about Reuter, he was, in fact "A very bad man." William thought it unbelievable the man had not been fired for such a sordid history of violence and misconduct. Why would he not have been dismissed? William discovered the answer toward the end of the information. Reuter had been transferred after each incident, given stern warnings by his superiors and allowed to keep his job. The Game Department managers recommending dismissal had continuously been dismissed and overruled by one CL Reuter, Senior, Head of the Texas Department of Game and Fish.

On a whim, William Travis performed a quick history of the Reuter family. He discovered the family were descendants of one Clause Lon Reuter, an immigrant that had settled in the New Braunfels area in the middle nineteenth century. That settlement occurred under the auspices of the German immigration company Adelverein. Searching further, William thought it interesting and appropriate the meaning of the German sir name Reuter was "highway man, or thief."

William, researching further, discovered the telephone and email trail from JD Sneed led to a young computer hacker going by the online name of Icracker, aka Timcan. His real name was Timothy Collins, a nineteen-year-old high school dropout living in his mother's basement.

Commander Houston had already monitored the young man's home computer, entering through the extra firewalls and security in about an hour. The young man was obviously quite gifted, as most hackers only took of few minutes for the powerful program he was running to penetrate. Houston identified the exact date and time stamp when the dashcam was edited. He was able to identify the program used to alter the digital sound tract. The program was widely available and known on the open market as Garage Sound.

Commander Houston thought while he was in the young man's system, he would simply restore the file to its original data. The computer now sat in the basement of his mother's house with the file stored on the hard drive exactly as it had been delivered to him. The altered version was also stored in the system. To anyone who might query the system, the original file appeared to have been permanently deleted. But the original data was there, awaiting discovery…a binary *smoking gun.*

On the recording not five but six gunshots could be heard.

A trial could be easily won with all this truth, William thought. How to best use the information was the question. What could he possibly use without incriminating himself? The information in the file and bringing to light the truth it contained is what would require wisdom and cunning on his part. William knew there was much at stake. On one hand his career, possible disbarment, criminal charges against him personally. On the other hand, a man's life was in the balance. Considering that fact, his decision was not that difficult.

He would take Bryce's advice for now. "Always pursue the hacker." Perhaps he might come forth with the evidence willingly. Removing the question somewhat…why and how this information was in his possession.

How had David put it? "As wise as a serpent, yet as innocent as a dove."

Chapter 60

Present Day

The buffalo seemed calm for the moment. They had not noticed the three men with bows at the ready, moving stealthily toward them as they grazed on the rich Texas grassland. The wind was light but just enough to not give the hunting party away, if they were careful. Moving downwind away from the herd, the three crawled through the grass on their bellies. Once well downwind from the small group of huge bulls nearest them, the stalk began in earnest. They were brave and fearless like a pride of lions, patient, deadly, in no hurry. The wisdom they possessed of what must be done to be successful gathered from years of experience, years of failure.

To hunt and kill a two-thousand-pound animal with arrows was a dangerous thing. Many strong Warriors attempting to do so had been killed by the beasts.

For the little band of Comanche, sustenance and survival was in the balance of the outcome. For the animal, its very life was in the balance. All the buffalos' senses and defense mechanisms came into play. The animals were continually vigilant, wary of scents, wind, completely aware of natural cover, predators…and man. A buffalo would fight to the death to protect the herd or a calf. The three brave men knew they must be cautious.

It took the three Warriors two hours to come within range of a bow shot. One of the bulls seemed to become aware of their presence. It began pacing, testing the wind with its great nose, even using its large tongue to detect sound and taste on the wind.

238

The huge animal froze, standing motionless. The hunters knew the beast must have winded them. The hunting party in turn froze, sinking into the high grass, disappearing. They waited for the animal to make its decision. Was there danger? Should the wise old bull sound an alarm...and run?

The three waited another full hour. Patience was what was required now. The beast eventually resumed its grazing, a mistake on the part of the beast. It would cost the animal its life.

Three Warriors, three bows, three arrows, communicating through signs, the arrows were all loosed simultaneously. All met their mark, penetrating deeply. Now the fight would begin. This one would not give his life easily. The three men arose. The beast spotted them, though his vision was poor. He could see the danger. Bleeding profusely, the huge creature charged.

Recognizing the danger, the three brave Warriors reacted as planned. Arming themselves with sharpened lances they moved quickly, each running in a different direction, confusing the beast.

The bull turned left first, toward the threat, then right, toward the other movement, then detecting movement, he straightened his charge, the target in sight now. With amazing speed, the animal charged. The Warrior froze and took a stance, knowing he could not outrun the beast. He planted the ten-foot lance firmly in the ground behind him; its sharpened point he aimed directly at the center of the charging angry beast.

Tosahwi prayed.

The other Warriors ran directly toward the bloody scene. They were slow, much slower than the charging beast. They would not close the ground in time to help.

Time slowed as Tosahwi stood his ground, the collision unavoidable. Lowering the lance slightly he adjusted his aim. He could now see the wild eyes of the great beast as the last few seconds were passing. He saw the rage, the nostrils puffing great wisps of bloody breath, the sound of the hooves pounding the earth thundered in his ears. The smell of the animal arrived on the wind just seconds before the impact.

Tosahwi took in a final breath before the collision, bracing himself. The lance sank deeply into the underbelly of the charging animal, finding its mark. The weapon pierced the beast's huge heart. Tosahwi instantly dropped to the ground below the great bull, as it flew, tumbling and clawing, a loud bawl escaping its lungs as it came to rest in a great cloud of dust and grass and blood.

As his sons raced to the scene, they could not see Tosahwi. The huge animal covered him completely. The Warriors noticed a bloodied arm and a foot protruding from under the buffalo. The two attempted at first to roll the huge animal over; it was simply too heavy, so they began frantically to dig.

Hearing muffled sounds, the two Warriors quickened their pace. More of the arm revealed, slowly a shoulder, both covered in blood. The Warriors could not tell if the blood was from the animal or the Shaman. Finally, there seemed enough room to take hold of the exposed leg and arm. With the two Warriors scraping and digging, they pulled Tosahwi from under the belly of the huge beast.

He was still breathing. Tosahwi was amazingly still alive!

After a few moments, he slowly rose from his prone position in elation and relief and gratefulness, a smile breaking across his face. Tosahwi stood raising his hands high and letting out a War Cry. The Warriors joined in, in jubilation.

The three knew that if not for the Great Spirit, Tosahwi could have never survived such a thing.

Giving thanks for the life of the huge beast, the three began the work of dissecting and processing the enormous animal. It would take two full days to move the tremendous amount of meat, hide, and bones to the cavern. The women were waiting with the necessary tools and racks to begin drying the meat. This mighty animal would bring a special level of strength to each soul that would partake in the consumption of its glorious body.

The little band would feast tonight in the warmth of the cavern. The roasting fires would burn brightly in celebration. The story would be told over and over again. This tale would become lore for generations to come. The day Tosahwi, the great Shaman, defeated the charging beast, with a bow, and a lance, and a fervent prayer.

Chapter 61

David sat astride his horse, studying the ground around the kill site. It was a beautiful Texas winter day, the sky a light pearl blue. The wind was light for West Texas. The faint breeze moved the tall grass in gentle waves, giving it the appearance of how the ocean looked on a light wind day, David thought, it's surface in constant movement. Jason, his ranch foreman, also studied the soil, rock, and grass surrounding the site of the possible buffalo kill.

There wasn't much left to see. The dried blood trail from where an animal had been shot was easy to see. Then a trail of blood about fifty yards long was clearly seen, as the animal evidently ran for its life. The area they now observed was possibly where the animal had died and been field dressed. It contained a large area of matted grass, scuffed rocks, and dirt where it appeared as if someone had dug into the ground. Dried blood coated all the surrounding grass.

There was a slight trail through the grass, heading south. It looked as if someone had walked back and forth to the site repeatedly. That trail disappeared once the surface of the ground turned from grass to hard pack and then a solid rock surface for one half of a mile. It was impossible to pick out the trail in any direction beyond the large rock surface.

"Could it have been something other than buffalo that was shot, Jason?" David asked curiously.

"I just don't know, Mr. Ross. That's a lot of blood," Jason answered.

"Yes, it is. And you've attempted a count again, I'm sure?"

"Yes sir, although it's hard to get an accurate count. These buffalo can really move if disturbed. I keep coming up with a different number. I've tried three times in the last two days. On the first day, 398; 397 the second day, and 398 again today."

"I see what you mean. I'm pretty sure we haven't lost three animals, have we?"

"No sir, but I have yet to count 400 buffalo."

David, thinking through the process, said, "Well, I would really like to know what happened here. Let's call Steve. I'll go up with you both at first light. Maybe we can get a better count from the air, before they begin to move in the morning. I'll have Steve meet us at the barn with the chopper at 6:30." David turned his horse, heading back toward the ranch.

"There is one other thing, Mr. Ross."

"What's that, Jason?"

"Well, I'm not sure how to say this, sir."

"Come on, son, out with it."

"It's something else I saw. Now don't think I'm cracking up or anything, sir, but yesterday…I think I saw an Indian."

David reined his horse around, looking directly at Jason. "When and where, son?"

"Yesterday morning, just below here, out toward the south in the little canyon near the big cavern," Jason said. "He was dressed in a full native get up. He even had a bow and a long spear. I thought I was watching something out of a western movie for a minute. Then he just vanished into the brush."

"Its OK, Jason, you're not cracking up. What you saw was real." David said. "But let's keep a lid on this for now."

"Yes, sir, Mr. Ross, understood." Jason stared in wonderment across the open plain before them. Taking a deep breath, he seemed relieved that Mr. Ross believed him.

David raced his horse across the open grasslands, a little trail of dust rising behind him and drifting in the light wind toward the caverns. Jason watched, admiring Mr. Ross and his skill as a rider.

David thought he needed to talk to Sana. More importantly he desperately needed to find Tosahwi.

Later That Evening

The West Texas wind whistled through the trees as it swept down the little canyon. The few remaining leaves and a few small branches were torn away from the large trees, landing along the riverbank and occasionally on top of the snug little lodge. Sana and Abby sat on the large buffalo rug in the warm lodge on the banks of the San Saba River. David and Old Grandmother were seated across from them. Grandmother began serving her stew from the large cooking pot. The fire crackled, giving off its warmth and the light fragrance of oak wood burning.

The four had begun meeting together each evening for a meal and to visit and catch up on the latest developments.

Sana had moved back into her dormered room in the ranch house. Grandmother had moved into the lodge. She loved being back on her Homeland, as she called it, referring to the old camp of her people.

"Is there any news of Tosahwi?" David asked, as he had been asking every day.

"You seem so anxious, my son," Grandmother said. "Have you considered praying for the Great Spirit to send him to you?"

David looked across at Abby and Sana, surprised by the question.

"I apologize, Grandmother. To be honest with you, I have not done so."

"It is a thing you must learn," Grandmother said. "However, I have interceded for you, David. Tosahwi will meet with you tonight."

David was stunned at the reply. He knew what Grandmother said would take place.

Abby and Sana were also surprised at the news. David could see the excitement in Sana's eyes.

"It is a good thing," Grandmother said.

Judge Connelly ordered Tabbananica's English lessons to continue, and Abby reported they were going very well. She had been allowed a two-hour session each morning with Tabba. The judge had also allowed Sana to attend the English sessions as translator.

Sana was continuing to hunt and prepare meals for Tabba. He had refused the food of the white man.

"He is much happier and content with the Comanche food," Sana reported.

The order from Judge Connelly was allowed on a motion presented from William Travis. Said motion objecting to the prison food as being spiritually and culturally unclean for a Comanche Warrior. The judge had agreed, but only after sampling the meals offered by the prison and those Sana prepared.

"Tabba is reading on a second-grade level already," Abby proudly reported.

The knock on the door was gentle but still alarmed the four.

"Come in, my child," Grandmother called out. The door opened slowly as the man entered the lodge.

Tosahwi had to duck slightly to enter the six-foot-tall doorway. The man was imposing, astounding…or beautiful might have been a better word.

He removed the large buffalo robe draped over his shoulders. His buckskins were adorned with incredible detailed beadwork. The breastplate over his chest was made of bone and decorated with colorful beads. His medicine bag hung around his neck, dangling as he moved across the lodge toward Grandmother. His long black hair was flowing and peppered with grey. His facial skin was weathered and wrinkled, although his features appeared still strong. In the man's eyes, David could see wisdom…and cunning.

Tosahwi gazed into David's eyes for a moment as he entered. David returned the gaze, never wavering from the deeply personal eye contact. There seemed to be a mutual understanding or respect, David thought, incredibly without any words being spoken.

The smell of the outdoors and the wild followed Tosahwi across the room.

To Abby, the entire atmosphere in the room seemed to change as Tosahwi entered. The man exuded a presence, a power, a knowing. Even his gait as he crossed the room appeared somehow regal, even graceful. Tosahwi carried himself in a way she had never seen a man do so, perhaps as a king might. Abby was enthralled with this presence. He seemed a figure come alive from some artist's masterpiece…or an ancient character arriving from some other time… in this unassuming little lodge on the banks of the San Saba River.

Tosahwi gazed at Abby for a moment, and in that moment she felt the man read her. His gaze seemed to peer deep into her soul, with a knowing look he seemed to feel her pain for a moment. He seemed to know her wounding, her loss, and even acknowledge it.

Abby released the breath she had been holding.

Tosahwi embraced Grandmother while speaking in his Native tongue.

"It is good to see you, Old Grandmother…It has been many moons."

Grandmother smiled and laughed out loud as tears of joy rolled down her face.

Sana also rose to greet him. Tosahwi took her in his arms, lifting her like a child.

"And you, Little One, the boys are making you too heavy for me to lift!"

Sana and Grandmother laughed. Sana's heart rejoicing, her friend, her leader had found her across the years.

The man turned toward David and Abby who had also risen to greet him.

"*David J. Ross, it is an honor to meet you. Thank you for what you have done to help my friends. My Family.*"

Grandmother translated. David and Abby smiled and motioned for Tosahwi to be seated. The group all settled in as Grandmother served the delicious stew.

She began the song of gratefulness and thanksgiving. The others joined in. The sounds echoed along the riverbank and into the trees outside the lodge. Those songs also echoed within the hearts of David and Abby. The two sat in awe, watching, listening, to a way of life, a reverence, that had disappeared from the modern world in which they lived. Each person was moved deeply within their soul at the simple song of worship.

Tosahwi ate as if he was famished, slurping loudly, a compliment to Grandmother who smiled. David and Abby watched and listened in fascination as the three Comanches continued to eat and laugh and catch up. Again, the rhythm and beauty of the language was captivating to Abby and David as they listened.

After the meal was finished, David, desperately longing for a chance to speak with Tosahwi about the attack on the highway, stood. Tosahwi turned, rising also, and looked at David, peering deeply into his soul. David could sense the man reading him. Then Tosahwi began to speak, as Grandmother translated.

"*David Ross, I did see the entire battle on the highway. I was standing above the scene only a few feet into the brush. The Ranger fired on Tabbananica. It was a mistake on the part of the Ranger. Tabbananica is a Warrior.*

"*I will go to the place of the white man's court and tell the man who is trying to have Tabba killed. That man is a bad man. He does not have the truth in him.*

"*The truth will set Tabba free…The Truth sets all men free.*

"*I have other news for you, David. The People have all awakened. They are hungry and in need of shelter. I ask for your blessing. With your permission, may The People exit the cavern now? We need only a small piece of land to survive.*"

David was shocked at the revelation, an eyewitness! More people? He had so many questions. How and where to house them? Also, how to keep their presence unknown to the public? How to protect them? His mind racing, he began to develop a plan.

Grandmother translated what David spoke to Tosahwi. "It may not be safe for *The People*, Tosahwi. We need to proceed carefully. Let us consider the future and where the people should live. This land is large, my friend; however, as you know from what has happened to Tabba, we still have enemies. I have a place of shelter that is very secluded. I need more time for its completion. Please remain hidden. Within one month, it will be prepared for you and *The People*."

Tosahwi replied as Grandmother translated. "*We are grateful for your concern, David Ross. One moon is not a difficult thing for us to do. The plan is a good one.*"

"How many have survived and awakened?" David asked.

"*We are nineteen in total, including Sana and Tabba,*" Tosahwi said.

"It is a good thing. I am happy for *The People*," David said.

A knowing, a communication beyond words, had taken place. A respect or admiration shown on the faces of both men.

Tosahwi reached into his medicine bag and removed the cell phone belonging to JD Sneed. "*I think you also need this box. It belonged to the man who is trying to kill Tabbananica,*" Tosahwi said, smiling.

Chapter 62

February 13

From the basement of his mother's home, Timothy Collins read the message that flashed on his screen and then unexplainably disappeared.

"I know you edited the dashcam," was all it said.

Someone was in his computer. How could that be? His security was state of the art. More importantly, someone knew about the video. He knew he should never have trusted that DA dude. Suddenly, one thousand dollars didn't seem like much money. He wondered what should he do now?

Another message flashed across his screen. "You will go to jail."

Timothy jumped from his chair, unplugging every piece of hardware, computers, routers, Wi-Fi, and gaming devices. Running up the stairs, he located the electric panel for the home and turned off the power to the entire house. His mother was at work and would not return for several hours. Maybe it would be long enough.

Timothy's cell phone buzzed. He glanced down at the TXT message displayed across the screen.

"That won't work."

He began to cry. Then he panicked. Where could he go, who could he trust?

Timothy's thoughts drifted again to his father. He had left them three years earlier. He had started a new family and now had a one-year-old son. His dad hadn't even bothered to call him in over a year. His father's new wife hated him, and she showed that hatred every time he attempted to see his dad. His mom had a new boyfriend, the fourth one this year.

Timothy knew this day would eventually come. He turned the power back on to his home and grabbed a backpack he kept at the ready. It contained an extra set of clothes, his laptop, the money he had left over from the deal with the DA, and the gun he had taken from his father's closet.

Placing the backpack over his shoulder, he grabbed his skateboard and headed out the door. He needed to think. He needed someone to talk to.

He had thought often about Mr. Clark, his shop teacher from high school. When he made the decision to leave school, Mr. Clark was the only teacher or coach that seemed concerned at his decision. Mr. Clark had met with him, given Timothy his cell phone number and said, "You can call me anytime day or night. Don't ever think no one cares about you."

He wiped the tears from his eyes as he walked down the street toward who knew where.

Maybe he should call Mr. Clark.

Commander Houston watched as the young man headed down the street in the direction of Little Grove. He would allow plenty of room before following. There was no chance of losing him, Commander Houston watched the GPS display on his laptop as it showed in real-time the location of Timothy's cell phone. That phone, Commander Houston could see, was tucked in Timothy's back pocket.

Commander Houston followed at a comfortable distance.

Timothy headed for the coffee shop. On entering, he chose a chair in which he often sat in the rear of the building. He quickly logged onto his home computer through his cell phone and started the program that would wipe the hard drives clean.

He had no way of knowing the program would stall after thirty seconds.

Staring at his contact list, Major Lynwood Clark's phone number was glowing in the dim light of the back corner. Timothy began to tear up again as he thought of his life…and what a complete failure it was. He truly felt like no one on the planet cared about him or his pitiful life. He thought of the gun in his backpack. No one would miss him. The hurting would stop.

Maybe one last call, he thought.

Mr. Clark answered the phone on the second ring.

"Timothy, it's good to hear from you. How are you doing?"

"Hi, Mr. Clark. Uh, ok, I guess…I, uh, need…" The tears were coming again. As he tried to compose himself, Mr. Clark sensed the distress in the young man's voice. Mr. Clark knew it was important to keep the conversation going.

"Listen, Timothy, I was just heading to town. Can we meet up for a coffee?"

"I guess so. I'm already at the coffee shop."

"Great! I'll be there in ten minutes. I need some help with my laptop. Oh, and I also heard of a computer security firm that is looking for someone with your kind of talent. You interested?"

"Um, I'm not sure...I gotta go." Timothy ended the call. He was overcome with emotion.

It was the first kind word or compliment he had heard from anyone in a very long time. Looking up from his chair, he wiped the tears away again. A man was walking directly toward him. He started to run, but the man was smiling.

"Timothy, I'm Commander Bryce Houston, United States Naval Intelligence. Could I share a moment of your time?" Commander Houston could see the raw emotion on the young man's face. He quickly decided to change tactics, seeing the need to soften his approach.

"Your system security was one of the best I have ever seen, son. I am impressed with your abilities. You know, if you are interested, we are always on the lookout for talent. We meaning Naval Intelligence."

Timothy was shocked at the comments. He sat in silence wondering what was next.

"I do need your help in a more pressing matter, as you know. But let me first offer some assistance. I can see you're worried."

"Well, you did say I was going to jail," Timothy said.

"Listen to me, Timothy, if you cooperate, I can cut a deal and you will actually be rewarded for helping us. You will save a man's life, if you're interested."

"And the jail threat?" Timothy asked.

"I needed to get your attention," Commander Houston replied.

"Who again is us?" Timothy asked.

Major Lynnwood Clark entered the coffee shop. Seeing Timothy talking with the man, he walked quickly across the room.

"Well, if it's not our computer whiz. You OK, Tim?" Mr. Clark looked questioningly at the two.

"Commander Bryce Houston, Untied States Naval Intelligence. Retired as of recently. I was just visiting with Timothy about his abilities."

"I'm Major Lynwood Clark, United States Marine Corp. Retired also, now a high school teacher and friend of Timothy's."

Timothy was shocked. Mr. Clark had just referred to him as his friend. Timothy continued to fight back the tears.

"So, what's going on here, gentlemen?" Mr. Clark asked.

Commander Houston thought a moment and decided it was a good thing the major was here; he decided to go ahead with the sensitive subject.

"Well, to tell you the truth, we need Timothy's help. Have a seat, major, please."

Commander Houston described in detail all that had occurred, including Timothy's role in the editing of the video. He emphasized the significance of his possible testimony against the DA and the fact that a man's life was in the balance. It all depended on Timothy and his willingness to testify. That testimony might occur in a court of law, but more likely behind closed doors before the judge presiding over the case.

"Well, Tim, looks like the ball is in your court," Mr. Clark said.

"And what'll happen to Sneed if I tell the truth?" Timothy asked. "That man lied to me. He said it was a training video. He told me that none of what was on the video really happened. Said they were all actors. That he wanted to see if the other trainees noticed the editing. That bastard is a liar and I hate him. He also used my mom…to get to me." Tim continued.

"She can't help it." The tears beginning to flow. "She needs a good man. She never finds anything but users, like this bastard Sneed. Yes, I'll testify against him."

"Timothy, there is more. After this all settles down, which will be quite soon, would you be willing to go to Maryland with me?" Commander Houston asked. "I would like to introduce you to some particularly important people. They will be extremely interested in your talents and abilities. You will need to take a series of tests, tests designed to determine just how good you are with computer security and cyberwarfare."

Timothy was taken aback at the possibilities. "What does that mean? Sounds like you want me to find bad guys?"

"If you perform well on the tests, we will send you to school, computer school. There you would learn, well…I am not actually allowed to name the programs. We consider them weapons. And yes, you would be finding bad guys, where they hide in the cyberworld. You could detect the plans they have to hurt people, our people. And your information would play a huge part in neutralizing them."

"Neutralizing them?" Timothy asked.

Looking around the room, Commander Houston lowered his voice and said, "Let's just say with your help, their plans for evil will not succeed."

Timothy looked across at Mr. Clark with a questioning expression.

"Your call, my man. Sounds bad ass to me!" Mr. Clark said.

Timothy's entire demeanor changed when he considered these new possibilities.

It was difficult for him to comprehend the change of circumstance that had come about in the last few minutes. He thought for a moment about what he had just considered with his father's gun. How could life, his future, change so suddenly? In this unbelievable moment, he had learned a life-long lesson, a lesson that in the future he would share with many young men.

Never give up. No matter the circumstances, which are certain to change. Never give up.

Tim took a deep breath and wiped the few remaining tears from his eyes.

"Yes, sir, Commander Houston, I'd love to take the tests. I'll help any way I can."

Chapter 63

Friday, February 15

After more than two weeks of delays, primarily requested by the prosecution, the courtroom was full. Normally Judge Connelly's court sessions, even for major crimes, never drew much of a crowd. Today was different. Among the observers was one Mrs. Mary Running Deer and her assistant, Brenda. Also accompanying her were some fifty tribal members from the Comanche Nation of Lawton, Oklahoma. Many of the tribal Elders and elected officials were also in attendance.

The local, and even national press, had set up their huge production and transmission units around the normally peaceful little town square. The few motels and restaurants of Little Grove were bursting at the seams with visitors and locals alike. It wasn't the trial per se they had all gathered to see. It was the Native American couple that had reportedly traveled through time and awakened in a cave in Texas. That couple was who they had all come to see.

Judge Connelly had ordered that no cameras would be allowed in the courtroom. That did not prevent CNN, FOX and other news crews from assaulting the little courthouse lawn. Reporters, with sound and camera crews following behind, interviewed anyone who happened by. They were each looking for a story that could be fed back to the network. The reporters were not getting much the producers in New York felt like they could use until the Tribal Delegation from Oklahoma arrived in chartered buses.

The Native Americans began to set up teepees and tents on the courthouse lawn. Soon a large fire was started. The tribal members began a ceremony of some kind. There was dancing. The sound of songs being sung and drumbeats could be heard from inside the courthouse.

Mrs. Hantaywee, seated at the defense table, began to softly sing along.

The traditional dress of the participants in the square was stunning. The colors and bead work a beautiful display. The cameras moved in. The producers in New York let the live feeds run for over an hour. Interviews from the Tribal Council members were conducted, all were gathered in support of Tabbananica. According to the interviews, this trial was yet another story of injustice imposed upon the Native American community.

The previous few days the news had spread across the nation like wildfire. More specifically the news spread across the Indian reservations of America.

The People had a cause.

Over the last several days more than one thousand Native Americans had descended on the small town of Little Grove, Texas. The town was overwhelmed with the crowds. It was quickly agreed that the local municipal golf course could be used as a campground for the Native Americans. The town council set up water stations and porta potties along the first fairway. Tents and teepees lined the remaining fairways. It was quite an unusual scene. Groups of entire families gathered around fire pits, talking and sharing meals together. When court was finally convened on Friday morning, all the Native Americans had gathered around the courthouse square.

From a historical standpoint, this was the largest gathering of Native American people in the state of Texas since the "Great Raid" led by Topusana's grandfather, the great Comanche Chief, Buffalo Hump.

The news coverage grew each day, as did the crowd supporting and sympathetic to Tabbananica and his pregnant wife, Topusana.

Inside the courtroom, the jury was seated in the jury box. Jim Bob Skaggs, the foreman, whispered to those jurors near him, seeming to project his self-importance to any who bothered to look his way. JD Sneed stood at the prosecutor's table next to Dr. Nina Rainwater who sat ready to translate. William Travis stood alongside Grandmother at the defense table. Tabbananica stood tall and strong, his beautiful long hair flowing down his back. He was a fierce looking man, even though the shackles and jumpsuit he wore identified him easily as the accused. The sketch artists were furiously at work detailing the scene.

Judge Connelly began the proceedings. "Is the prosecution ready?"

"Yes, Your Honor," JD Sneed replied.

"You may proceed with your opening statement, Mr. Sneed," continued the judge.

The district attorney rose and slowly paced the floor in front of the jury box.

"Ladies and gentlemen of the jury, I intend to prove the accused, Tabbananica, of capital murder in the death of Officer CL Reuter. He has also been charged with the crime of attempted capital murder of Officer George Bryant. That attempt to take the life of both officers you will see in living color before your own eyes as it happened. This will not be a difficult case to prove. The evidence is overwhelming. You will see with your own eyes the murder and the attempted murder…as those events occurred.

"I must also inform you, the accused has concocted a long story about his identity."

"Objection, Your Honor." William Travis rose from his seat and addressed the judge.

"Sustained. Mr. Sneed." A stern look from the judge was included in the reprimand.

JD Sneed continued, "Ladies and gentlemen of the jury, it will be up to you to decide if the accused is who, in fact, he claims to be."

"Objection! Your Honor, my client's identity is not on trial here."

"Sustained. Mr. Sneed, move on. I'll not allow those kinds of statements."

"I will let the dashcam video speak for itself. Reasonable doubt will never even enter your minds. The accused is guilty, guilty of capital murder. In addition, he is guilty of attempted capital murder," continued the prosecution.

"The man he killed in cold blood was a good and decent man. A public servant with years of service to the public and the state of Texas. The man he wounded that day lost his leg in the attack. He will never be the same man.

"You men and women of the jury have been designated 'Death Qualified.' The decision you will face upon completion of this trial will be the most important decision a jury could ever hand down. The question that will be before you is should we put this suspect to death for what he has done?"

"Objection!" responded William, rising from his seat.

"Sustained! Mr. Sneed, rephrase."

"Sorry, Your Honor. Ladies and gentlemen, for what he has been accused." Several of the jurors looked confused not understanding what was just stated and subsequently corrected.

JD Sneed attempted to make eye contact with each jury member. Most looked away. He needed to know who was with him. Mr. Jim Bob Skaggs was right there following his every word. He knew he had the foreman on his side already.

"It is a heavy decision you must make. Please do not take your decision lightly. You will have the power, the power to end a man's life. The prosecution believes the burden we carry is difficult but must be done. I know you will, in fact, come to the correct conclusion. The law allows for death to take place in Texas, in the most heinous cases. I know you will do the right thing. Thank you for your service to this community and to the cause of justice.

"Your Honor." JD Sneed, while ending his statement, seemed to put on a false sense of humility, attempting to win over some of the women with the weight of the decision before them. He laid out the heavy burden and responsibility he bore as prosecutor and that they as jurors also must carry.

None the women looked at the prosecutor. They fully knew the weight of the decision that lay ahead. Each felt as if manipulation shouldn't be added to the burden. In fact, some jurors, especially the women, were repulsed at the possibility of sentencing a man to death. Sneed, in his attempt to manipulate, had won over none of them.

William Travis could have made several other objections. While watching the jury himself, he knew he did not need to do so. To allow the district attorney to keep talking was, so far, a good defense.

William Travis had learned much from his years before naval courts and judges. One of the things he knew was points of law sometimes became secondary. Watching the jurors, or judges, was of the utmost importance. How to win them over was much more important than constant bickering over legal points. He was already revising his strategy. One thing was certain. He would do his absolute best to see that the video was never viewed by this jury.

JD Sneed, in his arrogance, thought he had swayed every single juror with his eloquence.

Then something quite unusual happened.

Several Native Americans had entered the foyer outside the courtroom and were listening as JD Sneed completed his opening statement. All of them began to boo loudly as Sneed was ending his comments. The tribal members outdoors took up the booing, following the lead of those inside. Soon the crowd noise could be heard by all within the courtroom. Loud booing and hissing echoed throughout the building.

Judge Connelly banged his gavel; however, none of the noise originated from within the courtroom. He spoke loudly over the crowd. "Order!"

JD Sneed moved toward his seat, turning red with embarrassment, or anger, it was difficult to tell. An aide rushed to his side, reporting on the commotion.

"Sir, the Indians outside are booing you."

"I will put a stop to this unruly crowd today!" Sneed raged.

As William Travis began to speak, the crowd outside, prompted by those in the foyer, quieted.

"Mr. Travis, you may proceed with your opening statement," Judge Connelly ordered.

"Your Honor, ladies and gentlemen of the jury. My client is innocent. The defense will prove over the next few days his was an act of self-defense. We will show that the officer's knowingly fired upon Tabbananica without warning. Make no mistake," William Travis peered directly at JD Sneed, "you will see exactly what happened. It was unfortunate. The situation should have been handled much differently than it was by law enforcement. When law enforcement personnel make mistakes, as these men had a history of doing, it can be costly. We will show you these costly mistakes."

Again, William Travis was staring directly at JD Sneed who showed a slight twinge on his face as William Travis smiled inwardly.

Sneed wondered if somehow the defense had discovered the history of Officer Reuter, or even something on the video they had missed in the editing. JD Sneed was so upset he didn't even object to the statement.

"Ladies and gentlemen of the jury, a man's life is in the balance. The truth must be known. There are many doubts that will arise as the prosecution presents its evidence.

"Listen to those doubts. They will speak to you loudly. Doubts will arise in your mind. I ask you to listen. Give those doubts a clear chance to speak to you, to your heart.

"These doubts will be reasonable, sound; they will exonerate Tabbananica. You will soon see. He is not guilty. That is all, Your Honor."

A loud roar of applause echoed through the courthouse square and enveloped the courtroom. Everyone in the room, from the judge to the lawyers, court reporter, and observers sat in awe at the strength and intensity of the sound level.

Tabbananica smiled.

As the noise began to subside, Judge Connelly banged away on his gavel, calling for silence. The order was heard by all of those inside the courtroom, but none of those who were cheering outside. The judge wondered how he was going to handle the outside disruption.

As the cheering faded away, the women of the jury thought about what William Travis said. He did not attempt to manipulate. The man simply asked them to listen and do their job. That job was, as instructed by the judge, to look for reason to convict or reasonable doubt.

"Mr. Sneed, are you prepared to begin prosecution?"

"I am, Your Honor."

"Fine, you may call your first witness," Judge Connelly stated.

"Your Honor, the prosecution would like to begin with the viewing of the dashcam recordings—" The booing could again be heard throughout the courtroom before JD Sneed could finish his response to the judge. The hissing and booing grew louder by the second, hindering the judge's ability to discern the response from Mr. Sneed.

William Travis had hoped for more time. He was surprised the prosecution was going directly to the dashcam video.

"Your Honor, I object," William Travis yelled from the defense table.

"On what ground, counselor?" the judge queried to a raucous round of cheering from outside the courtroom.

"Your Honor, the defense believes…let me rephrase. The defense has evidence that the dashcam video has been tampered with… and is inadmissible."

The noise of the crowd outside the courthouse overwhelmed those inside. Judge Connelly banged his gavel loudly, calling for order.

Continuing to pound his gavel, Judge Connelly motioned for the opposing counsels to approach the bench. "Court will recess now. I will see what can be done about the crowd. We will reconvene at 1:30 p.m.," ordered the judge.

The judge rose. The bailiff yelled, "All rise," as His Honor exited the courtroom. The noise level outside and inside the courthouse was astonishing. Inside the courtroom, the noise reverberated off the walls and hard surfaces of the room, creating a scene of confusion for all within the building.

The jury, looking confused, was instructed by the bailiff to return at 1:15 p.m.

William Travis and the defense team made a hurried exit to William's office across the square. They were followed by the huge crowd of Native Americans singing a victory chant in unison. Dr. Rainwater, the translator from Utah hired by the prosecution, purposefully fell in step with the defense team walking alongside William Travis. She entered his office with Grandmother directly behind her; they were both singing along with the crowd.

William, once inside, looked directly into the stunningly beautiful eyes of Dr. Rainwater and asked, "Did you make a wrong turn out there?"

"Yes, I did a couple of weeks ago," she said, smiling with incredibly inviting eyes, William thought. "I just fixed that, however, with my resignation as translator for the prosecution."

William paused a moment, thinking through his options and how to proceed. In his pocket, he felt the cell phone belonging to JD Sneed. He had a perfect explanation for how he was in possession of the email trail and the altered files of Timothy Collins. He had hoped to let JD Sneed hang himself with a day or two of lies from the prosecution. William thought that option must be secondary for now. Freeing Tabba was why he was here.

Keep your eyes on the goal, counselor, he said to himself as he gazed again into the beautiful eyes of Dr. Rainwater.

JD Sneed, upon exiting the courthouse, was pelted with a combination of tomatoes, half eaten hot dogs, and a chocolate shake that caught him squarely in the chest. He screamed and swore at the crowd that followed him. All the activities were caught live and in color by the ravenous news crews that lined the square. The producers in New York were practically drooling over the scene.

Grove County Courthouse
1:30 P.M.

Sheriff Fred Mason, along with William Travis and Timothy Collins, the young computer hacker, sat awaiting Judge Connelly in his quarters. The sheriff had in his possession the entire investigative reports on the crime scene and murder. He also had the computer files from Timothy Collins's editing of the dashcam recordings. JD Sneed had not arrived for the meeting. He had sent an assistant with a request asking for more time before any evidence was brought before the judge. Judge Connelly had denied the request. The judge entered the chambers and seated himself at his desk.

"Counselor, this better be good," he said gruffly.

William Travis pressed play on the video display, and the judge viewed the first three minutes of the edited version that had been presented by the prosecution. After a ten-second pause, the actual version of the crime scene played across the display. Judge Connelly did not comment.

"What else is there?" the judge asked.

William Travis slid two single sheets of paper across the judge's desk. The judge quickly examined the papers. "Your signature appears on both of these documents, Fred. Did you actually sign both of them?"

"No, I did not," replied Sheriff Mason.

"Counselor, you will have my ruling on this request at 10:00 a.m. tomorrow. We will recess until Monday morning."

"Thank you, Your Honor," William Travis said. The three men rose and exited the chambers as JD Sneed was just arriving in the hallway.

Chapter 64

Saturday, February 16
10:00 A.M.

William Travis, along with Sheriff Fred Mason, had presented the evidence concerning the dashcam video to Judge Connelly in his quarters the previous afternoon. William had decided he would not speak this morning, unless asked a specific question by the judge. In some circumstances, he thought it best to let the evidence speak for itself.

JD Sneed was present and had attempted unsuccessfully to block the judge's consideration of disallowing the video.

Judge Connelly had immediately ordered a recess in the proceedings, until he ruled on the admissibility of the evidence presented before the court.

The respective counsels now sat in the quarters of Judge Connelly. They were also joined by the attorney general of Texas, Nathan Lincoln, and several of his assistants, along with Timothy Collins and Commander Bryce Houston.

The purpose of the meeting was to hear the official ruling on the motion filed by William Travis to not allow the dashcam video as evidence.

Judge Connelly had reviewed the edited version of the crime scene video and the unedited version. He knew the district attorney considered himself above the law. This, however, was inexcusable and, quite frankly, the act constituted a felony.

The altered video evidence had been turned over to Sheriff Fred Mason by young Timothy Collins. Sheriff Mason's department led the investigation. The sheriff, seeing the necessity of circumventing the district attorney's office, had directly contacted the Texas Office of the Attorney General. Attorney General Nathan Lincoln had traveled to Little Grove immediately.

In exchange for the information, Sheriff Mason had asked young Timothy not be prosecuted for any possible charges. The attorney general had agreed.

Attorney General Nathan Lincoln was considering convening a grand jury for the purpose of presenting evidence and a possible indictment of JD Sneed. He knew proceeding down that road would not be beneficial to the state of Texas or the history of convictions JD Sneed had compiled. He knew many inmates would be overjoyed if actual charges were filed against a sitting district attorney. For now, his plan would be to jail JD Sneed and let him worry in a cell for a few hours, then have him released. Although a quick poll of public sentiment might change his plan of action.

The more immediate issue Nathan Lincoln was considering was how to proceed with the trial. He knew he would remove District Attorney JD Sneed from the prosecution team. His office would take over the prosecution of the case. Although they had all been following the case in the news, none of his staff was prepared to go forward without some preparation time.

He was subject to Judge Connelly's rulings. A request for a long delay would mean the judge would most certainly declare a mistrial.

Judge Connelly entered from his private office. "Good morning, gentlemen. This is not a difficult decision. The dashcam video will not be allowed as evidence in this trial."

"Your Honor, this is outrageous—" JD Sneed attempted to speak.

"Silence!" Judge Connelly spoke, his voice raised in anger. "I'll hear no more of your disrespect, Mr. Sneed!"

"Mr. Travis, Mr. Sneed, could you give us a few moments alone?" Attorney General Nathan Lincoln spoke abruptly.

"Certainly, sir," William Travis replied as the two attorneys rose and exited the judge's chambers.

Exiting the quarters, William Travis turned and looked directly into the defiant eyes of JD Sneed. JD Sneed still had no idea what was about to become of his career, his defeated appointment, and even the distinct possibility that he might soon be incarcerated.

"If you have illegally obtained evidence, I will see you in an orange jumpsuit soon," JD Sneed threatened.

William Travis being as *innocent as a dove,* said, "I have no idea what you are talking about, sir."

After a long fifteen minutes, the door to the judge's chamber opened and Sheriff Fred Mason motioned for JD Sneed and William Travis to re-enter.

Young Timothy Collins had exited with Commander Houston by an outer door. Attorney General Nathan Lincoln started to speak but was interrupted by JD Sneed.

"We need to get this crowd problem under control and continue this trial immediately," he demanded.

"I think you should be quiet for a few minutes, sir," the attorney general said calmly.

JD Sneed glared at the man, his insolence showing.

"This is exactly how we will proceed. Mr. Sneed, you are hereby removed as prosecutor of this case."

JD Sneed stood and started to object, until Sheriff Mason placed a strong hand on his shoulder and forced him back into his chair.

"Further, you are also herby removed as District Attorney of Grove County, Texas," the attorney general said.

For the first time in many years, JD Sneed was quite afraid.

The Attorney General continued. "My office will designate a new prosecutor by the end of the day. The charges of capital murder will be dropped. We will, however, proceed with the charge of attempted murder against Officer Bryant. The charge of murder, as it relates to the attack on Officer Rueter we will also proceed with. Perhaps we have enough to convict on the lesser charges. We do still have a body and that evidence is about all you have left us, Mr. Sneed."

"And why have I not been included in this ridiculous decision?" Sneed said.

The attorney general continued, ignoring Sneed's comment.

"You, sir, and your disrespect of the law have caused this decision. Just to review, a witness has come forward and testified to the editing of the dashcam video, a procedure for which you evidently paid one-thousand dollars in cash to have performed. That dashcam video evidence has now been ruled as inadmissible. It is obvious what you attempted to conceal, the unwarranted firing upon the defendant by Officer Reuter.

"The defense is also in possession of Officer Reuter's personnel file. The file to which you repeatedly blocked access in discovery. They also possess an original record and an altered ammunition dispensary record, which were just released to me by the defense, as evidence. I personally do not think the case has a snowball's chance in hell of a conviction. If a law enforcement officer had not been killed, I would probably drop all charges."

"And exactly how is the defense in possession of those files without having committed a crime?" JD questioned, leering at William Travis.

William sat in silence.

"They possess the files by doing their homework, despite your attempts to stop them. I believe it is not a crime to peruse a cell phone recovered on a public property. Did you not, in fact…um…leave your cell phone on a public roadway?" Nathan Lincoln asked.

"That data was not on that phone!" JD Sneed protested. "It's not possible!"

"That's quite enough, Mr. Sneed. Save it for your attorney, which I recommend you retain immediately," the attorney general said sternly.

"In addition, the video of you paying the young man in front of his computer was quite revealing. The grand jury will meet beginning Monday to consider the evidence of your felony acts. I expect an indictment to be handed down soon. The judge has agreed to continue, without delay. We will resume the trial on Monday morning, and you, sir, are under arrest. Sheriff, would you read the man his rights and get him out of my sight."

Sheriff Fred Mason cuffed JD Sneed and began to lead him away.

Judge Connelly spoke, addressing JD Sneed. "Do you understand by your actions you have just given every case you ever prosecuted grounds for appeal?"

JD Sneed, his anger rapidly turning to fear, sweated profusely. The room seemed close and uncomfortable. His heart skipped within his chest; his breath became short. He wanted to loosen his tie, attempting to raise his hands but quickly realized they were bound behind his back. The reality of his future crumbling to pieces before him sunk deep within his mind. How could this be happening? He felt the pain of the handcuffs cutting into his wrists. He felt for a moment what many he had prosecuted must have felt. For the first time in many years, JD Sneed was very, very afraid.

The sheriff and JD Sneed paused a moment before the judge at the question directed to Sneed. For the first time in his twenty years as a lawyer and a prosecutor, JD Sneed could not form a response. No words would come. A huge painful lump formed in the front of his throat. He simply could not reply. He managed to swallow hard, as he stood in silence for an awkward moment.

Then the sheriff led him away.

Chapter 65

Sunday, February 17

The hunting lodge was nearing completion. Its location adjacent to the entrance to the sixty-four-thousand-acre buffalo tract was in one of the most isolated locations on the ranch.

Tosahwi, Sana, Abby, and David stood outside the lodge, admiring the huge structure. David and Abby had spent the entire day getting to know the survivors of the attack on the San Saba band of Comanches.

David and Abby Ross were in awe. Nineteen Native Americans had escaped the battle on the San Saba. They had awakened from the Dream Time here on the Ross ranch in Grove County, Texas, near the former Home Camp of the Comanche.

The group consisted of Tosahwi, his wife, and his two sons and their wives, two old grandmothers, four children all under the age of seven years, all girls. The little girls were found by Tabba, hiding in a cleft along the riverbank after the battle. In addition, there were the five grandchildren of Tosahwi, ages two through seven. Tabba and Sana completed the nineteen Comanches that had escaped the attack on the San Saba band of Comanche. The survivors had been rescued after the massacre, by Tabba or Tosahwi. All had escaped a certain death from the white soldiers.

All had escaped into the Dream Time. The nineteen Native Americans were healthy, hungry, and in need of shelter, food, and clothing.

The construction foreman reported to David that all bathrooms within the lodge were functioning. There was heat and hot and cold water.

"Mostly just painting and flooring yet to go, Mr. Ross. We can work around, um, your guests."

"That's fine, we'll put everyone on the second floor for now, then switch when you're done downstairs," David said.

Sana and Abby were busy showing the group how to use the showers and toilets. The two had hastily made up the beds and had the entire group unloading towels, soap, and staples, even toilet paper.

The Comanches had laughed and pointed to one another as Sana explained the new method for personal hygiene.

Most thought the old way far superior. Sana knew an area outside would be designated and the old ways would survive for now.

David, translated by old Grandmother, spoke with Tosahwi.

"My Friend, it is a small thing for your people to live here for now. The log shelter is yours. You may hunt the deer and small game. However, for now please do not kill the buffalo."

"*Yes, my Friend,*" Tosahwi said. "*The females are all to birth soon. The Comanche way is to always honor the animal. It is a good thing you are asking. This has forever been the way of the Comanche. In the fall, when the days grow shorter, we will see if the numbers have grown. That will be the time for the taking of the buffalo.*"

The two men paused, staring into one another's eyes. There was a knowing and wisdom shared between them.

Tosahwi could see David J. Ross was a man familiar with the earth. He knew this man was a respecter of the gifts given from the Great Spirit.

Likewise, David saw the wisdom in how Tosahwi lived with and upon the land. This man, he thought, was also a caretaker, a steward of the Creation.

The two respectfully admired one another.

"*The People are grateful to you, David Ross, although they are not used to living inside such a great shelter as this. Some may prefer to set up their own teepees. Grandmother has shown us the new material for doing such. It is a new way* The People *from Oklahoma are building their teepees. She says the new canvas hides will be arriving soon.*"

"It is your choice, my Friend. A new storm is coming tomorrow. The ice will fall, and it will be very cold for a week or more," David said.

Tosahwi again considered the man. He also was aware the winter was coming with the cold and ice. This man was indeed listening to the earth, he thought.

David had checked the weather forecast on his cell phone just this morning.

The information that both men had obtained came from completely different resources; it was amazing that both were accurate.

David had cut two cords of wood and stored it along the huge front porch. The two men worked together building a large fire in the massive fireplace of the great room. Sana and Abby were just finishing up the unloading of the supplies. They had each person comfortable and settled into their own rooms.

The fire seemed to draw each person from their hurried activities into the great room. Without any instruction, *The People* gathered around the warmth of the fireplace. All seated themselves on the floor in a circle.

Old Grandmother, speaking in her native tongue said, *"It is time to bless this new home. The Comanche people of the San Saba now will have a new beginning. Let us give thanks to the Great Spirit. Your very lives have been in His hands and continue to be so. Let us be especially thankful for our new friends David and Abby."* Old Grandmother, Mrs. Hantaywee "Faithful One," began the songs.

The humility of *The People* was unmistakable. The sincerity of the worship unmatched by anything David or Abby had ever felt or known. The songs enveloped the room, the beautiful lilting tones were reverent.

Each member of the little tribe rose one at a time. Moving to David first, then Abby, each laid their hands on the two while the songs continued among the others. Each person, with their hands on the David and Abby, whispered a special blessing on each of them.

David and Abigail Ross were both moved to tears by the pure act of love and gratefulness from *The People*.

As Sana laid her hands on David, she saw.

The vision was pure, clear, and unmistakable. The worship of the people continued, but Sana's heart was breaking. Her secret tears would not stop for days.

Chapter 66

Monday, February 18

The cold air had indeed settled in from the north. A light dusting of snow covered the quaint courthouse square. The smoke from the many wood fires burning outside the tents and teepees set up on the golf course just one half a mile away drifted throughout the downtown area. The smell of meat cooking and wood smoke filled the atmosphere.

Barriers had been erected around the entire courthouse lawn. Sheriff Mason had stationed all available personnel along the street front surrounding Courthouse Park. The crowd of Native Americans had filled the streets encircling the courthouse, but no one was permitted to enter the lawn area or the courthouse itself without an identification badge. The authorities had hastily put together the list of approved attendees from both the prosecution and defense. The courtroom itself was packed with one hundred or more of the approved observers.

The prosecution, now led by Assistant Attorney General Mrs. Beverly Burnett, was prepared and ready to continue the proceedings. William Travis stood at the defense table alongside Grandmother and Tabba. Sana sat directly behind William Travis. She was accompanied by David, Abby, and Dr. Nina Rainwater of the Shoshone Nation.

The entire delegation of tribal leaders and members from the Comanche Nation of Lawton, Oklahoma, had received badges and were permitted to enter the proceedings.

As the jurors filed into their seats, Jim Bob Skaggs, the foreman, looked toward Topusana with lust in his eyes. The man had attempted to attract her attention several times during the proceedings.

Sana could feel the man's eyes on her and smell the death that seemed to surround him.

Tabba also had seen the look in the man's eyes. He could also smell the pungent odor of death on the man, even from across the room. What were these Texans thinking? Why would they allow such a crude man a place of honor, a place of judgement?

Tabbananica the Warrior stared the man down, looking him directly in the eyes. Catching the look, Jim Bob Skaggs shuddered in his seat.

Tabba, now also sensing the fear in the man, thought it would be a good thing to kill this man. If he continued to stare at his wife in the way he was doing, Tabbananica would do so.

Jim Bob Skaggs quickly looked away from the fierce stare of the man. The judge, as far as Jim Bob was concerned, needed to wrap up this trial and lock the crazy Indian away for a very long time. Then he could focus his advances and desires on the cute, vulnerable Indian woman. He knew he was a persuasive man. He would turn on the charm and seduce her soon enough. Jim Bob Skaggs looked her way again, smiling.

Tabba thought to himself as he caught the look again, if only I had a war club.

Judge Connelly called the proceedings to order.

"Is the prosecution ready to proceed?"

"Yes, Your Honor," came the reply from Mrs. Burnett.

"Mr. Travis, is the defense ready to proceed?"

"Yes, Your Honor."

"Ladies and gentlemen of the jury, you have been instructed as to your new guidelines and duties. This trial will proceed; however, the State has replaced the prosecution team. You jurors need to be aware I have ruled the dashcam video of the crime scene inadmissible. The district attorney has been placed under arrest for his involvement in tampering with that evidence."

A gasp escaped from the observing crowd. Several reporters ran from the room at the news. The Native Americans present began to talk among themselves. A distinct grumbling from the observers in the crowd was obvious.

The judge banged his gavel. "Silence! If you want to remain in this courtroom," he commented directly toward the onlookers.

"Jurors, are there any questions before we begin?" Judge Connelly asked.

Jim Bob Skaggs, seeing the opportunity to impress, raised his hand.

"Mr. Foreman, is there a problem?" the judge asked, rolling his eyes.

Jim Bob Skaggs stood and paused a moment for effect. During the pause, he again looked with lust upon the beautiful Indian woman Topusana, even allowing his eyes to rest upon the outline of her breasts.

Tabbananica, Voice of the Sun, saw the look from the jury foreman, as did Abby and Sana.

The courtroom was completely quiet.

Tabba rose from his seat in defiance. The War Cry cut through the silence of the courtroom like a sudden booming clap of thunder echoing through the building. The windows vibrated from the purity and the intensity of his voice. The crowd was stunned, as were the legal teams, court officers, everyone within the room was shocked and in awe at the strength, power, and effect of the man's voice.

Tabbananica, the Warrior had spoken.

Some observers ducked down in their seats, as did the judge.

Jim Bob Skaggs stood trembling, urine spilling on the floor around his pant legs.

As the sound of the War Cry echoed through the courtroom, Jim Bob Skaggs attempted to cover his crotch and the accidental release. He blurted out, "You filthy damned wild ass Indian!" Jim Bob Skaggs ran from the room his head lowered, his hands covering his crotch. The act did not conceal from most in the room the distinct wet outline soaking through his pant leg.

Judge Connelly banged his gavel as a roar of reply emanating from outside the barriers that encircled the courthouse enveloped the courtroom. The response from the Native Americans gathered in support of Tabbananica grew like a huge wave cresting into one long continuous War Cry.

The People had heard the call from Tabbananica.

The drumbeats were taken up; his Brothers and Sisters would not be quieted for hours.

William Travis and the entire defense team heard the comment from the jury foreman. Also, within earshot was the judge. The court reporter dutifully recorded what was said. Mrs. Burnett and the entire prosecution team also heard the racial slur from the jury foreman.

William Travis asked immediately to approach the bench.

The judge motioned for both teams to come forward.

"In my quarters now!" he ordered. The noise level in the courtroom resembled that of a football stadium, the judge thought, as the legal teams followed him out of the courtroom and into his quarters.

The sounds of drumbeats and war cries in the judge's private quarters were still loud and raucous as they echoed through the square.

William Travis sat quietly in the judge's chambers, he would make no motion for mistrial, knowing full well the possibilities.

"Mr. Travis, does the defense desire to proceed?"

"In light of the evidence we possess, yes, we are willing to proceed," answered William Travis. "We do have an alternate juror ready to serve." He was thinking of Lupe and the opportunity of the jury becoming more favorable to the defense due to the outburst of the foreman. William Travis was also considering carefully his next move. This trial could end here and now.

"I am inclined to see your position, Mr. Travis," the judge said.

"Mrs. Burnett, may I ask your position as prosecutor?"

The assistant attorney general was dumbfounded as to the sequence of events that had just unfolded.

"Your Honor, the prosecution believes a mistrial is certainly in order." Her thought process was to start over with a fresh jury and the time to prepare would benefit the prosecution.

"You don't sound too convinced, Mrs. Burnett," Judge Connelly said.

"Well, we obviously will have the right to retry the case, perhaps with a new jury at some point in the future," she said with a questioning look.

"If you can obtain a new indictment," Judge Connelly stated. The inflection of serious doubt was in his voice. "Normally, I would need a few moments, but not under the circumstances. Considering evidence tampering, your request for a new translator, the jury situation, I see no way to proceed fairly with this trial. I will hereby, declare this case a mistrial."

"For the record, the defense objects to this ruling, Your Honor," William Travis said.

"That is duly noted in the record and understood, Mr. Travis."

By objecting, William Travis further assured that Tabbananica under the Double Jeopardy clause of Constitution of the United States would most likely never be brought to trial again for the current charges.

To the echoing sounds of drums, chanting, and much of the crowd outside dancing the ancient dances, Judge Connelly entered the courtroom, followed by the legal teams.

The mistrial was officially declared, and the jury released from duty.

Tabbananica was ordered to be released immediately.

From the defense table, Grandmother began the song of victory. Singing along with the crowd outside the courtroom.

When Tabba exited the courthouse with no shackles and dressed in his traditional clothing, the more than one thousand tribal members erupted in celebration. The barriers surrounding the courthouse lawn were breached and the celebration began in earnest.

The fires would burn throughout the night. The live feeds to major news outlets would also run for hours. Interviews with legal experts and pundits would continue for days. Most agreeing, Tabbananica would in all probability, not be tried again.

Later That Evening

The fire burned gently, glowing and crackling in the wood stove, filling the little lodge on the San Saba with warmth. The twins occasionally wrestled with one another inside Topusana's womb. Tabbananica thought the boys felt strong under his hand as he gently rested it upon his woman's belly.

Chapter 67

Over the last two days the tribal members that had gathered in Grove County from across the nation's reservations had begun to pack their belongings into their pick-up trucks, vans, and trailers. The feeling was somewhat somber as families said their good-byes and headed out on what was, for most, a long journey home.

The People had won a great victory. Some of the older ones sang as they packed belongings…the old songs. The songs that were reserved for victory over one's enemy.

The golf course was covered in firepits, with rutted trails crossing the fairways from the group's activities. The tribal leaders from Lawton had agreed to send dozens of workers from the reservation to repair the damage to the course. Within the next few days, the work would be completed.

The television crews had assembled their gear and trucks and by the day after the mistrial was declared had moved on to other more pressing stories and locations.

The news crews, however, did a very thorough job of reporting exactly what had caused the declaration of the mistrial. That statement made by the jury foreman, which so prejudiced the jury, along with evidence tampering by the prosecution the Honorable Judge David Connelly felt there was simply no way to move forward.

The news coverage concerning a sitting district attorney, one JD Sneed, being incarcerated and removed from office also played repeatedly on the networks.

Attorney General Nathan Lincoln was viewed quite favorably for his actions in dealing with the unscrupulous prosecutor. He gave repeated interviews from the steps of the Texas State Capitol in Austin. His only request in granting the interviews stipulated the flags of Texas and the United States must be captured in the background as he spoke.

Nathan Lincoln was up for re-election in a few short months. Based on the positive news coverage he received, he made a very astute political decision. JD Sneed would remain incarcerated and prosecuted to the full extent of the law.

Seeing the public sympathy toward Tabbananica, he also concluded new charges would not be pursued against the man. It was easy to defend his decision, even to the law enforcement unions. There was simply not enough evidence. And what evidence was available in no way favored the prosecution. The officers had fired on the defendant without warning.

Many Native Americans watched in anger and heartache at what had been said. Jim Bob Skaggs was hounded by the news crews for an interview. Several news outlets both nationally and locally had staked out the man's home and funeral parlor. They were hoping to get a word or two from him. Several attempts to discuss his statements with the press were broadcast, showing Jim Bob Skaggs sometimes attempting to cover his head with his jacket and running from the cameras. A few other bits of video showed his defiant dressing down of the camera crews and reporters, many expletives being used by Mr. Jim Bob Skaggs in the process…all those moments and words caught on video and broadcast to the nation.

The pursuit by the news crews would end soon enough, he thought. He was looking forward to the new trial that was certain to come. He was sure he would again be selected to serve. He was an upstanding citizen…that psycho Indian would soon be the one to get exactly what he deserved.

Jim Bob Skaggs's pastor had called expressing the need for a meeting of the church board again. How dare they point fingers, he thought.

Meanwhile, The Man watched every piece of news that could be found concerning Mr. Jim Bob Skaggs of Little Grove, Texas. The Man thought this attitude and behavior was what had caused and continued to be the root problem on his reservation and those of his brothers and sisters across the nation.

Prejudice, racial slurs, and insults should have no place in the complex problems of society. Men who used their little positions to inflict heartache and pain on people simply attempting to survive day to day needed to be silenced. This modern world where there seemed to be no consequences for those causing the deepest wounds and hurts was inexcusable. It was time, The Man thought, time to silence the arrogant. The world should know and see; sometimes there is a price to pay.

The Man was a Warrior. No Warrior would ever allow the openly slanderous insult to have such a crude voice against his *People*. His family.

He loaded his four-wheel-drive truck. The drive to Texas and back would take a few days. The Man knew he would need an alibi. He had spent enough time in the white man's prison. This time he would plan better.

Entering the Tribal Store, he stopped and visited with a few friends. The Man bought supplies for his hunting trip. He talked with the Native hunting guides while he sat and enjoyed a cup of coffee. The Man informed the little group of his planned direction of travel and general area where he would be hunting. In the event he did not return, they would know where to look for him. He made certain those in the group knew his planned return date. All agreed to meet again in five days. They would be aware if he did not return as planned and be prepared to help if needed. This was common practice among the Tribe.

The Man saw the look of his Elder. The knowing was in the older man's eyes. Perhaps the Elder had seen what was to come.

The Man knew his alibi was completely intact.

3 Days Later

Jim Bob Skaggs had just exited the processing room in the rear of the funeral home. The young woman had died in a one-vehicle rollover forty miles north of town. To his surprise the corpse had no visible injuries. The neck fracture had cost the young woman her life. Jim Bob thought she was a beautiful woman. He had not begun the embalming process yet. He hated to. She was still so…fresh.

As his hands ran over her lovely body, the old temptation and the voices urged him on. Jim Bob Skaggs once again listened to and obeyed the voices of evil.

The remorse and slight twinge of guilt always left him famished. He thought he would remove the evidence after a quick meal. He might even enjoy a little repeat visit with the young woman…if the voices kept suggesting he do so. He locked the door to the processing room securely behind him. He headed toward the town square just down the street.

The arrow silently pierced the abdomen of Jim Bob Skaggs. The modern razor-sharp steel broadhead sliced through skin, tissue, and liver efficiently. He fell stiffly to the concrete sidewalk. The tip of the broadhead penetrated a full inch into the man's spine rendering him unable to move. His arms and legs became stiff, completely frozen. No matter how hard he struggled, Jim Bob Skaggs could not move. The pain was hot and searing, the slightest attempted movement increased the intensity of the white-hot pain. Lying on the concrete, his head angling awkwardly down, he could see the last few inches of the arrow with its brightly colored fletching protruding from his abdomen. He could also see the blood, his blood, covering the walkway beneath him and flowing into the grass adjacent to the sidewalk. Several flies buzzed in and around the pool of blood they had quickly discovered.

He knew he would die right here on the sidewalk. Fear permeated his entire being. He could see the man walking away from him with the bow. He knew his words had cost him his life.

As Jim Bob Skaggs lay dying on the sidewalk, his only concern was the evidence. He would now be found out. The voices that normally were only in his mind seemed to take on shape. Dark forms encircled Jim Bob Skaggs. Straining to move, he attempted to escape the figures, the pain unbearable at the effort. Jim Bob Skaggs, with his eyes wide open, breathed his last breath.

What would the church folks think? His last conscious thought.

He began to realize he should have been much more concerned with the darkness that had enveloped the unseen world of which he was now becoming aware.

The Man walked the one hundred yards to his truck and loaded his bow in the rear seat. The Man replaced the missing arrow on his quiver with one from a new box he had purchased. None of the new arrows matched the one he had fired. As he drove away, he began to sing the Song of Victory. This song concerning victory...over evil.

The Man had no idea how great an evil he had just removed from the earth.

The investigators found no leads. They never even determined the direction from which the arrow had been fired. All cameras in the area showed nothing of the murder scene.

The investigators thought perhaps they had over one thousand suspects, although most of the Native Americans had left town prior to the incident. The case would go cold in a few short months. It would never be solved.

The news crews returned, however, upon the discovery of the condition of the young woman's body that had been under the care of Jim Bob Skaggs. A long-time employee of Skaggs's was not surprised at the news. The employee revealed Skaggs's unusual behavior and insistence on personally processing any women brought under the care of the funeral parlor. The employee also thought it odd the door to the processing room was kept locked and ordered off-limits when Skaggs's was embalming young women. The gruesome details spread across the nation once again. DNA from the scene of the necrophilia or as many considered, the rape, was a perfect match to that of Jim Bob Skaggs.

The public disgust and outrage eventually led to a second crime. A few days after the discovery of the young deceased woman's rape, the funeral parlor belonging to Jim Bob Skaggs was burned to the ground.

That crime, too, would remain unsolved. The investigators quite frankly were not especially motivated to find the arsonist.

****

The Man entered the Tribal Store at the agreed upon time and date. The men sat in silence…acknowledging one another with knowing looks. The Elder greeted The Man in the customary way.

"Your hunt was a success, my son."

The Man allowed a few moments to pass. There was no need for conversation to be rushed. Pouring his coffee, The Man seated himself at the table.

"Yes, Grandfather," The Man said. The smell of the wood stove was pungent this day. Steam rose in little clouds of vapor from the coffee cups around the table. The wind could be heard humming through the cracked single-pane windows. The sound seeming to add to the comfort provided by the wood burning stove. The other men reflected in silence, all inwardly rejoicing, as they quietly sipped their coffee. After a few moments, the Elder replied, "It is a good thing when the voice of evil is silenced."

The Warriors seated around the table all nodded in agreement.

****

From his home on the reservation, Tenahpu, (the meaning of his name translated to English was "The Man") watched the news coverage of a funeral home in Texas burning. The building collapsed around itself in the video. The firemen surrounding the scene evidently allowing the fire to burn out. No firehoses were pumping onto the burning building. Its destruction would be complete. The footage of the scene the following morning showed there was nothing left of the structure but an ash pile.

The Man raised his hands...and began to sing his song again.

PART THREE

Chapter 68

March 1

Tabba, Tosahwi, and David sat their horses, watching the buffalo herd as the animals grazed around the lake. The wind whipped the grass, making little ripples in its surface as the wind moved across the pasture. Many of the calves were coming early. The buffalo were nervous at the presence of the men on horseback. Many of the bulls snorted and pawed at the ground, challenging the unknown figures.

Today, they had counted 114 new calves. It appeared the herd would grow substantially. Many of the buffalo cows were still heavy with unborn calves.

The men moved away slowly and quietly, attempting to not disturb the creatures.

Once outside the pipe fencing, they were free to talk, although the conversation was limited.

"Cattle do well, David," Tabba said in broken English.

"Yes, the numbers are high on calves this year. If the rains come, we will have a record sale once they get some weight on them," David said.

"The rain will come, David," Tosahwi stated matter-of-factly. David caught the look in the man's eye. It was not a question in the mind of Tosahwi…it was a certainty.

David was amazed at the ability Tabba and Tosahwi possessed with horses and livestock. The two seemed to instinctively control their mounts with precision and the slightest touch. The horses responded immediately to seemingly indiscernible commands. All the impressive skill taking place without the need of a saddle as the two men rode bareback.

Their insight into the breeding and birthing of the cattle was beyond any ability of the ranch hands that had worked the ranch each spring.

"You know, David, the true abilities of the Comanche remain in our love and appreciation of quality war ponies. *The People* have always had a special way with horses. It is a gifting from the Great Spirit," Tosahwi said in perfect English.

David could certainly see that gifting as he admired the skill the men displayed simply moving across the open plain before them.

"The wild ponies should be in this area. Perhaps soon we will cross the sign of their trail," David said.

The three men moved along under the wind-swept Texas sky, observing, thinking, and planning for the future. Descending into a shallow valley, David thought there was nothing he could see that gave away the year and time they were now living and breathing and moving through. The blue sky, the little prickly cactus blooming, the feel of the wind on their shoulders, the warm sun on their backs, and the open prairie before them.

Not a sight or sound was out of place. He was in awe as he rode along with the Comanche Warriors…his friends.

No one spoke for over an hour as the three moved along, searching the skyline and the ground for signs of the wild ponies. However, communication was taking place.

Trust was being shaped. Iron was sharpening iron.

The creation was showing the three men her very best. Suddenly Tabba, with a light touch to the side of his mount, galloped away at full speed.

The wild horse herd in the distance bolted at the lead of a magnificent stallion. A cloud of dust formed at the rear of the galloping horses. Tosahwi, with an indiscernible nudge, accelerated his mount quickly. David, with the spurring of his horse raced away. Both in pursuit of Tabba and the stallion. The chase was on.

To the lead stallion, this romp was not a challenge. Tabba knew this about the stallion. Racing across the prairie, his mares followed. With the blood in his veins pumping, his heart racing…the thrill of being wild and free and able to escape at will, even the swiftest of pursuers, this was but a game to the stallion.

Tabba could quickly see this one would not be caught this day. This stallion was ruler of this kingdom.

Tabba simply could not believe the beauty of the animal, the strength and speed, the grace of the animal's stride; he knew this stallion was a rare sight to behold.

He slowly turned away from the stallion, angling at the mares toward the end of the herd. David and Tosahwi following in understanding, slowly widened their own pursuit. They would attempt to separate a few horses from the stallion. The strategy worked. Five or six of the group peeled away toward the east as the main herd raced across the prairie toward the north. The three men were close behind the few horses that had turned away. They could all hear the nickering of the stallion leading the other mares to safety.

Urging his mount, David loosened his rope. He was closing fast as the few mares that had separated from the main herd became confused and began to slow. Tabba, his lasso at the ready, closed on a beautiful mare quickly. The rope launched through the air, gracefully encircling the mare's neck and settling into place. Tabba expertly began to slow his mount but continued to run with the mare. Drawing alongside the horse, Tabba began to drive her away from the other few horses. Continuing to slow, the two horses were now at a slow gallop. The mare, her eyes wild and rolling, seemed uncertain. The presence of Tabba's horse settled her.

David and Tosahwi had broken off their pursuit of the other horses and now followed closely behind Tabba as the lassoed mare continued to slow.

David had never witnessed such expert horsemanship in what he saw next. Tabba slacked the rope he had used to lasso the mare. The mare continued stride for stride with Tabba's mount. Rising from his seat, Tabba stood in a low crouching position on the back of his horse. Waiting for the perfect timing of the move, pausing a few seconds, Tabba lept from his mount onto the back of the wild mare. The animal never lost a step. The mare continued right along with Tabba's mount keeping in perfect stride with the other two riders galloping close behind.

David could not believe what he had seen. Tabba had taken in the slack of his braided rope and urged the mare ahead. The beautiful mare sped away from the three horses, leaving them in a trail of dust.

Tabba whooped a cry of what David thought was the sound of pure joy.

Tabba was blessed to have caught the mare. He knew she would be an excellent mount for years to come. David and Tosahwi followed in the distance at full speed, unable to match the speed of Tabba's new mount. Tabba's previous mount dutifully fell in stride with David and Tosahwi. The two men slowed their mounts to a trot as Tabba headed in the direction of the hunting lodge.

Tabba knew he would return for the stallion, having never seen a more beautiful animal. The Warrior also knew this one would be difficult to capture. It would take precise timing and planning. But it could be done.

David and Tosahwi turned to follow Tabba.

"This is a good day," Tosahwi stated.

"Yes, my Friend, a very good day." The two men gazed into the knowing eyes of one another.

Like all men who consider the future and what may come of their life's work after they leave this Earth, David was considering the future of the ranch. What he was seeing from his Comanche friends was very encouraging.

Their skill, their knowledge, their giftings were beyond compare. More importantly, the respect and care these men showed for the land and the animals that lived upon it was what convinced David J. Ross more than anything.

He now knew in his heart what he would do, what actions he would take concerning the future of the ranch.

He would see William tomorrow. They would begin to work out the details over the next few days.

Chapter 69

Sana sat in front of her computer in the public library, finishing the history paper assigned to the class. She enjoyed chatting with her professor and other students, all of whom were hundreds of miles apart. She was again in awe of the technology in this new world in which she was equipping herself to live. She had taken twelve hours of online classes in addition to this Texas History class.

The paper she had just completed contained information and insight that, according to her professor, sounded "Like she had actually been there."

She *had* been.

With the tutelage from Abby, Sana was maintaining a perfect GPA. She intended to use her education in a way that would benefit the San Saba Comanche Tribe most effectively. Sana was beginning to understand how important education would be in attaining her goal for *The People*.

A Homeland and sovereignty for her tribe.

Dr. Nina Rainwater was assisting Sana with studies of the current history and status of the major Indian tribes in the United States. The pattern of failing government-run programs was consistent and astonishing to Sana. Many of the tribes were not doing well.

Casinos had been built across the nation on tribal lands. Hotels, restaurants, even shopping malls had been constructed. The profits from the development never seemed to benefit the tribes. Exorbitant interest rates were charged by fund managers, debt was a heavy burden on local tribal councils. Outside management firms skimmed profits, and Nevada corporations mismanaged and outright stole hundreds of millions of dollars. The result was the average tribal members struggled in poverty, lack of education, and many of *The People* even struggled with enough food to feed their families.

The economic development of tribal lands appeared to be benefiting several corporations and banking institutions. That development was not, however, benefiting those for which it was intended, Native American families.

Dr Nina Rainwater, along with Abby, encouraged Sana to think differently.

Sana was doing just that. A plan for the future was growing in her heart and mind. She thought she would never want to abandon the traditions of her people. How could she possibly set her little tribe on a foundation of financial security? Was there a path forward in the new life they had all been given? Casinos or shopping malls were far from the dreams she hoped for her people. Could the old ways and the brave new world she and Tabba had awakened to co-exist? The one thing still foremost in her mind remained, their need for a Homeland.

She hurried to the downtown coffee shop, anxious to share her new thoughts with Abby and Nina.

As she walked along, the vision came to her as a gift. She paused along the courthouse square, closed her eyes tightly, and saw the future. She saw her future and that of her sons, and her little tribe.

Topusana was once again comforted deep in her soul…at the vision she had been granted.

Chapter 70

March 4

Nan Chisholm, Abby's friend and art dealer from New York, listened quietly as Sana explained her reason for the decision. Grace had joined Sana, Abby, and Nina Rainwater. The five women sat in the cozy little breakfast nook overlooking the San Saba. The painting was displayed on a tripod in the center of the kitchen. It was difficult for Sana to concentrate on the conversation. That embrace from Prairie Song...she could still actually feel. That loving touch radiated forth from the painting. As Sana peered into the not so long ago past, her thoughts seemed to remove her from the comfort of the room, the present, and transport her instantly to the frozen prairie and her former life.

It was still beyond her comprehension that the moment had been captured by the man. The man Tabba had met on the prairie, Karl Bodmer.

Sana realized from her recent vision her little tribe would soon need a school.

Abby had continued the English lessons with Tabba. She had also begun to teach the seventeen other survivors who had awakened. Sana, Grandmother, and Dr. Rainwater had also been assisting in translating and teaching. The group met each day in the hunting lodge. Two hours each morning was followed by meal preparation, lunch, and then another two-hour afternoon session. The younger children were learning rapidly. The children picking up the new language much more readily than the older ones.

All *The People* were working together, making a concerted effort to feed, clean, and in general, make certain the little tribe was safe, sound, and well fed. It was much like how they had lived in another time. However, with the benefits of modern technology, running water, heat, and electricity, the little tribe had much more time available for education.

Sana knew the English classes would soon turn to reading, math, history, and more. A school for *The People* was at the heart of her vision.

She admired Abby so much; she too wanted to learn and learn quickly. Topusana wanted to become a teacher…just like her mother, Abby.

"Sana, selling the painting will not be difficult. I believe it is such an important piece that placing the piece at auction is not necessary. The moment I mention its existence and publish your intent to sell, a bidding war will quickly ensue," Nan said. "I would hope that one of the major institutions would be interested, or perhaps one of the many college collections. I will contact a few of the curators I know personally, and we will know quickly where we are market wise. One thing we may be able to secure as part of any sale to an institution would be having one of the many talented artists that work for the museums recreate the painting for you. I have seen this done in the past, and I can promise you the work will be perfect. You may not be able to tell the difference between the original and the copy, except for the signature."

Nan continued. "Speaking of the signature, there may be some additional value if you sign the original painting, Sana." Nan had thought through this topic and possibility while discussing it with her fellow experts. She could not begin to imagine the added value of a classic from one of the Masters, if the subject had autographed the piece. This was the first time in history that this had become a possibility.

Sana was amazed at the revelation of the painting's value, as were the other women. But the concept of paper dollars and their value was difficult for Sana to comprehend. What she did know was the painting could be traded for a school, and that was all that mattered in her mind.

"What do you think?" Sana asked the group.

Grace spoke first. "Sana, you would receive the funds…possibly ten million dollars for the building of the school, enough for construction, and permanent funding for its operation. You would have an exact replica of the painting to hang in your room. I think it's a wonderful thing for you to go forward with. *The People* will benefit for generations."

"I agree wholeheartedly," Nina Rainwater said.

"Mother, what are your thoughts?" Sana asked.

"I could never imagine a better investment, or a more generous and honestly, a more forward-looking plan for your 'New Beginning,' Sana. I love the way you're thinking. It's a wonderful plan!"

Grace, observing and listening, thought inwardly for a moment.

Since her first meeting with Topusana, something within her soul had changed. A monumental shift in her entire life, even the questions she had begun to ask herself…that were so introspective. For the first time in her life, Grace desired to be a part of something that mattered. Something that brought significance to her as a human being. All the dreams she had chased, even her success, had left her empty and searching. Searching for purpose. Having seen her new friends Sana and Tabba struggling just to survive, Grace Ross desired deeply to be a part, a part of helping to contribute to this fascinating story. Perhaps she would find significance in giving her talents, lending her life to the needs of others. She had observed from a distance, it seemed, her mother, Abby, doing that very thing. Giving of her life, her talent, her resources, her very self. Grace thought her mother, Abigail Ross, was perhaps the most content person on the planet. After hearing again, the generosity, the hope that Sana held for the future, Grace decided to share her inmost hopes, dreams, and plans she had already put into action. Somewhat nervously she stood before the women in the little breakfast nook and opened her heart.

"I've also been thinking about how I may have a role in what's happening here on the ranch and with *The People*," Grace said. "I was going to save this news as a surprise for Mom and Dad later this week, but since we are on the subject. I have sold my home in Malibu. Mom, I'm coming home."

Abby's eyes filled with tears of joy at the words she thought she would never hear. Hugs of joy spread throughout the room.

"My plan is to use the proceeds of the house sale to build an art studio here on the ranch. I'm thinking near the school, making it part of the campus. *The People*, your people Sana, will also learn and develop their creative giftings along with their overall education. I can build a sculpture studio anywhere. Home, here among *The People,* seems the most beneficial and logical place. Now, I'm thinking it may also need a few classrooms."

The tears slowly ran down the face of Grace Ross.

"Perhaps I can finally now do something with my life that matters," whispered Grace.

Sana was stunned at the offer of generosity and love from Grace. She looked directly into the beautiful eyes of Grace and could see the emotion, the desire to simply help.

Sana moved toward Grace and raised her hands to Grace's face and held them along each cheek in an intimate graceful touch. "Grace, your life does matter. Sometimes our human spirits deny our unique giftings. You are now finding your true path. It will be an honor to walk this path beside you, my sister." In that moment, a new bond formed between Grace and Sana. A lifelong knitting of hearts had taken place again in the quaint little nook, along the banks of the San Saba.

Nan Chisholm, breaking the silent moment said quietly, "With your permission, Sana, I will proceed?"

"Yes, Nan, let's move forward as the young children are already in need of the school." Feeling her belly, she added, "More students will be added soon."

The smiles and the excitement level in the room was electric. The plan, or the *vision,* was unfolding and being revealed.

The vision was accurate and comforting not only to Topusana but to the others to whom it was slowly being unveiled.

The Comforter was indeed at work.

Chapter 71

March 24

David and Abby sat at a corner table of the Driskill Grill with William Travis and Dr. Nina Rainwater. The old Driskill Hotel, built in the 1880s, was one of William's favorites in Austin. With its beautiful façade and rich history, William thought it the perfect setting for what he had planned.

David was always in awe of the hotel and its history. His great-great-grandfather Sullivan Ross had held his inaugural ball in this very room. The history of presidents and world leaders meeting in this place gave the quaint little dinner party an atmosphere of significance. As David reflected on the history, he knew the magnitude of their recent decisions would correct some of the unjust decisions of his ancestors.

The future of *The People* was in the balance and the decisions David, Abby, and Topusana had made and put into effect over the last few days would affect generations to come.

This was now William and Nina's second double date with David and Abby; however, William and Nina had been seeing one another every day since the trial had ended. The two were absolutely enchanted with one another. Abby could see instantly it was more than a date. It was plainly obvious the two were head over heels in love. Abby ribbed David under the table, indicating William's nervousness. David questioned what she was trying to say, a puzzled look on his face.

William could hardly contain himself. As the dinner came to a close, he felt for the ring box in his coat pocket. Yes, it was still there. He was completely captivated by the natural beauty of Dr. Nina Rainwater. But over the last few weeks, he thought it was her intellect that attracted him more than her physical appearance. Nina held, not one, but two doctoral degrees. One degree was from the University of Utah in Native American linguistics. The other in psychology from UC Berkeley. She had used her training and expertise to build a consulting firm based in Salt Lake City. Nina had a wide-ranging list of clients, including several government agencies and tribal councils from across the nation.

Nina, too, was drawn to William Travis, physically, intellectually, and idealistically. The man was absolutely gorgeous with his sandy blond hair, beautiful blue eyes, and with the physique of a man in his twenties, even though William was now in his sixties. His intellect was off the charts. The raw attraction she had for William made her feel and act like a schoolgirl. She was enjoying that feeling immensely.

The two discussed at length the large population of Native American veterans, several of whom William had represented. They would talk for hours about possible solutions and activism toward their respective causes. Being extremely like-minded, both were drawn to one another's thinking and philosophy. The deep discussions actually stimulated both of them, in their minds and hearts.

William Travis had decided years ago he would never love again in the way he had before the loss of his wife. The emotional cost was, he thought, just too high. From the first moment he saw Nina Rainwater those thoughts simply disappeared.

Nina, after a failed marriage, could never quite find a man that possessed the qualities she was looking for: intellect, good looks, and a heart for something bigger than one's own self-interest. She had found all of that and more in William Travis. She placed her hand on his inner thigh under the table. Desire rising again, her heart skipping, her mind imagining his touch. She hoped the dinner wouldn't last too long.

William looked at Nina. Nina, seeing the "look," leaned toward him and whispered in his ear. "I know what you're thinking. Go ahead and think. Perhaps what you're thinking will soon become more than just thought." A longing look swept her own face, and she gazed into the eyes of her new love. William swallowed hard.

He admired her regal appearance. She was again elegantly dressed in a stunning white dress that rode low across her shoulders, revealing her beautiful, smooth, flawless dark skin, and more…the curve of her breasts and cleavage the dress discreetly revealed. Her elegant chin seemed always slightly raised. The way Nina held herself, a Native American woman proud of her heritage. She exuded a balance somehow of intellect, beauty, and…sexuality. William tried not to stare. Gold and silver Native American jewelry adorned her body, bracelets, a delicate necklace, earrings. The beauty was natural and stunning; however, her insight and ability to know his thoughts were simply captivating, William thought.

She whispered lightly in his ear, "It's OK to stare."

David began to see what was coming and smiled at his life-long friend. William took a deep breath.

Reaching into his coat pocket, William Travis removed the little box, opened it, and set it on the table between him and his future wife, Ms. Nina Rainwater. The beautiful combination of diamonds, turquoise, and gold glittered in the soft light.

The quiet of the pause was worth a thousand words…a thousand proposals. William Travis had rehearsed his speech over and over. But no words would come. He sat in the stillness of the moment unable to speak. Staring into her eyes. Staring into the heart and soul of this woman. Nina, while peering deeply into his eyes, gave her reply without words. She took the ring, and with the assistance of William, placed it on her ring finger. Tears flowed freely from both of them. They stood and embraced one another.

The kiss was deep and intimate. The emotion of the two washed over them. Years of heartache, and loss, the searching, the deep longings that all human beings carry, were ended.

Two souls, with some divine intervention, they would both agree, had discovered one another.

Abby held David's hand under the table, the tears coming for her also. The two looked at one another and smiled. Abby whispered they should go. The four embraced. Words of hope and congratulations were exchanged. Abby and David were honored to have been a part of the special evening. William and Nina made an awkwardly hasty exit to the knowing smiles of Abby and David.

Abby and David exited the beautiful hotel, pausing in the heavy atmosphere of the Austin night. The warmth and humidity felt familiar and comfortable, even refreshing somehow. Awaiting the valet, under the beautiful exterior of the Driskill, David reached for Abby. She received his intimate kiss, open, sensual. The two held the embrace while Abby whispered softly into David's ear, "Take me home, love."

David dialed Steve's number. "I think we can depart a little early. We'll meet at the airport in fifteen minutes."

The jet landed after the short twenty-five-minute flight from Austin. Abby sat next to David in the truck as they drove along the highway toward the ranch house on the San Saba.

"I think Tosahwi would say 'This is a good day,'" David said.

Abby, smiling, placed her hand gently on David's inner thigh, and said "I'm glad we got away early, aren't you?" The kind of look she recognized so easily was growing across David's face.

Chapter 72

May 1

The behemoth stood tall and stark across the West Texas sky. The huge two-inch steel cables were now securely attached to the pylons driven deeply into the caliche ground surrounding the structure. The welders and roustabouts busily went about their duties of securing equipment, even welding toolboxes and equipment into place on the giant platform. The sky was aglow, the sun reflecting a crimson tint from the West Texas sand held aloft by the constant wind.

Drilling would begin within hours.

The land, one mile by one mile, containing 640 acres, or exactly one section located in far western Andrews County, David and Will had obtained in a quite unusual way. It had been deeded to himself and William Travis upon the recent death of a long-time friend of David's father, one Sergeant Dan Walker.

David's father and Sergeant Walker had served together in Korea. Both sailed together on the naval destroyer *USS Fletcher*.

David and Will had come to the aide of Mr. Walker years ago. The section of land Mr. Walker had purchased after his tour of duty in Korea and subsequent discharge from the Navy due to the injuries he had received in the line of duty, had been under constant attack. Mr. Walker had been continually harassed over the years by oil companies both large and small. The land, in most probability, contained a huge amount of oil beneath it.

Mr. Walker simply did not want the drilling activity on his land nor the complicated life that oil money was certain to bring him.

He preferred a quiet, simple life of raising a few cattle. He enjoyed daily his life's dream of riding his horse on his West Texas ranch and relishing in the life he had so narrowly escaped losing as a young man in a faraway place.

As often happens with the unscrupulous when they do not have their way above board, they ultimately resort to other tactics.

One company attempted to stake a claim on the mineral rights supposedly granted on the land from a previous owner. Mr. Walker, while unable to afford the legal counsel necessary, came very near to losing those mineral rights and the land. That would have most certainly occurred if David Ross, with the assistance of William Travis, had not intervened. It would take two years of legal maneuvering to rid the land of the false claims and subsequent clouding of the title those claims had caused. Mr. Walker eventually prevailed. The man lived out his life peacefully on his beloved little ranch in far West Texas. He was forever grateful for the financial and legal assistance David and William had provided him. Upon his recent death, the one section tract of land was bequeathed to David Ross and William Travis.

A note in Mr. Walker's own handwriting attached to his Last Will and Testament said, "OK, boys, drill away!"

The huge deposits of oil beneath its surface had never been developed. At the angst of the largest corporations in the world, the independent driller retained by the newly formed Ross & Travis Energy Company would begin exploration within hours.

David and Will stood observing the huge structure. "The oil is there, isn't it?" William said more as a statement than a question.

"Yes, it's there. Look around us." The pump jacks ran 24/7 on all the surrounding properties. Some of the neighboring wells produced hundreds of barrels per day...per well.

"The only question really is, how much is down there?" David said.

As he reflected, David thought about the technology the driller would employ. It was the most advanced in the industry. There would be one well head, but five or more horizontal well holes would be utilized. The technique of drilling horizontally and angling downward into the depths of the earth would reduce the environmental impact on the land. It was an expensive process; the costs would soar into the millions quickly. The potential upside was perhaps in the hundreds of millions.

The excitement for the project was growing between the two friends. The kinds of resources that could become available to them both were limitless.

The men knew any windfall would primarily be given away to their respective causes.

The solid foundational character and goodness of the two men would be proven soon, proven to the innumerable recipients of their generosity: children's hospitals, cancer research centers, universities, veteran advocacy groups. Multiple charities across the nation would be forever grateful for the philanthropy these two men would soon disperse.

The New Comanche Nation headquartered in Little Grove, Texas, would, however, become the primary beneficiary of the massive oil reserve that lay beneath the surface.

This well would take fifteen million dollars to complete. David, ever the prudent businessman, borrowed nothing for the project.

Upon completion, the production was estimated at eleven hundred barrels of oil per day. Gross income of fifty-four thousand dollars per day. That number would be multiplied fivefold. Within the next year four additional wells would be drilled on the one section ranch. The net income from the oil production would exceed one hundred million dollars annually.

David soon realized the San Saba Comanche Tribe would become the wealthiest Indian tribe in the United States. The little group that had survived the attack on the San Saba was, indeed, now a people with which to be reckoned.

Chapter 73

June 4

William Travis sat alongside Topusana as they appeared before the full panel of the Texas Land Commission. William had worked tirelessly over the last three months. Even gaining an audience with the commission was a minor miracle.

The men and women listened intently to the presentation. Many of the individual members had followed the news of the San Saba Comanche. Several had feared this type of action might be requested. Despite the stonewalling William Travis had received in every other state agency, the Texas Land Commission had a policy in effect for securing a position on their agenda by any Texas resident. William Travis followed their set procedures, and now was before the full Commission.

His request was concise and to the point.

There were survivors from the Comanche Nation. Their lands had been stolen. They had never been compensated in any fashion by the state of Texas for their Homelands.

The Texas Land Commission managed thirteen million acres of land. Much of it was currently for sale. Many state parks and public lands within Texas were managed by and under the authority of the commission.

William Travis was before the panel in an advisory capacity, having been retained by the San Saba Comanche Tribe.

What he was proposing were reparations. Reparations in the form of land. This, he stated, was to be a friendly first inquiry as to the possibilities and the position of the independent members of the commission.

"Gentlemen, my client can show immeasurable damage. Damage to these few survivors, both in life, culture, and loss of their rightful Homelands.

"I realize this is a first step. The question before you is, will you consider any tract of land currently administered by your commission?"

"What consideration are you asking for, Mr. Travis?" the chairman asked.

"Establishment of a reservation for the San Saba Comanche Tribe," William Travis replied.

"Do you have an area in mind, sir?" a member asked.

"I do indeed. Big Bend National Park."

The room grew silent at the suggestion.

"That's over 800,000 acres, sir." the commissioner said.

"I am well aware of that. And every acre of that land was once a very small part of the Homelands of the Comanche People. All that land lies within the state of Texas. It is one of the few undeveloped tracts that would meet the needs of the Comanche People."

The commissioners were shocked at such a bold request. The room again fell silent for several moments as the individual members digested what had been proposed.

"Has this tribe been designated *officially* as a State Designated Tribal Statistical Area (SDTSA) by the state of Texas or gained federal recognition from the Bureau of Indian Affairs in Washington?" the commissioner asked. The commissioner knew fully the answer to the questions he was posing. Texas had no governmental process in place to comply with what he was asking, nor was there any procedure within the current state bureaucracy by which the San Saba Comanche might pursue that designation.

The man had done his homework. William Travis would give him credit for the most revealing question he could ask.

"Not yet, Commissioner. However, that work, on the federal designation and application is underway, and we expect a decision from the BIA soon," William said.

"Until such designation, I see no need to pursue this request."

"Sir, I understand that. My client is very interested in the possibilities and what your position may be on the matter. Some indication on the part of the Land Commission would help us determine our strategy in the future."

"By that I take it to mean should you come before the commission in the future with a legal request or with a team of lawyers?"

William Travis looked the man in the eye. He appreciated his directness.

"I can see, sir, you are a man who doesn't want to waste time in niceties, which I appreciate. That is exactly what I would like to determine, Commissioner."

The commissioner looked down the elevated platform to his colleagues and replied. "Let me first say thank you for your directness, Mr. Travis. But may I pose a question to you before I answer?"

"Absolutely, sir," William said.

"What do you suppose your great-great-grandfather would say to such a request? The man was a hero. A brave individual who fought and died for this great state and its establishment. As I understand our history, he also fought in several battles against those you are representing, and was, in fact, severely wounded in one of those…skirmishes. Is that not correct?"

"Yes, that is true, Commissioner. To answer your question, the commander of Texas troops at the Alamo, William B. Travis, was in support of many of the agreements and treaties offered to *The People*. In fact, he reprimanded many of those who simply changed their minds after the violation of those agreements and treaties or for their refusal to ratify those treaties. War for my great-great-grandfather was always a last option.

"I believe if he were here today, he would, as an attorney and statesman, absolutely be in favor of such a request, in favor of the state of Texas honoring even a fraction of what it had once agreed to."

The commissioner was impressed by such an answer.

"Thank you for your honest appraisal of the question, Mr. Travis. I will be just as forward and honest with you. We, as a commission, have discussed this in closed session. I want you to know exactly where we stand as a public body.

"We will oppose you at every turn, sir. I will make certain every request is denied. Texas fought the war against the Comanche, and we won it."

Sana was shocked at the commissioner's statement. His words seemed to sting within her heart. She rose from her seat, staring directly into the commissioner's eyes as she questioned the man.

"Was it a war? Or was it extermination? Or perhaps genocide? Did you lose any children in this war? I did," Topusana stated.

Topusana turned and exited the meeting room. She exhibited a sense of pride and honor, even nobility as she walked regally from the commission chambers.

The room became quiet. The few words she had spoken had impacted the mindset and position of several of the commission members. After an awkward few moments, the Chairman replied, "I would say bring on the lawsuits. We will never consider the request unless ordered to do such. Is that a clear enough answer for you and your client, Mr. Travis?"

"Crystal clear, Mr. Chairman. Thank you for your time today."

"Furthermore, Mr. Travis, you should know, as I am sure you do, Big Bend National Park was deeded to the National Park Service by the state of Texas in 1944. We do not own the land, nor did Texas retain any control over it. Your request for reparations from Texas on that land may be somewhat misguided, sir."

"I understand that perfectly. If I may, there have been seven instances of the National Park Service closing national parks and transferring ownership of those lands to other entities. In all those instances, the states in which the transfers were accomplished supported the action of the Park Service. Obviously, if we had your support, the request would have precedence."

The commissioner looked surprised at this information. The commissioner had no idea a land transfer from the Park Service was even a possibility.

"We will not be supportive of any type of transfer requested by your clients. Is that clear enough for you, Mr. Travis?"

"Very clear, sir."

William Travis would use this position and public declaration of such to a decided advantage in the court of public opinion for the San Saba Comanche Tribe.

William knew the eight-hundred-thousand-acre tract of land that was once a small portion of the Comanche Nation would soon become a battleground. Texas would obviously once again fight to prevent any form of restitution to the Native Americans from whom it had been stolen.

Many of those individuals entering the battle for this land on behalf of Texas had never seen, nor traveled, nor lived on that parcel of land now known as The Big Bend.

The small band of Comanche survivors, including Topusana and Tabbananica, however, knew most of that country by heart. As history recorded, those survivors had spent years living in and on and within its boundaries.

Their fight for the land was not about a piece of paper or boundary lines on a map.

This fight for the Comanche survivors was, today, about recovering a small piece of their once sacred Homeland.

****

The Man watched the news coverage of the proceedings from his home on the reservation. The comments from the chairman of the Texas Land Commission stung within his heart, within the hearts of all Warriors who listened to the unjust attitude and position.

The Man began to plan. It seemed another hunting trip would soon be necessary.

Chapter 74

Nina Rainwater was also hard at work with her own research. Her labor and experience with other Native American groups across the nation gave her much insight into the process of gaining federal recognition for Native American peoples. With her expertise and contacts at the Bureau of Indian Affairs, she was certain the San Saba Tribe of Comanche would soon be granted federal status.

In her research, she had discovered Texas had, throughout the later portion of the twentieth century, fumbled through the process of exactly how to administer the one remaining federally recognized tribe.

She had learned that in 1965 the Texas legislature established a Commission for Indian Affairs. Its sole purpose was to benefit financially, culturally, and educationally the Alabama-Coushata Indians living in the big thicket area of far East Texas. Most legislators did not consider the tribe viable, as the majority of its members were of less than 25 percent Native American ancestry. Many were 12.5 percent Native American, meaning one great-grandparent was Native American. None of the tribal members were 100 percent Native American. Texas had adopted a management style from one administration to the next similar to many governmental programs. That being, "Perhaps if we ignore the problem, it will go away."

It did not. In 1967, the Tigua Indian community of far West Texas was added to the oversight of the Texas Commission for Indian Affairs. The following year, the Tigua would gain federal recognition as an official tribe.

In 1975, Texas was still struggling with how to manage the few Native

Americans living in Texas, the legislature officially changing the name of the commission to the Texas Indian Commission.

In 1977, much to the dismay of Texas politicians, the Kickapoo Tribe of Eagle Pass was added to the jurisdiction of the Texas Indian Commission. The Kickapoo subsequently gained federal recognition as a tribe in 1984.

In 1985, the three tribes were so dissatisfied with the effort, or lack thereof, on the part of the state of Texas and its Texas Indian Commission, the tribes all petitioned the federal government to extend federal trust protection to each of them. The federal government approved the request. Thereby, those few tribes would now be administered by the Bureau of Indian Affairs in Washington, DC.

The move by the tribes set in motion the demise of the Texas Indian Commission.

In 1989, the Texas legislature moved that the Commission change its structure and become an advocacy office to represent the interests of Native American cultures within the borders of Texas. Much to the dismay of civil-rights activists and Native American support groups, the Texas legislature failed to act on the legislation and any further funding of the Texas Indian Commission. The bill was allowed to die in committee. Also dead was any further funding concerning oversight of Native American peoples living in Texas.

The Texas Indian Commission officially closed its doors in August of 1989.

Nina understood completely what was now common knowledge among Native American advocacy groups. Over the last century and a half, Texas had failed to address the problem of assisting the Native peoples and cultures whose land they had inhabited by force, and whose people they had imprisoned, enslaved, and attempted to commit genocide against.

Nina Rainwater saw the opportunity the history afforded.

Texas would have no voice or political opportunity to deny the application for federal recognition to the San Saba Comanche. The state had no agency nor advocacy in place to even consider an application, nor representatives from such to either oppose or support the federal recognition of the San Saba Comanche Tribe.

The federal government, and the life-long friends of Nina Rainwater at the Bureau of Indian Affairs, would determine the fate of the nineteen-member tribe unhindered by the state of Texas.

Nina would use scientific facts rather than politics. She would utilize the exact science of DNA blood quantum testing.

Chapter 75

June 8
Lawton, Oklahoma

Tabba, Sana, and Tosahwi sat quietly as the tribal official signed the required paperwork. Old Grandmother, Mrs. Hantaywee, sat beside Sana, holding her hand.

Tosahwi spoke. *"Thank you for your assistance, Grandfather,"* directing his statement to the tribal Elder assisting them. The two men made eye contact, the pain of what was about to take place shared between them.

David and Abby waited in the outer office with William and Nina Rainwater.

Mrs. Mary Running Deer had facilitated all the required approvals throughout the Comanche Nation governmental structure.

With all the necessary documents in hand, the group loaded into a tribal van and began the long drive to the outskirts of the reservation. Their destination: one of the many old tribal burial grounds.

Heat waves shimmered off the surface of the highway as the van made its way across the reservation. Dry thunderstorms dotted the skyline to the north and west. Distant rumbles of thunder could be heard even inside the van as it traveled along the pot-filled pavement. Exiting the highway, the entire group observed the conditions in which many of the tribal members lived. David noticed again the ill-repair of the homes and especially the suffering condition of the horses.

"Is there no grass for horses in Oklahoma?" Tabba said in disgust.

The question from Tabba was quite sincere.

Grandmother replied. "Only when the rains come does the earth feed the animals. Otherwise, they are much like *The People.*"

The group traveled along in silence, reflecting on what Old Grandmother had said.

"How are they alike, Grandmother?" Sana asked.

"They are both trapped within the confines of life on the reservation. The horse is no longer free. This is also true for *The People.*"

Dr. Nina Rainwater thought how profound the truth was that continually came forth from Old Grandmother. All silently agreed with the statement.

Sana decided this day she would do everything in her power to see these living conditions never occurred within the New Comanche Nation. She was also considering how she might assist *The People* of the present Comanche Nation and how they might work together to improve the life within and on the reservation.

The red dirt road they now traveled on left a trail of rising dust that could be seen for miles. The gust front from the storms swept the trailing clouds of dirt across the road. The dust cloud rotated and swirled, flying away behind the van as if escaping from some unseen pursuer.

The men, seeing the dust cloud drawing near, arose from the shade of the tree, awaiting the arrival of their brothers and sisters. No words were spoken among the men. These Warriors knew this would be a difficult day.

The Comanche believed the site of the dead was forever a sacred and holy place.

Only with the fervent prayers of Grandmother and Tosahwi would the men even dare such an act.

The van pulled to a stop in the cloud of red dust. The little delegation exited silently.

Small gravestones dotted the little cemetery. The wind had settled; the heat and humidity were stifling. The untended graves were overgrown with brush.

The names were recognizable to Tosahwi, Sana, and Tabba. Those markers were all that was left of many friends and family members, the only evidence that these people had ever lived, or loved, or existed. A simple stone marker.

Tears began to flow down Sana's face. She felt deep in her soul the loss of each friend. As she read the names one at a time, she paused before each gravesite. She attempted to picture each person's face in her mind. It wasn't difficult for her to do so.

From her perspective, she had seen these friends and family members just a few short months ago. Kota, Maguara, Tahsi. In her mind, at the reading of each name, there seemed a sharp painful reminder of where she had come from and what she had escaped.

Tabba and Tosahwi slowly made their way through the tangled brush covering the overgrown graves, stopping in front of the great Chief's marker.

"Buffalo Hump, Grandfather To Us All," was engraved on the small granite stone.

The men lit the small sacred fire as instructed by Old Grandmother.

There was no song for what was about to occur. The little group encircled the fire as Tosahwi began to pray. The ceremony was somber and the prayers heartfelt and sincere. Tosahwi prayed for understanding and grace. He acknowledged that the Great Spirit knew what was about to take place, and that this act would benefit His Children.

He acknowledged the forgiving power of the Great Spirit. He praised Him for what He was creating again.

Tosahwi spoke his last prayers in English. A request for the blessing of His Children. A request for faith to be present in each heart. A request that His will be done this fine day.

Finishing his prayers, he nodded in the direction of the men.

The Warriors began, very carefully…to dig.

The Man dressed in jeans and a long sleeve flannel shirt. He kept a bandana tied around his face with a straw cowboy hat drawn low across his eyes, the dark sunglasses completing his outfit. The dress concealed his identity completely. It also concealed the tears that sprung forth from his eyes as he watched his daughter weeping among the stone markers that identified her friends and family.

The Warriors and The Man located the wooden casket and gently loosened the soil surrounding it. The men carefully dug around the outer perimeter of the casket. The soil they piled to one side of the grave in a great red hump. The Man gently swept the remaining dust and dirt from the top of the cedar box casket and released the cover.

The forensic technician from the tribe removed the top piece of the casket and without looking at the Great Chief, covered his face and the remains of the upper torso with an ornate burial cloth.

The technician set up his equipment and performed the procedure. The DNA evidence obtained would be properly documented. A digital video recording of the procedure was made for posterity. The samples were properly labeled and sealed in three separate medical kits. The DNA strands of Buffalo Hump would now be forever preserved.

Tosahwi stood over the open casket of his lifelong friend. He knew in his heart the spirit of the man was long departed. He seated himself on the mound of earth adjacent to his friend's grave. Pausing, he closed his eyes…and listened.

The wind whistled through the broken-down barbed wire fence surrounding the little cemetery. Tosahwi could hear the faint voices. The voices sang the old songs. The songs of long ago. He attempted to recall as many memories as he could flush into the forefront of his mind. The voices in the wind reminded him of many things. The two had spent many good days together. With his eyes closed, a slight smile grew on the face of Tosahwi.

The Dream Time had separated the two men just a few months ago. Yet the 174 years that had passed on Earth and the separation time had brought seemed like a thousand years to Tosahwi.

"I miss you, my friend. This new time is much different than how we lived. In many ways we are no longer free. I long for the day when you and I might ride out again across a frozen prairie. The buffalo before us. Our women in the warm teepees, awaiting our return. I will see you again…soon…very soon, my friend."

Tosahwi sat in silence beside the grave of his dearest friend. The wind whispered the old songs in his heart. The tears fell from his face onto the red dirt he was seated upon.

Tosahwi knew it was time to move again. The Dream Time was calling to him.

He sat in silence for a moment, then rose and nodded to the Warriors. The men slowly closed the wooden casket and lowered it gently into the shallow grave.

The Warriors and The Man, along with Tabba and Tosahwi, began to cover their friend with the earth. Each knew in his heart that Buffalo Hump, their grandfather, really wasn't there in the box. They knew his spirit now walked with the Great Spirit.

The songs in the wind grew in volume. The Warriors began to sing along with the voices in the wind.

Once the grave was filled, The Man gently raked the disturbed soil, smoothing it expertly. Whispering inwardly a prayer of thankfulness.

The small group of men lingered in the shade of the trees surrounding the little graveyard. The Warriors, along with The Man, had laid to rest, for the last time, the remains of their grandfather Buffalo Hump. It was an honor for these Warriors to have been chosen for the task.

The men would soon speak of the experience…the hope and promise the future held for their brothers and sisters of the San Saba Comanche Tribe. The Man would consider the effect of silencing the voice of evil. Tomorrow they would gather once again over coffee at the Tribal Store.

Though the process was somewhat uncomfortable and unnerving, the little group of friends and family departed the old burial grounds with the overwhelming presence of hope. That hope enveloped them as they rode along in silence. Each heart seemed to understand the significance of what had been done. Traveling along the bumpy red dirt road, Grandmother began to sing, breaking the silence. The others, one by one, joining in, following her lead.

The Man watched from the stone markers as his daughter, Topusana, and his son-in-law, Tabbananica, drove away. He removed the bandana and sunglasses. His face and eyes were coated with the red dirt that had clung to the tears he had shed in silence under the bandana.

The results from the DNA testing of all nineteen members of the San Saba Comanche Tribe would show each of them to be of 100 percent Native American Ancestry. Many were direct decedents of Buffalo Hump.

7:00 A.M.
The Following Morning

Tosahwi was seated in a chair at the circular table toward the rear of the Tribal Store. He and the Elder conversed in their Native tongue, talking of the days ahead concerning the future of the little tribe from the San Saba.

The wood burning stove gave off a scent of wood smoke as it glowed in the corner of the store. The smell of strong coffee and bacon cooking permeated the atmosphere of the room. The Warrior, George Ten Bear, had just joined them, seating himself facing toward the door, ever vigilant.

The door opened wide as Tenahpu entered. He took a deep breath. This setting reminded him of a different place and time…so long ago. He thought of his grandfather, remembering the days they had spent together in the tribal store in New Mexico. Tenahpu closed his eyes, remembering.

His Comanche name translated meant "The Man." Tenahpu acknowledged his brothers with a nod. Moving to the coffee pot, The Man poured himself a cupful of piping hot coffee, then moved toward Tosahwi. The shaman rose from his chair and embraced The Man.

"*The years have been kind to you, my friend,*" The Man said.

"*It is good to be with you again, Tenahpu,*" Tosahwi said. "*I know the years in this new time have been difficult for you. But now you are free from the white man's prison. Free to be a Warrior. Free to be a protector and defender of* The People."

"*This thing you say is true, Tosahwi. Freedom is a good thing,*" The Man replied.

The others listened quietly, nodding in agreement at the truth of what was said.

The Elder spoke. "*There are others who will soon rise up against our people, Tenahpu. I fear your actions have not yet convinced many of the white leaders. I have seen this clearly. Your protection will be needed for a time.*

"*We must be vigilant. You must be fierce. It is a thing the whites will soon take note of and understand. It is exactly how the whites behaved toward our people when they were building their nation.*"

Tenahpu turned and addressed the other men and Warriors present. "*These few survivors are all that is left of my family. I will defend them until the day I breathe my last. It is why I have come to this time. Tosahwi's plan is good. He alone had the knowledge to send me into the Dream Time ahead of the others. His wisdom will indeed be seen forever as a very good thing.*

"*I have been told of my grandsons. They will enter the world soon. Perhaps one day I will meet them.*"

"*It is best for now that you remain hidden,*" Tosahwi replied. "*The whites have no idea that the survivors have a protector. You, Tenahpu, were the fiercest of all Warriors. You must use your skills to defend the defenseless.*"

"*I understand,*" The Man said. "*If I must remain hidden for all my days, it is a thing I can do. I learned much in the training I received in the white man's army. Ranger school focused much on tactics. It is the best strategic factor to possess against an enemy, the element of surprise. The whites have no idea that I even exist. It will remain this way. I will remain hidden. It is also a thing that brings me deep satisfaction as a Comanche Warrior. Protecting our family, my brothers, is the purpose of my very existence.*"

The brothers and Warriors again nodded in agreement. The men sat in silence for a few minutes. The wind whistled through the thin cracked panes of the windows, and the smoke occasionally rose from the stove. A knowing, an awareness, wisdom, and purpose permeated the silence. The Man drank slowly from the steaming coffee cup, enjoying the quiet reflection. The soft, scarcely discernable, yet distinct sound of drumbeats could be heard in the wind.

Chapter 76

June 23

The militia members gathered in the old barn located twenty miles outside of Austin, Texas. The property records showed the land was owned by a Texas LLC; the members and managers of the LLC were all names of deceased game wardens from across the United States. The tax payments made on the property were always paid in cash by different militia members each year. The farm was isolated, completely overgrown and neglected. Neighboring landowners had concluded over the years it must have simply been abandoned by heirs of the original landowners, and had given up on hopes of ever purchasing or leasing it for farming. The gunfire that seemed to erupt from the property a couple of times a year was unexplainable to them.

The militia needed a place to practice with the sniper rifles, ARs, and other weapons they were amassing. Those weapons needed to be used and kept in good working order. The leaders also thought the boys needed the bonding time the rifle practice seemed to produce.

This meeting, however, was unscheduled. The men had a specific purpose. The degenerate imposters had killed a son. One of their own. A swift response was needed.

The fools in the legal system had failed to mete out justice. These men were determined. They would not fail to do so.

Chapter 77

It had been exactly one year since Topusana had exited her little cavern in the Texas Hills. Now six months pregnant, she was glowing with radiant beauty, healthy, and looking forward to the special blessing of motherhood.

The Bodmer painting had been sold within one day of its rumored offering and possible sale. The buyer, a private collector, requested to remain anonymous. The buyer had paid eleven million dollars for the piece and agreed to the commissioning of a replica. Nan Chisholm had refused any commission or fee on the sale. However, the buyer insisting, also rewarded her effort in the sale quite handsomely.

Sana's excitement grew as she observed the construction of the school. The project would take another few months to complete. With direction from Abby and invaluable input from Nina Rainwater-Travis, the final design would include eight classrooms, a gymnasium, a cafeteria, and even a small auditorium.

The excitement was contagious this beautiful morning as the four women toured the construction site. The school would be built near the hunting lodge David had completed. The little settlement was beginning to resemble a combination of the old ways and the new. Tosahwi's sons had constructed teepees with the new material David had purchased. They, along with the old grandmothers, preferred to live in the teepees rather than the rooms in the hunting lodge. Six teepees now lined the side of the hunting lodge.

The construction of Grace Ross's studio and Educational Art Center was also underway. It could be seen in the distance, one half mile down the road toward the highway. The beauty and the natural lines of the structure were already beginning to show. The women thought the design perfectly matched the serene surroundings and setting. From where the women now stood, the buffalo could be seen in the distance on the other side of the great fence. The blue Texas sky and summer sun shone down on the scene. To the women it seemed there was an unseen hand covering and blessing all that was taking place.

****

The regiment of game wardens and militia members concealed in the underbrush awaited the signal to begin the raid. The men moved about semi-concealed. Their movements were clumsy and uncoordinated. Their steps left little trails of dust rising in the air. Sounds of branches breaking reached Sana as she became aware of their presence.

The Man had seen the militia group approaching the lodge. He took up a concealed position to the rear of the group of armed men. His silenced sniper rifle was locked and loaded, trained on the apparent leader.

Turning to run toward the hunting lodge, Sana once again let out a War Cry. This time, *The People* received the warning in time. The children were quickly gathered. Teepees emptied and doors were bolted. Abby, Sana, Grace, and Nina ran toward the lodge.

CL Reuter Sr., noticing the activity, gave the order. The raid began. The militia quickly surrounded the four women and ordered them to lay on the ground.

Nina Rainwater-Travis activated her cell phone video, refusing to comply. She was promptly wrestled to the ground by two game wardens and handcuffed. A warden placed his boot on the back of her neck, forcing her face into the dirt.

Abby managed to gain control of Nina's cell phone as it continued to record.

Sana, while rushing to the aid of Nina, was knocked violently to the ground by a game warden. Clutching her abdomen, attempting to protect her unborn sons, she fell to the hard rock surface. Once Sana was knocked to the ground, the warden brutally drove the butt of his rifle into her forehead. Sana lost consciousness instantly. Blood poured to the ground from the open wound the rifle butt had caused. As she lay unconscious, she was handcuffed by the game warden.

The Man opened fire. The silenced green tip round entered the warden's chest, easily penetrating the Kevlar body armor. His fall to the ground in a shallow depression went unnoticed by the other wardens. The Man quickly, expertly, removed the barrel of his rifle, replacing it with another.

Abigail Ross was also violently shoved to the ground and handcuffed. She attempted to stand, rising to her knees, she screamed at the wardens. The scene seemed surreal to her.

"What do you think you're doing? This woman is pregnant. This is private land. You have no authority to be here," Abby anguished.

The boot of a nearby warden caught her squarely in the ribcage, several ribs breaking at the impact. Abby rolled back onto the ground, the pain excruciating. Grace rushed to her side; however, while attempting to assist her mother, Grace was pinned to the ground by another warden and handcuffed. Grace began to yell for help as this horrifying scene continued.

Nina located the cell phone Abby had dropped and continued videoing the actions of the wardens.

CL Reuter Sr. threw a copy of his search warrant issued by a judge in Austin, on the ground next to Abby.

"This will go a little smoother if you simply comply with my instructions. Illegal hunting and poaching have been reported at this location. I suggest you open up all the facilities, or we will break down every door here," Reuter stated.

Nina and Grace, attending to Sana, screamed at Warden Reuter. "This woman your officers injured is pregnant! She needs medical attention now!"

Sana, beginning to regain consciousness, lay on the ground, clutching her abdomen, the tears beginning to flow. The fear of the white soldiers returned to her mind.

Reuter spat on the ground in the direction of Topusana. "She looks fine to me," he said.

The four women huddled together, Grace and Nina attempting to comfort Sana. Abby began to struggle to breath. She knew something had happened to her lungs. She began to pray, please help us, Lord.

Nina continued to record the activity at the scene.

"The white soldiers have returned?" Sana asked, the fear in her eyes...a fear like nothing the other women had ever witnessed.

The game wardens began a door-to-door search of the hunting lodge, reporting to Reuter that everything seemed to be bolted from within.

The men were secretly hoping for an encounter with Tabbananica.

This was the unspoken primary reason the men were here.

They had come for Tabbananica.

Inside the main lodge, Old Grandmother picked up the phone and dialed 911.

The dispatcher had a difficult time understanding but finally got the facts. The white soldiers were raiding the hunting lodge on David Ross's ranch. Several women were injured. The dispatcher immediately called Sheriff Mason and relayed the information.

Grandmother gathered the women and children and quickly led them into the safe room. Tosa, son of Tosahwi, and his brother Neeko gathered their weapons. The two Warriors took up defensive positions outside on opposite ends of the lodge. The Man seeing their positions also moved onto a small piece of high ground, a perfect firing position.

Sheriff Fred Mason was at a loss to understand what was happening. He ordered three available units to the scene. One unit was close by, approximately fifteen minutes away. Then he called David Ross. The two men couldn't quite understand what could be happening, but both agreed to head to the lodge. Hanging up, Sheriff Mason also ordered the dispatch of an ambulance to the scene.

The helicopter was parked at the ranch house. David and Steve quickly boarded and began the ten-minute flight to the lodge. The sheriff would not arrive for another twenty-five minutes.

As the chopper approached the lodge, David could clearly see Topusana, Nina, Grace, and Abby on the ground toward the side of the lodge guarded by several men in uniform.

David Ross's blood came to a boil as the chopper was setting down. Two wardens with weapons drawn ordered David and Steve to the ground as they exited the chopper.

David Ross refused the order and walked directly to the nearest warden, demanding to know what the hell was going on. The warden continued to point his weapon at David Ross ordering him to the ground. CL Reuter, from the front of the lodge, directed his officer to hold his ground. The warden pumped the slide on his weapon…chambering a round.

Seeing the threat to Mr. Ross and having seen in the past many men executed in this very fashion…Tosa the Warrior acted. He loosed his arrow. The arrow sliced perfectly between the ribs of the officer, severing arteries as it traveled through his torso. The shot was a complete pass through. The arrow penetrated the ground a few feet from the warden. Tosa recognized the warden as the one who had shoved Topusana to the ground. The warden stumbled and fell dead at David's feet.

CL Reuter froze, fear now overcoming him. His arrogant demeanor evaporated instantly as his man fell dead before his eyes.

"Ross, what the hell are you doing? Order them to stand down," Reuter yelled.

"Have your men move away from the lodge and drop all of their weapons and I will do so. Otherwise, each of you will die right here and now," David spoke coolly.

CL Reuter hesitated, playing the scene out in his mind; he knew several would die. Reuter swallowed hard; he knew he would die. He gave the order. "Men, every weapon on the ground now!" The other officers gathered in the road fronting the lodge and quickly obeyed the order, each eager to comply with David Ross's instructions.

Tabba arrived at the scene upon his mare. He raced the horse across the front of the lodge grounds toward Sana. He leapt from his mount, drawing his bow, standing in front of and between the women and the wardens. Observing Tosa and Neeko, Tabba released the tension on his drawn bow, quickly quivering the arrow. He knelt to the ground to evaluate Sana's wounds.

David saw the handcuffs on Abby, Grace, and Nina. "The keys, now!" David ordered, moving quickly toward the uniform who was evidently in charge. Reuter slowly reached toward his belt, removed and held the keys high.

David Ross purposefully walked toward the man and took the keys from his hand, then delivered a mighty fisted blow to the face of one CL Reuter Sr. Blood and teeth spattered across the ground as CL Reuter fell unconscious. The warden nearest Reuter made a move toward his weapon. An arrow from Neeko's bow instantly penetrated the man's neck. The arrow passed through the soft tissue and arteries, then exited and landed near Nina.

A bullet from the rifle of The Man simultaneously penetrated the Kevlar jacket the warden was wearing. Scarcely slowing, the armor piercing green tip exploded within the warden's chest cavity. The warden fell in a shower of blood, dead before reaching the ground. The Man quickly changed barrels again and inserted a new cartridge of 308 caliber bullets.

Another officer moved to aid the fallen man. An arrow from Neeko's bow instantly pierced the warden's upper leg, severing arteries. That arrow, after exiting the warden's leg, bounced along the rocky ground and came to a stop in the brush near where Sana lay. The wounded warden fell to the ground, writhing in pain, blood flowing profusely from the arrow wound. He lost consciousness and died within a few moments.

David Ross, his voice booming across the scene, said, "All of you men freeze. Do not move a muscle or you will surely be fired on."

Three men lay sprawled across the ground, dead. A fourth also lay dead near the handcuffed women. The remaining wardens and all militia members froze at the command of David Ross.

"Now all of you, face down on the ground, hands behind your heads."

All complied.

Tabba gently lifted Sana from the ground. Seeing the severity of her head wound, he called out to David. David turned and raced to where Abby had fallen. Seeing her clutching her side and her labored breathing, he gently lifted Abby from the ground, and both men carried their injured wives toward the helicopter. David placed Abby inside the helicopter, as Tabba struggled with the door of the chopper on the opposite side of the aircraft. Steve jumped into the cockpit and began the start sequence.

The militia captain, seeing the opportunity, slowly reached for and drew the revolver from his ankle holster. He carefully took aim and fired the Smith and Wesson .38 caliber revolver at Tabba. At the report of the pistol shot, The Man identified where the shot had come from and opened fire. The green tip bullet penetrated the Kevlar jacket, killing the militia captain instantly.

Sana saw the bullet fired at Tabba exit the barrel of .38 caliber pistol. It seemed to fly across the scene in slow motion. As Tabba lifted Sana into the rear seat of the helicopter, the slight downward movement of his body as he knelt to lift her caused the bullet to miss him. As Sana's body was raised by Tabba slightly higher, into the exact position where Tabba had been a milli-second previously, the slow-motion bullet entered Sana's chest just above her heart, with a dull thud.

The sound of sirens could be heard in the distance as Steve lifted off. He was unsure who had been hit. He knew someone had been. It was clearly evident from the blood covering the side window of the aircraft. Steve knew every second counted. He swore under his breath, then silently began to pray. As the helicopter flew on a direct line toward the hospital with five souls on board, one of those souls departed across the heavens.

Tabba felt Sana's spirit leave her body.

He knew she was gone.

Mrs. Nina Rainwater-Travis continued to record the activity at the scene. Nina put the phone down momentarily, then located and removed all three arrows that had been fired from the direction of the lodge. She hastily placed them inside her pant leg, she would later burn them in the stove located in the little lodge along the banks of the San Saba.

The first sheriff deputy arrived on scene, his weapon drawn. He ordered the men on the ground to stay exactly where they were. The militia members complied. The deputy trained his gun on the militia and radioed the other units. Those units could now be heard approaching in the distance.

Seeing the surrender of the white soldiers, the Warriors Tosa and Neeko stealthily exited the scene. They moved silently through the brush toward the safety of the large cavern an hour away.

The Man also moved away from the lodge, completely concealed by the terrain and brush. He slowly made his way toward the small caverns in the shallow canyon just a mile to the north.

The Man began to pray. He knew his daughter had been severely injured.

****

Sana was instantly in the presence of her grandfather Buffalo Hump. He held her hands and the warmth of his spirit comforted her soul as the stars floated by.

Suddenly, in the blink of an eye, Sana stood alongside a beautiful river.

Teepees and lodges extended across a pristine meadow as far as she could see. A light snow was falling, the ground covered in white. She smelled the smoke from a thousand lodge fires. She could hear the singing of the river as it laughed along its course. She could taste the fresh snow-laden air.

Her grandfather released her hand. Sana entered the lodge before her.

Love filled not only the atmosphere, but also her entire being.

She sat at His feet. No words were needed.

There was only Love in this place.

Chapter 78

June 24
9:15 A.M.

William Travis arrived at the hospital twenty minutes after David's helicopter landed carrying Topusana, Abby, and Tabba. He entered the waiting room and solemnly greeted Tabba and David.

The three men were escorted to the surgical waiting area by a charge nurse who promised to report back as soon as Sana and Abby's condition could be updated. Both women had been rushed into emergency surgery, their condition was unknown.

The three men sat in silence, their minds racing. Tabba wondered how these men could continue the concerted effort to harass and threaten the existence of the little tribe of survivors? Tabba also thought that inwardly peace was a difficult thing to obtain. The warrior inside of him could never let such an act of cowardice be tolerated.

William reflected, how could this level of prejudice, racism, and hatred still exist in our modern world? Sadly, he thought, not much had changed in the last two hundred years.

David remained silent. The anger within his own heart rose to a level he had never felt. He had heard Abby's labored breathing as he held her in the helicopter. He knew from experience her lung had been punctured.

Tabbananica needed to speak with William Travis. He needed to know what consequences he might face were he were to take action. In his Warrior's heart he knew these Texans should die.

William could read the look in Tabba's eyes.

"I know, Tabba. It would be an easy thing for you to kill these men. I am asking you not to do so," whispered William.

Tabba looked surprised at the request.

"And you also, David. Whatever it is you are contemplating, please put it away for now. The girls are our immediate concern for the time being."

June 24
11:00 A.M.

Dr. Blake entered the waiting room. "Gentlemen, please follow me."

Following the doctor, the men entered the surgical recovery room. Pulling the curtains back that encircled the area, the three men were relieved to see Abby sitting upright, resting, and awake.

David gently took Abby's hand as Dr. Blake began to speak.

"Abby was fortunate. She has three broken ribs, two of which punctured her right lung. Mr. Ross, this is an injury that sometimes can cause death, depending on which way the bones are forced after the break. It is obvious she was on the ground, the impact a downward blow when she was attacked. The surgery was successful, and I believe she is out of danger. She should recover fully and be back to normal in a few weeks. We will, however, keep her here for several days so I can observe her condition and monitor her improvement."

"Thank you for your help, Dr. Blake," David said. "What about Sana?"

"Sana is still in surgery. I'm going in now to assist. I will report to you as soon as possible."

"My sons?" Tabba spoke softly.

"I do not know, Tabba. Her injuries are quite grave. I will tell you her condition as of now is serious. However, it appears the bullet may have missed, very narrowly, the major arteries in her chest. I also know she has gone into labor. We're doing all we can to not deliver the boys." Dr Blake turned and walked quickly toward the operating room.

"Is there anything we can do, Dr. Blake?" William asked.

Dr. Blake turned to the men. "Two things. First, pray." The men all peered at the doctor intently with questioning looks.

"And?" William asked.

"Find out who did this to these defenseless women and pursue them to hell and back. No matter the cost."

Tabba saw the look in the man's eyes. A look he knew well. A look Tabba had only witnessed on the battlefield.

William Travis looked Dr. Blake directly in the eyes.

"The man who assaulted Topusana was shot through the heart with an arrow and is dead. The warden who shot her with the gun we have yet to identify."

"And Abby's attacker?" Dr. Blake questioned.

"I will deal with him," David said.

Tabba again recognized the look from David Ross.

Chapter 79

Three Hours Later

The investigators and law enforcement personnel gathered in the Grove County Sheriff's Department headquarters. Sheriff Mason was livid. "How can you conduct an undercover raid in my county without even a phone call?" He addressed the question to CL Reuter, the director of the Texas Department of Game and Fish.

Reuter spoke through a swollen face. The bruising continued to rise. His words were slurred due to several missing teeth along one side of his mouth. "The Game Department doesn't answer to local law enforcement." The pain on the man's face was evident as he spoke the reply.

Acting District Attorney, Mrs. Beverly Burnett, spoke next. "I'm curious if you revealed to the judge that issued your warrant, the recent history here involving your department? And your immediate family?"

Reuter did not reply. His silence indicating the truth. In all likelihood, he had not.

"Have you made an arrest for the murder of my wardens?" Reuter asked insolently.

"I'll not reveal any information to you or your department, involving the ongoing investigation. That is a precedent you have set between us and our agencies, I believe," Sheriff Mason retorted.

On a thorough search of the lodge, the only persons present were two elderly Native American women, Old Grandmother, and four young Comanche children. Also remaining were the wives of Tosahwi's two sons and their five young children. None of whom revealed any information as to a possible suspect. Nor would they ever.

The investigators from the Grove County Sheriff's Department and the Texas Department of Public Safety (DPS) had no way of knowing if there were other Native Americans that had left the scene. They were unable to verify how many Native Americans were present at the time of the raid. Nor could they determine how many Comanche actually resided on the Ross ranch. The investigators were told most were visitors from the Comanche Nation. Though the statement was true, the investigators assumed the report referred to the Lawton, Oklahoma, reservation. Those interviewed by investigators claimed to not speak English.

Old Grandmother translated all questions and answers from the witnesses. Most of her translations were somewhat accurate.

The testimony from the wardens present seemed to conflict. None of the wardens heard any gunshots with the exception of the one revolver shot from the warden that had been killed by a NATO 7.62 bullet. None could identify the direction from which the arrows had been fired. None could identify a shooter or his possible location.

The investigators also could not locate the arrows that had been fired at the game wardens. Sheriff Mason was completely perplexed.

Compounding the investigation was the lack of any dashcam video. Reuter, against every law enforcement agency's training protocol, had left the vehicles far from the actual raid. The sheriff had five officers of the Texas Department of Game and Fish in the county morgue, and virtually no suspects or evidence.

Sheriff Fred Mason also knew he most likely had an illegally obtained search warrant on his desk. That warrant issued by CL Reuter's half-brother Judge Donnie Reuter.

Further complicating matters, the sheriff had learned Judge Donnie Reuter was under investigation by the FBI for his ties to a Texas militia group.

The Texas Department of Public Safety investigators, along with the Attorney General's office personnel, lashed out at Sheriff Mason on the evening news coverage, demanding an arrest be made, and quickly.

Chapter 80

June 25
The Following Morning
9:00 A.M.

The meeting held the following morning in David Ross's study was to devise a strategy. Present were William Travis, David Ross, Commander Bryce Houston, and Nina Rainwater-Travis. Commander Houston had already analyzed Nina's cell phone video. Now the others viewed the recording as Bryce commented while the clip played.

"It is fascinating to me that you were able to record the assault on Topusana and Abby.

"Evidently the phone was on the ground, facing up during each incident where a militia member was shot. Although, the warden as he handcuffed Sana can be seen falling sideways away from her. There is no evidence of the bullet impact, which means there is no forensic giveaway, referring to the direction in which the shot originated.

"It is also amazing that Nina captured the shot from the warden who fired at Tabba. The video follows the direction in which the shot was fired at the helicopter, and clearly shows Sana being hit by that gunfire. The video again does not show the warden being killed by the arrow. Nina as you panned back toward the warden, who fired the revolver at Tabba and Sana? It does show the hole in his vest. He was also shot by a sniper that was at the scene somewhere."

"So, what do we do with the video? The investigators have no idea it exists," William asked.

"Use it to your advantage," Commander Houston said. "There is no doubt the investigators know there was a shooter at the scene, so the bullet hole in the Kevlar is not a giveaway. This video clearly shows excessive force and refusal to aid an injured woman who is obviously pregnant. It clearly shows the violent attack on both Abby and Sana, and the unwarranted firing upon Tabba and Sana. Furthermore, the pleading for assistance from Grace and Nina that is refused by CL Reuter Sr. while he evidently spits on them, literally, will cause any jury member's blood to boil. It causes mine to do so.

"I have also positively identified through evidence on the video, eight of the twelve wardens that participated in the raid. I'll be investigating their backgrounds. The little information I have been able to determine at this point, shows a connection," Commander Houston said.

"To what?" David asked.

"Some type of militia. A simple social media search reveals that connection. I'm triangulating their cell phone history and locations over the last couple of weeks. I'll soon have some answers on their recent movements and activity. By the way, the judge who issued the search warrant is the half-brother of CL Reuter. My source at the FBI says he is under investigation for his ties to a secret militia.

"I'd wait a few days just to see what type of false narrative the game department and the prosecutors come up with. Let's see who buys into that narrative as far as investigators from Department of Public Safety and the sheriff's office," Commander Houston said.

"And then?" Nina asked.

"And then, release the video to the press," William Travis said.

"These men are fighting our people in the old ways, with bullets and brute force. We need to fight back in the new way," Nina said.

"How is that?" David asked.

"Through the press and a team of lawyers. We need to file suit for damages in an amount that will break the budget of the State of Texas," Nina said.

Two Hours Later
Grove County Hospital
11:00 A.M.

Tosahwi continued his song quietly. He stood beside Topusana's hospital bed. He was amazed at the healing abilities of the whites. The medicine was indeed powerful. Tosahwi would have never been able to save her life; the wounds were too severe. Even with all the giftings he had been granted, to save her would not have been possible.

The confusing array of tubes and chords, along with the sounds the little machines made, fascinated Tosahwi. However, none of this medicine could replace the purpose of the Great Spirit. Tosahwi knew in his spirit Topusana no longer indwelled her body. What he was praying over was simply an empty vessel. Perhaps, she would return soon. Tosahwi sang softly.

Dr. Blake Tower knocked gently at the door. He entered the room with Abby, Nina, David, Tabba, Grace, William, and Old Grandmother following close behind.

Dr. Blake briefed the group on Sana's condition.

"It is simply a miracle that Sana survived the surgery. The contractions have ceased. The heartbeats of the boys are strong. It may be a little premature, but it appears to me Sana will recover. Her sleep is quite deep due to the anesthesia and pain medications. I don't expect her to be fully awake for several hours. I will leave you to be with her now." Dr. Blake exited the room.

Old Grandmother began the songs softly. Nina and Tabba sang along. Tosahwi began the prayers. The songs resonated deep within the spirit of Topusana. She sang along in her heart with her loved ones.

****

Sana longed to stay here, to never leave this lodge, this Love, His presence. The peace she felt while in His Lodge was beyond anything she could ever describe. His eyes were like fire. His clothing like the sun. His healing touch miraculous. Sana noticed His name was written across His thigh. Only she understood the meaning. The two sat together for what seemed like many days. They watched her life. They laughed, rejoiced, observed. Topusana knew He was proud of her. The difficult days of her life unrolled like a scroll before them…without tears. Purpose and understanding of those days she clearly recognized in her soul.

On the seventh day without words, He communicated to her it was time to return. She knew deep within her being she had not completed her purpose. Sana understood.

She rose. He remained seated a moment, drawing something in the soft sand. Sana peered down and saw her new name drawn in the sand. He stood.

Sana kneeled before Him in worship. Taking her hand, He helped her rise. He touched her abdomen…and blessed her sons. Topusana now understood further.

A future Nation rested within her womb.

Purest Love surrounded Sana as she exited the lodge.

Once outside the lodge, her grandfather greeted her again. He was standing beside a great tree. Holding his hand was Prairie Song.

Mother and daughter embraced. Complete comfort permeated Topusana's soul.

She held tightly to Prairie Song's hand. A communication took place. It was without words; however, somehow complete knowledge sprung forth and blossomed. Their hearts and souls and minds melded together in a beautiful burst of love and understanding.

As the two departed, Sana noticed the wave from the woman on the other side of the river. Then she recognized the warm soft lovely face of her mother, Kwanita. Sana returned the wave as a peace and understanding flooded her heart and mind.

Topusana and Prairie Song, mother and daughter, traveled across the heavens in an instant. Sana gazed into the knowing eyes of her beautiful daughter. For the first time, Sana understood what it was Tosahwi had attempted to teach her about letting go. She then let go of Prairie Song's hand…and her life. A new level of comfort filled Sana's heart and mind and soul concerning her daughter.

A young soldier had come to escort Prairie Song home. This young man touched Prairie Song's face gently, with a questioning loving touch. Prairie Song nodded her head, indicating her readiness.

Topusana made eye contact and recognized instantly the heart, soul, and even the face of the young soldier.

He took Prairie Song by the hand. Then Jonathan Ross escorted Prairie Song across the stars to her home by the beautiful river.

Sana was alone for a moment. She then descended into the little hospital room. She took one physical step downward. She felt the pain instantly as her spirit re-entered her body.

****

Old Grandmother continued the songs. Her eyes closed, her hands raised in deep worship. The others in the room emulating Grandmother, also closed their eyes, raised their hands, and sang softly.

Sana's soft clear voice joined them.

She sat upwards, slowly opening her eyes. The light in her eyes glimmered with life. Topusana joined in the worship, as did the two sons within her womb.

The tears from all within the room flowed freely. Tears of gratefulness.

Topusana was alive.

Chapter 81

June 30
5 Days Later

The meeting took place in the command center that had been set up in the basement of the Grove County Courthouse. The investigation teams from the Texas DPS, Sheriff Mason's investigators, the State of Texas crime lab personnel, and the legal team from District Attorney Beverly Burnett's office and several assistants from the attorney general's office, along with representatives from the governor's staff were all present.

After days of investigation, Sheriff Mason had not a shred of evidence with which to proceed with charges, nor any suspects to charge. The investigators could never locate the arrows that had been fired at the game wardens. Nor could they identify a location of the shooter. The forensics inexplicably could not match the bullets fired to one single gun. Each bullet had substantially different barrel pattern marks. None of the suspects at the crime scene tested positive for gunpowder traces.

Sheriff Mason addressed the meeting.

"We have nothing. No murder weapon. No suspects."

"Bullshit! Arrest someone! Arrest David Ross. Call the press and announce it. We need a suspect," yelled the head of the Texas Department of Public Safety.

"That kind of mindset is exactly what caused these deaths, sir," said acting District Attorney Mrs. Beverly Burnett. "I'll have no part in making a false arrest just to appease your political base."

At that moment, an aide rushed into the room, interrupting the meeting.

"You all need to watch FOX, or CNN, or whatever. It's on all the networks!"

The investigators and prosecutors watched in awe, or in most cases disgust, as the video of the raid played across the video display that had been setup along the front wall of the meeting room.

Sheriff Mason switched channels and the video played in its entirety on CNN. After a silent pause and even the wiping of a tear from the commentator's eye, the coverage switched to the broadcast studio. The commentator, after composing himself began his interview with William Travis, attorney for the plaintiff, the San Saba Comanche Tribe.

Mrs. Beverly Burnett gathered her team, then paused before exiting the room. Glancing at Sheriff Mason, she motioned him to silence the news.

"Gentlemen, it does appear some arrests need to be made. My team will evaluate this evidence and issue warrants for the crimes I see being committed during this so-called raid."

"Bullshit! You will not turn on our own men," the lead investigator from the Game Department said.

"From what I have just seen, you better pray she survives, or the charges will include murder."

*****

The Man watched the video of the attack on the women of the San Saba Tribe as it ran repeatedly on all major news networks. What kind of cowardice did these men possess, he wondered. The Man recorded the entire broadcast. Playing the video repeatedly, several of the game wardens' badges revealed their identities. The Man began to write the names of the men on a scrap of paper. One man, CL Reuter Sr., was shown spitting toward the women on the ground. His badge number and name were clearly visible in the video. The Man added the name to his list.

The Man would meet again with the other Warriors tomorrow at the Tribal Store. It appeared another hunting trip was in order.

The Man thought that very soon those in positions of power would begin to note there are consequences to prejudicial actions and decisions. Many would become cautious in the future; their intolerance and attitudes toward the Native American people would soon begin to change.

The Man would find himself quite busy over the next several weeks and months.

The commissioner of the Texas Land Commission would be reported missing. Never to be found. The head of the Texas Department of Game and Fish, CL Reuter Sr., would die in a hunting accident. His gun had reportedly accidentally discharged while exiting his vehicle for a deer hunt. Three game wardens had all suspiciously lost their lives in the line of duty. All had participated in an early morning raid on the Ross ranch several weeks prior to their untimely deaths.

The Man thought that many people throughout history had also been motivated to reconsider their thought processes...by the actions of a handful of brave Warriors.

Chapter 82

July 3

Just ten days after the attack on the hunting lodge, William Travis filed a civil lawsuit in federal court in Austin, Texas.

He named every individual member of the Texas Game and Fish Department who had participated in the raid, along with the game department as a whole. William Travis also named the State of Texas.

The suit asked for damages in the amount of five hundred million dollars.

Criminal charges were also filed by Grove County District Attorney against the officer that had assaulted Abby. The officers that had attacked Sana and Tabba had been killed at the scene.

Texas Attorney General Nathan Lincoln was extremely upset over the criminal charges against the game warden…prior to viewing the video.

Nathan Lincoln held meetings with the governor, the Texas comptroller, and a team consisting of the governor's closest inner circle of attorneys and staff members. In short, most agreed that, in light of the evidence, the Game Department and the State of Texas would not prevail in the case.

The governor suggested a meeting with the plaintiffs. The sole purpose would be to negotiate a settlement, and to do so quickly. Five hundred million was certainly an absurd amount. Perhaps, he thought, a more reasonable amount could be agreed upon. He would be entering the presidential race soon. He needed this problem to go away quietly.

Prior to the proposed meeting, the governor sat in his office going over the evidence William Travis had turned over to the attorney general.

Nathan Lincoln addressed the governor. "The search warrant will most surely be deemed as illegal. Reuter using his half-brother as the issuing judge will be ruled against immediately. Sir, that fact alone will make the use of force and retaliation by the plaintiffs justifiable."

"I understand, Nathan; I went to law school," the governor replied. "What have we done about the Militia problem?"

"We seized all their property. My office has made several arrests. However, the FBI is now involved, as is ATF. The number of weapons and ammunition discovered removed the investigation from our hands. None of this helps us."

"Meaning?"

"The settlement number will be very high, sir. Considering that fact, I received a request from William Travis this morning. He would like to meet with you and me prior to meeting with the plaintiffs," Nathan Lincoln said.

"Let's do it. I can't afford the biggest settlement in the history of Texas to be paid out on my watch," the governor said.

Nathan Lincoln replied, "We need to have the acting land commissioner in the room with us."

"I think I understand," the governor said.

The Following Day

William Travis entered the governor's office and was greeted with a warm welcome.

Present in the meeting was Texas Attorney General Nathan Lincoln, along with several of his assistants. Also in attendance was the newly appointed acting Commissioner of Public Lands Mrs. Ruth Duncan. Mrs. Duncan had served on the land commission for four years. She had met William Travis and Topusana previously. She well remembered the day the two had appeared before the commission, and her emotions as Topusana had exited that meeting. Also, in attendance were William Travis's legal assistants.

Pleasantries and introductions were made. The governor seated himself at the head of the large conference table and got right to the point.

"Mr. Travis, let me first say I deeply regret the actions of the game department. However, the requested settlement is a little on the high side, wouldn't you say?"

"Depends on the jury, I suppose. Do you realize this is the second time in the history of my clients that they were attacked by Texas militia members?"

The governor had done his homework. What William Travis was saying was quite true. None of this would play well in the public's eye. Nor the voters' eyes. He knew public sympathy ran very high toward any Native American injustices.

"I agree, Mr. Travis. Let's get to it, shall we? What can I do to settle this here and now? I'm sure we all understand the state doesn't desire to go through this circus act, the press...all of it."

William Travis opened a folder and slid the contents across the table.

"This is our proposal. Non-negotiable. I'll give you the simple details, and you can discuss this with your team.

"Texas will pay my clients 200 million dollars. Furthermore, the land commission will support, along with the governor's office and every agency within the Texas state government, the transfer of Big Bend National Park from the National Park Service, to and for the benefit of, the establishment of 'The San Saba Comanche Tribal Reservation.'

"That's 60 percent less than we are asking in damages, and some land you don't even own.

"I need an answer within twenty-four hours. Thank you for your time, sir," William Travis said. He rose from his chair, turned, and exited the governor's office with his assistants.

The remainder of the meeting was short. The governor and the attorney general knew any jury would be sympathetic to the rights of the landowner, the Ross family, and the Tribe. He also believed any jury would clearly see through the real intention of the game department and the decision made by CL Reuter Sr. to retaliate at the death of his son. These facts, along with, ironically, the video of the raid showing the brutality of the game department and the refusal to assist an injured pregnant woman whose injuries were caused by the game wardens conducting the raid, led the two men to come to the only logical conclusion possible.

"What do we do about the deaths of our officers?" the governor asked.

"We could ask for some level of cooperation from the tribe," the AG said. "However, sir, they were all militia members killed during an illegal raid on private property. In Texas, among your voter base, this will not play well to pursue what many see as the 'defender' of the Ross family and the tribe, and frankly, justice."

"By defender, you mean the unidentified shooter?" the governor asked.

"Yes, sir, and we still have found no evidence concerning who that might have been, or even if this was the work of one sniper. The ballistics report suggests as many as three snipers at the scene."

The governor paused a moment in thought. "Perhaps others will think twice before attempting this kind of action in the future."

"I believe that the defender's actions show this was clearly his intent. You are thinking exactly as he would want you to, sir." Nathan Lincoln said.

"I understand, Nathan. And the law enforcement unions?" the governor asked.

"That's a pretty small number compared to those voting private landowners in Texas."

"Understood."

"Can this land transfer actually be done, Mrs. Duncan?" the governor asked.

"Yes, there is precedent, sir. It will take some help from your friend in the White House, but it can be done," Mrs. Duncan said.

"Any other input?" The governor glanced around the table to his staff. There was no response.

"What do I pay you people for? Just as I expected…I see I'm on my own here. Can we keep the terms of this settlement undisclosed?" the governor asked.

"I think so. These records can be sealed; however, the two hundred million coming from the state can in no way go unnoticed and will need approval of the legislature," Nathan Lincoln said.

"OK, folks, this meeting is over. Thank you for your input," the governor stated rather sarcastically. The staff members and aides all filed out of the meeting room.

"You two stay," the governor said, indicating the attorney general and the governor's own personal attorney and financial advisor.

"What's my net worth as of today, Ann?" The Governor directed his question to his attorney and financial advisor.

The woman made a few clicks on her phone and replied, "About forty billion as of this morning."

"Will I ever catch up to the mayor from up north?" the governor said, smiling.

"Not if you continue to fund Civil Rights settlements," she replied.

"Let's do this. Nathan, have the agreement on my desk in the morning. Make damn sure the settlement is bulletproof and sealed by the court. I will fund the dollar amount personally. Make sure that transaction can't be tracked. In a few days, leak information that indicates there was no monetary consideration granted in the undisclosed settlement made with the San Saba Comanche," the governor said.

"Yes, sir. And for the record, I'm with you on this, sir. This is a good decision. You do need to file your election status in Iowa in a few days," Nathan Lincoln said.

Chapter 83

It usually took two to three years or more for approval and federal recognition of a Native American tribe. The process was normally delayed by the blood quantum testing of applying tribal members. Many applicants had come forward over the last twenty years or so, out of pure greed. Casinos were usually at the heart of the applicant's intent. The pitiful unjustified applications had cluttered the already overburdened system. However, with the expertise and contacts of Dr. Nina Rainwater-Travis, the application of the San Saba Comanche Tribe had been designated as a top priority.

The DNA testing was before the committee. Also, the evidence of the distinct history of the members and their occupation of the geographical area were noted of importance. The application also included the proposed membership criteria. Due to Dr. Rainwater's expertise, the application had included every requirement needed for approval.

The period of public notice had been complied with. The committee was set to hold immediate hearings. The only public entity registered to testify was a lobbyist hired by the state of Texas.

The lobbyist would, on behalf of Texas, vehemently oppose the action.

Texas, as a state, could still not quite come to grips with how to co-exist with *The People* from which they had historically stolen the lands of Texas.

Promptly at 10 a.m. on July 8, Committee Chair Jim Black Bear of the Sioux Nation called the meeting to order. Calling the only registered commenter, the lobbyist hired by Texas, the lobbyist was welcomed to the microphone. The man droned on and on about Texas being exceedingly benevolent and caring toward the Native tribes already granted federal status. He was interrupted only once during his presentation. A committee member asked if the man had seen the video of the assault on the homesite of the San Saba Comanche by the Texas Department of Game and Fish. The man said he had not.

The lights were dimmed, and the full twelve-minute video was shown before the hearing.

The raw emotion on the faces of both the committee members and those in attendance of the hearing was unmistakable.

All in attendance easily recognized the prejudice, injustice, and outright abuse, as well as the impact the militaristic action had on the innocent victims of the San Saba Comanche Tribe.

This was nothing new to the Native American community, from Wounded Knee, to Sandy Creek, the Trail of Tears, and countless other injustices, the behavior of the Texas officials was simply history repeating itself in a most egregious way.

As the video ended, silence fell across the meeting room. No additional words were needed.

It was obvious to every single committee member. The little tribe needed federal trust protection.

The lobbyist was offered the opportunity to continue his presentation. He quickly declined and abruptly exited the hearing room.

The vote for approval of federal recognition and Federal Trust protection was unanimous. Dr. Rainwater-Travis was extremely grateful for the quick action on the part of the BIA. She and William had much more work to complete. An abbreviated political structure had been submitted with the application. However, a complete constitution was needed, and elections would need to take place.

William Travis had obtained birth certificates for Tabbananica and Topusana, or *Sana Nica* as her knew birth certificate stated. In the tradition of many Native American tribes, the combination of their names seemed to blend well and retain their Comanche heritage. Sana Nica would soon be inaugurated as the first modern-day Chief or (*Akima*) of the San Saba Comanche Tribe.

The greatest need of the little band of survivors at this moment in history was a designated Homeland.

Chapter 84

September 30

Sana was just settling under the buffalo robe. The lodge was warm and safe. She snuggled closely to Tabba and drifted off into the deep comfortable sleep she had never remembered enjoying in her former life.

The pain came suddenly, sharp and intense.

Tonight, the boys would enter this beautiful new life.

Tabba, like all fathers-to-be, raced around the room uncomfortably. In his old way of life, he would never have been a part of the birthing process. Inwardly, he was glad he would witness the miracle of birth.

Outwardly, Tabba was terrified.

Sana dialed Abby on her cell phone while Tabba loaded a few things into a small satchel.

Abby and David arrived in the truck in just a few minutes. The drive to the hospital took forever, Tabba thought. The others in the truck seemed calm and collected.

David enjoyed the innocent naïve behavior of Tabba. Looking his friend in the eye, David said, "Just breathe in. Now exhale…it's going to be just fine."

At first, Abby thought he was speaking to Sana. Then she smiled at David in the rear-view mirror, understanding his coaching was directed at Tabba.

Tabba had never imagined the process of birth and what the mother had to endure. Sana was escorted into the delivery room at the hospital. Tabba observed the needle being inserted into Sana's arm. His head became heavy, and his vision seemed to blur as he also watched the many wires and monitors being attached to her skin. Tabba understood none of what was happening. He jumped at the sound of his beautiful wife crying out in pain as a full contraction came upon her.

A nurse, noticing his reactions, quickly directed him to a wheelchair against the wall. Tabbananica the Warrior slid into the chair, his breath becoming short, his knees becoming weak. David again moved to his side and whispered, "Just breathe deeply, my friend."

The nurse directed the men out of the delivery room to watch from a viewing window, stating, "We just need one patient here tonight, gentlemen!"

Sana and Abby actually smiled at Tabba's reaction. Then the pain came again, quickly this time. The nurse called for Dr. Blake.

The labor was uncomplicated, a miracle as far as Abby was concerned. After two hours, the boys were delivered just one minute apart. Sana was simply amazed at the level of attention and care both she and her sons received. The many births she had attended in the past were excruciating, pain-filled events. The outcome never certain. Many mothers in her former life did not survive the birth of children. She held her sons close as Tabba and David entered the room.

Tears of joy flowed from Tabba's heart as the two boys were held high by Dr. Blake.

The boys were perfect in every way.

Topusana, though exhausted from the ordeal, also was filled with wonder. The miracle of life was indeed an astounding thing to witness. Tabba had seen the boys take their first breath.

Abby and David joined Tabba and Sana with the two boys in the little hospital room. The four friends hugged, took photos, genuinely each heart overcome with gratefulness and the honor of calling one another friends... family even.

Abby broached the subject first. "Sana, any thought of names yet for the boys?"

"This was decided months ago, Mother," Tabba said. "The eldest is to be named David, the younger will be named William."

The room became still and quiet at the pronouncement.

David Ross took in a deep breath. Raw emotion shown on his face. The memories of Jonathan's birth became clear in his mind. The heartache, the loss, of his only son flashed across his mind. As David considered what had just been said, he realized how significant to him the names were. His name would be carried forward.

It seemed strange to him that at his son's death, one of the things that troubled him most was his name just ending. No son would carry on the family name. It seemed to David so deflating, for some unknown reason this fact still troubled him. After all these years, he had decided that maybe it wasn't so important. But something deep within was healed at the words Tabba spoke.

David Ross took the young child into his arms.

"David, I am so very honored to meet you," he said, fighting back the tears.

Chapter 85

October 7

The new school had been completed just over one month ago. The timing was perfect to begin the first ever school year of the San Saba Tribal School.

Abigail Ross was enjoying immensely her role as headmaster. However, regardless of her expertise and thirty years of experience and certification, the school had been denied accreditation from the state for grades Kinder through Eighth. The reason given from the State Board of Education for the denial: "the proposed school was not *racially diverse*."

Nina Rainwater-Travis was appealing the decision. Through the BIA, she had applied for and received federal funding for meals, utilities, transportation, books, and even funding for six employees. It seemed Texas still could not quite come to terms with its past or how to move forward into the future concerning the Comanche Nation. Many of those in positions of power maintained the same mindset of their ancestors.

Sana was initially responsible for the nursery program. The boys were healthy and vibrant. Sana was in awe at the strength of the two and the rate at which the boys were growing. She reflected on the beautiful night the twins had come into the world. Topusana was grateful. She constantly whispered her gratefulness to the Great Spirit, God the Father.

Grace had completed the art studio and four adjoining classrooms. Every student attended art class each day. Many of the classes were also attended by the students' parents. The sons of Tosahwi, Neeko and Tosa, along with both of their wives, were extremely gifted in both painting and sculptor work. Grace thought the work was simply incredible.

Grace was beginning her own dream. She had already been in contact with the galleries she was acquainted with back in Los Angeles. She was amazed at the natural gifting and talent the students and their parents possessed. She knew without a doubt the work of *The People* was both extraordinary and quite marketable.

Tabbananica had overseen the construction of a huge barn designed specifically for the breeding of horses. The great stallion, as of this day, was still free. Even with all Tabba's skill, he had not been able to capture the beautiful horse. The other Warriors had named the stallion *Shadow*. Tabba accepted their good-humored teasing.

"Were you able to come near the stallion's *Shadow*, today, Tabba?"

This was often the question around the evening fires *The People* enjoyed daily.

An enormous round pen was being constructed on the open prairie, the home of the stallion. Perhaps with the camouflaging of the pen and the building of a huge V-shaped fence, the stallion could be driven into the trap.

Tabba knew if he could capture and tame this wild stallion, his breeding would produce some of the greatest horses, or the term he preferred, *war ponies* on Earth.

The buffalo herd had grown by more than 300 animals. The first hunt would take place the following month. David required a Native American guide for each permit sold. The Warriors of the tribe had been granted a great responsibility. It was an honor for each man. Their knowledge, insight, and proven stewardship of the land was foremost in the granting of this oversight. David J. Ross was quite proud of the Warriors. He knew the management of the herd was in very capable hands.

Tenahpu, The Man, watched as his son-in-law rode across the prairie again this morning. The Man knew Tabbananica all too well. He would capture the mighty stallion soon enough.

The Man moved silently for a full mile, rising to stand beside the small elevated rock outcropping. None would detect his movement, nor would he leave the slightest sign of a trail. Tenahpu was an expert at evasion and resistance. He could see the children playing, his children. He could also make out the distinct figure of his daughter, Topusana. He was amazed at how much his daughter resembled her mother, Kwanita. The Man knew the children would be safe under her care. He would, however, continue to provide a deadly, stealth layer of protection for all his little tribe. One never knew what the white man was capable of.

The Man knew he would remain unknown and hidden for many years to come. Carrying two rabbits, he moved down the little draw and entered the third cavern in the shallow canyon nearest the school. He would eat and rest throughout the remainder of the afternoon. In the late evening, he would resume his nightly oversight of them all. Any and all that entered the new Homelands would be scrutinized and observed closely.

****

The tribe was enjoying a time of growth, (they now numbered twenty-one souls), in addition, Tosahwi's daughter in-laws were both now expecting new ones. Peace had settled upon *The People*. A sense of hope and prosperity permeated every facet of this new life, this new Nation.

Chapter 86

October 9
Channel Islands National Park

David and William had sailed to the very tip of the island chain. William had always wanted to visit the rookeries of seals and sealions on San Miguel Island. The sail out had been pleasant despite the ten-foot swell. The trimaran lay at anchor, riding the swell inside the little protected cove. David explained the small tropical storm two thousand miles away just east of the Hawaiian Islands was the cause of the swell.

"There is nothing between here and there to alter the swell of the ocean waves," David said. William had not thought of that, but picturing the Pacific in his mind he clearly understood what David was saying.

The hike among the magnificent animals was exhilarating. Thousands of sealions lined the beaches and fished along the shoreline of San Miguel Island.

The weather was perfect, the Pacific sun shining overhead as the two friends hiked the entire island. The men stopped for a drink of water and yet a few more pictures. David admired William's enthusiasm as he pointed and commented in his animated boy-like wonder at the incredible scenes before the two.

The getaway had been planned for months, the two men having had quite a busy year. With the beginning of the school year, their wives were both occupied and busy. Will had, over the last several months, completed the drafting of the tribal constitution. The two friends needed some much-deserved down time.

They had camped one night off Santa Rosa Island and hiked through the beautiful and rare Torrey pines. David had hoped to spot one of the island foxes. The elusive little animal, however, did not show itself this time. William was overwhelmed with the landscape, plant life, Torrey pine forests, and seascape of Santa Rosa Island. Lost in the unparalleled beauty of the environment, he took hundreds of photographs. William couldn't wait to share this wonderful place with Nina.

David had promised at least a dozen times they would all return soon.

Carefully working their way through the maze of sealions, the men finally arrived at the dinghy. The two launched through the surf, riding the face of the large breakers at an angle. David thought the swell had grown since their landing earlier in the day.

Will tied the dingy securely as David had shown him with a bowline knot. David checked Will's technique. "I think you've got that one down, my friend."

William was again beaming like a boy scout. David smiled at the light in his friend's eyes.

The men settled in for a beautiful evening of grilling fresh-caught tuna steaks, followed by homemade chocolate chip cookies the girls had sent along for them. The sailboat lulled the two as it rose and fell on the Pacific Ocean swell. David's favorite blended whisky topped off a perfect day at sea.

The men talked long into the evening.

"I think we should write a book about all of this one day," Will said.

David pondered the statement. "I'm not sure which category it would fall under, my friend. If we told the story exactly as it happened, most would think it was fiction."

The two smiled at the truth of the statement.

"I've got to get myself one of these sailboats," Will said. "Although, I think I'll just hire a crew and point where I would like to go."

"Well, you certainly have enough money to do just that."

The conversation grew thin as the activities of the last three days seemed to hit them all at once. It was a deep satisfying kind of tired.

"I think I'll turn in early," David said.

A soft snore from the cushioned cockpit was the only reply that came from his life-long friend.

As David moved toward the steps of the cabin, he could feel the little breeze coming out of the east. He decided he would need to check the anchors every few hours during the night.

****

Somewhere out over the Great Basin, the largest watershed in North America, the wind in the upper atmosphere shifted. The high-pressure area that normally stalls over the four corners region began to back itself toward northwestern Arizona. The circulation around the high pressure began to move the winds across southern California toward the west. The unsettled atmospheric winds rose upslope against the eastern slopes of the mountains of southern California and the Baja peninsula. Those winds grew dramatically in force as they descended the western slopes of those same mountains toward the Pacific. It would take only twelve hours for those winds to reach hurricane force. By 7:00 the following morning, the winds were blowing a steady sixty miles per hour at many of the airports along the southern California coast.

The topography of the Channel Islands formation actually caused those winds to accelerate to even greater speeds as the wind whipped in and around the jagged coastlines of the Islands.

David had struggled and fought the anchor lines most of the night. He decided it would be much safer to move away from the rocky shoreline. He had spent the entire night trying to prevent the boat from being driven into the rocks. Even with the engine running and his largest anchors set, the boat could no longer hold its position.

At 7:00 a.m., the sky finally lightening enough to grant him some visibility, he decided to let loose the anchors and attempt to ride out the storm at sea. Moving away from San Miguel Island with only a tiny storm jib up, he met the worst sea conditions he had ever experienced in his life. Observing the conditions, he decided to activate the onboard EPIRB (emergency position indicating radio beacon).

This device would broadcast his position to the satellites one hundred miles overhead. The Coast Guard stations in District 11 picked up the emergency signal immediately.

David turned the trimaran into the swell. The storm nearly two-thousand miles away had strengthened considerably, as had the huge swells now arriving along the southern California coast. The wind David was recording atop the mast of the vessel was seventy-four knots. This offshore wind driving directly against the oncoming swell from the west had caused the swell to grow and steepen. He quickly found himself facing steep twenty-foot waves, the tops of the waves being blown into a brutal driving sea spray. The boat rose steeply at an angle up the front of each wave, then crashed down off the backside of each wave with an alarming and unbelievable force. The noses of the three hulls penetrated deeply into the water off the backside of each wave. He thought the boat would never take the beating the ocean was about to unleash. David ordered Will to harness himself in. David did the same. The men were now tethered to the boat. Both had dawned survival gear and life jackets. David prayed the hull would stay together.

Taking the microphone, he made the call. "Mayday! Mayday! Mayday! This is the sailing vessel *Abigail*...Mayday! Mayday! Mayday!"

To David's surprise the call was answered from the naval air station located at Point Magu, just over sixty miles directly east of their current position, the radio operator seeing in real-time the location of the vessel.

After describing the sea conditions to the Coast Guard, a decision was made by the commanders on duty. A helicopter would be dispatched within minutes. Now being daylight, the primary deciding factor—the only factor—that allowed a rescue to be attempted.

Thirty-five minutes later the helicopter was on site attempting to hover above the sailboat. The wind was ferocious, the seas estimated at twenty-one feet, the worst conditions the crew onboard the helicopter had ever seen. They knew if they couldn't get the two men off the boat, they would most likely perish at sea.

The plan was for a rescue swimmer to enter the water, then have the men abandon the sailboat one at a time, hoisting them from the water in the rescue basket.

The decision was ultimately up to the rescue swimmer. The pilot, continuing the hover, dipped between the swells expertly only eight feet above the trough. The timing was perfect.

Giving the thumbs up, Petty Officer Caleb Kekoh of Honolulu, Hawaii, entered the angry waters and expertly made his way to the sailboat. The pilot ascended quickly as the next wave crested below the helicopter.

David unleashed William on the signal from the swimmer. Timing the swell, David pushed William off the stern of the boat as it began to climb the next wave.

The temperature of the water instantly took William's breath away. He attempted to stay afloat, his arms and legs heavy from the shock of the cold water. William fought against the incredible strength of the ocean. The temperature of the water at 57 degrees was numbing. The sea water instantly filled his boots and clothing, chilling his extremities and making it extremely difficult to attempt to stay afloat. His arms and legs quickly became heavy and useless. Fighting the wind and waves, William began to take into his lungs the sea spray, choking, struggling with all his might. He became exhausted within a few moments of entering the water. Finally, he surrendered to the waves, thinking there was no way he could survive the tempest.

Petty Officer Kekoh watched a moment, fully knowing the man needed to stop fighting the sea in order to rescue him. Upon the total exhaustion of the survivor, Petty Officer Caleb Kekoh latched onto the man the instant he saw him surrender to the waves. Moving away from the sailboat, Caleb expertly assisted the floating of the survivor, keeping William's head above the water. Both men floated on the sea, becoming a part of the raging tempest, rising with each swell, descending into each trough. Caleb Kekoh allowed the wind and waves to take them where it pleased. As he relaxed—he knew not to fight—Caleb, with William Travis floating above him, calmly awaited the lowering of the rescue basket.

The crew and pilot worked together in amazing harmony. They expertly plucked William from the crest of a wave. It took all of William's strength to just lay in the basket, hanging on desperately as he was hoisted into the buffeting chopper, exhausted. Peering out the open door, William could see the sailboat below, tossed to and fro by the storm, and his friend David fighting, doing all within his power to survive. William vomited a huge amount of sea water, struggling to breath, then lost consciousness for a few moments. Mercifully.

The helicopter pilot saw if first.

Quickly responding, he climbed the helicopter forty feet higher. David also saw the rogue wave. There was nothing he could have done.

The wave was estimated to be thirty-five to forty feet in height by the flight crew. The pilots watched as the wave caught the forty-four-foot sailboat at an angle, despite David's best effort to correct his heading. The boat rolled into the wave initially, then was tossed through the air as the wave broke. The boat rolled over ninety degrees to the starboard and seemed to hang in the air. Then the breaking wave flung the sailboat over backwards. The vessel landed upside down in the water as one ama separated itself from the vessel. The crew watched in desperation as the man that had been on the stern of the boat and had evidently just unleashed, disappeared from sight. No one on the rescue helicopter could spot the man…anywhere. He seemed to simply vanish into the churning, angry waters of the Pacific Ocean.

Petty Officer Kekoh frantically searched the waters surrounding the sailboat. The flight crew also continued scanning the waters. The man had a survival suit and life jacket on. Petty Officer Kekoh knew if he wasn't in sight on the surface of the water, he had to be trapped beneath the vessel, underwater.

For the next thirty minutes Petty Officer Kekoh dove repeatedly under and around the hull of the sailboat, to no avail. Suffering himself from complete exhaustion and hypothermia, he was ordered to the rescue basket. He never saw the man, David Ross, again.

Becoming low on fuel, the helicopter was ordered to return to base with the sole the survivor.

A second helicopter had been dispatched and arrived on scene as the first helicopter departed. The second flight was designated not as a rescue flight, but as a recovery flight. The recovery flight spotted the body a full hour later, floating in the water some 400 yards from the capsized sailboat.

David Jonathan Ross had perished instantly. The huge rigging of the boat causing traumatic blunt trauma as it evidently had struck the man across the back of his head and torso as it collapsed around him. There was nothing any of the rescue crews could have done to save the man.

Chapter 87

October 10

Old Grandmother had kept the fire burning all night in the little lodge on the banks of the San Saba River. She had prayed with all her heart and soul.

She knew that sometimes the Great Spirit could delay His purpose. In her heart she knew He had said no to her prayers. It was not hers to question. Only the Great Spirit knew the number of days each of His children were given.

Abigail Ross had struggled through the night also. She had felt this awareness before. The day Jonathan had died. The awareness had returned this morning.

She knew.

The confirmation came again in her front yard as Mrs. Hantaywee, the Faithful One, climbed the steps of her home. She was softly singing the songs of mourning. Her arms opened wide, welcoming Abigail Ross into a loving, protecting, embrace.

Sana, from her dormered room at the top of the stairs, was awaiting Grandmother's arrival. She too, as she descended the stairs, began the songs. She had never spoken of her vision concerning David.

It was, however, true and accurate.

The phone rang. William had decided to make the call to Abby himself.

October 15

Abby stood regally, adjacent to the grave site, peering through the flowers draped across the casket. David was gone, only five days now. It seemed already to have been much longer, she thought.

The words her friend and pastor spoke seemed to run together, the language seemed to not make sense. The cloud of confusion echoed in her ears like some sort of terrible dream. Abby closed her dry eyes. She had no more tears. Her heart was empty. Feeling her hands grip tighter, she felt the return snug grip within each of her hands. Glancing to her sides, she again realized she was standing between Sana and Grace. Both women, her daughters, weeping, holding her hands, also holding her upright, apparently.

As the pastor's words faded, Abby could hear something else from some other place within her heart. She could hear the voices singing in the wind.

Old Grandmother, Hantaywee (The Faithfull One), began leading the songs of mourning.

As Abby gazed upon the serene setting, the casket, the river, the flowers bowing in the wind...the words came to her from deep within her spirit.

Little pieces of her memories floated across her mind. She well remembered the day that she and David had discussed how reverent Old Grandmother's life seemed. Abby remembered wishing she knew the songs.

Those songs came to her now. Softly she sang along with the wind. Abby was accompanied by the trees. She was joined in harmony by the gurgling of the river, even the flowers seemed to sway in time with the ancient songs. Peace like a river filled her very being, attending her soul. It is well...she thought...it is well with my soul.

Chapter 88

May 9, 1847

Buffalo Hump stood tall and fierce, his stature and appearance true to the heart of the great Chief. Wearing nothing but a partial buffalo robe across his loins, brass rings encircled his powerful forearms and biceps. A beaded breastplate adorned his chest. His long flowing hair fanned out in the gentle breeze that drifted down the San Saba river valley.

Gathered along both sides of the riverbank were hundreds of Comanche Warriors. The scene before John O. Meusbach (El Sol Colorado, The Red Sun) would be forever burned into his memory, he thought, as he stood among the impressive, fearsome group of Native Americans.

The treaty would be the third that Buffalo Hump had agreed to. The first between himself and Sam Houston in 1838 was never ratified or honored by the Texans. The second between him and the United States of America in 1846 was immediately broken by the United States Cavalry and the Texas Rangers.

This treaty, the first between a private party, the German Immigration Company Adelsverein, and the three Comanche Chiefs present: Santa Anna the War Chief, Old Owl, and Buffalo Hump the leader of the Penateka Comanche. The treaty would allow the German immigrants to settle within the designated three-million-acre tract lying between the Llano and San Saba Rivers.

The Comanche Nation would agree to allow the Germans to settle and not be interfered with by the Comanche. In exchange, the Comanche would be allowed to survive, hunt, and live upon the land, unfettered. The Comanche would be allowed to enter the German settlements unhindered. A payment of two thousand dollars would be given the Chiefs.

As the men stood together along the banks of the San Saba, Buffalo Hump considered the future. He knew "The Red Sun," the name *The People* had given the man with shining red hair, was an honorable man. Perhaps this time, this agreement—not with the Texans, but with the Germans—would be honored. He desperately needed the peace to be upheld. However, Buffalo Hump was no fool. If the Germans did not honor the agreement, he would have no choice. War would come again.

However, history would prove this to be the only treaty concerning the Comanche Nation that would remain unbroken by either party, with regard to the settling of Texas lands.

Buffalo Hump gazed down the river; he could see the old camp of his family. Most had died in the raid by the white soldiers, many of the deaths those of his own close family. He sadly thought of Prairie Song, remembering her kind spirit, his heart turning over in his chest.

He scanned the hills above the riverbank toward the north. He had climbed the little canyon the day before and covered over the entrance to the cavern where his granddaughter Topusana now slept in Dream Time with Tabbananica. Buffalo Hump alone knew this cavern was also where the silver coins from the "Great Raid" were hidden.

If the peace failed, perhaps those in the Dream Time would awaken far enough into the future that they might have a chance at a new beginning.

Epilogue

Five years Later

My boys, David and William, would turn five in just a few days. I was simply amazed at how time seemed to slip by so quickly. The boys would begin kindergarten next week. I swaddled little baby Abigail in the soft deer skin. Baby Abigail, the name with which they had all begun to refer to my newborn daughter.

I paused, closing my eyes…seeing.

My mother Abigail was so looking forward to the daily time she would enjoy with her grandsons as their teacher.

Mother's life was full of promise and hope and even contentment. A life my father, David Ross, would have desired for her. She would honor his memory by living well, despite such great loss.

The buffalo herd had grown to almost four thousand animals. As my husband, Tabbananica, rode across the ridge above the buffalo herd each morning on his great stallion Shadow, he was continually awed at the sight before him, as was I, as I watched him from the school.

The men of the tribe had decided to discontinue all public buffalo hunting. The animals were healthy and vibrant. The hunting of the animals would now be reserved for tribal members only.

The sacred hunt took place each fall. Our entire tribe participated in the traditional hunt. For one full moon, thirty days, we lived in the old ways, moving our teepees daily, following the herd, processing the buffalo. I enjoyed immensely living in the old ways, as did all the tribe.

We were in touch with who we were as a people. We lived in tune with Earth, living as protectors and possessors even of the traditional ways of *The People*. The younger children were learning, learning the old ways. Learning the traditions and respect of Earth and her offspring.

My Friends Mr. and Mrs. William Travis had adopted the four young girls found along the riverbank after the attack on the San Saba tribe. Mrs. Rainwater-Travis had become an official member of the tribe. William Travis was designated as an honorary lifetime board member of the San Saba Comanche Tribe. He continued to serve our little tribe as designated legal counsel. William and Nina had built a beautiful home adjacent to the little settlement near the hunting lodge.

I watched as Old Grandmother slowly crossed the highway toward our home. She, too, was teaching one class per day at the school. Each student was proficient in both English and the Comanche language.

She entered the great room, awaiting the drive the three of us made each day together.

My painting shone brightly in the morning light that streamed into the room from the east.

"Mother and Daughter" hung above the great rock fireplace, the signature of Karl Bodmer I could see clearly in the magnificent custom frame.

My father, David Ross, revealed in his last will and testament that he was the anonymous purchaser of the original painting, when sold by Nan Chisholm. It was bequeathed, a gift to me, Sana Nica, and my husband, Tabba Nica.

Additionally, the will bequeathed almost the entire two hundred and fifty section Ross ranch to the San Saba Comanche Tribe, including all revenue from existing and future oil production.

The People, my people, now at long last possessed a Homeland.

One section of land (six hundred forty acres) surrounding the ranch home was set aside for my mother, Abigail Ross. It included the cavern sites up the little canyon above our home.

One section of land surrounding the art studios was bequeathed to Grace Ross. The new gallery had been completed four years ago. The stunning, beautiful works of several tribal members were continuously on display in the new gallery.

In addition to our current land holdings, William Travis had begun a land acquisition program. The San Saba Comanche Reservation was growing. We, under the sound direction of William Travis, were silently acquiring adjacent ranchland. Using income from our oil revenue, he began to purchase any property as it became available, expanding our land holdings toward the south and west, toward the Big Bend.

The ceremony would be conducted in just a few days. I would travel to Washington, DC, where I would be a guest of the White House. The former governor of Texas, now President of the United States, would himself execute the documents. The transferring of the former Big Bend National Park to *The People* of the San Saba Comanche Tribe would, in a few short days, become a reality. The settlement program I had developed along with the leaders of The Comanche Nation of Lawton, Oklahoma, would begin within the year.

The one-half interest in the one section of land in Andrews County owned by my father was bequeathed to my mother, Abigail, and my sister, Grace Ross. The other fifty percent interest in that ranch already belonging to William Travis.

My mother and I were quite surprised at how much time and effort it took to give away fifty million dollars per year. Forty percent of the donations went each year into the permanent fund of the San Saba Comanche Tribe.

I could see it made their hearts glad to give so generously. They both knew the deep spiritual truth that David J. Ross had taught us all. It was indeed more blessed to give than to receive.

The vision had come to me just this morning. I had just swaddled Baby Abigail. Closing my eyes, the vision was pure and clear, just as the water that flowed along the San Saba in winter. The Man I saw was seated on a buffalo robe. The firelight reflected off the walls of the cavern. The dim light illuminated the familiar features of his face. His muscled arms rippled as he reached for the rabbit that sizzled on a spit over the fire. The Man gave thanks for the bounty the earth had provided. He gently removed the rabbit from the spit. Rending a hind quarter from the animal, he leaned against the wall of the cavern, savoring the delicious meal. He ate slowly, methodically. It was his way. He was in no hurry. I could see the pure meat of the fresh roasted rabbit seemed to strengthen more than just blood, muscle, tendon, and bone. This Man possessed abilities and an inner strength beyond compare. The Man began to sharpen his arrowheads as he ate.

Comfort. The knowledge revealed to me through the vision brought comfort. In an instant I had seen the answers to many mysteries. The pieces fitted together neatly. The reason those who had attempted to bring harm to us…had met with tragedy.

I now knew we had a Protector.

As *Akima* (Leader) of my people, this knowledge of a Protector among our little tribe brought a level of relief and security. I had not felt this level of comfort in so long. I gazed at the painting across the room. I could feel the embrace of Prairie Song.

Now, I knew, this Protector would defend us when necessary, in the old ways.

We now possessed one of the most effective and deadly military resources ever to walk the face of the earth.

A Comanche Warrior.

My father, Tenahpu (The Man) was alive!

A few notes on the novel

My hope as an author is that you have escaped within the pages of *A New Beginning*. I certainly did as I created my characters and the scenes within the work. In creating a work of fiction based on actual and imagined historical events, it is quite difficult to recall all the research sources I studied. I have read innumerable magazine articles, public records, scoured online resources, and spent many days reading an old encyclopedia set. (I still enjoy the glossy pages and wonderful photographs these treasures contain.) In short, I am certain that there may be an idea here or there that stuck in my mind from a history book, or research article somewhere, that I used to complete a sentence in the novel. I can assure you this is purely the process of creativity.

The Karl Bodmer painting "Mother and Daughter" is fictional. It does not exist. If you are an artist and are interested in creating the piece, contact me at sghightower@yahoo.com for permissions info.

"The Battle on the San Saba" is a fictional event. This will help the history buffs.

The cavern where Topusana awakens is a real place. I explored the caves as a young man. If you think you know the location…you are probably incorrect.

My second novel, a prequel and wonderful story of the Native American generation prior to the characters introduced in *A New Beginning: The Smoke of One Thousand Lodge Fires,* will be completed in late 2020 and published in 2021. You may see excerpts, or pre-order at www.stevenghightower.com.

I do have limited availability for signings/speaking engagements. Please see the contact info on my website listed above, or visit my Facebook author page facebook.com/anewbeginning2020 to make a request.

Special Preview to Book Two of
A New Beginning Series

I awoke with a start. It was impossible to know how long I had slept, but I knew it had been a long full night of sleep. My body was rested; I felt strong somehow. I again gave thanks for the life and nutrition the beautiful fish had given me.

Rising from my little sleeping room, I flicked the flashlight on and made my way to the spring.

I drank deeply of the cool, refreshing water. The little spring formed a small pool of water about five feet across and ten feet long. I shined the light into the little pool and saw my reflection. My long dark hair and thin features stared back at me. I was taken aback somewhat at what I saw. I was seventeen years old, but I looked forty. Lines of worry and heartache shown upon my face. I thought for the first time in my life that I looked like a man.

What would this day bring? I needed to return down the mountain. I had promised to meet with coach Tower. I needed desperately to speak with Nita. More than anything what occurred to me was that I would today... start my new grown-up life as the man I had just seen in the pool.

All at once, many decisions seemed clear. I would face Bear Woman; I would not become a foster child. I was able bodied, intelligent, and could work as hard as any man. Thanks to my grandfather, I possessed skills that many of my peers had forgotten. I had also completed the training my grandfather had initiated. I had only one feat to complete to gain the title he had desired to place upon me. That long honored tradition was within my reach. With a definitive victory over an enemy, I would sing the song. The song of victory over one's enemy. Upon completion of whatever possible victory awaited me, I would become an Apache Warrior.

My grandfather had instructed me to be patient. I was not to pursue some invented victory. He said it would come to me when the time was right. The Great Spirit would show the way.

Rising from the pool, I made my way back to my little sleeping room. I gathered my things. The bow, quiver, war club, and the beautiful knife. I stowed the little cook stove on the high rock shelf. As I placed the stove upon the shelf, my hand grazed something else. It was soft to the touch. I removed my hand and looked around the little room for something to stand on. I spotted a square stone about a foot high against the wall. I gathered the stone and moved it into position below the rock shelf. Standing on the stone I could now see what it was I had brushed against. Shining the flashlight up and down the little shelf my heart lept at what I saw.

My grandfather's medicine bag! It was beautiful, ornately decorated with the finest hand painted bead work. I lifted the medicine pouch and could detect immediately it was filled with something. Gazing farther down the length of the shelf I again was stunned. A book— or a scroll was a better word—lay tucked in the back corner of the rock ledge. In awe at this discovery, I stepped off the stone, and moved the rock step over to my left. Stepping up again I could now reach the scroll. I carefully lifted it from its resting place. With my right hand I gently lifted the medicine bag. Gingerly I stepped from the stone with the treasure I held in my hands.

As I beheld these ancient items, I knew in my heart they had been left for me.

I whispered a prayer of gratefulness and said aloud, "Thank you, Grandfather."

I sat in my little room and read by the light of the small flashlight for hours.

The old parchment papers were bound with leather loops and were contained within a thick leather binding. The lettering appeared to be some type of heavy paint, the calligraphy on the pages stunning. On the left side of each page, the information was printed in Apache along with sketches of each subject. On the opposite side of each page, a handwritten translation in English written in the easily recognizable hand of my grandfather.

I understood immediately the knowledge within these pages had been gained over centuries. This written record of wisdom was priceless. Not in a monetary way, but rather in the immeasurable value of the wisdom the pages contained.

I closed the scroll, knowing I needed to make the long walk down the mountain. I carefully placed the scroll-book back into its hidden resting place. Once again, I gathered the tools of my grandfather, the tools all Warriors carried.

A whirlwind of knowledge, wisdom, healing, medicine, water sources, and enemies, rotated in my mind in a deluge of thought and consciousness. I had only scratched the surface of what the scroll contained. It would take me years of study to comprehend and put into practice what I had read over the last few hours.

The scroll-book was a complete manual of the old ways. It was like being filled with a delicious meal. Like a sampling of the finest fare.

This book had the ability to feed one's soul.

The last few pages contained an incredible mystery. Something I had never thought possible. I read in utter amazement.

The instructions were clear and succinct. The ingredients for the "Medicine" precise. The explanation given in my grandfather's hand lept from the page into my heart and mind. The words before me in writing, I could somehow hear him speaking.

"Dak, this medicine requires faith to succeed. It is not a mountain of faith. It is not a great river of faith, nor a mighty ocean of faith. To succeed in this ceremony, you must have a tiny seed of faith. Once the seed is planted, and you genuinely believe, this thing can be done."

I knew then. A soon as the words were read, I knew, I would travel into the past.

The medicine of "The Dream Time" would take me there.

****

Using the flashlight, I made my way out of the large room, up the snowy river, and across the shallow ledge. I turned off the light and covered the last two hundred yards using the growing reflected light from the entrance. I paused just inside the cave and listened. For what I did not know. I sensed something amiss. I had heard the faintest of movement outside the cave. I waited... now just two steps from the entrance. I heard again the sound that was out of place. The scraping of a footstep. Heavy clumsy steps on rock. The sound was moving away from the cave.

Who could possibly have followed? Who might be up here among the high peaks after the heavy wet snow?

I chanced a quick peak out the entrance. Just a milli-second to peer in the direction of the sounds.

I jerked back quickly. Had he seen me?

I held my breath, then drew an arrow from my quiver. Skillfully I knocked the arrow in the bow string. The footsteps had stopped. No further sound came from outside the cave. I drew the bow and stepped out of the narrow entrance.

There below me just thirty yards away, staring directly at me…stood the cruel animal.

The man who had killed my mother.

The man froze. Then began to laugh. "You. The little suckling appears. Put your toys away."

He sneered at me like I was some kind of insect. Like he could squash me with his filthy boots on a whim. Those boots had tracked the same mud they now held, into our little home. They had lowered my mother to the floor in agony. Those boots had destroyed the door to my room. I did not waiver in my aim.

"You killed her," I spoke through gritted teeth.

"What can you do about it, little sprout? You are just a scared little boy. Put your toy down now!" the cruel animal screamed at me with the voice I had heard before. "You will die here today just like your grandfather did. He was a coward. You are nothing, his little mite. You have no courage, neither did your mother."

The words he spoke stung within my heart. How could this man say such things? I knew the truth. I knew the man was lying. But these untruths hurt. The words wounded something deep within me. The lies also awakened something deep within me.

My mind refocused. The animal reached behind his back and drew his long knife. I said nothing of the lies. I spoke not a word of the pain he had caused. I focused, my training rote.

"See the arrow hit its mark, Dak. In your mind see only the kill zone. Place the arrow perfectly in your mind first…then allow your body to obey what your mind has already seen."

The cruel animal started toward me with the knife. There was no doubt in my mind, he would kill me. I released the arrow…

About Steven G. Hightower

Steven was born on the plains of West Texas, where many of his stories take place.

Within these pages you will find many of Steven's experiences. He has sailed oceans and piloted across continents. He has sung his songs to listeners, fortunate to share his stories musically.

Life has been an incredible blessing to him. Through this amazing walk we call life, he has discovered his true gifting. He is a storyteller. He has always loved geography and history, embellishing the honest and true while giving it new life.

He is incredibly grateful to the people in his life who have simply been kind. He is trying his best to become like you.

Steven invites you to enjoy this gift…the gift of a good story, well told.

He lives in the mountains of central New Mexico, along with his wife, Ellie. They have two children and five grandchildren. They are the greatest blessings in his life.